To Siouxsie with love.

With thanks to Mum, Dad, Chris, David, Galen, Caspar, Lachlan and Katarina.

In memory of Gran, Grandad, Kitten and the Baggins.

Keep your blade, mind and tongue sharp,
but share them with no one.

With a salute to my vigilant readers, who left no typo unturned: Kate (and Rebecca) Alcock, David Woods, Paul Leeming and Maggie Milne.

And a hearty hail to my long-suffering cover artist:
Oliver Flude.

Chapter One: Shatter

The molten fist exploded scant inches from Saltar's face. The heat singed his hair and started to blister the wood panelling on the wall.

Saltar swayed out from under the creature's fiery grasp and kicked it from the back and side to keep it off balance. The leather of Saltar's shoe charred from even this briefest of contacts with the man of magma.

'By the madness of Wim, what is this thing?' Saltar sweated, now that he'd put a bit of space between himself and the assailant, who had come from nowhere.

'You're the Battle-leader,' the Scourge grumbled as he disentangled himself from the chair he'd collided with in getting out of the monster's way, 'so you tell me. Never seen the like. But it's intent on getting a hold of you. Just as well, really, or I'd probably be dead by now.'

Rather than taking time to turn around, the incandescent rock flowed backwards and created new facial features for itself where the back of its head had been an instant before. It was on Saltar again in moments, not allowing him any real respite. If it were not for reflexes and instincts honed during countless lifetimes in battle, Saltar would have been swamped there and then. As it was, the Battle-leader himself could also move his body in near impossible ways. He adopted the elemental fighting form known as Water and swept away round the room as lava lashed after him.

Deceptive drifts and loose fluid movements found Saltar atop the ancient table along one edge of the throne room, where he kicked a vase of fresh flowers towards his attacker. Water splashed down its front, and steam and a roar of pain rose from it. However, although the red of its torso darkened momentarily, it seemed otherwise unharmed, and it certainly hadn't slowed in its pursuit of the Battle-leader.

'Scourge, it's very nice to see you again and all that, especially when we thought you were lost to us, but for Shakri's sake *do* something! I can't keep this up forever.'

The Scourge, God Slayer, Consort of the Goddess of All Creation, and erstwhile Commander of the feared Guardians of the King of Dur Memnos, picked up the chair with which he'd been wrestling, hefted it at the molten creature's head and cursed as it had no effect.

'Look on the bright side! At least the Captain of your Guard's stopped screaming. He was giving me a real headache. And it's no doubt a blessing for him, as he wouldn't want to be awake having had half his face burnt away.'

'Thanks. That's a great comfort, Scourge, really!' Saltar bit back. 'In case you hadn't thought it through, his screams were our main hope of attracting help from elsewhere. Now, unless you've got something constructive to say…'

Saltar was forced to break off as lava erupted towards him. It was only by dropping flat to the table that he avoided death. Even so, a glowing gobbet fell on his tunic and immediately set it alight. He tore buttons apart with scrabbling fingers and threw the incendiary article of clothing into the creature's shifting face. The tunic burnt to a crisp in a matter of seconds but served as distraction enough to mean its heavy fists smashed into the table rather than Saltar himself.

'Shakri be damned!' Saltar cried as he slipped on the shaking, polished surface of the table. His arms flew wide as he sought to keep his balance, but even water has to obey the natural law of gravity.

'Hold on!' the Scourge shouted as he yanked down the nearest tapestry from the wall and flung it over the main part of the animated, burning mass. 'There you go! Now don't say I haven't helped!'

'Great! Let's get out of… oh, no!'

The Chamberlain skittered into the room, followed by a large enough number of guards to block the doorway and prevent Saltar and the Scourge from exiting the room cleanly. The tapestry went up with a whoosh and quickly burnt away as the flaming creature fought its way free.

The Chamberlain titled his head on its side as he considered the intruder. 'And what do we have here, milord, hmm?'

'I was hoping you could tell me, Chamberlain. After all, nothing's meant to be able to get into the palace without you knowing about it, now is it? More important than that, how do we fight it?'

The Chamberlain hissed as he was forced to duck a bright and blinding piece of igneous matter. A young guard lunged bravely at the molten figure, only to have the edge of his blade run liquid and leave him with a useless weapon. The magma then ran up over the hilt of his sword and up to his elbow. The smell of cooked meat filled the room and then the guard started screaming. He released his sword but could not shake the magma from his arm. It dissolved his lower limb clean away and then splattered to the floor where it sizzled for a moment before it began to cool.

'Get back, all of you!' Saltar shouted as the King's guard dragged their delirious comrade back from the horror. 'Chamberlain, I want answers, and I mean *now*!'

The Chamberlain flinched and flexed his limbs as if making ready to leap away in an instant if his person were threatened again. 'It must be of magical origin, hmm? Its substance will not last long in that state. It must cool, hmm? We will avoid it. That is the best way. But such a thing cannot possess magic of its own. There must be a mage somewhere near the palace. It is that practitioner who must have arranged to get this thing past my wards, hmm?'

The creature moved for Saltar again but the Scourge was ready with another tapestry. Saltar skipped around his attacker and grabbed a jug of wine from a side table. He didn't hesitate to douse the ancient fabric.

'That'll stain, you know!' the Scourge observed, and heaved the material onto the advancing inferno.

'Shut up! Everyone out! Now! We won't get another chance.'

The guards tumbled out into the corridor beyond, followed by the quick, jerky movements of the Chamberlain. The Scourge and Saltar came hot on his heels and wasted no time in sealing the door behind them. They moved off down the corridor before speaking further.

'Get water!' the Scourge ordered a sergeant among the guards, who immediately picked out others to go with him. 'Quickly! That door won't hold it for long!'

'Chamberlain, do you know the whereabouts of Kate and my son? And what about Mordius? Are they safe?'

The Chamberlain was clearly agitated, his spidery limbs constantly twitching and his beady eyes never coming to rest in one place. Magma came spreading out from under the door and flames licked up the wood. It boomed as it was struck from the other side and then cracked.

'I-I do not sense anything, no, I don't. But we must fear, yes? If there is a mage nearby, then why have they not come to add their powers to the fire golem's against you, hmm? Surely they cannot think the Battle-leader will be easily overcome, even by a golem? No, this golem must be here as a distraction only.'

Saltar didn't waste a second and set off at a flat run. He didn't know if the Scourge and Chamberlain had chosen to follow him or stay and stop the golem from burning the palace down, but at that moment he didn't care. All his thoughts were bent upon the woman and two-year-old child who gave his life its entire meaning.

His mind raced. Where had this threat to his family come from suddenly? They'd had years of peace since their defeat of the despotic necromancer Voltar, who had stolen the throne of Dur Memnos and taken the world to the brink of destruction. Voltar, with the God of Death Lacrimos at his side, had started a war of attrition that had lasted generations against the neighbouring kingdom of Accritania; in a self-deifying attempt to wipe out the populations of both kingdoms and, ultimately, precipitate the overthrow of the realm of Shakri, the Goddess of Creation. As the most powerful and ambitious necromancer on the continent, Voltar had come perilously close to becoming the ruler of both life and death, and the supreme will that defined all reality within the cosmic void. If it had not been for Saltar's adamantine, irreducible will set in opposition to Voltar's own, all would have been lost.

Yet life in all its previous aspects had been preserved and Saltar had taken on the leadership of Dur Memnos to oversee and safeguard its reconstruction. He'd become known as Saltar the Builder by many of the people, although to his mind he did nothing more than ensure that the people had the peace, freedom and security they needed to build their own lives. More than that, Saltar even saw himself as slightly selfish in how he oversaw the reconstruction since the safety of his own family was his main motivation for making changes to the wider society of Dur Memnos.

Once Voltar had been defeated, Saltar and Kate had quickly got married, and a year later they had had a son they named Orastes. They'd then had two years of happiness as they'd watched both Orastes and the reborn kingdom of Dur Memnos grow and flourish. There hadn't been a single day of darkness in all that time. There'd not been one instance of a town or village being plagued by a necromancer and animees, an unholy demon or an unnatural conjuration.

The Scourge, their old comrade-in-arms, had then suddenly appeared out of thin air in the middle of the throne room of the palace. They'd been delighted to see him, of course, but somewhat amazed since he'd died in the arms of Lacrimos before being chosen to be Shakri's consort. The Scourge had admitted somewhat sheepishly that he'd been arguing with Shakri and that she'd thrown him out of their home. She'd stripped him of his near divinity and as a punishment returned him to the mortal realm.

That had been a week ago, and at the time Saltar had struggled to hide his smile of amusement as he'd listened to the tale of domestic woe from the grizzled, old soldier, but now Saltar had to wonder if the Scourge's appearance had been some sort of warning or omen. Could Shakri have foreseen that Saltar would soon need help? Had she foreseen that the Scourge would need to be there to save Saltar's life once the golem appeared? And what further help would Saltar need?

If it was the Scourge who had been sent, then the danger must truly be great indeed, for the Scourge was no ordinary man. He had been the commander of the King's Guardians and bane to every necromancer no matter where they hid. In sacrificing his own life, he'd managed to murder the God of Death, Lacrimos himself, as reality and meaning had unravelled into the void around them. He was the only mortal ever to be known as God Slayer. Once dead, he'd become the near-divine consort of Shakri herself. And now he was returned to mortal life.

No, this was no ordinary man. The threat to Saltar's family, if not Dur Memnos itself, must truly be terrible if the gods themselves were taking a hand. Now panicking, Saltar tried to take the stairs three at a time.

'Kate!' he shouted hoarsely, fear choking him. 'Where are you? Mordius!'

Lungs burning, he reached the landing at the top and hurtled round a corner towards the rooms where his family took its residence. He collided with a guard standing stupidly in the middle of the corridor and went sprawling to the floor. He swore and struggled to his feet, waving the guard back from him.

'Where are they?' he asked urgently.

The guard was young. His face was pale with terror. He pointed a shaking finger towards the open door to Orastes's nursery. Saltar pushed the man aside and moved quickly to the threshold. There, he suddenly hesitated as he saw splatters of fresh blood on the floor. A moan escaped his lips as he saw the mutilated bodies of two guards lying on top of each other just inside the room.

Kate's head came up. 'He's not here!' she said, her voice shaky with panic.

Saltar didn't know whether to sigh with relief that Kate was unhurt or cry out in anguish that his child was missing. 'Where is he? Who did this? Mordius, tell me something, now!'

'I-I don't know,' the diminutive magician stammered. 'Kate and I only just got here. We've been searching the room, but there's no trace of Orastes.'

The Scourge shouldered his way past Saltar, who was already turning to leave. 'Not so fast, Saltar. This room still has much it can tell us.'

'You!' the Battle-leader of Dur Memnos shouted at the guard stood gawping just outside the door. 'Get the palace sealed and searched. Now! Stop standing there like a village idiot. Muster the guard! Do I have to do everything myself? Find out how whoever's responsible got in. That'll be how they're leaving too, and we can start after them before they get too much of a lead.'

The guard fled and was soon hollering for his comrades to turn out.

'Have either of you moved anything?' the Scourge asked Kate and Mordius.

'Where's the god-cursed Chamberlain?' Saltar spat. 'Does anyone know which way they went? Did you see anything! Answer me, Mordius, damn it!'

Mordius shrank back, shaking his head, distressed and at a loss.

'Is our child safe?' Kate asked in a high-pitched and querulous voice. 'Saltar, what's happening? I don't understand what's happening.' Her eyes became confused, unfocussed and then tearful.

As if magically summoned by the use of his name, the Chamberlain came creeping with surprising speed around the edge of the door. His face was twisted in pain and he held livid, burned hands out in front of him. 'Milord, I was ensuring the creature in the throne room would never be able to pose a threat to anyone again. But where is the child?' he then asked agitatedly as he beheld the bodies.

Saltar moved to Kate and put his arm around her. 'Everything is fine, my love. I won't let anything bad happen.'

Ignoring his retainer's injuries, Saltar turned on the Chamberlain: 'Get me reports from those manning each of the gates into the city. I want to know if anyone unusual has been seen leaving Corinus, especially if they were carrying any sort of baggage about the size of a small child. When the guards have finished searching the palace, have them search the city, house-to-house. Tell them to batter down doors as necessary, and anyone who resists. If there are any of my Guardians in Corinus, tell them to start searching the countryside, and to get the message out about the kidnapping.'

Mordius then heard the question the Scourge had asked him before. 'We looked to see if the boy had hidden himself somewhere, but otherwise haven't touched anything.'

'Now, hang on!' the Scourge warned Saltar. 'May I remind you *I* command the Guardians. Let's just think this through first. Let me read the room to see what we're really up against.'

'Kidnapping?' Kate asked tremulously. Pain and conflict began to war across her face. Then she became strangely composed. 'But what do they want? Death?'

'Enough!' Saltar roared at the others in the room. 'You will all be silent and do as I say!' His eyes and tone threatened such murder that all except Kate could not help being suddenly frightened of him. The Scourge cleared his throat uncomfortably but at a glare from Saltar decided to hold his tongue.

'Chamberlain, why are you still here?' Saltar growled.

The black-garbed retainer bowed fluidly, his expression schooled, and disappeared without a word.

'Saltar, my love,' Kate said curiously, 'why don't you listen to the Scourge? He is the commander of the Guardians – if anyone can read this room and tell us who has stolen our dear child, it is him. Beyond that, he was *my* commander, the closest thing I've ever known to a father, and a man who has sacrificed himself so that all might live, so that you and I might have the chance to know peace and raise a family. It is beyond trust. If he thinks we should listen, then we *will* listen!'

Saltar ground his teeth. 'We do not have time…'

'My friend,' Mordius said quietly, 'we have had more years of peace than we could have hoped for. We always knew this day would come, that forces both mortal and supernatural with interests at odds to our own would eventually seek to strike against us. We must consider why they have chosen to attack by taking your son. They must know that such an act will provoke the rage that has long slept within you, that you will tear the realm apart looking for your son, that you will not rest, not think about anything else, not listen to anything else until you have retrieved him. They are using your son to distract you from whatever they really want. They will triumph, they will destroy us all, unless you can master the rage within you, my friend.'

'Mordius is right,' the Scourge nodded. 'The fire creature in the throne room was a distraction. The taking of Orastes is likely to be another. Our enemies work by slight of hand, bluff, subtlety and a cunning understanding of mortal desires and responses. It suggests great age or intellect. We must be wary, therefore, and make sure we understand as much as we can from every trace of our enemy's passing. You *must* give me some brief moments to read this room.'

Saltar fought for calm. 'Be quick!' he ordered and went to pace in a corner of the room like a caged animal. His hands twitched at his sides, so he tried folding his arms as he strode, then gave that up and thrust his hands behind his back.

The Scourge hunkered down as he considered the bodies of the slain guards. 'Their blades are clean so either they faced someone so adept that they couldn't land a blow or they were taken completely by surprise by a number of foes. Given their blades are unsheathed, they clearly weren't caught unawares. And yet they failed to call out to Kate and Mordius, whose rooms are not far away. It reeks of magic. Were they somehow paralysed and then cut to pieces while they were held immobile? What sort of magic would allow that, Mordius?'

Mordius half-shrugged and his face reddened with embarrassment. His role in the palace was that of magical advisor but this was the first time he'd really been called upon for anything in the last several years. Never a self-confident individual, the small man was pained whenever he might seem inadequate to others. 'W-well, it is unlikely to be a priestly form of magic, since the balance prevents the gods from interfering so directly in the affairs of men. They would not be capable of holding a man still so that one of their followers might kill him… unless the magic was more indirect than that… say, a glamour or a web of befuddlement. Theoretically, a priest might…'

'Look!' Saltar interrupted, unable to contain his irritation. 'We already know there's some unholy magic at work because of that fiery golem in the throne room! Get on with it!'

'Okay!' the Scourge said, finding it equally hard not to rise to Saltar's impatience. He deliberately took a moment to scratch his stubbled cheek as he thought. 'But we now know the magic-user had to have entered the palace themselves. They wouldn't have been able to incapacitate these guards if they hadn't been here. Looking at the contemptuous way in which one body has been dumped atop the other, I'd say we're looking at someone who considers non-magic-users a long way beneath them. We're looking for someone who sees themselves as not only very powerful, but also more *worthy* somehow. They are arrogant and cruel, whoever they are.'

'Cruel?' Kate said numbly. 'And they have Orastes. Shakri watch over him!'

'How many of them are there?' Saltar demanded.

'I think the magic-user will have brought a few lackeys with him… or her. They will not have wanted to deal with the guards and try and catch a child at the same time. They will not have known exactly how much resistance to expect… unless they have an insider working for them.'

Saltar's eyes narrowed. 'An insider?'

The Scourge nodded. 'Let's face it, Orastes is usually with at least one of us. Was it coincidence that they struck when he'd been put down for a nap and there were only the two guards around? How did they know to have the golem appear in the throne room, exactly where you were?'

'And if I may say, the magic required to animate a golem requires a lot of time and preparation,' Mordius supplied. 'Such preparation would go hand-in-hand with considerable advance planning, and planning would demand information concerning the palace and its routines if the enterprise were not to be a complete waste of effort.'

Saltar looked to the Scourge for him to continue.

'We are dealing, then, with an organised and well-resourced enemy. I suspect, however, that they will have entered the palace as a fairly small group so that they could move with speed and in silence, and keep the risk of being observed to a minimum. Of course, there may be a larger group waiting to join with them, either in the city or somewhere in the countryside.'

'Well, which is it?' Saltar pursued relentlessly.

The Scourge sighed. 'If I had to guess, I'd say they'll be trying to get out of the city as quickly as possible. The Chamberlain's spy network being what it is, they wouldn't be able to stay hidden in the city long, and they certainly wouldn't be able to find anywhere secure enough to keep us permanently at bay. No, they'll be trying to get to somewhere defensible, or trying to disappear in a remote part of Dur Memnos or some other kingdom.'

'Somewhere defensible,' Saltar repeated intently. 'Holter's Cross is the closest. If I discover any suggestion that the Guild's mercenaries have had a hand in this, then I will personally see to the complete destruction of their enclave! Not one of them will be left alive!'

Holter's Cross was close to a city in size and served as a haven for mercenary companies all over Dur Memnos and beyond. In return for sanctuary, the companies were sworn to undertake only those commissions that came to them via the Guild of Brothers who ruled the city. Inevitably, therefore, Holter's Cross was always well-defended by its own standing army, and was a constant source of unease for the ruler of Dur Memnos in Corinus. Such was the strength of the Guild that any attempt by the Memnosian army in Corinus to march on Holter's Cross would probably only succeed in destroying both armies. When the necromancer Voltar had been on the throne, he'd kept his people fighting Accritania for generations and had been the main client of the Guild, all of which had served to keep the kingdom together. The Guild had even pledged not to take on any commissions that conflicted with the interests of the throne in Corinus. Saltar had extracted Guild Master Thaeon's personal promise that the arrangement would remain in place once Saltar had defeated Voltar. But the Guild Master was a pitiless old crow who could not be trusted, especially since the number of mercenary commissions had fallen to almost nothing during this era of peace. Peace was certainly not good for Guild business.

'They wouldn't dare, surely!' Kate gasped.

'It's enough for me,' Saltar said decisively.

'Well, it's not for me!' Kate replied with a barely contained anger. 'I want to hear how our child is, thank you very much! Scourge, what else is there? You don't… you don't see any of his b-blood, do you?'

Saltar looked chastised for a moment and then was all concentration as he waited on the commander of the Guardians to speak.

'There is no blood, Kate. All there is is that forlorn rag-doll soldier there on the floor. Was it a favourite of Orastes? Did he sleep with it?'

Kate rushed over to the doll and picked up the half-chewed, damp comforter. She held it to her cheek and then hugged it to her chest as if it were Orastes himself. Her eyes were wet again as she said: 'Yes, it was the only thing he ever wanted. It got so dirty I was a bit embarrassed by it, but he refused to be parted from it. He would have screamed the place down if they'd made him leave it behind… but we didn't hear anything, I swear!' Her features then went through another lightning quick change in response to the storm of emotions she was experiencing: 'I will not allow this!' she snarled.

She tore at his soul. Saltar went to his wife again. 'And I swear that I will bring this world to its knees, if I have to, to ensure he is returned safely to us. You must believe that.'

Kate nodded mutely. The Scourge spoke into the silence. 'So they either gagged your son or used magic on him to keep him quiet. Magic is the more likely. There is no more to say really.'

'Right, then I have weapons to get and a force of men to gather.'

'I will go with you,' the Scourge said an instant later.

'There is something more…' Mordius murmured.

They all stopped and turned to look at the thoughtful mage.

'What!' Saltar demanded.

Mordius blinked and ended his preoccupation. 'Well, what is it they want exactly? It can't be ransom, for there are much easier targets in the merchant district of Corinus. I can't believe it is the Guild of Holter's Cross looking for political bargaining power. They know you would not forgive such an act and the magic used is not their style. I'm not aware of us having any other political enemies, so the perpetrators must be after something else. We spoke before of them seeking to distract you. Distract you from what?'

'Go on!' Saltar ordered.

'I can only think that there is something yet to come, something bigger, deeper… darker. They want you out of the way before they put their larger plans into effect. They must see you as a principal threat. We know they have dark magic at their command and are allied with something… older.'

'So a demon, then? Or do you think our friend Lacrimos is up to his old tricks?' Saltar shrugged. 'Whoever it is, they're going to get exactly what they asked for since I'm not going to waste a moment longer standing here and engaging in speculation. I am leaving to hunt them down and make them regret ever having been created. And you and Kate are going to stay here.'

'If you think for one second…' Kate began to shout in fury.

'I really think that…' Mordius ventured.

'Hear me!' Saltar bellowed over them. They quieted, but the look in Kate's eyes warned him he would have to speak quickly. 'Mordius, you will stay here and liase with the temples to discover what agencies may be arrayed against us. Demand access to the library in the temple of Cognis. If they seek to deny you, use the city guard to force the issue.'

'And Kate,' he said gently to the woman with the blazing eyes and carved features who owned his heart, 'someone must remain to rule in Corinus. I do not trust the Chamberlain, and Mordius does not have the experience to direct the wider military. It can only be you. I know that it is against every thought and instinct of a mother to sit and wait when her child is lost. But I would never ask you to remain idle. Rather, I am putting the entire resources of the kingdom at your command so that you may bend everything we have and are towards finding our sweet Orastes.

'The Scourge and I are the best equipped of all of us to take up the hunt while the spoor is still fresh. You must see why this is the only way. It is always my desire to have you at my side as life-partner and help-mate, but we must make this sacrifice for a while if we are to make sure we are united as a family again one day. Please, do this for me!'

Her features did not soften and she continued to gaze at him in silence for a few moments. He could not read what she was thinking. Finally, she gave a curt nod. 'Then come, husband, and let us arm the kingdom and its Battle-leader once more, for our lives will be nothing but misery and war until we have conquered this new foe.'

He loved her with such intensity and pride at that moment that his chest hurt and it was all he could do to hold himself back from crushing her in his arms and spending the rest of his life in her embrace. Her face forbade him and he dared not reach for her; for he knew he would not be able to leave her once he had clasped her to him, and she would not be able to let him go. Faces grim but resolved, they strode from the room side by side, yet an armslength apart.

⁂

The Chamberlain and the sergeant of the palace guard who had overseen the water detail that had finally extinguished the fire golem found Saltar and the Scourge in the royal armoury. Saltar did not look directly at them as he continued to concentrate on assessing the heft and balance of a set of particularly wicked-looking throwing knives.

'Report, Chamberlain!'

'Milord, the guards at the gates to the city have nothing unusual to report, hmm? The only people coming in and out have been local traders and an occasional group of entertainers with commissions from wealthy houses, you see. Everyone had their documentation properly checked, but then the guards *would* claim that, wouldn't they, lest they expose themselves as negligent. It would appear that either the guards have been inattentive, our adversary was well-disguised, some other means to leaving the city was used or our enemies are, in fact, still in the city… hmm?'

The sergeant scraped his foot. Clearly he had something to say that he considered important.

'Well, sergeant?'

The sergeant brought his heels together. 'Milord, I had the palace searched, as per your instructions. I also took the liberty of questioning the palace guard. They said no one of any significance came in through palace entrances today…'

The Chamberlain tutted quietly. 'Yet how are they to know, hmm? Perhaps magic was used on them.'

The sergeant was clearly wary of challenging someone as dangerous as the Chamberlain.

'Go on, sergeant!' Saltar ordered, testing the edge of a blade with his thumb and idly watching the blood that began to bead from the invisible cut.

'Milord, we therefore decided to search the corridors that have flagstones in the floor. We found one that was loose, with an entrance to the catacombs beneath it.'

Saltar sighed. Corinus was built upon a hill that was honeycombed with tunnels and caves. During Voltar's reign, the outdwellers, the poor creatures who existed outside the city walls, had used the catacombs as their home and had fed on the dead as they could, what with the widespread shortage of food that had been a fact of life – and death – back then.

The irony of course was that Saltar and his companions had used the self-same tunnels to get into the palace to confront and ultimately defeat that deathmonger Voltar. When Saltar had taken over the leadership of the kingdom, he'd had the cave system largely cleared and sealed up. But there was no way the myriad entrances could all have been found, and now his enemies had apparently used the tunnels against him.

'Scourge,' Saltar called to the commander of the Guardians, who was experimentally twirling a bolus. 'How many men do we take with us?'

'The fewer we are, the faster we travel.'

'Hmm. But what if we come up against significant resistance?'

The Scourge gave an unconcerned shrug. 'It's never stopped us before, has it?'

Saltar regarded the sergeant. The man was on the short side but had broad shoulders and a wide chest. Despite his heavy build, though, he had arrived silently. He was light on his feet and clearly had the sort of balance and poise that would make even a dancer envious. This man would be formidable in battle. His face was criss-crossed with scars showing his experience and that his rank had been conferred based on merit rather than the privilege of birth. His entire life could be read there – obviously it had not been pretty – so he would have to be open and honest. He could be trusted, and Saltar needed all the trustworthy men he could find right now.

With his many lifetimes of experience, Saltar had the ability to weigh up a man in seconds and anticipate the secrets of his heart. That ability had never let him down except when he tried to read the Chamberlain, which always made Saltar uncertain about his courtier, always made him wonder if the Chamberlain was more than just a man, was perhaps as old as Saltar himself.

'What is your name, sergeant?'

'Marr, milord,' he shrugged. 'It is not a decorous name, to be sure. I'm happy with Sergeant, if it please, milord.'

'Very well. Sergeant, I want you to hand pick five men that you know and trust and have them ride out with you within the hour. They are to be provisioned for a long, hard journey, but for the sake of speed should travel light, understood?'

Marr's eyes did not flicker, which pleased Saltar. The Sergeant was not a man to be caught off-guard. 'Yes, milord. Permission to begin, milord?'

'Very good, Sergeant. Follow on as quickly as you can. The Scourge and I will be at the home of the outdweller known as Trajan. He is their unofficial leader. If we are not there, he will tell you in which direction we have gone. Dismissed.'

Marr nodded and hurried away. The Chamberlain's hard, glittering eyes watched him go, and his hands clawed involuntarily. Then he turned to Saltar and smiled so that his small, sharp teeth could be seen.

Does he think to ingratiate himself with me, or is he trying to intimidate me? Either way, Saltar didn't like it and he shifted the knife he held so that it fit more snugly in his palm. Saltar's instincts screamed at him to strike, and he knew that any hesitation might prove fatal. As if the Chamberlain suddenly sensed the danger, he took a step back and bowed low. 'Dearest lord!' he wheedled, staying in his bow with his eyes carefully down. 'I would only beg that you consider taking these other two with you.'

'What other - ?' the Scourge began as Lucius and a portly, middle-aged man came hurrying in.

'Now what?' Saltar asked coldly, wondering whether the Chamberlain conspired to delay his search for his son as long as possible. 'Lucius, get out of here!'

'I came as quickly as I could!' Lucius panted, shifting the heavy greater lute strapped to his back into a more comfortable position. 'I can help.'

The Scourge chuckled. 'Really? What would you do? Serenade our enemies to death?'

Saltar experienced a dizzying moment of déjà vu. Surely he'd heard the Scourge say such a thing to Lucius before. But his memory was vague about those final days. Lucius had helped them before, hadn't he, when they toppled Voltar? Shaking his head, he turned back to the array of weapons and selected an iron-shod fighting staff. 'Ready?' he asked the Scourge. 'Kate and Mordius will have prepared our horses.'

The Guardian nodded and began to push the others aside so that he and Saltar could exit the armoury.

The panting individual next to Lucius finally caught enough breath to struggle out with: 'I've been sent to you by the High Priest of Shakri. He sensed a disturbance at the palace and sent me to be of whatever service I can to the Battle-leader and the most revered Consort of the Mother of Creation. It was I who bid Lucius bring me to you. He is a faithful member of our temple's congregation.'

'I might have bloody known!' the Scourge shouted. 'You're a no-good, Incarnus-bred priest! It's not enough that she kicks me out, but now she has to send an overfed, wittering fool to plague me, get in my way and trip me up.' He went for his blade and it was only Saltar's quick, restraining hand that stopped him pulling the weapon free of its scabbard. 'Get away from me or, so Lacrimos help me, I'll carve your fat frame thin. I will not have her keep a watch on me as if I were some possession, pet or child! I am no longer her consort and want no part of her or her fawning priesthood!'

Saltar could tell that the Scourge was working himself up into a killing rage and that there would be no reasoning with him, so he grabbed the Guardian around the arm and physically dragged him towards the stables. The priest shook with fear and cowered as they passed. The look that Saltar gave Lucius was all that was required to make it clear that Lucius should not dare to speak a word or attempt to follow them.

'Damn it, Scourge, enough of your self-indulgent domestic squabbles! My *child* has been taken. Who knows what's happening to him! Take your anger out on the gods-cursed magic-user who's responsible, not a witless, harmless priest.'

Chapter Two: And Fall

The three lords had always been. Even Larc's grandfather, the lords spare his recently departed soul, had only ever known the rule of the Three. They were ever-living. The large mountain valley was all any of the Brethren had ever known. They lived and died in the flat-bottomed river valley bounded by mountains and escarpments, and never dared venture beyond, for as they all knew there was only chaos and the void outside of the valley.

The lords preserved the people of the river valley. In times past, it was said, they had raised the landscape as a natural barrier against the unfettered nightmare forms beyond. They had then stationed the spirits of the dead at the boundaries to guard against any encroachment by the enemy without. At the same time, the lords were forced to forbid the Brethren from seeking to venture from the valley, since it could only result in death… or worse. It was in the Brethren's own interest to be so forbidden. It was for their protection. In that sense, being *Owned* by the lords was one of the sacraments every member of the Brethren experienced during their lives. Larc still remembered how proud his grandfather, parents and people were when on his thirteenth birthday, the age at which he left his childhood behind and became a man, he was admitted into the holy presence of one of the lords to confirm his Ownership. Of course, Larc didn't really remember much about the holy lord himself, since he'd been too terrified to look upon the true face of divinity.

Those had been the happiest days of his life. Having reached adulthood and confirmed he was Owned, he had then been permitted a mate. They'd given Sarla and Larc to each other, which had been more than either of them had ever had before, so they'd been grateful to the lords, even if the smile Sarla had given him in the early days had not been that happy or friendly. In his sinful heart, Larc himself had hoped for another, a woman called Lillian from the other end of the valley, a woman with hair as flaxen and buttery as the thick honey that the rare mountain bees produced one month in the year. But it wasn't to be, and the wisdom of the lords had ultimately led Larc to an enlightenment of sorts, for he and Sarla had come to find comfort in each other.

A year later and Larc and Sarla were rewarded for their faithfulness – for Sarla had become pregnant. Larc had been so proud that his friends told him he now had the chest of the eagle. He'd woken up with a grin on his face everyday, set out to hunt the rock rats in the boulder fields earlier than any other, then come home with the last of the light and a weary but loving smile to his beloved mate and their bright, warm home.

He'd never known her more beautiful. And she'd had a special place in the hearts of all the Brethren, for she was to produce a precious new life for the community. The lords explained how few the Brethren were compared to the infinite chaos beyond, and how absolutely necessary it was to preserve and increase the lives of the Brethren. They said the enemy would come one day, so the Brethren needed to multiply and become strong. That was another reason why the Brethren needed to be kept in the valley – they were Owned by their community, since every life was of such importance to the community.

Every life was so important. It had been a tragedy when Larc's grandfather had died, for he had been the oldest person in the valley except for the lords. No one in the community could think of life without him and his stories in the great community hall every night. Everyone's life was lessened by his passing.

And his grandfather had been done the greatest of honours, for the lords had sent not two but four of their magicker-retainers to ferry his corpse to the enormous House of the Dead atop the main mountain ridge. There, the whispers went, the dead were reborn so that they could act as nighttime guards along the borders of the valley. It was also said that some of the spirits of the dead were freed by the magickers so that they could find their way back to the community by possessing the bodies of as yet unborn children. Larc had always hoped that his grandfather would possess the baby growing in Sarla's stomach, for then his grandfather would become a part of his life again. Larc missed the knowing, forgiving and all important presence of his grandfather so much, as was only right and proper. Of course, Larc had never spent much time with his own father since, as a virtuous man, Larc's father would never seek to challenge the long-established, more valuable place and will of Larc's grandfather. Age and seniority were everything to the Brethren, since the greater the longevity of the people, the more numerous and strong they would become. After all, were the holy Three not the oldest among them?

The departure of his grandfather had been a terrible blow to Larc, even though he'd already become a man, but he had managed to cope with it by thinking of the rebirth the magickers promised. But what Larc had then suffered had plunged him into an all-consuming and inconsolable grief. It had utterly undone him and made him vulnerable to sin. He did not know how he stood on his feet anymore. The sin had clearly taken control of him for now he stood in the darkness at the base of the escarpment staring up at the silhouette of the House of the Dead dominating the skyline. He was even considering the forbidden act of climbing up to the top! He so desperately wanted to see them again! He knew it was wrong but could not help thinking it.

He knew he was flawed or lacking in faith somehow. Maybe a fundamental lack of faith had been his original sin, and that was why he'd been punished. Perhaps that was why Sarla and their baby had been allowed to die, why they had been taken from him. He must have transgressed in some way, left his thoughts open to the corrupting whispers of the chaos spirits that swirled around the perimeters of the valley.

His life was precious, yes, but it was clear to him now that he was no longer deserving of it. He began scaling the escarpment, uncaring of the damage he did to his nails and hands as he clawed his way up through the rock field. His hands began to feel wet, then sticky, and he knew it was blood, but that only meant his grip was better and he could haul himself closer to the dead and his worthy punishment.

All the Brethren knew that the reborn dead at the top of the ridge would not hesitate to kill anything they came across. They were there to keep the enemy out and the misguided in. They would even kill friends and family, it was said, so that the spirits of such friends and families could be freed in order to possess the bodies of unborn babies in the community. Such rebirth allowed tormented spirits to forget their troublesome memories and find a new and happier life in the community. It was a kindness really, the last of the sacraments.

What should have been the happiest day of his life had been the end of his life. Instinctively, he'd known something was wrong when Sarla had turned so pale. The wise woman attending the birth had looked worried. He'd dashed from their stone cottage, straight to the magicker temple. It had been late, but he'd been so beside himself with terror for Sarla that he'd forgotten to show obeisance as soon as he'd come within sight of the temple. There had been screams for help – probably his own – and then he'd hurtled through dark corridors, up and down, bellowing for the aid that was the due and preservation of the community.

The next thing his torn mind remembered was the cottage again. A burning torch, jumping shadows, the wise woman standing back against the far wall as the magicker crouched over the wan, wracked Sarla and chanted in a deep, throbbing voice. A hand resting on his forearm. A face close to his. A shaking head. And something in the magicker's eyes, something that was even worse than what was happening, something that was worse than losing Sarla and the baby, something that told him he would never know them again, something that killed him in a moment. A flicker of emotion across a face, whether a badly thrown shadow or not, something less than an instant but an infinity and eternity of meaning. The magicker had looked at him with… sympathy.

Sympathy! How could a magicker look at him with sympathy now, when Larc had defined himself and his life on what was meant to be an absolute faith, a faith of which the magickers were meant to be holy guardians? Just as the enemy would eventually come, so would their god, the magickers preached. The god would save them all. Magickers had even gone into the chaos and the void lately, it was said, to prepare the way for the god. Surely they would only have done that if they'd had the same faith as they espoused! Surely. The community waited and prayed for the return of the magickers and the deus ex machina. The Brethren lived faithful lives, so that deus ex machina was of itself a divine inevitability, surely! It was self-fulfilling in its absolute divinity, wasn't it?

Wasn't it? Where then did sympathy sit? Even a man who'd lost his grandfather, mate and child would not require sympathy if their spirits would always be returned to him. Why then had a guardian of the faith offered him sympathy? It was a betrayal, and it was beyond all compass. It annihilated all meaning and self. Larc no longer knew who he was or where he was. His name and thoughts had no meaning.

All he saw was the House of the Dead. It was pitch black down in the valley but the enormous mausoleum stood out against the starlit sky. A gentle moaning drifted down from the heights, but he assured himself it was the wind and kept climbing. As he came closer, he realised the building was even bigger than he'd always thought, bigger than the lords' temple even, so big it could only have been built by a god. It was an ancient edifice that had stood looking out over the valley of the Owned since time immemorial, or far longer than any of the Brethren could remember anyway. It had been a permanent part of the landscape of Larc's life; it had been familiar and reassuring because it had represented the watchful care and protection of the Three. But now it loomed before him dark and forbidding. He slowed his approach, terrified beyond telling.

He should not be here. For such a transgression, there would be no forgiveness or sympathy. There would only be death. He pondered the prospect of such an end and the promise of forgetfulness, and realised it did not scare him. In fact, it would be welcome, for he could not live with the anguish of the loss of Sarla and his child. His life was empty and bereft. In fact, it was not life, it was merely existence. In all the ways that mattered, therefore, he was already dead and this was the right place for him.

He stepped forwards woodenly, peering through the dark, trying to catch signs of any movement. Entering the large expanse of the lee of the House, a clammy coldness began to take hold of him. He shivered but could not shake off the fingers of its icy grip. Unsighted, he half-ran and half-stumbled towards the titanic wall of the House, but it offered him no shelter: he was exposed. And now the wind rose, its distant howls like those of a pack of hunting dogs that had found his trail and were coming ever closer to their prey. He fought to control the panic in his throat. Instinctively, he knew that his absence was now discovered and that they had set off in pursuit. It was not for him to decide how the life of one of the Owned would be administered. They would dispose of it as they saw fit.

If he was to see Sarla, he knew he would now have to move quickly, but his limbs were as heavy and lifeless as stone. The magickers must be reaching out for him, trying to paralyse him where he was. He growled and performed the mental shrug he'd copied as a mannerism from his grandfather. It gave him just enough manoeuvring space to focus in on himself, find his core and release his limbs from their burdened state. He felt an echo of the consternation of the community's questing magicker and allowed himself a small, self-satisfied smile.

Pushing himself, he got to the corner of the building and peeked around it. Motionless figures stood scattered along the ridge, looking out away from the valley. Some of them swayed slightly on their feet, as if finding it hard to keep their balance. Halfway along the adjacent wall, the giant doors to the House stood open. There were no guards in evidence; after all, what did the dead need to guard against? Larc wiped sweat from his top lip, his mind racing.

Would Sarla be inside? Or would she be outside, standing a silent vigil with the others? He daren't approach any of them out here because they would all come for him at once. He had no choice.

He crept forwards a pace or two and then stopped to be sure no one had seen him. Then another step, and still: like the grey, near-invisible mouse who lived under the floor of Larc and Sarla's cottage, a creature he'd studied time and again on long, quiet evenings when it had ventured out for crumbs of food.

He trembled, his every sense alert for any hint of danger or change. The wind on this side of the building was stronger than on the leeside and covered the slight scraping noise his feet made on the stony ground. He feared a sudden lull, but he knew the pattern and feel of the wind in the mountains well enough to know that any sudden stillness now would be down to the use of magic. But who knew what the dead were capable of, what fell powers were theirs to command? And might the magickers be able to communicate with the dead they Owned, even with the House so far from the community? Were they simply waiting for him to enter the House so that he would then be trapped within?

He gathered what he could of the fickle wind around him and blew through the open doors to the mausoleum. He rushed deep within, swirling all around before the wind could lose its impetus in the confined space. It was a place of untold horrors, but he managed to rush past most of them before they could settle into his numbed mind. Still, he could not completely ignore the images of decayed and fragmented bodies struggling and failing to rise. Were there tormented spirits trapped in all this animated detritus? How long had they been like this? Decades, lifetimes, longer? Apparently, the dead gradually declined and eroded even after having been raised by the magickers. Was this the fate that awaited his grandfather and dear Sarla? He could not conscience it.

The air began to leave him and he now found it difficult to pick his way through the twitching limbs and half-bodies all over the floor. Quickly! he told himself, the skin at his temples pulling tight with stress and hurting his scalp and jaw. His life suddenly felt very fragile.

Unseeing eyes turned towards him and fingers and arms began to reach. He moved faster now, no longer caring what he trod on. Desiccated lungs wheezed and tried to call the dead vigilantes outside. His right foot fell through a chest cavity and he had to lift the animated cadaver with his leg before he could kick it off him.

He found the next doorway and pulled himself into the room beyond. It was the last room left. Thankfully, some of the roof had fallen in, so that there was enough grey light to see by. Stone tables and plinths stood in ranks along the length of the charnel space, fresh and whole corpses laid out and statuesque. He could see her. He stepped quickly before his courage deserted him.

Larc laid his hands on his beloved and shook her gently, trying to avoid looking at the sunken shape and stained area of smock where her abdomen was meant to be. 'Saaarla! It's me! Wake up, wake up. Sarla, please!'

Her eyes snapped open and he had to hold onto to her with all his might to prevent himself from stepping back in horror. This wasn't her. Now he saw her more clearly, these empty eyes and this stretched face were not the warm and happy features of the being he knew as Sarla.

Her arms rose as he leaned over her and the backs of her hands brushed his cheeks; then they moved back down and her fingers encircled his throat. She'd done this to him when she'd been alive. He smiled. He couldn't breathe, though, and she still refused to look at him. He put his arms inside hers and slammed his forearms against her elbows, sure that would break her grip.

'Gaack!' he managed as he sought to flex his throat enough to grab a vital breath. But she instantly squeezed harder. She meant to kill him. He made a fist and smashed the meat of it into her face. She didn't make a noise even though cartilage and bone gave way. He began to cry.

'Ba-by!' It was the last he had. At least he would die in her embrace… if that was what she wanted. Her nails bit deep into his neck and blood trickled down his chest. Spots appeared in his vision and then he lost his sight.

The pressure lessened and then stopped. He blinked. He was lying on the floor. She looked over the edge of the table and down at him without any emotion. He'd broken her nose, and felt awful despite what she'd done to him.

'Sorry. I'm so sorry,' he rasped painfully. 'If there'd been anything I could have done… anything… to…' he trailed away.

There was no blink, no light of understanding in her eyes. Slack and dead. He pushed himself up awkwardly and she rose to a seated position. She put her arms out in a plea.

He shook his head: 'I don't-don't have our child. Is he not with you?'

She remained mute, her eyes reflecting nothing.

'My love!' he half-sobbed. 'What have they done to you? What have they done to us?' He put his arms around her stiff torso and hid his face in her hard shoulder.

Larc rallied after a few moments and leaned away. Her mouth hinged open and shut as if she was trying to speak. He pushed carefully against her chest. As it sprang back, air filled her lungs.

'Leave!' she sighed. 'Before it is too late. Bring our boy to me. I love you. I fade. It is difficult to stay, to be here, to be… don't… who am… help me!'

Her cruel hands began to seek to strangle him again and he lurched away. He stopped and stared at her in agony. She leaned forwards and tried to come after him.

He fled from his beloved, the woman who was everything to him. What help was there? He banged into a half-standing animee, blundered on and, as he left the House, careened into an undead sentinel just outside the door.

'Ahh!' he yelped in terror, scrabbling away from the clawing thing.

Now they were all turning towards him. He did not know where he was going, but simply ran, ducking and dodging, slapping away blackened hands. He was suddenly teetering at the edge of a shale precipice and over-balancing. 'Help!' He fell forever, sometimes buried, then churned back up above the loose stones, suffering large stones as they clattered and battered him, having his ears deafened by the angry mountain as he was violently thrown out of the valley of the Owned. Their sanctuary was no longer his.

He couldn't think. He was bruised and dazed. Small pebbles continued to trickle and bounce down around him. Louder stones still clacked above and he rolled painfully away in case one should be about to find his vulnerable head.

Larc had come down the far side of the ridge. These were the wastes of chaos, nightmare and the void. There would be demons and the lost god out here. Magickers were out here searching. He would join them and do whatever was required to bring help for his dead wife and child. Even if it meant submitting to an eternity of slavery and torture, it would be worth it. What else was there?

Chapter Three: Onto hard ground

'Throw you out, did she?' cackled an old man on a doorstep not far away, showing off pointed brown teeth.

The Scourge pulled his horse up and leaned forwards on his pommel. 'Trajan, that you? I swear there's less of you each time I see you.'

'Wouldn't be surprised, what with all the toing and froing I have to do! Food ain't what it used to be either,' mourned the elder.

The Scourge smiled, rarely having seen the head of the outdwellers sat anywhere other than at his customary perch in front of the door to his small, dark house. During Voltar's time, this stone dwelling had been one of the few buildings to exist outside of the city walls. It was the traditional home of those who lived in the catacombs beneath Corinus to feed on the bodies of the dead interred by the indwellers above. There'd been no other reliable source of food back then, and the human instinct for survival always defeated a sensitive morality in a straight fight. Shakri would even have approved in some ways, the Scourge reflected. Life was sacred to her and she refused to judge those who did whatever was required to survive, to preserve their sacred spark.

'Starting to get some new neighbours for yourself, I see,' observed the Scourge and nodded towards the new row of houses being built by Memnosian soldiers not far away.

Trajan hawked and spat into the loosely cobbled road. 'Seems that way. Gotta have somewhere for folks to stay out of the weather now that the catacombs have been closed to them, haven't we?' Then he pulled a clay pipe from inside his none-too-clean shirt, tapped it out and proceeded to tamp a small wad of tobacco carefully into the bowl.

The wind soughed. Saltar shifted impatiently in his saddle. The Scourge sent him a warning look and then commented to Trajan: 'To be sure, things have changed, some for the better I'd say.'

'Praps, praps not,' Trajan replied evenly, for all the world like he was idly passing the time of day with a neighbour. He put the pipe stem in the gap in his bottom teeth and waited.

The Scourge sighed to himself. The cantankerous old scrotum didn't get any easier with age. 'What would be better and worse, to your way of thinking?' he asked, pulling his flint and tinder pouch from his saddle-bag and dismounting from his horse so that he could light Trajan's smoke.

After an elaborate few minutes of striking sparks and shielding them from the wind, the Scourge finally had the man satisfied. 'Much obliged! Well now, young Scourge, seeing as I'd heard you were dead, then I'd say you looked to be in better shape than I'd expected. Asto the worse, well, your being around has never been an omen of the gods' imminent blessing being visited on mankind, now has it? Put plainly, there's always a heap of trouble coming if you and I are having to converse.'

The Scourge stared at Trajan in shock. It took him a second to recover himself. The old man was absolutely right.

Frustrated with the cryptic references of the two, and now their strange silences, Saltar demanded of Trajan: 'Do you know of any foreigners who might have entered the catacombs in the last few days? They will have ridden out of here in some haste but a few hours ago.'

Trajan looked at only the Scourge. 'Did you hear something just then, Guardian?'

The Scourge got a grip on himself and decided to move things on more quickly, before Saltar took it into his head to throttle answers out of the old man. 'Dear Trajan, this man is a father. His child has just been stolen from him. He is beside himself with worry. He cannot help but suffer from a certain distraction right now. Can you help us at all?'

'How is your child, the rat-boy?' Saltar asked Trajan grimly. 'I feel him watching us with his beady eyes from inside your small house.'

Trajan's eyes were dragged almost against his will to Saltar. The old man suddenly looked fragile and exposed, there on his step. He shivered slightly against the cold edge of the breeze. Trajan blew lungfuls of smoke out in front of him, to obscure Saltar's gaze and break the spell of the dreadful moment. 'I remember you now,' came the outdweller's croak through the haze. 'Those last days were dark. So much screaming and death. My boy took you into the catacombs, as I recall. Risked his life.'

Saltar's eyes remained unforgiving. 'All lives were in the balance. If you had not acted then, we would not be bandying words here now. I am asking you to act again, Trajan, for lives are in the balance.'

'All lives, think you?' asked Trajan contemplatively.

'Praps, praps not.'

Trajan chuckled without any real mirth. 'Hmm. Then it may help us all to know that six men in black robes and turbans rode through here within the last handspan of hours.'

'Jaffrans!' the Scourge gasped in confusion. 'Surely not. They have no reason to move against Dur Memnos, certainly no interest in making an enemy of us.'

'They are heathens,' Trajan shrugged, as if that were sufficient explanation.

Saltar frowned. He did not know much about the remote but large island of Jaffra across the Sea of Tears to the east. To be sure, Jaffrans were famed seafarers, who often brought their spice ships into the Memnosian port of King's Landing for the purposes of trade, but they rarely ventured very far inland, and certainly not in any numbers. They followed some sort of orthodoxy that meant they preferred not to mingle with other races; and they were never to be found in any of the drinking dens that characterised the seafront of every Memnosian port.

'No Jaffran embassy in living memory has ever presented itself in Corinus... and I've been alive a long time,' Saltar mused. 'They would stand out immediately if ever they came here. They would not have the local knowledge required to find somewhere safe so that they could observe the comings and goings of the palace.'

The Scourge's eyes narrowed suspiciously and he watched Trajan carefully as he said, 'But there are plenty of Memnosians who are mercenary enough or desperate enough to help them, wouldn't you say, Trajan? I imagine food is harder to come by now that there aren't piles of bodies lying around because of the war, eh? Indeed, didn't you say something to that effect when we first stopped by? Are any of the outdwellers close to starving, Trajan?'

Trajan's eyes also narrowed. He removed the pipe from his mouth and said in a very deliberate tone: 'No outdweller can have been involved without my permission. And if I had any issue with how Corinus were being run, then we all know I would have more direct and effective ways of dealing with it. I certainly wouldn't need no foreigner to be doing my dirty work for me. That, I swear on Shakri's holy menses. If it turns out that some Memnosian *has* been involved in this dark business then, mark me, it won't be a Memnosian from around here. It will have been a rogue mercenary out of Holter's Cross, either that or a dry-throated and desperate pirate from King's Landing. Now, given it will be one of the latter, those that have run the kingdom so poorly for so long only have themselves to blame if their lack of vigilance has brought them and their troubles to my doorstep.'

The Scourge sighed and hung his head. He should have known better than to take such a tack with the old man. They were now unlikely to get anything more of use out of him. Saltar's knuckles cracked loudly as they tightened around the reins to his horse. His jaw clenched and his neck corded. He strained as he fought to hold back his unreasoning rage and fear. In a strangled voice, he finally managed:

'I apologise if we have insulted you with our speculation. We will remove ourselves now, in order to pursue these bastard offspring of Lacrimos. Good day, Trajan. I hope not to have to trouble you again anytime soon.'

The old man considered Saltar with calculating eyes, sucked on his withered cheeks for a few seconds and then apparently came to some sort of decision. 'It is not everyday that the Battle-leader of Dur Memnos offers an apology. I worry when such things happen. It tells me that this is no ordinary day and that we do not live in ordinary times. I will send my boy to your wife and tell her what I have told you. I will also ascertain what has been seen and heard in the city in the last few days. Besides, if too much starts to go on without my knowing of it, then the outdwellers will quickly decide that I'm slipping and that my bones would be of more use to them for making stewing stock.'

The Scourge nodded his respectful thanks to Trajan. 'A sergeant-at-arms should be leading five men through here soon.'

'Very well,' the old man grumbled. 'I will also direct them, but that is all. I don't know what consorts you have been used to of late, Scourge, but I am no wench set to waiting upon your pleasure. You're sucking on a teat that dried up years ago.'

The Scourge winced. 'Perhaps I owed you that one. Farewell, you old crone!' He kicked his horse on down the road.

Saltar's spirited horse was quickly vying for the lead, as impatient as its master. It rarely got enough exercise, what with Saltar too often cooped up in meetings and dealing with the intricacies of running the kingdom. Finally free of Corinus, therefore, the horse demanded its head, and Saltar gave it willingly. 'Faster!' Saltar whispered to the horse and then shouted across to the Scourge:

'We must assume they make for King's Landing. Will they be going cross-country?'

'It may be shorter in distance, but is a longer journey in time. No, they will go north to Holter's Cross and then east to the coast!'

'Then no more talk and pontification. Let's do this, Scourge! If you can't keep up, I'll leave you behind. And we will ride through night and day until we have hunted down our prey.'

The Scourge was about to answer that the horses wouldn't last long at such speed, that perhaps they should give the soldiers time to catch up in case they were ambushed, that they should think the Jaffran threat through more before... but then he told himself he should just shut his yap. Why was he constantly trying to delay them taking action? What had happened to him? When had he become so fearful, so henpecked? That bloody goddess had much to answer for. Saltar's child had been taken from him, for crying out loud! Why couldn't the Scourge stay connected to and focussed on that? Was there some agency deliberately seeking to keep him mentally distracted? If so, what force could be at work here, for surely not even Shakri would stoop so low as to put bothering him over saving the life of an innocent child?

⁂

Kate was in no mood to be thinking anything but blasphemous thoughts about the gods at that moment. How could they have permitted her child to be taken from her after all she'd done for them? Hadn't she risked her life time and again to preserve their pantheon? Hadn't Saltar and all those he loved similarly been put at risk? And more than that, wasn't she Shakri's own daughter? Hadn't Cognis, the hoary, old god of knowledge and wisdom, dandled her on his knee when she was a child? Is this how they treated their own family, then? Did they have so little understanding of love? No, she couldn't believe it, for Shakri was love itself. Something else must be going on.

'Mother of Creation, answer me in my hour of need!' she shouted at the ceiling to the empty room. Only her echo answered her.

'Incarnus! I want vengeance on those who have wronged us!' The shutters to the room rattled, but there was no other sign that anyone had heard her.

She suddenly felt small and alone. She put her arms around herself and rocked backwards and forwards on her feet slightly. She realised she was humming the silly tune she always used when bathing Orastes. He would watch her with his wide, blue eyes and listen intently whenever she sang it. It stopped him play-fighting so she could get him properly washed. Where had it come from? Wasn't it something Lucius had composed?

It was at about this time she would bathe Orastes every day. But where was the maid heating the kettle of water over the fire today? Where was Orastes now? She barely had the courage to ask herself the question, for the answers that came to her only served to increase her terror. She tried not to think about it but then feelings of guilt that she dared neglect her son came crowding in. She hummed even more loudly and hung onto it for all she was worth, somehow knowing that if she did not her thoughts and sense of self would be lost completely. Slowly, the suffocating darkness receded and she found she could draw a new, shuddering breath into her chest.

She needed to find different answers than these, answers of her own if the gods would not or could not provide them. She secured the last buckle on her green leather armour, which was stiff with a lack of use, moved her arms in big circles and twisted left and right at the waist. The creaking and groaning of her second skin was terrible to hear. She should never have laid it aside, but Saltar had taught her to dream and then believe peace and happiness were possible. Deep down, she'd always known it could not last, and perversely it was now something of a relief that the wait was over. No longer did she have to watch over her shoulder in fear that some predator was stalking her and waiting for its opportunity to strike with maximum impact. She'd survived the first encounter and was now hunting her enemy. She would track it all the way back to its lair and end the struggle once and for all, no matter the outcome. The fight for existence was joined once again and she felt more alive than she had in several years. Her eyes were bright and there was a fierce hunger within her.

As she worked to make the leather armour more supple, she now found the joints and muscles of her body beginning to protest.

'By the premature ejaculate of Wim!' she cried. 'I'm too soft!'

When she'd become pregnant with Orastes, she'd eventually had to give up her training, and after his birth she'd only returned to light and irregular martial practice. She would need to harden herself quickly if she was to have any hope of bringing dangerous foes to bay. What had she been thinking to let herself become so weak? Why had Shakri decided on such a form of motherhood in a realm that always sought to prey on the vulnerable? Why create the urge to procreate and the parenting instinct? All it brought was pain and loss ultimately, whether to the parent who lost their child or the child who saw their parent die of old age, if they were fortunate enough to reach old age of course.

Curse the ways of the heart that it could allow such things to happen. The flaw was in her, she knew. But the gods had probably designed mortals with such a flaw precisely to stop mortals from becoming divine themselves, to prevent them from challenging the balance of power. She felt on the verge of some sort of dark revelation. Would she have to challenge that very balance of power to guarantee the safety of her child and those she loved? Was this the sort of dilemma Voltar had found himself in? Had they completely misunderstood him and what he was trying to achieve? She now feared they might have.

But what hope did she, one woman, have of shifting the entire cosmic balance of power? It was unthinkable, unimaginable, impossible. She wished Saltar was here to tell her what to do.

No, enough of such dependency: it did neither herself nor those she loved any favours. She would have to be of an adamantine mind and body if she was to win through all that was arrayed against her. She put on her second leather glove and splayed her fingers out so that their tips came right to the ends. Then she tightened it into an uncomplaining, compact fist.

Determined, she strode away from the room. Mordius was waiting for her in the antechamber. He stepped forwards, and then hesitated as he beheld her demeanour. There was a nervous wariness on his face. How she hated his cowardice.

'So we depart for the temple of Cognis, then, Kate?' he snivelled.

Quelling her impulse to kill him where he stood, she grimaced. 'Am I right that the priests of Cognis have fore-knowledge, Mordius? Should they, in fact, already know that we have need of them?' And, sadly, I have need of you, at least for now.

The magician nodded silently.

'Well, given that they haven't presented themselves at the palace yet, then they would seem disinclined to offer us much help or support. Such an attitude towards the throne is a little... disappointing, wouldn't you say?'

'I – ah... their first loyalty is to...'

'Because *I* find it disappointing, I can tell you that, if not a little treasonous. And then I cannot help wondering if they had fore-knowledge of the kidnapping. In fact, I cannot help wondering if they are somehow complicit in all this!'

'Kate, fore-knowledge doesn't really work like...'

'Oh, quit your whining, Mordius! I'm not in the mood for it right now. Honestly, you're worse than the Chamberlain. At least he usually knows what's going on. We'll be taking most of the palace guard with us on our little visit to the temple.'

'Kate, no! Relations between the throne and the temples have always been predicated on trust and respect. We can't just march in there and start making threats and demands.'

'No, Mordius, you're wrong. That's precisely what I can do and intend to do. Just as someone marched into the royal palace unchallenged and took Orastes from me. You see? You stand there wittering on about trust and respect, when that was the last thing that was afforded me and mine! Are you so insensitive, so selfish, Mordius? Do you not stand with us, Mordius?'

Mordius blinked wide-eyed and shook his head. He struggled to speak, as a fish struggles to breathe out of water. 'I – I will do whatever I can to help you, you know that…'

'Good, then you can help by getting out of my way before I walk over you, and then you can use whatever existing relationship you have with the flaming priests of Cognis to get us an invitation to meet the High Priest. If that's going to prove too difficult for you, then you're of no use to me and I'll have to take matters into my own hands.'

Mordius took a deep breath and released it slowly. He raised trembling hands in a placating gesture. 'Yes, of course, you're right. We need to find out what they can tell us about both Orastes and those working against us…'

'Glad we agree on something!'

'…but, remember, there is more than one way to skin a priest.'

Kate smiled grimly. 'Now you're talking, Mordius. I suppose we could flay the skin from them, or cut it away with a knife, or just peel it away as you would with a piece of fruit. What would you suggest? Tell you what, let's try them all. Maybe we can come up with some other ways while we're at it, but the results are largely going to be the same, aren't they? Yes, it might be fun, but we really haven't got the time to get too creative. Let's keep things simple, instead. Are you coming or not?'

Mordius followed slowly after the leather-clad woman, no longer recognising her, and more terrified than he had been in a long time. What was happening to everyone?'

❧ ❧

It was late afternoon but the landscape was already hovering in gloom. Saltar squinted up at the hazy, ineffectual sun. Its umbra flickered like a glittering candle. True, winter was probably only a month or so away, but surely the autumn could muster more of its bronzed glory than this! He shrugged it off, content that the world around him seemed to understand his mood and increasing sense of foreboding.

The Scourge rode just off Saltar's left shoulder, eyes staring straight ahead. It was reassuring to have this relentless warrior at his side once again, but not for the first time Saltar wondered at how the Scourge's miraculous return to the world of the living had all but coincided with the Jaffrans kidnapping Orastes. And the Battle-leader knew enough of the gods to be fairly certain they would take it upon themselves to have a hand in such matters, whether those matters might be considered mortal or not. Shakri, the Mother of Creation and the goddess of love and life, had never got on with her dark brother, Lacrimos, god of war and death, and both were quite capable of interfering in the affairs of this realm purely on the off-chance of gaining some small advantage over the other. At the end of the day, it was characteristic of the gods to see mortals at best as mere agents of divine will or pawns, and at worst as play-things or insignificant specs of dust. No wonder the Scourge was still angry at the gods despite the apparent honour he'd received as Shakri's consort.

Saltar allowed his mare to drift closer to the Scourge's destrier. 'What was it like being Her consort? Where is the pantheon of the gods? Can you describe it?'

The Scourge scowled at the ruler of Dur Memnos.

'This is not the time to be coy, Scourge. Anything you can tell me, no matter how seemingly unconnected, might help in finding Orastes. You cannot expect me to leave any stone unturned, even if it means I have to treat you and your delicate feelings somewhat unkindly.'

The Scourge's scowl remained, but softened slightly. His tone was surly at first but gradually became more even: 'The word consort is misleading in some ways. It wasn't so much of a physical thing between us… as… as a kind of meeting of, well, minds or essence… spirit, I guess some would call it. I don't think I'm describing it very well. Look, the pantheon isn't a place as such – it's not like you just walk along and meet one of the gods there or anything.'

'So what is it, then?'

'Well, it's, it's as if they're all aspects of the same essence. Each of them is different, to be sure, but still the same, even Shakri. For a while, I shared myself with the aspect called Shakri, but I don't know if you'd call it love, really. It's much more than love in some ways… but maybe less in others, I'm not sure.'

'Different but the same,' Saltar murmured to himself while the Scourge indulged in his own personal reverie. What was he reminded of? It was like the paradox that lay at the foundation of the necromatic magic Mordius had used to raise him from the dead so many years before. Perhaps there were similar paradoxes at the roots of all magic, divinity and reality. Ultimately, such paradoxes unravelled themselves, as the tension at their heart slowly tore them apart. Perhaps Voltar had had such insight and used it to take them all to the brink of the void, to take them so close to the end. The throne room in Corinus was all that had been left of Shakri's realm, hanging there in eternal nothingness.

If paradox lay at the foundation of everything, then everything would eventually unravel, everything would come to an end. It was a terrifying thought. One day, there would be no gods, no mortals, no reality. In fact, one day there would be no one day.

Surely there had to be a more permanent and universal dynamic! Surely there was a dynamic that didn't rely on paradox! There had to be something more enduring, something eternal, didn't there? But if even the gods weren't eternal, what was?

Saltar realised he now had a headache. He'd been about to ask another question concerning the gods when he suddenly changed what he was going to ask. 'Scourge, why am I having so much trouble seeing you? Have we entered some sort of murk? Have my eyes become misted? I can hardly see the road.'

The Scourge spat over the side of his horse and wiped his mouth. He began to reach for his blade. 'I don't like the taste of this. It doesn't strike me as natural. Night should be hours away yet. Stay close. I can hardly see you and we don't want to get separated.'

Saltar peered through the increasingly opaque fog at the silhouette of the Scourge, even though he couldn't be more than six feet away. He felt boxed in and the sound of his horse's hooves echoing back off the grey walls only added to the effect.

A caped, shadowy figure carrying a half-lance approached the outline of the Scourge. Although the Scourge's sword was drawn, he didn't shift his body position as if he were aware of the closing attacker.

'Look out!' Saltar shouted in panic.

In silent horror, he watched the half-lance plunge through the Scourge and out his back. The Guardian arched in mute agony and his antagonist capered like an uncoordinated shadow-puppet.

'Show yourself!' Saltar screamed in impotent fury, slashing with his staff and only finding air. He couldn't trust his own eyes in such an ether it seemed. 'Scourge!' he yelled, but all sound was deadened as if its energy were leeched away the instant it left his mouth.

Yet laughter came to him from his left. Saltar strained to see, but his sight was completely occluded – was it in his eyes or this heavy atmosphere that the cataracts lay? A voice drifted towards him, again from the left.

'Show? Show? You are a simpleton! You are not worthy of vision or this realm!' came the clammy accusation. 'I, Visier, will only permit such vision as it illuminates the arrival of the god.'

A point came spearing in at Saltar's chest, visible only at the last moment as it was about to penetrate him. Saltar had already adopted the stance required for the elemental fighting forms known as Wind, and twisted his torso at the waist so that the weapon could only glance through his leather armour and bounce off his ribs. The Battle-leader had already shut away the part of his mind that understood pain, for he knew the wound would not be fatal.

His opponent was clearly a master of the visual dimension. He had a type of magic that could manipulate, obscure and blind the sight of others. Saltar refused to be debilitated by this one sense. His hearing would suffice – after all, the sound of Visier and the attack had both come from the left, so that sense could probably be trusted to be accurate.

Saltar sent a sudden zephyr to that side of his body and felt his staff make contact with something. There was a gasp. Swirling, Saltar became a series of strong gusts that kept his opponent on the back-foot. Drawing greater and greater momentum from the dispersed magical energies of Visier's artificially created space, Saltar quickly whipped himself up into a devastating tornado form. He battered the magic-user mercilessly, blows cracking on skull and limbs without surcease. An eddy or flurry would pull Visier's defence one way and then leave him open for the full and unforgiving force of the whirlwind coming in close behind.

The fog separated like a ripped curtain and the inert, bleeding, broken form of the assassin could be seen flickering on the ground. The Scourge stalked out of the fading shadows around them and savagely kicked the magic-user in the head. The rays of the setting sun cut through the mists of Visier's magic and the world could now be seen.

'You're alive!' Saltar said in wonder.

'Of course I'm bloody alive!' the Scourge harrumphed. 'No thanks to this excretion of Lacrimos!'

'I'm not sure he's actually got anything to do with Lacrimos,' Saltar mused. 'He didn't use a death-magic or anything I've seen before. How was he able to change the nature of light? Mordius could have probably told us.'

The Scourge crouched, pulled back the sleeve of Visier's black robe and checked his pulse. 'He can tell us himself. He's still alive. That turban of his probably saved his life. So, do we set up camp for the night? It'd give this fellow time to come round, us time to torture him, and time for Marr and his men to catch up with us – we might need them if this is the sort of ambush we're going to be running into from now on.'

Saltar fretted at the loss of any time. He feared that his son was in some sort of increasing peril. If they didn't find the kidnappers soon, they might *never* find them. He looked off down the King's Road anxiously and then back at the swarthy Jaffran, trying to decide on a course of action. The information they got from this Visier might end up saving them a lot of time. And they might not get such an opportunity again.

'Okay, search him properly and then bind and gag him. If he's a magician, we don't want him mouthing spells before we even realise he's awake. Meantime, you can tell me how it is I saw him run you through, only to have you standing in front of me now full of the joys of life.'

'Eh? You saw what? Look, that fog was full of phantoms and strange shapes. At one point, I thought I saw a legion of demons all around me. I'd say this magician was more than capable of a few illusions.'

Saltar nodded and wondered why the Scourge had avoided his eyes when giving his explanation. Surely the Guardian wasn't hiding something from him, was he? If so, that would be out of character for the usually frank and direct Scourge. If the magician were truly capable of illusion, could he have swapped himself for the Scourge? Was it actually the Scourge that Saltar had smashed to the ground and was ordering to be tied up? Saltar narrowed his eyes and began to watch the Guardian intently.

There was a shiftiness to the other's eyes. Was that a sidelong glance he was throwing? The Scourge had never displayed such behaviour before. Saltar casually brought his staff across his body and balanced his weight.

The Guardian shot to his feet and faced the Battle-leader. His hands did not move for any of his weapons. Anger and frustration distorted his features so that he was barely recognisable. 'You don't understand!'

'Then why don't you explain it to me!' Saltar said dangerously.

The Scourge ground his teeth. He was apparently going through some inner conflict. 'I am cursed!' he said finally. 'Will you not be satisfied with that, damn you?!'

'No. I will *not* be satisfied with that. What's happened to you? I don't know you at all. Who are you?'

Fear and grief now transformed the old warrior's face. 'No! Don't say that! You don't know what she's done to me! I am destroyed. There is nothing left to me.'

'Explain!' Saltar barked, trying to force coherence from the being in front of him, fighting to drag meaning out of its nihilistic self-division.

'I – I cannot die!' the Scourge moaned barely audibly. 'It's worse than death!'

Saltar frowned. What on earth did this creature mean? 'Shakri has done this to you, I take it, as some sort of punishment? It makes no sense.'

The Scourge was close to sobbing. 'They said it was divine love. She said I could stay with them forever. We would not be undone. He would know her and all would be well. I... I... are them... is us. Please!'

Saltar thought furiously, putting his all into the act. 'I was wrong. I know you. There is no doubt now. You are the Scourge.'

The Scourge stood transfixed.

'You can die. It is harder for you than most, but there is no question that you can die.' For a warrior like the Scourge, the hazard of life and death, definition through violence and struggle, was all-consuming. To take the resolution and meaning represented by death from him was to erase the larger part of who he was. What remained could hardly sustain itself. It was a tragically cruel sentence that the gods had passed on the Scourge. 'I could strike your head from your shoulders, break open your skull and reduce your brains to a puree. They would have little hope of reconstituting you,' Saltar confided.

The Scourge blinked and Saltar's words worked a sort of magic to reset the warrior's features and re-establish who he was. 'That bitch!' he snarled. The man was nearly himself again. He looked confused. 'What were we talking about?'

Saltar was shaken to the very foundations of his being. Had the paradox under-pinning reality been about to unravel before his eyes? What would have happened if he hadn't intervened at precisely that moment, if he had chosen the wrong place and side for the tipping point of the balance? Could Shakri's reality really be fragile? What had happened to make it so? He wondered if he'd half imagined it, but then what was it Visier had said in the darkness? Something about the arrival of *the* god? Was there a malevolent god working to seize or destroy Shakri's creation? It could not be Lacrimos, for he had as much interest in preserving the balance as Shakri did, and Visier had used a type of magic seemingly entirely alien to this world. And how was the kidnapping of his sweet and innocent son connected to all this?

The magician began to move slowly. Realising he hadn't seen to binding him properly yet, the Scourge used his foot to roll the man onto his front. Kneeling swiftly, he used a piece of whipcord to secure his hands. The man groaned and tried to open eyes swollen closed by the beating he'd taken.

The Scourge pulled his neckerchief free and began to roll it so that it could be used as a gag. Suddenly, Visier bucked and twisted onto his side. His face was contorted in agony. The Scourge cursed and stepped back shaking his head.

'What's going on?' Saltar demanded.

'Must have had a tooth loaded with poison for just this sort of situation.'

'Can't you do anything?' Saltar asked irrationally. 'He's got to tell us how to find Orastes.'

The Scourge shook his head and watched the magician's death throes without emotion.

'Damn it!' Saltar shouted and turned away before his anger and frustration could get the better of him. He wanted to shake the Guardian, scream in his face that he was useless, punch him until he was unrecognisable. He began to shake, feeling a killing rage start to build in him.

'Wait, I'll search his body and see if there's anything that can help us,' the Scourge said in ignorance of Saltar's temper.

It was enough to give Saltar pause and get his trembling under control. What was he to do now? Get back on his horse and ride through the night? There was nothing to keep him here anymore, no evening to be had torturing answers out of Visier. If Mordius had been here, of course, then he could have simply raised the assassin from the dead and compelled the spirit to give them the answers they needed. This wasn't the first time he'd wished Mordius was with them, he realised. Had it been a mistake to leave him back in Corinus, particularly when they were faced with a magic they didn't understand? They didn't really have much of a defence, did they? Uncharacteristically, Saltar began to doubt himself. What's the matter with me, he worried. Since when was I plagued by fears and phantasms? What's happening?

'I'm still searching him, that's what's happening!' the Scourge called back testily.

Saltar blinked. He hadn't realised he'd spoken his question out loud. 'Err... right. Good. Let me know if you find anything. I take it we shouldn't waste the time burying or burning the body, right? Let's just leave it here by the road and get going… right? What do you think?'

The Scourge stood up and studied Saltar. 'Nothing.'

'What?'

'I haven't found anything on the body. As to what I think to riding on, I don't think much of it. It's about to get dark and there's hardly any moon, so I don't think we'd make that much progress. Plus, any ground we made up during the night would be offset by the fact our horses would not be fresh come the morning. Potentially, riding on now will lose us more than we can gain.

'I mean, just look at the horses. They're in a lather and we should wipe them down before the sweat starts drying on them. Otherwise, they'll catch a chill and decline all the faster. We don't want to ride them into their graves, Saltar!

'And you can be sure that those we hunt will not be making these sorts of mistakes. Everything we've seen tells us that they have planned and prepared all this in ruthless detail. Look at the fact this Jaffran had nothing about his person that might provide us with any information. Someone clearly anticipated the possibility of our defeating him. I've told you before, we are up against an experienced, sophisticated mind. Be in no doubt then that those we're after will have spare sets of horses waiting for them along the way, and that the best we can hope to achieve is not letting them get even further ahead of us. We must accept that we are not going to be able to overtake them, and that we need to make decisions based on a longer game.'

'This is no *game*!' Saltar sneered.

'Stop it! You know what I mean. We have to start thinking more. We can't keep reacting and lashing out. We need to sit down right here and give ourselves the space and time to think properly. Otherwise, we'll just run blindly into any snare or ambush they choose to set for us.'

'Have you finished?'

'No!' the Scourge said with a stubbornness to match Saltar's own. 'You also need to look at yourself, Saltar. Your face is grey and shows only frowns and worry lines. You'll ride straight into Lacrimos's realm with your horse if you carry on driving yourself like this. You've got to get a grip. Do you know what *I* think?'

'Oh, do tell!'

'I think you've forgotten what it means to be alive.'

Saltar licked his dry lips. 'What are you talking about?'

'You still think you're an animee that doesn't need any rest. You can march forever without let-up, to the ends of the earth and the end of days. You are an implacable force who need not fear either the goddess of creation or the god of death. You can fight anyone or anything and triumph through force of will!'

'Shut up.'

'No, you should listen. You have been gulled, Saltar! You're none of those things! You're just a man now. You have to accept that.'

'No! I'm the eternal Battle-leader of Dur Memnos. I have lived countless lifetimes. And you are a mighty slayer of gods, Scourge!'

'No, Saltar,' the Scourge said shaking his head sadly. 'You are just a man. You may be handy with a weapon, but your flesh can be torn and your bones broken just as easily as any other man's. Physically, you are no better than any other soldier. And psychologically you are no different to the rest of us. You are a father who fears for his son, a husband who fears for his wife, a friend who fears for his companions...'

The Scourge broke off as Saltar's fist smashed into his jaw and laid him out cold next to Visier's dead body. Wincing, the Battle-leader rubbed his sore knuckles. The pain only proved to him that everything the Guardian had said was true. With a sigh, he sat down next to his friend to wait for Sergeant Marr and his men to arrive.

Chapter Four: Where There Is No Rest

Larc stumbled along yet another ravine, praying that this one wouldn't just end up leading into another dead end or a switchback. He'd long since lost all sense of direction and had no idea if he was simply treading the same ground over and over. Was he damned to walk these twisting, confounding ravines until he collapsed from exhaustion or dehydration? He'd found the odd patch of old snow in deep shadow, but it seemed to have very little moisture in it. If anything, it sucked away what little water he had in his mouth and left him more parched than he had been before.

He knew he should be marking each ravine where he could, but he hardly had the energy to pile stones on top of each other anymore, and anyway he suspected there was a devil in the wind that came barrelling along the narrow passes, a devil who took delight in dismantling anything Larc could build. After all, these were the chaos wastes, so they would defy any attempt to navigate them rationally.

At one point, he'd found himself in a ravine with relatively shallow sides. He'd struggled up one side to see if he'd be afforded any sort of view by which to orient himself, only to look out over an endless field of deep contours and sharp ridges. He was reminded of nothing more than the surface of a giant brain laid bare to the elements. He was trapped in a maze of corridors that had no end… no end except madness, death or a doomed return to the very valley he'd been trying to escape in the first place.

There'd been no safe progress to be made along the top of the shallow ravine, so he'd descended back into it, resolved not to waste any further energy on even short ascents, and continued on his way. He'd walked a whole day through and then lay down on the floor where he was to snatch a few hours of fitful sleep. Neither the unforgiving stones beneath him nor the tormenting wind stopped him sleeping so physically drained was he. He'd had a fleeting worry that he'd die of exposure and never open his eyes again once he'd lain down, but then the concern had escaped him and he was left to his tortured dreams.

He awoke shivering, his leather tunic unable to keep the cold fingers of the wind-demon off him. He came out of the foetal position in which he'd slept and stretched out his stiffened limbs. He lay looking up at the spiralling stone-grey sky and failed to discern any direction to the movement of the clouds. There was no sun, so nothing to steer himself by; not that the knotted ravines would have let him keep the golden life-giver always to his right or left side anyway.

Knowing that the heat at his core wouldn't last long if he didn't get moving, he got to his feet. His body creaked and groaned. Today would be harder than the day before, for it was now even longer since he'd last eaten and his strength would only continue to fade. In his hand, he still carried the palm-sized stone he intended to throw at any rock-rat he came across, but thus far it looked as if nothing could survive in this environment.

He took a small, swaying step and waited for his body to rediscover its balance. Another halting step. He would continue to push on, no matter how slow his progress, so long as his body sustained him. This was the path, this was his existence, if he was to have any hope of finding the lost god and having his wife and child returned to him.

Larc realised he was limping. The leather on his right foot had worn through and the stone was starting to rub his skin raw. He swapped the leather on his left foot with that on his right to ensure his feet would become equally damaged and he would not need to waste energy limping. He laughed. He was actually working to damage new parts of himself! Only in the chaos wastes could such insanity seem so sensible.

He walked on, limp-free for the time being, and concentrated on his environment once again, searching for anything that might be a distinguishing feature to stick in his memory and help him know if he revisited a place or not. Would he spot that strangely shaped out-cropping if he came back through here? Probably not. He needed to find something else. What about that greenish lichen? Maybe.

Sighing, he trudged on. Then he came to a large single piece of rock blocking the way. It was nearly three times his height and there were no gaps between it and the edges of the ravine for him to squeeze through. He contemplated turning back, but could not remember having seen a side-route off the ravines he'd been traversing in a long time.

He regarded the giant shard of rock again. It was fairly pitted and would not ordinarily pose too much of a problem for an experienced climber like himself. But he was dangerously light-headed and his limbs were heavy with fatigue. Even a small fall could result in a crippling injury that would quickly prove to be the end of him.

Taking a few deep breaths, he found hand holds on the rock and began to haul himself up. He gritted his teeth and tried to ignore the shaking in his arms. He had to be up the rock quickly before his muscles spasmed, cramped or failed through over-exertion. 'Come on!' he shouted at himself and gasped in triumph as he made the top. He lay on his back a while, heaving in large lungfuls of air, and then rolled across the top of the rock and lowered himself down the kinder far side.

He blinked with large eyes and lurched forwards. There was a small river twenty metres ahead of him. He scrambled to it edge and plunged his head into it. Life! He gulped in overly large mouthfuls and revelled in the pain of the frigid water crashing down the gorge of his throat and into the empty basin of his stomach.

Before he drowned himself, he pulled his head back out and happily wiped the grit from his eyes so he could look on where he was with clean and clear eyes. There were green mosses and small bushes up and down the course of the river. Maybe there would be some fruit or edible plant he could forage for! His stomach growled in anticipation. He drank more water to quieten it. Besides, the water was so sweet that it was as good as eating to him.

The river chuckled and he had a giddy urge to join it in laughter.

'Where have you come from then?' asked a young voice.

Larc jumped in fright – he'd been so intent on slaking his thirst that he'd neglected to check properly whether there was anyone else around. And the noise of the river would have been enough to cover the whisper of leather shoes on the stone path running alongside the water course.

He cursed himself for a fool and prepared to spring away at the slightest suggestion of an attack. He peered up and around cautiously and beheld a woman of about his own age not more than ten metres away. She was dressed in a simple brown robe and carried a basket of herbs, but he remained wary. This could well be a demon in disguise.

'You're all wet!'

Larc didn't understand the harsh grunting noises being made. Maybe it was all the utterance the creature was capable of, or maybe it was the true language of the demons. He decided it best to assume he was being issued some sort of challenge, and tried to think how he should respond.

'Are you heading for the temple?'

Larc nodded, which seemed to please the woman-demon.

'I see. Then maybe we can travel together. We don't get many visitors, to be honest, and the priests are a fairly quiet bunch. Maybe you can tell me what's going on in the outside world. Here, would you mind? I've been out all day and I'm tired.'

The woman-demon held out its basket to Larc and he realised he was being offered something. He edged closer carefully and looked more closely at the plants that had been collected. Reaching out a tentative hand, he took a piece of edible moss he recognised and put it in his mouth.

The woman-demon laughed and he was suddenly afraid he had been tricked or poisoned. 'It's not for eating, silly! It's for dying garments. What's your name?'

Beginning to realise the boy didn't understand everything she said, and wondering if he was simple, the girl touched her chest and spoke more slowly. 'I'm Vasha. Va-sha!'

'Vasha!' Larc said hesitantly.

'Yes, that's right. And who are you?' Vasha asked, pointing at Larc and putting her head on its side.

'Larc!'

'Larc,' the woman-demon said with a funny twang in her voice. 'Come on then, before it starts getting dark. Actually, I'm a bit surprised they haven't already sent someone out to find me. Brother Altor always frets that I might get attacked by a mountain lion or something. He's funny like that, but nice.'

As the woman-demon spoke, Larc began to realise he could pick out the odd word she said, now that he had an ear for her strange intonation and accent. She had thrust her pannier into his arms and turned away to walk up the incline of the path. He hurried after her.

'It's only a mile or so now,' she said, clearly happy to have someone new to talk to. 'We'll be in time for the evening meal, I think. You must be famished. You don't seem to have brought anything with you and the nearest village is at least a day's journey away. So, what is it you need to ask of Cognis?'

Larc realised he'd just been asked something. 'Cognis?'

'Of course Cognis. Or do you want to join the temple? It would be nice if they accepted you, cos then I could show you around and we could be friends, yes?'

'I – I don't know.'

She looked a little crestfallen at that. 'Oh, I see.' But then she rallied. 'Don't worry, Cognis has all the answers. You'll like it at the temple, you'll see. And it's always warm and there's always enough to eat. The priests know everything about everything, you see: what you can eat, what the best things to grow are, how to call the animals to them, everything! The only thing you have to do every day is pray and study, and that's not too bad really. They're very good teachers, of course.'

Larc smiled despite himself. Vasha's apparently innocent enthusiasm was slowly beginning to lift his spirits. If she was a demon, then she was certainly a very strange one, or one more artful than he could ever hope to fathom. Content to listen and provide the occasional, monosyllabic answer, he allowed his mind to relax and drift for the first time in what seemed a lifetime.

It was so strange to be walking alongside the pure, rushing waters of this river, having a harmless conversation with someone like Vasha, while still being in the chaos wastes. How was it that he could find a measure of peace when fell creatures of nightmare could be over the next rise or just beyond the next bend? It all seemed so surreal. Were they seeking to raise his hopes so that, come the time, the distance that he fell, the horror that he experienced and the pain that he suffered would be all the greater?

'Altor says the temple is remote so that the priests can remain undisturbed in their holy contemplation, research and devotion. But they seem more devoted to their books and scrolls than they are to people, if you ask me. They're very nice, but the temple's a bit isolated, a bit... lonely. There aren't many acolytes my age. There's Peevis, who's nineteen, but he's always mean to me. How old are you then, Larc?'

Larc blinked. 'My life has spanned fifteen summers.'

Vasha giggled. 'You speak funny. I'm fourteen! I didn't know you were just a boy though. You look older somehow, more serious. Do you know you've got lines on your forehead?'

He turned on her. 'I am no boy!' he said hotly. 'I am a hunter, a man! I have taken a mate, had... had a child!' Then in quieter tones: 'A son.'

Vasha stopped, her mouth in a fixed oh of surprise. She stared at him with wide eyes. Unable to face the questions in her gaze, he walked on, his head hung low.

Her footsteps pattered after him. Much to his relief, she didn't ask him anything.

'This way,' she said quietly and led him up a steeper path.

Regretting how he'd upset the mood, he sought to be more conciliatory with the woman who was helping him. 'Sorry. I've lost my wife and child. I'm searching for them. Maybe this priest, Cognis, can help me? Or Altor?'

Vasha giggled nervously. 'Cognis isn't a priest, silly! He's the god of wisdom, knowledge and… and… wait, I always forget this last one… exp-experience! Yes, that's it. Surely you've heard of Him! Where are you from, Larc?'

He hesitated. The things she said confused him. He'd never heard of Cognis. Was Cognis the demon who owned this region, or had Larc just discovered the lost god of the Brethren? He dared not believe his luck. And if Cognis was all-knowing, as Vasha insisted, then this god would be able to tell him how to find his beloved Sarla and their child again.

It seemed too good to be true, which made him wary once more. Cognis might still prove to be a demon, a demon who would no doubt want to know how to get to the valley of the Brethren. Vasha was probably owned by this demon and leading him even now towards a betrayal of his people.

God or demon? He needed to find out before the temple had him trapped. 'I'm from a village a long way away, Vasha, so we don't get to hear much about Cognis. What is he like? Does he live in the temple? What does he eat? Tell me everything!'

Her initial answer was reticent and vague, as if she were hiding something from him. 'Well, I'm not sure really. I haven't seen Him myself, but all the priests say they have and I've seen His statue. He's quite old, I think. After all, old people seem to know lots… until they get really old, when they sometimes forget things, like Brother Melitus. So Cognis can't be too old, I suppose. He has this big, white beard… I… I don't know really…' she tailed off lamely.

'Does he live in your temple?' he pressed.

'Er… umm… well, there's the altar… and I think there's a holy place behind that, but I've never been allowed to go in there. Brother Altor says he often feels the god guiding him when he's studying quietly in the library. So Cognis must have powers or be invisible sometimes.'

Larc frowned. What she was saying now seemed more childish than evasive. She was younger than him, after all, and didn't seem to have lived half as much as he had. 'Does he eat the flesh of the dead and drink the blood of the living?'

He turned to see that she had now backed away from him. Her young face was hurt and disgusted. 'That's a horrible thing to say! He's not like Lacrimos! He's gentle. Why would you ask something like that? You and your people must be very mean. They shouldn't let you get married so young either. It's wrong. Everyone knows that!'

The woman – though he thought of her as more of a girl now – had clearly taken leave of her senses. She was completely irrational. And who was this Lacrimos? Another demon? It had to be, because all the Brethren knew there was only *one* god. Therefore, Cognis and Lacrimos had to be demons.

Pleased with his discovery, but conscious he would still need Vasha's help, he tried to calm her. 'So Cognis is kinder than Lacrimos, is that right? I don't really know very much about them.'

'Clearly! Haven't you got teachers where you come from? You're un-unedu-cated! And, anyway, what happened to your wife and son? How did you lose them? Bit careless of you, wasn't it? Did they run away because you said such horrible things?'

He bit his tongue, knowing she spoke out of upset and anger. He held the silence while she glared at him and then said softly, 'No, they died. If I can find the god, though, he can return them to me.'

She gasped and shook her head. Her eyes watered as she said, 'Larc, it's forbidden. Necromancy is outlawed. I'm sorry about your w-wife and p-poor…'

'But your temple has the outlawed knowledge required to perform such necromancy, surely! Is Cognis not the god of all knowledge? Even knowledge of necromancy must be holy to him. His priests *must* guard and protect such knowledge. It is their religious duty.'

'I-I have no idea. Even if they did, I don't think they'd let just anyone have it. Brother Altor says knowledge is power and that too much knowledge is a dangerous thing. The more mortals know, the more they usually destroy. Only the gods are meant to know everything. When mortals seek to know too much, they challenge the power of the gods themselves, they challenge the balance.'

'The balance? What's that?'

'I'm not sure. Brother Altor can explain it better than me. Yes, he'll help you. Come on, this way.'

They rounded a bend in the path and Larc was presented with a view of humble buildings perched on a ledge high above them. A rock face towered behind the temple, and Larc wondered if the priests had also tunnelled into the mountain itself. That aside, the overall impression given by the scene was one of harmony with nature – the colour of the temple's stone walls blended with the surroundings – where the constructions and ambitions of Man did not seek to compete with the majesty and scale of the god's creation.

The temple of Cognis more than spoke of peace with the universe: it was the embodiment and physical expression of the divine artistry and eternal design of the balance between god and man, creation and chaos, reality and meaninglessness.

'Oh! I see!' Larc breathed, completely forgetting himself.

Lichens and mosses softened the harsh edges of the human habitation and provided a deceptively simple frame to the setting. Trees climbed and curved exquisitely, in understated but perfect counterpoint to the deliberate lines and blocks of conscious will and intent. The patterning throughout, though, was a melody for thought and senses.

Time seemed suspended here. Was this place not eternity? He held his breath, sure that the voice of god was about to whisper at his ear.

Sure that the voice of god…

The voice of god…

The voice…

Of god… would speak

His mind nearly unravelled there and then. Only silence. No voice. Not even a whisper. The silence was a discordance, if absence has a sound. A painful rushing and thunder in the inner ear. Blood bubbling, churning and boiling in his veins and trickling out of his ears, his nose, his eyes, his mouth, his lower regions, his bowels. He nearly vomited his intestines onto the dusty pebbles of the path just in front of him.

'What's happening?' Vasha screamed in the distance.

Such a beautiful scene, with such a composition of the visual and kinaesthetic must surely combine the aural aspect. Why were there no birds singing with enough joy to burst their hearts? Why did not the wind sough or sigh with contentment? What had happened to silence the world?

Larc tasted dust in his mouth, blood in his throat and bile in his stomach. By force of self alone, he wrenched the world back into a place, any place, he understood. It slammed back with a force that threw Vasha to the floor and pushed him onto one knee and elbow. He helped her up and wiped the bright red trickle away from where she had bitten her lip.

She clung desperately to the v of his arm. 'Larc, something terrible has happened.'

'I know. There is something wrong with the temple. Come, Vasha, I fear we are the only ones who can bear witness to what has occurred.'

The closer they got to the temple, the slower each of their steps became. The last five paces were so extended and anguished that they thought they wouldn't or couldn't arrive. 'Asymptote!' Vasha whispered to him, but he didn't know what she meant. He was too busy mastering himself to pay attention to anyone else. Every hair on his body stood upright and pulled his skin so taut that he expected to be torn apart every second and left a bleeding hulk with no skin on.

'The Three protect me!' he whined in desperation and the agony lessened.

Vasha was gifted no reprieve, however, and her eyes began to roll back in her head. He caught her and pulled her back and away from the temple. He checked she was breathing comfortably and then turned back for the holy place with grim determination.

His muscles swelled and his sinews stood out too far from his skin. He sunk his knees low, locked his hips straight with his back and pushed forwards, not caring if it would be the death of him. He broke the inversion and suddenly found he could walk with as little effort as a puissant god. For a fleeting moment, he was intoxicated with his own power, and then he was just Larc again, a fifteen-year-old that some people considered just a boy.

He walked as bravely as any boy-cum-man could through the gates of a sacred precinct. Plants in terracotta pots had withered. The water in the well had been turned into a fetid steam. The walls around the central courtyard had been so cracked that not a single, regular brick-shape could be discerned. His skin itched and became covered in small blisters.

He considered turning back, but what was there to go back to? Taking a deep breath, he walked into a central building. It had an impressive domed roof, but he paid it no attention. In front of him was a grisly pile of bodies piled one atop another. He stood rooted to the spot, unable even to blink. You're suffering from shock, a small voice inside him said, you've seen worse, much worse. He didn't know how much time passed. A drop of congealing blood finally broke free from the end of a finger-tip where it had clung for an age, and landed on the glazed eyeball of a face just below. The drop didn't spread or swim: it just sat there viscously, as bulbous and bloated as a blood-toad. Stillness and silence returned.

All Larc could hear was his ragged breathing, which he irrationally tried to keep as quiet as possible. Nine, ten, eleven bodies, or did I not count that one before? Five, six, seven, eight, nine, ten, eleven, twelve, thirteen! I should start again. Oh, what does it matter how many there are? Dead is dead. Besides, that limb's not connected to any of the bodies, and I'm sure I counted it as a whole body before.

The kills were fresh! That made Larc try to slow and quieten his breathing again, but for more rational reasons this time. The killers might still be close. Maybe he should simply leave while he still had a chance. After all, only magickers, monsters, demons or gods could be responsible for such carnage, and he was defenceless against such a threat. By the Three, if such a number of the followers of the demon Cognis could not mount an adequate defence, then how could a mere rock-rat like himself?

But rock-rats survived surprisingly well. Move quickly and stick to the shadows as much as possible. He scampered to the altar at one end of the chamber and twitched the curtain behind it. The coast clear, he ducked through and quickly took in the small, dusty antechamber that presumably constituted the holy of holies. There were large books open on reading stands, their beautifully illuminated pages making the room seem more bright and alive than it otherwise would have done. He ignored the gaudy tomes and dashed over to the small, dark bookcase in the corner. A rare, metal lock kept it sealed. Larc smashed through the absurdly fragile fretwork of the doors to the case and grabbed the slim, unremarkable volumes within. He threw them into an empty and overlarge book bag that lay conveniently nearby and then went looking for the kitchens to the temple complex. He had soon procured for himself two loaves of unleavened bread, a handful of tomatoes, a side of beef and some green vegetables or fruit he did not recognise. A mere two minutes after having entered, Larc the rock-rat exited the temple of Cognis laden with the means for his own future survival.

⁂

Mordius sighed with relief to see the main doors to the temple of Cognis stood open. That was one potentially bloody confrontation avoided.

'Kate, let's take four men with us and leave the others outside. No need to cause any unnecessary tension by taking them all inside, eh? They'll still be close at hand if we should need them. And I'm not even sure all fifty would fit in the temple courtyard.'

She studied the necromancer, briefly enjoying watching him squirm. But what he said made sense. 'Fine. Captain, bring three of your men inside with us. Have the rest of them shut off the street.'

'Kate, I really don't think...' Mordius began and then tailed off as she levelled her threatening gaze at him. 'That is, I really don't think we need waste any more time out here on the street. This way!'

They filed through the arched entrance and down the corridor through the outer wall. There were murder-holes high up in the corridor walls, for the use of concealed temple archers, but the holes had long since become festooned with cobwebs. One of them provided a home for a nest of house martins.

The group emerged into a small, colonnaded courtyard surrounded on all sides by two-storey stone buildings. The architectural style of the place was at once familiar and foreign – this was reputed to be one of if not the oldest buildings in Corinus. It was the precursor, the progenitor, the ancestor to all the future generations of construction that followed it. Looking upon it, even in its weathered condition, the group felt their own transience, youth... and insignificance. This was from an era they knew nothing of – only the tomes and documents written by the builders of this place, and held in this place, recorded anything of that older time.

And the buildings still stood. The style of the place was relatively humble and unadorned, apart from a few now faceless statues, and otherwise spoke of a strength designed to carry the weight and burden of eternity. The pillars of the place were short and squat, but none of them were bowed. The bricks of the walls fit together with all but invisible lines, the walls tapering slightly as they rose so that their vanishing point was in the midst of the heavens. There was a power here that was fundamental.

Mordius turned on Kate. 'You see!'

'Okay, okay,' Kate nodded, once more the young girl who had learnt at the knee of Cognis. 'I see. I will commit no blasphemy here.'

A priest of Cognis appeared, peering oddly at them through pieces of glass balanced on the bridge of his nose and somehow held together by bits of wire connected to his ears.

'The Raiser and the Green Maiden here together! Oh my!' he twittered and then hurried away.

'Now what?' Kate asked, but no one had an answer. The courtyard had an eerie silence about it.

Then there was a shuffling in one corner and they peered into the shadows to see the priest supporting a bent over elder. They waited awkwardly and one guard half-started to bow before he realised none of his fellows were doing the same. He straightened back up with a slight blush to his cheeks.

The elder finally reached them. His eyes were the blue of a child's, for all the age of his body. A slight smile crinkled his face as he regarded Kate, as if he knew her. In fact, he had the look of someone who knew nearly everything, Kate thought to herself, someone who unsurprisingly reminded her of Cognis himself.

The guard who'd attempted a bow earlier took a step back, as if he feared to be in the presence of the high priest, and lowered his eyes to the ground.

'His Reverence, Reader Philasteres, High Priest of the temple of Cognis,' the younger, but by no means youthful, priest said by way of introduction.

'I am a Guardian of Dur Memnos. Why did this priest call me the Green Maiden? Where did such a name come from?'

Mordius cringed at Kate's blunt and peremptory manner. And it was Mordius that the high priest chose to address first in his unexpectedly mellow voice: 'Why, hello, my dear friend Mordius. I would say it was good to see you, but it does not bode well that you are accompanied by Kate clad in her green leathers.'

'How do you know my name?' Kate demanded. 'What do you mean that it doesn't bode well?'

The high priest smiled again, indulgently this time. 'How to explain? Hmm. I know your name because you are famous for your garb, Kate. Indeed, you have long been of great interest to the temple of Cognis for your part in the defeat of the King. We would love to hear and document account of those final, dark days, for we possess few facts about them. They represent something of a gap, shall we say, in our history, and an all important gap we suspect. But that is, perhaps, for another time.

'As to how things bode, the urgent nature of your questioning and your martial aspect can only mean that there are troubles afoot in the kingdom, no? You see, I am nothing more than a fairground confidence trickster, peddling second-hand knowledge and informed guesses to unwary customers. For a small consideration, I can read your future in your palm if you like.'

Kate's eyes narrowed. He was mocking her, but also seeking to distract her by it, as any good trickster would. And had he just set her some sort of puzzle, to trap her into sharing some knowledge with him? Typical of a priest of Cognis! They loved such conceits. She wanted to throttle him, but decided that he'd find it too hard to answer her questions if he had a broken neck. She could try some other physical torture, but doubted his heart could take it. Grinding her teeth, she remembered back to when Cognis had played all sorts of games with her as a child. Trickster, fairground, distraction... sleight of hand. The customer invariably took their eye off the target at a key moment, often just for the need to blink. She decided to refocus on her original target.

'Why did this priest call me the Green Maiden? The Raiser and the Green Maiden here together, he said, as if it were a prophecy, foretold or some such. Do you have foreknowledge, yes or no?'

Philasteres's eyes twinkled. 'Perhaps. Would you like me to read your palm after all? What will you pay me? Gold, silver?'

The man was insufferable, but she had him now. 'As you know, good priest, gold and silver are all but worthless compared to the value of knowledge. A man or woman with an abundance of knowledge can create as much gold and silver for themselves as they could ever want. Why then would I offer gold or silver?'

'Quite so, quite so!' the elder said, his head bobbing merrily. 'Are you then a woman with an abundance of knowledge who might trade in kind with a man with an abundance of knowledge?'

Kate smiled. 'Yes.'

Mordius sighed with relief. Blood had been avoided for a second time.

'After all, did you not tell me that you were interested in my account of the final days? But I will need to settle that account with you at a later date, I fear, for I do not have the necessary time now. My son has been kidnapped...'

The priest with Philasteres gasped, but the high priest showed no obvious reaction.

'... and we do not know who or what is responsible. We cannot apprehend their motives. If you have foreknowledge, then we would ask you share it with us.'

The eerie silence returned to the courtyard, as if the world held its breath to listen. None of them dared speak as they waited on the ancient priest. He closed his eyes slowly and rested unmoving. Finally, he sighed and began to speak. 'It is not clear what I should and should not reveal. You ask of hidden and secret things, some of which pertain to the sacred secrets of this temple and the power of its priests. To share them with the uninitiated would normally be a blasphemy, but we have reached a nexus, where a number of paths are possible. The paths twist and turn so that I cannot see too far ahead, cannot see which hazards lie along each path, cannot see where the paths ultimately lead. Not to share my knowledge with you might be more dangerous than otherwise. Or all the paths could lead to the same end – it is not clear.'

'So, you *do* have foreknowledge then, limited though it may be. Tell me, did you know they would take my innocent Orastes? It cannot be blasphemy to help return him to me. It cannot therefore be blasphemy to tell me who has taken him and what they want.'

'We knew only that dark days were coming. We did not know what events would mark their beginning. Now those events are known, perhaps we can more easily read what is to come, more easily read the Pattern.'

'Pattern?' Mordius prompted quietly.

Philasteres waved the question away as if it were a bothersome fly and tightened the grip of his other hand on his assistant. With a jump, the assistant realised he was being asked to explain: 'To the best of my knowledge, what you hear now has never been shared with anyone outside of this temple before. I must have your solemn vow that you will not disclose it to any other!'

The palace guards did not hesitate to swear it upon their hearts.

'I swear it by all creation!' Mordius said with a serious frown.

'I so swear, except that I will share it with my husband and the Scourge, and them I will bind with the same vow!' Kate decided.

The assistant paused significantly.

'Come along!' Philasteres muttered. 'You really do have a flair for the dramatic, don't you, Spinderus? Kate's in a hurry, you know.'

'Very well!' Spinderus said, only slightly flustered. 'The more that is known of a situation, the better its outcome can be predicted. The more that is known of an object and its environment, the better its use can be understood. The more that is known of a person, the better their behaviour can be anticipated. The more that is known of all these things, the better the future can be read, particularly when we also ponder the threads and patterns of history and current events. A knowledgeable person will often seem mad, prophet-like or divine to the truly ignorant. They will seem like they have foreknowledge, when all they have done is develop and practise their ability to read the Pattern of human history, society and the gods.'

'Oookay!' Mordius said with deep creases in his forehead and chewing on a thumbnail. 'And what does this nexus represent then?'

Spinderus took a deep breath, letting them know the answer was not going to be short or simple. 'If you think of our world as a tapestry being woven with the threads of our lives, and history being the recognisable and occasionally repeated Pattern, then a nexus represents a change of some sort – the introduction of a new pattern or colour, or the breaking of a thread, for example. Remember, every new pattern, even one that seems localised, changes the entire and overall Pattern; it shifts the dynamic, creating a wholly different tapestry of meaning.'

'And how do you know that we're at this nexus now?' Kate asked curiously.

Spinderus looked to the Reader, obviously nervous of revealing much more. Philasteres nodded and said: 'Put simply, the coming of the nexus was read in the Pattern several years ago. We knew the nexus would be marked by the Raiser and Green Maiden attending the temple of Cognis together.'

'Several years ago?' Mordius repeated in astonishment.

'How is that possible?' Kate pressed.

Philasteres pulled an uncomfortable face. 'Every now and then, one of our number works too many hours in the library, forgets to take refreshment, gets too immersed in what they're studying, becomes overly tired and light headed, or falls ill, that sort of thing... and... and, well, they start shouting all manner of things, a lot of it rubbish! They're usually okay after a bit of air and a lie down, but the thing is, the thing is that some of the things they say seem to make a sort of sense and...'

'He means prophecy!' Mordius said with wide eyes. 'They have prophets here in the temple.'

'Shhh!' the high priest said, and then hastily added: 'I don't have a particular aversion to the word. I'm not squeamish about it or anything, but the term causes us some... problems when it starts being used too freely. It causes a great deal of excitement among the people and they all start acting strangely. They get this fervour and... and somehow feel compelled to come to the temple, and then we get loads of prophets popping up all over the place...'

'I can't believe I'm hearing this,' Kate said. 'Are you actually saying you don't want the people becoming too religious?!'

'... you have to understand this is a place of quiet study and contemplation, a temple of learning. When we get too many people traipsing through here, it's highly disruptive. Besides, I would have thought the palace didn't want the people becoming too agitated – civil unrest is in no one's interest.'

'I think the poor would disagree with...' Kate began hotly.

'Let's return to the prophecy in question, shall we,' Mordius squeaked, 'rather than get lost in issues of social equality and reform... please!'

Philasteres and Kate glared at each other, but it was the high priest who broke the gaze first: 'Don't get me wrong. I am open to the idea that these so-called prophets do actually speak in the voice of Cognis Himself. But as Reader of the temple, I must also consider the arguments of those scholars who point out that the revelations of these so-called prophets could just as easily be arrived at through methodical – and admittedly inspired – research.

After all, it's always pretty easy to predict that a period of relative peace will eventually be disrupted by some strife. There are those that are even more dismissive of prophecy than myself. They say that if you wait long enough, then nearly all prophecies, even the falsely produced ones, have a good chance of coming true or being generously interpreted as having come true. It's far from an exact science.'

'No, I'd say it's more a matter of faith,' Kate said with heavy sarcasm and obvious frustration.

The Captain of the palace guard cleared his throat.

'What?' Kate shouted, her eyes blazing.

The Captain paled but otherwise did not flinch. 'Maybe we should ask the holy Reader how it is that the prophecy of the Raiser and the Green Maiden is so well-known within the temple, when apparently there are a significant number who do not put much stock by prophecy.'

Kate blinked. She was silent for a second. 'Yes. Yes, that's a good question. She attempted a sweeter voice and was nearly successful. 'Good Philasteres, how is it that even your assistant is so aware of this prophecy that it was the first thing he mentioned when we entered this precinct? And while we're at it, is there more of this prophecy that you haven't told us about? I get the impression it's been documented. Is it in your library? And is it more than good fortune that it's been documented? Well?'

The high priest had closed his eyes. His breathing had again become heavy. A small snore issued from his lips.

'Unbelievable! He's asleep!' Kate said in consternation.

Spinderus suddenly stepped between the high priest and Kate, facing towards her. He drew himself up to his full height and looked down his nose at her through his funny lenses. His face was puckered in disapproval. 'You forget yourself, Guardian! The lack of respect you show towards His Reverence is intolerable. You have made him over-tired with your ungracious demands. I am terminating this audience.'

A dangerous anger flashed across Kate's face. Mordius covered his eyes. He couldn't bear to look. All was quiet. He decided to risk a peek through his fingers. He gulped. Kate's hand had moved to the hilt of the slim dagger she wore at her waist. The guards had tensed.

'If you do not step back right now...' she said into the hush.

'You wouldn't dare!' Spinderus said in a high-pitched voice.

'If you do not step back this instant...'

'This is sacrilege!'

'... then your over-tired priest will collapse without your arm to support him, won't he?'

Spinderus yelped and moved back to clasp the elbow of the high priest. Philasteres opened his eyes, apparently alert once more: 'Ah, there you all are. Now, where was I? Yes, the prophecy. Well, we document every prophecy as a matter of course. Better to be safe than sorry, eh? What makes this one special, though, is that it came from young Averius, and he has foretold things before, things that have always come to pass. He is an unassuming and modest scholar. He is not the type to make things up just to gain attention, status or influence within the temple. Added to that – and I don't think he'd mind me saying this – although he is diligent and methodical, he is far from being a brilliant scholar, certainly not the type who could read the Pattern with any great insight or understanding. In short, as a prophet, he is... well, very credible. We pretty much all believe him, you see, even the more sceptical among us.'

Then, with an almost youthful excitement, the high priest added: 'We may as well get started then. This way to the library!'

'But Your Reverence...!' Spinderus began to protest.

'Yes, yes, Spinderus, I know! We don't normally allow the uninitiated into the Great Library, but this occasion is hardly what you'd call normal, now is it?'

Spinderus blinked owlishly back at him, clearly at a loss.

'Spinderus, we are at a nexus! If the temple of Cognis cannot provide knowledge and advice of value at a time like this, then what value does it really have? The more information we can provide our friends from the palace, the more informed the decisions will be, and their decisions will no doubt affect us all. It's therefore in our own interest that we help them, Spinderus.'

They'd all begun to move after the old priest, when he stopped suddenly and they were all forced to bump into each other. 'And there was another thing you wanted to know about, wasn't there, besides the prophecy? Mordius, be a good fellow and remind me what it was,' he said, cocking his head because he apparently had better hearing in one ear than the other.

Mordius leaned forward slightly. 'We are not sure who it is moving against us. We have speculated that it is a dark and ancient enemy, but know little more than that. Its cunning seems more than human for it must have been planning this move for years. Who knows how long it has been waiting for its chance.'

Philasteres frowned deeply. 'Oh dear, that doesn't sound good, not good at all. We will have to go to the lowest levels of the library then, where we keep our most ancient texts, those that date back to before the founding of this temple even.'

Spinderus's mouth hung open in horror. Clearly, Philasteres was suggesting they break yet more long-standing traditions and protocols.

'Well, come on then!' the high priest exhorted them impatiently. 'What are you all standing around for? We don't have all day, you know.'

There was panic in Spinderus's eyes as he helped his high priest forward towards a large and heavy pair of ornate doors in one wall. The wood was silver with great age, and shiny where countless pairs of hands had touched the surface. The overall design of the carvings and reliefs defeated the eye and made Mordius's head ache at the temples.

Philasteres chuckled, 'One day you will see it, my friend, one day – when you are closer to my age, I think. Spinderus, what is it you tell the new initiates when you bring them into the Great Library for the first time?'

Collecting himself, the assistant priest began to speak in practised and sonorous tones: 'These hallowed halls contain everything: the past, the present and the likely future. They are the sum total of all mortal knowledge. In some ways, though, that knowledge is more than mortal, for the shelves, tunnels and levels of this catacomb are like the twists and turns of a giant brain that has been a sentient witness to our entire history. It is closer to being the all-knowing mind of an immortal than a mortal. It is Cognis!

'Are you keeping up at the back?' Spinderus chided, without ever having looked round.

The trailing guard, who had stopped to gawp at the rows of richly bound tomes lining this first room, jumped and wore the guilty expression of a schoolboy caught day-dreaming by his school master.

'Question?' Spinderus then asked, as Mordius began to open his mouth.

'Oh! Yes. Er... you said the library was sentient. How can that be?'

Spinderus sighed tolerantly. 'It is hard for the newly initiated... pardon me, the uninitiated in this case... to understand at first. The priesthood of Cognis effectively provide the mind of Cognis with its sentience. Our constant reading of the Pattern, the insights we have and our timely sharing of those insights all create an active sentience of sorts. We are like the lifeblood moving through the divine brain if you will. Our priests die and are replaced by the next generation, just as blood cells die and are replaced by new ones without the body ever being damaged. Come along, this way!'

'Oh, I see,' Mordius said with a shrug to Kate.

She leaned over with a gesture towards all the scholars sat engaged in silent study and whispered: 'None of this lot look too sentient to me. If this place is a mind, it belongs to a dusty and dim-eyed dotard.'

Mordius coughed to hide his snort of laughter and then quickly asked another question to distract the high priest Philasteres, who was eyeing him suspiciously. 'Your Reverence, I am surprised that there are so many reading lamps in here. Of course, the temple scholars require light to read by, but what of the risk of fire in this repository of priceless parchment?'

'Fear not, good Mordius, for do we not here possess the knowledge and invention of millennia? Examine the lights more closely and you will see there are no naked flames here. Truly, knowledge is its own best defence.'

Kate, Mordius and the guards gathered around a light attached to a wall and puzzled over it. The light was held in a glass ball around which a soft, constant glow formed a still and spherical nimbus. There was none of the fitful flickering or angry red of a normal flame.

'It's like daylight, like the sun. How is it possible?'

'Is it magic?'

'It is wondrous. It is the holy power of Cognis.'

'Or have the priests discovered how to isolate the divine spark gifted to all living things by Shakri Herself?'

Spinderus shook his head and tutted. 'The ignorant always ascribe a magical or divine cause to that which they do not understand. The lamp is naught but mortal invention. But let's not dawdle. If we were to stop at everything you didn't understand, we'd be dead of old age before we got to the records you require. And this is only the first level.'

They all hurried along after their guide, Mordius taking his turn to support the wheezing Philasteres.

'How many levels are there?' the necromancer called ahead to Spinderus, hoping he would slow down to answer the question, be reminded of the frail condition of his high priest and then start to check his pace more regularly. But down here Spinderus was all focus and intensity. Gone was the blinking, slightly nervous priest they had met in the courtyard. He was all busy confidence now. He was in his element.

'We do not know how many levels there are!' Spinderus called back, his voice echoing slightly against the long chamber's ceiling. 'There are limits on access to knowledge, even for the initiated. There are some things that are not for us mortals, a complete understanding of the divine being one. Then there are forbidden areas of magic which are best left buried as deeply as possible. Members of our temple are permitted access to a new level of knowledge for each year they study. We cannot allow the Pattern to be revealed too quickly to an immature mind, you see, for only trouble would otherwise result. Selecting a level at which to store a record therefore depends upon a combination of its content, age and significance when it comes to reading the greater Pattern.'

'Ah, I see now why you baulk at taking us down into the library,' Kate said. 'You fear what we might do with the knowledge we discover. And I also see why you are nonetheless prepared to lead us. As a priest of Cognis, you yourself thirst for new knowledge. Your high priest has given you a rare opportunity. How you must have dreamt of this day! Sneaking down to new levels must be your main temptation in life, your original sin. How the members of this temple must suffer! Dedicated to preserving and increasing the temple's knowledge, but never being allowed to enjoy that knowledge fully.'

'You understand much of Cognis, Kate,' Philasteres observed. 'He is a friend to you, it would seem.'

'No,' she said coldly. 'I understand much of *suffering*. And Cognis failed to guard my child. He guards his knowledge too closely. He is not a true friend to us mortals.'

'Blasphemy!' Spinderus choked. 'Cognis has given us so much. How dare you show so little gratitude!'

'Enough, Spinderus!' Philasteres barked. 'You are disturbing the sacred study of others.' Then he turned to Kate. He sighed. 'There may be some truth in what you say, Kate, but have you yourself not been complacent? In the last few years, how often have you worshipped at the temple? Can you truly say you have been completely faithful to Cognis? I think not.'

Kate's face was hidden by shadows. She did not speak. Philasteres called ahead: 'Lead on, Spinderus!'

After a second or two, the party continued in silence. They would travel along one long chamber, reach stairs at the end of it and then descend into a chamber that snaked back underneath where they had just been. As they moved deeper and deeper, the brightly bound leather tomes were replaced by faded scroll tubes and loosely gathered piles of parchment. The chambers became shorter and ceiling came down lower and lower.

Mordius had lost count of how many levels they'd traversed, how far they'd travelled back in history, and was beginning to lose a track of time. The tension was still there amongst the group, and he started to feel claustrophobic. When he could take it no more, he blurted out in a voice too loud for the confined space: 'Your Reverence, how long have we been in here? Surely the prophecy is higher up.'

Philasteres took a moment to catch his breath. 'We passed that long ago. We are searching first of all for texts that may allude to ancient enemies of mankind, be those enemies demonkind or something altogether different. Spinderus, take down that light from the wall, for if I recall that is the last that we'll find. There is only darkness beneath us.'

'Holy Reader, how is it that such old documents haven't turned to dust?' asked the Captain, stifling a sneeze.

Philasteres smiled. 'The atmosphere in the Great Library is ideal for the preservation of materials. The temperature is constant and the humidity is low. We have mutes here at the temple who spend all their time copying out and replacing the older parchments. There is less concern about the records where we are going, for they exist as skins and carved tablets. They were obviously produced to stand the test of time, as is often the way with rare knowledge.'

The light around them wavered. Mordius realised that Spinderus's hand was shaking. There was a glint of excitement in his eye. Clearly, he had not been this far before.

'Touch nothing!' Philasteres warned in a gravelly voice as they started their journey. 'And read nothing without asking me first! Although the old language will appear unfamiliar to you, it can still be affecting, much like a painting can cast a spell over its audience.'

It felt like they were descending into a tomb. The walls and the earth closed in around them. Mordius could hear his breathing becoming ragged. The air seemed thick down here, despite what Philasteres had said about the unchanging atmosphere of the library.

Mordius pulled at his collar, which suddenly felt too tight, and told himself not to panic or let his imagination get carried away. There was plenty of air down here, he told himself, it just didn't flow as freely as it did above ground. Sweat trickled down his brow – well, of course he was hot, what with all this exertion in such close conditions.

The light that Spinderus carried started to move into the distance, and the necromancer had to hurry to avoid being left alone in the darkness. He drew level with one of the guards, who seemed to be labouring. Mordius decided the chest plate the man wore must be heavier than it looked. Philsateres coughed and leaned heavily on the Captain, who was now aiding the elder.

Only Kate appeared unwearied. She strode ahead with her back straight and her eyes sweeping the shelves to either side of her. What she was searching for, he didn't know; and surely she couldn't know either; but her behaviour suggested that she believed she'd know it when she saw it; that her intensity of gaze and relentless force of will would force it out into the open. She was as unwavering and unstoppable in her course as the sun moving across the sky. Fiercely, she would blaze until her light had found out the darkest and furthest reaches of the universe. There would be no place her enemies could hide her child from her.

Yet all that meant she ignored some of the signs around her, just as humans crawling upon the face of the earth were of no moment to the sun. In some ways, she was blinded by her own light. Her strength was her weakness.

'Everybody just stop!' Mordius shouted with as much authority as he could muster. To his relief, they all did as he asked. 'Look, is it just me, or is the going strangely difficult down here? It's really stuffy, and yet His Reverence said the temperature in the Great Library is constant and the humidity should be low.'

No one replied.

'Shh!' Kate ordered. 'Do you hear that?'

'What?'

'A-a whispering, I think. Voices. Listen!'

Mordius held his breath and strained to hear. 'Yes. There's a noise. But I'm not sure about it being voices. And how could there be people down here anyway?'

Philasteres started to groan.

There was a sudden *whump* and the noise came closer. It was now a distinctive crackling sound.

'Noo!' Spinderus choked.

'I can smell burning! What...?' the Captain began.

'Run!' Kate shouted and started to push them back the other way. 'Captain, pick up the old man and carry him if you have to!'

There was another whump and a tremor ran along the floor.

'Move!'

The hem of Mordius's robe caught under his feet and he almost went sprawling. Kate grabbed him and began to pull the heavy material up over his head.

'What are you doing?' the magician yelped.

'Don't ask me why, but I'm saving your life. You can thank me later.'

Mordius was finally down to nothing but his briefs and then free to chase after the others. He quickly made ground on them, which was just as well because he felt an increasing heat behind them.

'Save the books!' Philasteres screamed as he suffered the indignity of being slung over a soldier's shoulder. 'Spinderus, do something!'

The priest hesitated. Another whump and he lost his balance. He grabbed hold of a shelf and dragged scrolls and parchment down with him.

'Get up!' the Captain bellowed as he hurdled over the prostrate follower of Cognis. 'The fire's exploding upwards floor by floor. We've only got seconds before we're all incinerated.'

'I've lost my spectacles!' wailed Spinderus. 'I can't see!'

'Use your other god-given senses!' Kate shouted. 'We can't wait for you or we're all dead. Up the stairs, quickly!'

They squeezed up the narrow, twisting staircase as the darkness behind them suddenly flared to white. A moment later came the noise: a concussion that shook reality from their grasps for a second. Mordius realised he couldn't hear anything anymore and fumbled blindly around him. He found the wall and hauled himself up to the next floor. Hands reached down to help him onto his feet and his vision began to clear.

'I heard Spinderus call out! Where is he?' Philasteres pleaded.

'Let's get moving,' Kate said. 'Captain, one foot in front of the other as fast as you can, if you please. If the old man starts to struggle, knock him cold.'

The party started to move, living from second to second lest the next be their last. The floor bucked and cracked wide; blue flames licking up around their ankles as if to grab them. They were forced to run with their legs spread wide or crab side on as best they could. The air became hotter and hotter – it was only a matter of time before the dry parchments around them spontaneously combusted.

A ball of flame took shape at the end of the corridor behind them. Mordius glanced back over his shoulder to see it accelerating after them. He wanted to claw past the guard in front of him, do whatever it took to hang on to his own precious, fragile life. It was now impossible to breathe – the fire consuming what little oxygen was left in the corridor.

'We'll never make it!' Mordius croaked, unsure that anyone would hear him over the hungry roar of the fire.

'Take your last breath and hold it as long as you can!' came a strained voice that might have been Kate's.

Mordius gulped a lungful of super-heated air and fought against his body's immediate instinct to expel the painfully hot gas. He put his head down and ran for all he was worth. But the flames were faster – racing along a shelf and leaping the gap to the next one with impossible speed. They swept past him and he felt every hair on his body burnt away in a flash. He held the scream in, knowing that to do otherwise would mean his certain death. Thick, black smoke now filled the corridor before him and he ran on unsighted.

He tripped over something heavy and unmoving in his path and hit the floor. He landed on his chest and was forced to exhale. Involuntarily, he took smoke into himself and immediately started to choke.

He knew he only had moments of life left. His limbs spasmed but he got them under control and with painful slowness got to his feet. The searing heat meant he had to keep his eyes closed as he staggered forward.

A wall. Left, a step upwards. On his knees now, another rising step. A hand found what remained of his hair and pulled him up. Parts of his scalp came away but he was dragged higher.

'Breathe!' came a harsh order.

Mordius coughed so hard that he tasted blood in the back of his throat. But then sweet, Shakri-blessed air filled him and cried out like a babe.

'I keep having to save you, but you're one tough, Incarnus-bred little bugger, I'll give you that!' Kate observed. 'Thought we'd lost you that time. Oh well, next time, perhaps. Come on, just thirty or so levels to go. Up!'

'What?' Mordius rasped, unable to recognise his own voice. 'We can't stay ahead of it.'

'These halls are larger than the ones below. The fire will be slower to make its way up. We can make it. We *must* make it!'

With that, she was gone, followed by the Captain carrying an unconscious Philasteres. He realised that they'd lost the three guards to the nightmare rising up around them, and felt an irrational pang of guilt that he hadn't tried to save whomever he'd tripped over in the murk. Of course, he would only have succeeded in dooming himself if he'd tried, but it still didn't sit well with him. Maybe he should have used his necromatic arts to bring back the guard from the dead. Yes, it was forbidden but what harm could it really have done? When someone died tragically before their time, who else could redress the situation except a necromancer?

Still, it was too late now, since the poor guard would have been consumed by the ravening flames. Mordius raised up his own protesting body and hobbled after Kate and the Captain. Then began the most hellish, temple-pounding flight of his life. He wove along misty corridor after misty corridor, careening off stacks of shelves as they jutted out. He'd long since gone past his pain barrier: if he went too far, he knew, he'd never find his way back and would be lost in Lacrimos's maze for all eternity.

They began to pass priests at desks, who looked up in annoyance and shock. Their eyes went wide when they beheld the manner in which their high priest was travelling, and even wider when they looked at Mordius. He realised his smoke-black, singed and semi-naked appearance must make him look like something from the pit.

'Fire! Everybody out!' Kate called.

'Get up, you dullards! Save yourselves!' the Captain shouted in his best parade-ground voice.

There was a terrible detonation that felt like the whole mount on which Corinus sat was being torn asunder. Pillars that had stood for millennia cracked, solid shelving that had housed priceless, tissue-thin manuscripts for centuries broke apart like tinder wood, and the catacombs, which had existed for aeons before the first foundation stone of the capital city of Dur Memnos had been laid, began to collapse.

Mordius flung himself after Kate and the Captain into the temple courtyard. Dust filled the air and the previously firm flagstones underfoot now felt out of kilter.

The Captain gently placed the Holy Reader, who had come to as they'd reached the higher levels, on his feet.

'Captain, see to your men and then the city!'

The soldier still had the wherewithal to salute smartly. 'Yes, milady!' Then he hurried away.

'Kate, help me!' Mordius croaked as he tried to haul a determined-looking Philasteres back from the doors to the Great Library.

'Priest, have you completely lost the wits Cognis gave you? Don't you understand there's nothing you can do in there?'

Philasteres shrugged off Kate's hand and turned on her. His eyes blazed with an alien intelligence. 'No, it is *you* who does not understand, daughter! You cannot even begin to comprehend what it means to lose the library. Don't you know that my mountain temple has also been destroyed? Don't you know that the lives of these priests are as nothing next to the loss of the sum of all knowledge? After all I have taught you, daughter, do you still know so little? Don't you know what will happen to *me* and this realm with the loss of the library?'

'C-Cognis?' Kate asked in the voice of a child.

Then Philasteres's eyes became all-encompassing. 'Ahh! Now I see it. We will be reduced to what we were before the Time of Breaking! That has been the intent all along. And by this we know the Enemy is returning! So little time!'

Philasteres made for the smoke-filled door once more and Kate barely had the strength to slow him down. 'Cognis, I beg you, who is the Enemy? What is happening? What must I do?'

The god-possessed priest broke step long enough to say, 'I don't know how it is possible for the Enemy to return.' He laughed – a sound so hopeless that it both broke her heart and terrified her beyond words. 'Don't you see? The irony? I, Cognis, do not *know*. Already I am diminished. But enough of me still remains to tell you that discovering how the Enemy returns will also tell you what you must do if anything is to survive. Go to the Old Place, where the Enemy is still remembered.' And, with that, he disappeared into the smoke, as if he himself had never been anything more than that.

Mordius sought to follow, but tongues of flame forced him back from the portal, tongues that both lashed out at him and gave voice to a deep, mocking laughter.

'Kate, what are we to do? Not one of the priests has escaped.'

'You're going to find this Old Place. Meanwhile, I'm going to have a serious chat with our good friend the Chamberlain.'

'You want me to travel with all this going on? On my own?' Mordius smiled in terror.

'Hmm. Where's Strap when you need him?'

'Someone call my name?' came a boyish, playful voice as Strap led his horse through the entrance tunnel and into the courtyard. 'Honestly, I leave you lot alone for five seconds and look what happens. And what's this I hear about the Scourge being back? No wonder we've got problems.'

Chapter Five: Nor Shelter

The Scourge was in a foul mood. Not only did his jaw still ache from where Saltar had hit him, but as he had lain unconscious Sergeant Marr and his men had turned up with both Lucius and that cursed priest of Shakri in tow. The fat fool had been all conciliatory concern about the apparent injury to the Consort of Shakri and, uninvited, had attempted to administer care to the Scourge; to the extent that it had taken three of Marr's men to restrain the Consort and prevent him from perpetrating much greater damage upon the person of the priest himself. Saltar had not tried to intervene, as he was equally unimpressed with the arrival of the royal musician and the priest – though the basis of his concern was that the two new members of the party were more than likely to slow them down.

So it was that their evening camp had been a difficult and tense affair. The priest and Lucius wisely kept themselves to themselves. The Scourge made Visier's body safe with water from the temple of Shakri, so that the assassin couldn't rise up during the night and attempt to slit their throats; then he went and lay down on the far side of the camp fire. With just a few words, Marr organised his five men to keep a guard through the dark hours. And Saltar prowled back and forth until all was quiet; then he threw himself on the hard ground to wait. A few short hours later and well before the dawn he was up and packing his horse. The Scourge joined him without speaking a word; clearly, sleep had also been impossible for him.

If it hadn't been for Marr's man waking his sergeant to explain they were striking camp already, and the noise of the resulting scramble, Lucius and the priest would have been left where they were. As it was, they'd been last away and been made to push their horses hard to catch back up to the group.

Now, a brooding Scourge rode next to Saltar at the head of the band, the Battle-leader setting a brisk pace. In his head, the Guardian tried to read through all that had happened and all that was implied by their encounter with Visier from the day before – the sort of basic process even the greenest of Guardians was trained in – but all that filled his mind was the feeling and knowledge of the priest's eyes on him. It was a small thing, like an itch, or a fly buzzing round the head, but left too long it could drive even the most disciplined of intellects to distraction... and the Scourge had known anything but self-discipline since his return to Shakri's realm. Just what was wrong with him? He didn't feel like his old self. He'd been clumsy in the extreme when he'd faced both the golem and Visier with Saltar. If Wim had been against him on those occasions, then more likely than not, he'd have ended up killing Saltar by accident or some such.

He sighed to himself. It was that bloody woman... goddess, he corrected himself... Shakri. She'd upset his equilibrium. His time with her amongst the gods must have changed him. Well, of course it's changed you, you idiot, he chided himself. It would change anyone. Who can think of life as a mortal in the same way when you've known the ecstasy of godhead? Who can fight for life as a mortal with the same sharp intensity, passion and belief when they have experienced a type of existence that makes mortal life seem trivial?

He shook his head, uncertain what to do for one of the first times in his life. He was desperately worried that he represented more of a hindrance or liability for Saltar than anything else... well, more of a liability than anyone except Lucius and that flaming priest, of course. Indeed, he'd become so lost in pondering his predicament that he'd failed to speak up when Marr had told one of his men – a square and reliable, but hardly quick-witted, soldier called Barris – to go scout the road ahead of them. The Scourge, with all his experience and roadcraft, should have been by far the better choice for such a role.

His reverie was broken when Saltar called the priest to join him at the head of their group.

'Good priest, we have not treated you well thus far. I am somewhat overwrought by recent events and have neglected to show you even the basic courtesies. I would be honoured to know your name and hear about the omens that prompted your high priest to send you to us.'

The priest, who'd been all agitation as he approached, visibly relaxed to hear Saltar start observing some basic protocols. The relationship between the throne and the temples had never been straightforward; and sometimes the only things that had kept the peace were the agreed upon forms, procedures and boundaries. The latter existed for the good of the kingdom, since without them surely only social upheaval, civil war and chaos would follow, or so the temple scholars argued.

Of course, it hadn't always been necessary to agree such essential protocols and principles formally, since Mordius had long served as a skilled interlocutor between throne and temple. He'd ensured that an *understanding* existed between both parties, without their ever having to start arguing over the finer points of written codicils and constitutions. But the recent behaviour of the Battle-leader had begun to put not only the status quo but also the future of the kingdom in jeopardy, as far as the priest was concerned. It had made him wonder if Mordius would not have been a better candidate for the throne. It was therefore a considerable relief that the quixotic Battle-leader had finally seen sense and become prepared to accept guidance from the temple of the goddess of all creation.

The priest was all smiling grace as he said, 'Milord, this humble servant of the goddess,' (at this point he conspicuously kept his eyes averted from the Scourge), 'is called Altibus. I am honoured to be in the company of both you and... and...'

The Scourge narrowed his eyes. Was this wheedling bureaucrat deliberately trying to provoke him?

'... your party. On behalf of my temple, I am here to serve in whatever way I may, milord, just as the exalted Nostracles was a faithful servant to you before me.'

'Is that so?' Saltar asked gently and with a raised eyebrow. 'Didn't Nostracles originally join you and Young Strap on the road, Scourge? He was always more your faithful servant than mine, wasn't he?'

'Indeed,' the Scourge growled. 'And let us not forget that Nostracles was ultimately stripped of his priesthood by Shakri Herself. I wouldn't go calling Nostracles *exalted*, if I were you, priest, unless it is your express purpose to commit blasphemy and follow in Nostracles's footsteps in that manner.'

Altibus suddenly looked faint. 'I... that is...'

'Because speaking from personal experience,' the Scourge continued, his voice grinding and painful to listen to, 'faithfulness is not the strong suit of our beloved goddess or Her followers. Not only did Her Wonderfulness abandon Nostracles, but also Her high priest before that. She claimed their acts lacked the required degree of faith, only then to go and reward them with a similar display of faithlessness. Hardly sets a good example, now does it? And she hardly treated me much better either, in case you were wondering, which I know you all were! Now, priest,' the rockslide demanded, 'just how are you going to make us believe you are a *faithful* servant? Do you really expect us to believe that you are beside yourself with fear for the safety of young Orastes?'

'That's a good question, Scourge,' Saltar nodded. 'Well, Altibus? Answer the man! Are you having any sleepless nights for worrying about what's happening to my son? Funny, because I distinctly heard you snoring last night. In fact, you were snoring so hard that at one point I thought you were going to put out the camp fire.'

Altibus quailed before the two men, but had no escape but to attempt to answer them. 'The ways of the gods are a mystery...'

'No,' Saltar said quietly, silencing the priest instantly. 'Try again.'

'I am a devout...'

'No. Last chance.'

The party had slowed and the others had caught up to the front. They kept a respectful distance, however, as they witnessed the confrontation. Marr had shaken his head each time Altibus had spoken. The priest mopped his clammy brow and looked to Lucius for help, but the one-eyed musician could only shrug.

Altibus licked his lips, cleared his throat and then said in a shaking voice: 'Your son's safe return is now my prime concern. As a priest of Shakri, my interest is in safeguarding life, particularly that of the innocent.'

Saltar smiled faintly. 'See, that wasn't so hard, was it?'

Lucius sighed with relief. Marr looked disappointed and the Scourge spat over the side of his horse.

'Okay, now we're all friends, good Altibus, how is it your high priest knew to send you to us?'

The party resumed its previous pace along the King's Road. 'In all honesty, I am not certain, milord. But High Priest Ikthaeon was very clear on the matter, almost… agitated, I don't think he'd mind me saying. He emerged from the holy of holies and immediately asked me which of our priests were in the temple. He then told me that he had a holy task for me that would involve me having to leave Corinus. I must say I was somewhat shocked, because I've never travelled much beyond the environs of the city, and I'd just started my annual review of the temple's accounts – very important work, you understand, for the central temple in all Dur Memnos – but High Priest Ikthaeon insisted that it was the will of the goddess Herself I undertake this task. I was to find the musician Lucius and convince him to bring me to you, so that we might join your group and provide… well, anyway, High Priest Ikthaeon made me swear I would not be deterred no matter what resistance

I met,' and here he couldn't help eyeing the glowering Scourge, 'and that I ensure both Lucius and I accompany you on this holy quest.'

Saltar meditated upon Altibus's words and left it to the Scourge to give an initial response to the priest's narrative; which the Guardian duly and ferociously did. Saltar chose not to listen and wondered at Shakri's apparent interest in his son's welfare. It wasn't like the goddess to trouble herself with individual mortals, since their lives and deaths were simply the realm's natural process of birth, procreation, dissipation and regeneration. As the priests of Shakri were so fond of saying, even in death there was new life, since worms and maggots always fed and multiplied on the dead. Could her care for Orastes actually be genuine? If so, what motivated it and why shift the balance in Lacrimos's favour by taking an overt hand in hunting down the Jaffrans? It didn't make sense. There was something missing. Something he didn't understand was going on, which raised the more likely possibility that Shakri was using them all as her pawns and manipulating events to serve her own ends. It would be just like the gods to consider even the life of an innocent child theirs to play with, no matter the consequences for that child. He felt the insane anger he normally kept under tight control surge and nearly break free.

He blinked rapidly and fought against the rage. He clenched his fists so tightly around the horse reins that the skin on the backs of his knuckles split open and the nails of his hands drew blood from his palms. He tried to detach his mind from his body by focussing as much as he could on what was going on around him.

The Scourge was ranting. '... only sent you because there were no other priests around in the temple at the time. And from what I can tell, you're just a clerk more used to spending his hours with pen and parchment than tending to the faithful of Dur Memnos. You have the well-fed look of a priest who has indulged himself and his appetites to the full, a priest who has grown fat while his followers have suffered. How will someone used to a soft and pampered life hope to cope with a hard life on the road, even when you can get your horse to behave because of your priesthood's affinity with all living things, and when you can use your powers to heal your saddle-sore arse every night? How will you cope when the killing starts?'

'K-killing?' Altibus blurted involuntarily, unable to combat or contradict the wrath and perception of his goddess's own consort.

'Yes, *killing*, you Wim-addled loon! What do you think this is, a picnic? This is a hunting party that will track down, torture and exterminate its prey!

If you cannot help us in that, then why are you here? Are you simply a spy for Her Holy Interference?'

Altibus's eyes were moist and his lower lip trembled but he met the Scourge's eyes as he replied: 'It is my holy vow not to be deterred, no matter what resistance I meet. It is only right that the Consort test my devotion to the Holy Mother.'

'Enough, Scourge!' Saltar said calmly, and the Scourge stopped. 'Your points are well made but if Altibus is a spy, then he seems a very poor one… that, or an exceptional liar. A Wim-addled loon, I believe you called him, so he is more likely to be a very poor spy and not too much to worry about. But this isn't getting us very far except to make all of us angry. Good priest, I am curious about your High Priest Ikthaeon's insistence that Lucius accompany us. Would you care to explain?'

Altibus smiled with relief at Saltar's intervention. 'I am sorry, milord, but the high priest offered no explanation.'

'Lucius!' Saltar called back down the line. 'Why are you here? Don't you have a concert to perform somewhere or something?'

The one-eyed musician trotted up to them. 'Saltar, I owe you, Kate and the Scourge everything. I wouldn't be alive were it not for you. You rebuilt the kingdom so it was a place in which I could perform my music both in safety and to appreciative audiences. Truly, you are the Builder they say, Saltar. And it is not just houses that you have built, but actual lives; and not just empty lives either. You have permitted our lives to have their own purpose and meaning. How could I not be here, then, when I might be of some help during your time of need?'

Saltar frowned. 'Exactly what help do you think it is you can render me, Lucius?'

Lucius looked apologetic. 'I do not know, but I have decided that even if there is only a remote chance of my being of any use then I must accompany you. Please, do no try and dissuade me, for I have decided this is the purpose to my life, and my purpose is my own. I can promise you that I will also do everything I can to avoid being a burden. If ever I fail to keep that promise, then I will not hesitate to leave.'

Saltar sighed. It seemed that he did not have any choice but to suffer Lucius's presence. The musician was not just one of his soldiers he could order to do this or that – no, he was a free man who could choose to do whatever he wished, as long as it did not involve breaking the law. 'Very well, but I cannot have you slowing down this group of trained men. The best way for us to ensure that you are no burden is to ignore you mostly. If your horse becomes lame, then you will be left behind. If you collapse from exhaustion, then do not expect help from us. If your canteen runs out of water, we will not be able to spare you any. Do you understand?'

'I do,' the musician said solemnly, and when there was no further comment from anyone drifted back to his place at the end of the line.

'And I have one last question for you, Altibus.'

'Anything, milord!'

'The Jaffran called Visier was some sort of magician, but did not use a type of magic with which I am familiar. He changed the very air around us, so that first it was gloomy and then there was nothing but a thick fog. There were shadowy demons all around us but they were illusions, seemingly. How can an individual have such power over Shakri's realm that he can bend the light and matter to his own will?'

The Scourge cursed himself for not having thought of this question. It was so obvious that it should have occurred to him even without trying to read through the events of the battle with Visier. He realised that he had a headache – when had it started? And it seemed to be getting worse.

Altibus whistled absently through his teeth as he thought about Saltar's question. They all waited, the Scourge the only one fidgeting. Finally, the priest said: 'Fundamentally, there are just two types of magic – that which changes the world around us beyond our control and that which changes us beyond our control. The force that changes the world around us is exclusively the domain of the gods and occasionally their priests. The force that changes us is most certainly not divine in nature, however. It is a magic performed exclusively by men and women.'

'Hmm, interesting,' Saltar mused. 'I assume the gods cannot change us if the balance is to be preserved, if we are to retain our free will, yes? Or is there something irreducible in the nature of each of us that is beyond the power of the gods?'

They all looked blankly at the Battle-leader except for Altibus, who appeared discomforted. 'We cannot answer and perhaps should not even speculate upon such a question,' the priest replied.

Saltar put the priest's censure aside. 'We can argue about that another time. If I understand what you are saying, either the world around the Scourge and I was changed or it was the Scourge and I that were actually affected by this magic.' Altibus nodded. 'Visier was either a priest and therefore able to change the world around us or was capable of a mortally-derived magic and able to affect us in that way.'

'Correct.'

'Hmm. Visier did speak of the *arrival of the god*, as if he was preparing the way for this being. Would that make him a priest of sorts? And do you know who this god might be?'

'Saltar...' the Scourge said faintly.

'The arrival of *the* god?' Altibus mused. 'As if there were but one? It cannot be one of Shakri's pantheon then. And the Jaffrans are not monotheists as far as I'm aware – those heathens have thousands of gods and will worship just about anything. It could be that a new cult has arisen on Jaffra and that there is some demon masquerading as the one-god or some such. It's happened before, you know.'

'I see,' Saltar said. 'But surely such a demon wouldn't have any significant power over Shakri's realm, would it? Its priests would be capable of little more than conjuring tricks.'

The pain in the Scourge's head became so bad that he could no longer follow the conversation. He put his hands to his temples to massage them, but could find no relief. He was finding it hard to see now.

'I suppose so,' Altibus conceded.

'In which case Visier was using some sort of mortally-derived magic. What can you tell me of such magic? Can anyone do it?'

Altibus pulled a face. 'Such magic is frowned upon by the temples, and is forbidden in most civilised kingdoms. Necromancy is an example.'

'Surely not!' Saltar protested. 'Isn't necromancy performed in the name of Lacrimos?'

The priest shook his head. 'Necromancers actually seek to steal the dead away from Lacrimos. Remember, the Heart of the necromancer Harpedon was an abomination that threatened Lacrimos's realm as much as Shakri's own. All mortally-derived magic is similarly dangerous and sacrilegious. It must be stamped out wherever it is found.'

'I understand,' Saltar said carefully, 'but Visier did not use necromancy or any other sort of death-magic, did he? Good priest, I need to know what we're up against. It could be extremely important.'

The portly priest became flustered. He refused to meet Saltar's eyes and his cheeks reddened.

'Altibus, my friend,' Lucius said gently. 'I know this man. He is a *good* man, despite his occasional, dark looks and sudden demands. You and I have vowed to help him in whatever way we can, and this is but another test of that vow. We knew it would not be easy. I also suppose you fear that what you reveal to us might put us on the path to temptation; but in following these

Jaffrans I think we are already on such a path. We need your wisdom to help us recognise the ambushes they may have set for us along the way.'

Altibus gave a shamefaced smile. 'You speak with the artistry of a minstrel, but there may be something in what you say. Very well, I will tell you what I know although it is little enough. The temple doesn't encourage the study of such an area, of course. It is said that some of the jungle tribes to the south have shamans who not only practise death-magic, where they contact their ancestors and so forth, but also some sort of blood-magic, allowing them to be imbued with various strengths and abilities when they consume the blood of jungle animals or… or tribesmen they have defeated in battle. They're just stories, I'm sure!'

'Savages!' Sergeant Marr spat.

'What say you, Scourge?' Saltar asked. 'Is there any substance to such stories? You must have seen and heard of many things in…'

The commander of the Guardians toppled out of his saddle and hit the road headfirst. Blood smeared across a number of flagstones.

'Scourge!' Saltar shouted in panic and vaulted out of his saddle.

The Sergeant was only a second behind him and already shouting at the priest. 'Get down here, you lardcake!'

'Noo!' Lucius moaned with tears in his eyes.

Altibus struggled down from his saddle. The Guardian was not moving. He reached out shaking hands towards the grievous head wound and then snatched them back.

'What is it?' Saltar demanded.

'He's… he's dead!'

'What?!'

'No, no, no!' Lucius protested.

'Shit!' Marr said. 'Wim must have heard his blasphemy.'

'Do something!' Saltar insisted.

Altibus looked up at the Battle-leader standing over him and shook his head fearfully. 'I-I can't!'

The Scourge groaned and rolled over. 'Oo! Terrible headache!'

'Priest, you're an incompetent fool!' Sergeant Marr decided for all of them.

'I swear he was… there was no emanation… or…!'

'Never mind!' Saltar said, pushing Altibus aside and leaning over the Guardian. 'Scourge, can you hear me? What's wrong? You fell off your horse.'

The Guardian's eyes finally stopped rolling around and his gaze drifted up to those huddled around him. 'Cognis! He's gone!'

'What did he say?' whispered one of the soldiers at the back.

'How can Cognis be gone?' Saltar pressed. 'Gone where?'

'I don't know, do I?' the Scourge said with more strength in his voice. 'Isn't anyone going to bloody help me up?'

'Stay where you are. Give yourself a second or two to recover. How do you know Cognis is gone?'

'I… I just know, okay? One minute he's there in the back of my head, along with all the other gods, and the next he's gone. I've been having trouble concentrating recently, and I think it was because he was under attack somehow.'

'But… but you know what this means, don't you?' Saltar said, aghast.

The Scourge nodded and winced at the pain it caused him. He put his hand to his head – his injury was no longer as livid and messy as it had been just seconds ago. 'All that we knew will start to diminish. We won't even know what it is we've lost. Soon, we won't even know ourselves, since it will become harder to retain and acquire knowledge. No mortal will survive, and that will threaten the gods themselves. I cannot see many of them surviving either.'

'How can this be?' one of the soldiers shouted wildly. 'It's impossible!' He began to shake.

Marr strode over to the man and struck him across the face. 'Get a grip on yourself! Or I'll have you wearing a baby's swaddling clothes! Understand?'

The soldier blinked hard and then nodded with his eyes down.

'But what can we do?' Lucius asked nervously.

Saltar looked at him in silence for a second while he thought. 'I can only imagine that something catastrophic happened to the entity Cognis or his temple. I now fear Mordius was right: the kidnapping of my son was intended to distract us and remove us from Corinus, to get us out of the way so that it would be easier to strike at Cognis. I hope Kate and the others are alright.'

They were all silent, none of them daring to suggest that they give up on their pursuit of the Jaffrans and Orastes.

'We have no alternative,' Saltar said. 'We must continue on this path, for all the signs are that the kidnapping and the disappearance of Cognis are connected. The kidnappers will give us the information we need to find the source of this trouble, to destroy the one-god if that is what we face. We must travel more quickly though, for we are being outstripped by time and events. At the same time, we must search out the temples of the gods of the pantheon to be sure they are safe. Do any of you see another way?'

None spoke.

'Very well. Scourge, stop laying about. Any more beauty sleep and you will be inspiring lust rather than fear in our enemies.'

❧ ❧

They rode hard through the late autumn landscape, leaning low behind the heads of their horses to stay out of the chilling wind as much as possible. Altibus was encouraged to ride towards the front so that they could shelter in the wake of his ample frame – after all, the priest could use his Shakri-gifted magic to stay warm, so it made little difference to him.

At least the Jaffrans will be suffering in these temperatures, Saltar thought to himself, the subtropical climes of Jaffra well known because of the spices and citrus fruit the island produced. Strange time of year for them to be travelling really, he pondered further, since Dur Memnos has no spare grain to trade at the end of autumn and hasn't yet begun to trap forest animals for their thick winter coats. That means these Jaffrans will have sailed in and been unable to do much trade – surely that would have drawn the attention of our kingdom's spies. And how had these Jaffrans travelled all the way to Corinus without being seen? Perhaps they'd donned Memnosian attire, but why then had they been reported as fleeing the capital in their traditional island dress? It didn't make sense.

As the sun was close to setting they reached the environs of the mercenary city, Holter's Cross. Their scout, Barris, was waiting for them at the side of the road.

'Milord, yonder city guards report five men in black capes and turbans turning east here, taking the King's Road towards King's Landing. They had what appeared to be a child with them.'

'It's them!' Saltar said with certainty. 'When did they come through here?'

'Mid-morning, milord.'

'So about six hours ahead of us. We'll ride through the night and be sure to catch them.'

The Scourge pulled a face.

'What is it?' Saltar asked.

'I'm surprised they'd let themselves be seen by the city sentries. It doesn't feel right.'

'Scourge, they're in a hurry and don't know the landscape well. They must know there'll be a group pursuing them and that they don't have time to mess about. Besides, I can't see any other option but for heading east, can you?'

The Scourge shook his head. He felt that a group that had shown such meticulous planning in attacking the palace and kidnapping a child would not then be so inadequate when it came to covering their trail. Perhaps the Jaffrans had deliberately allowed themselves to be seen going east only then to take another direction unobserved. Were they laying a false trail? But where would they be going if not King's Landing? He couldn't think. His thoughts felt so dull, so muffled. He sighed. He'd just have to watch the trail as best he could and try to spot any side-step, departure from it or diversion. 'No,' he said tiredly. 'Let's go!'

⁂

They pushed on into the evening and then into the kingdom of night. There was no moon, so they could barely see the rider immediately in front of them. Still, there was just enough starlight shining down from the constellation known as Shakri's Host to make out the edges of the road. Besides, the sound from the horses' hooves would warn them if they managed to stray, always assuming there was one of the party not dozing in the saddle and still attentive to such things.

Rising before dawn and riding hard through the day had taken its toll on man and beast alike. Their pace had slowed to a walk and even Saltar's eyes were beginning to droop. He barely had the energy to curse the shortcomings of his mortal body as he listened to the rumblings coming from Altibus's chest and noticed the hung heads of the others around him. If they were to be attacked now, they would have no chance! Maybe it would be better to be an animee again, to have the untiring strength of the undead: then he would have no trouble catching his enemies and retrieving his dear son. But if he were an animee, he would feel no emotion when his son smiled at him or squeezed one of his fingers in his chubby palm. He would have no inclination to hug the child to him. He would have no instinct to protect his innocent Orastes from harm.

They came round a long but gentle bend in the road. Lit up though it was, Saltar was halfway past the inn before he realised it was there.

'Awake!' he shouted, and a few of the party stirred and looked up. Altibus continued to snore.

'Shakri be praised!' Lucius breathed. 'Food and a soft bed.'

'Feed and rest for the horses!' the Scourge reminded him.

'Oh! Yes, of course.'

'Saltar,' the Scourge said more quietly to catch the Battle-leader's attention, 'before you suggest we only make this a short stop to gather information about the Jaffrans, be aware that the horses can't take much more. We've pretty much ridden them to a standstill. We might actually make better time overall by taking a few hours rest now. And the men need rest and sustenance if they are to be of any use in a fight against the enemy tomorrow. We don't want them so tired that they cannot even lift their weapons.'

Saltar sighed, knowing the truth of the Scourge's words, but not necessarily liking them any more for it. 'Very well. Sergeant Marr, could you and the men attend to the horses while I rouse those inside?'

The Battle-leader left his party to sort itself out and made for the main door. Lucius tried to shake Altibus awake without dislodging him from his saddle and sending him crashing to the earth. The Scourge followed Saltar.

The innkeeper was there waiting for them with a lantern when they entered. His hair and clothes were unkempt – clearly, he was a light sleeper and their arrival had awoken him.

'There are more of you,' he stated rather than needing to ask a question.

'Ten in total,' Saltar nodded. 'A meal and pallets if you have them.'

The innkeeper frowned and raised his lantern a little. His eyes widened as he recognised the Scourge. 'Gentlemen, welcome to the Stumbling Traveller. My humble inn is at your disposal. We have ample viands, though they are cold now. I will set candles, tap a new barrel and pull my sluggard daughter from her bed.'

'Good innkeep,' Saltar said quickly. 'We will only trouble you for a hand of hours, for time is against us.'

The innkeeper smiled. ''Tis a strange time of night to be abroad, that is certain. If I do not miss my mark, you have some interest in the dark-robed men who were in here this evening. They similarly chose to travel through the night.'

'They were here? Five of them?' Saltar pressed. 'Did they have a child with them?'

If he thought Saltar's question strange, the innkeeper chose not to show it. 'None that I saw, but one of the party mainly kept himself to the stables. They did not stay long.'

As the innkeeper stirred the fire in the hearth to life, Saltar and the Scourge were joined by Lucius and the priest. Sergeant Marr had decided that he and his men would eat and sleep in the stables – he knew better than to encourage a soldier to relax around alcohol.

The innkeeper's daughter deposited four foaming tankards of beer at Saltar's table and smiled at the Scourge. 'I'm Lamia. I was here last time you came through, Guardian. How have you been? There was a rumour you'd died. I'm glad to see there's life in the Old Hound yet!'

Altibus raised his eyebrows, while the Scourge lowered his. Lucius smiled and Saltar shook his head. They all looked at the Scourge, who refused to be embarrassed. 'Hello, Lamia. I am also glad to see you well. These are my travelling companions. Saltar… Lucius, a musician, and Altibus, a priest of Shakri.'

Lamia's mouth hung open. 'The Builder! Here!' she gasped, staring at Saltar, and then quickly performed a curtsy.

Suddenly, the innkeeper was there, trying to hustle his daughter away. 'Sorry if she's bothering you, milords! Come, Lamia, there's work to be done in the kitchens!'

'Guardian, I hope to see you later!' Lamia said with a far from innocent smile.

The Scourge caught himself beginning to return the smile. 'Err… yes… I hope so too!'

'I really don't think…' Altibus began.

'I knew it!' Lamia screamed, breaking free of her father. 'I turn my back on you for five seconds and you're eyeing up every tavern trollop in the kingdom! For all your protestations of love, you're just like any other glob-tongued, self-serving male!'

'Lamia, what are you…?' the innkeeper started to ask in confusion.

The Scourge surged to his feet. 'Shakri! How dare you!'

'How dare *I*?'

'You mean… she-she's the g-goddess!' Altibus squeaked in terror. Hastily, he shunted the table forwards, spilling some beer, and fell to his knees.

'You just can't mind your own obsessed business, can you?! You threw me out, and then think it's okay to spy on me! You have no right, none whatsoever!' the Scourge roared. 'Then in a fit of pique you think you can possess any mortal you want and put the entire balance in danger! You are a maniac! You will release this girl at once!'

Lamia's hands went to her hips and she stamped her foot. 'I will *not*! It was I who gave her life. She is my dutiful servant! She is mine to do with as I wish. And I was clearly *right* to throw you out. You cannot be trusted when your head is turned by a winsome wench less than half your age!'

'Why, you self-righteous bitch!' the Scourge choked, his face red with anger and veins pulsing in his forehead. Altibus sobbed where he was, his face pressed to the floor. Lucius was all but hiding under the table. The innkeeper had backed away as far as he could.

Saltar rose smoothly from his seat and slapped Lamia hard across the face. She cried out.

'You-you hit me!'

'Yes, and I'll hit you again. Leave this place. Surely you know there are more vital matters to attend to elsewhere. The realm is under threat from some other god, is it not?'

Lamia wobbled on her feet and then her eyes cleared and she caught her balance. Her father came to her, hugged her and led her away without a backward glance.

'Thank you!' the Scourge said shakily. 'You saved me having to do that myself.'

'What have you done!' Altibus wailed. 'You cannot strike the goddess of all creation,' he pleaded. 'You cannot! It is unconscionable, unthinkable!'

'Wait till he hears you once incapacitated her with a scythe,' the Scourge chuckled darkly.

'What?' Altibus whispered, looking faint.

'Enough,' Saltar said humourlessly. 'There is nothing to be gained by any of this. I only agreed to stop so we could get the refreshment we needed, not so that we could waste time with pointless recriminations over past misdeeds. I'm retiring now to the room that's been put aside for us.'

Lucius and Altibus indicated that they would also turn in.

'It's a shame to let this beer and the innkeep's hospitality go to waste. I will be there shortly,' the Scourge asserted.

'Very well,' Saltar replied. 'But we will leave with the dawn.'

***

The Scourge was left alone with his beer. Both the innkeeper and his daughter had disappeared and showed no signs of returning. He brooded over the unpleasant scene with Shakri and his mood became as black as the night.

She did not own him! She did not even have a right to his affections now that she'd thrown him out. So why was he so troubled by her? She'd gotten under his skin and he knew it. Even if he were to flay that skin from his bones, he knew, he still would not be rid of her. She'd gotten into his marrow, become a central construct within his mind, become a dimension of his soul. Curse her!

What really got to him though, as he wondered dully where the beer had gone so quickly, was that he did not entirely understand why she had thrown him out. Sure, he had a certain grumpiness about him that wasn't to everyone's taste, but it had never been that much of a problem for her before; if anything, it had only seemed to endear him to her more. He couldn't believe she no longer loved him. After all, she was the goddess of love as well as the goddess of creation. But maybe there was someone she loved more!… Someone other than *herself*, he couldn't help adding churlishly.

The door to the inn opened and closed and the Scourge looked up. A large barbarian with the twisted tribal scars of the south-eastern deserts stood taking in the room. A large, sheathed scimitar was strapped to his back, but his hands were well away from it.

The Scourge waved him over. 'Fanshy a drink?'

The barbarian nodded silently.

'Shee that barrel over there? Go pick it h-up and bring it h-over here!'

The barbarian complied, poured himself a tankard and drank it down in a single draught.

'Thirshty, huh? Have h-another. Come a long way?'

The barbarian nodded heavily. 'To be fighter in Holter's Cross. I am good fighter!'

The Scourge pushed his empty tankard towards the barbarian. 'That sho? Good for you! Not enough fighting going on down h-in the deshertsh then? Bit unushual that. What'sh happened? You h-all finally killed h-each other? You the lasht one left alive? Come to find more people to kill?'

The barbarian poured more beer for them. 'It's matter of honour.'

'Always is with you tribeshmen. Shomeone inshult your goat or something?'

The barbarian shook his head unhappily. 'It was woman. I must reclaim honour in battle.'

The Scourge laughed loudly. 'I'll drink to that! Take my h-advice, friend, never have anything to do with women. No good can come h-of them.'

The barbarian took a long draw on his beer. 'But what is alternative? Tribe is everything. Family is everything. Without women there is nothing!'

'Shure there ish!' the Scourge slurred. 'There'sh your honour, comrades, the fight and… and other shtuff. And there'sh drink! Oh! Don't mind h-if I do.'

'And there are gods. Life can be dedicated to them instead of mortal society.'

His thoughts increasingly muzzy, the Scourge nodded. 'Yup, good one. But not Shakri. She's all about love, and that'sh what causes ush the problems in the first place. Shtrikes me that Lacrimosh might have the right idea after all. It'sh not for nothing that he'sh worshipped by mosht warriorsh in the world. War, knowing yourshelf, knowing your fellow man and death: there'sh a kind of shimplicity and honeshty about such a short of life, a kind of peace really. Heh! Funny! Peace by way of embracing war and death.'

'To Lacrimos!' the barbarian toasted and gulped back more of the strong beer.

The Scourge didn't raise his beer but nodded his head. 'To Lacrimos,' the Scourge said reflectively. 'He'sh never been my favourite fellow, to be honesht, but at least you alwaysh know where you shtand with him and what he represhents.'

'I make oath to serve Lacrimos. You should also.'

'Maybe,' the Scourge conceded, staring deeply into his beer. 'Maybe.'

They continued to drink in companionable silence, each man lost in his own thoughts.

If she did love someone more than him, then why would she continue to stalk him in this way? She didn't taunt him whenever she appeared; rather, she behaved jealously. The more he thought about it, the less it made sense. Still, very little made sense these days. That could be down to the beer he'd had or down to the loss of Cognis, but quite frankly the things the gods said and did rarely made much sense at the best of times. It was a waste of time a sensible mortal trying to make sense of such whimsical and vain beings. They found amusement in the most ridiculous things, and sometimes the suffering of mankind. It wouldn't surprise him if Shakri had thrown him out just so that they could all watch and laugh at his pain. Yes, that had a sort of perverted logic to it. And Shakri would turn up now and then just to add to his mortal torment and make the divine belly laugh all the bigger.

The booze may have made him paranoid, but he probably knew the gods better than any other mortal so would be a better judge than most. Yes, curse these gods! Mortals would be better off without them. Perhaps it was for the best that this one-god was coming.

'Beer gone!' the barbarian declared mournfully, turning his tankard upside down and watching the last drip fall onto the table. He blinked and then smiled. 'Time you make oath.'

'Oath?' the Scourge asked wearily.

'To Lacrimos.'

'Oh!' he said, leaning back from the table. He pushed his chair away. 'I'm tired!' Then he surged to his feet, found his balance and pulled his sword clear of its scabbard.

The barbarian was already heaving their table over towards the Scourge, tankards flying everywhere. The Guardian stumbled back awkwardly and just avoided being knocked to the floor. His opponent was suddenly holding a giant, two-headed axe and was preparing to swing it. It burned with red runes, clearly some sort of supernatural weapon.

'You cheat!' the Scourge accused him. 'You had a shcimitar before! You can't jusht magic shomething out of thin air! You'll destroy the balance. What's the matter, Lacrimosh, so scared that you have to resort to such desperate tricks?'

'Fool! I am *restoring* the balance! My self-indulgent sister put everything at risk just so that she could play games with her latest bed-slave. She sickens me with her base appetites. Her behaviour is almost mortal! She is unworthy of worship! And you! You! Your return to the realm of the living threatens the balance even more. You died; and therefore are a destructive anomaly that must not be tolerated. You are a perversion! A mortal who cavorts and consorts with the gods and thereby corrupts both godhead and mortality. But I will restore the balance by ending you once and for all.'

The Scourge simultaneously froze in horror, as he understood the truth in Lacrimos's words, and quickened with a selfish rage and desire for his own continued existence. Tightly, he said: 'What else can I do, where else can I go, when I am used as a play-thing and then cast aside by the gods? And you expect me to submit to you? Ha! You're as bad as all the others. Don't pretend you're here to restore the balance. You wanted me to swear an oath and serve you! What game were you playing, eh? What would have happened if I hadn't seen through your ruse? Lacrimos, I will never bow to any god. You can try and take my life if you want, but if I recall you tried that once before and then ended up crying like a baby. And the way you carry on about Shakri's love life, anyone would think you have an unhealthy interest there. Do you secretly lust after your own sister, is that it? It's alright, you can tell me!'

With a divine roar that deafened the Scourge and left his ears ringing, the God of Death bunched his muscles and swung His mighty two-headed axe. His senses, co-ordination and reactions thoroughly impaired by alcohol and a lack of sleep, the Scourge never had a chance. His sword was batted aside as if it was nothing more than a child's stick and then the wide, flat curve of the axe was cutting through his middle. Blood sheeted out and drenched the god as the Guardian's torso began to separate.

'Aargh! That hurts!' the Scourge complained as blood also began to pour from his mouth.

'Now you will accompany me to my realm,' Lacrimos said with grim satisfaction.

The Scourge chuckled wetly. 'Wish I could oblige, but I'm already damned, you see!'

'What?' Lacrimos growled.

'We've fought before, you and me. Victory wasn't yours then and it won't be now. Perhaps that defining meeting established the pattern that will repeat itself forever more. For it seems I will now kill you again.'

'No! It cannot be!' Lacrimos said shaking his head furiously, but there was a certain shrillness in his voice.

''Fraid so!' the Scourge said, pulling the axe towards him and further into his stomach. Unable to anticipate such an act, and his hands slick with blood, Lacrimos lost his grip on his weapon. He stretched his hands out for it, only for the Scourge to whip the axe round and cut the hands off at the wrists. Blood spurted in thick gouts and Lacrimos's face morphed through a dozen emotions in the blink of an eye as the god realised he was facing his last moment. The Scourge hefted the axe and allowed its weight and gravity to deliver the final, crushing blow.

The large body of the barbarian crashed to the floor and the Scourge let the axe thump down with it. Loss of blood and the abuses of the evening meant he could no longer see straight. He felt no triumph at having defeated the god. After all, wasn't he already a godslayer? Instead, he felt hollow... and tired, *so* tired! He lay down next to the bloody carcass of the god and closed his eyes. He drifted away, no longer caring if his own body breathed or not.

Saltar felt ghastly. He knew he must look like something newly risen from the grave, but he didn't care. How could he sleep when who knew what was happening to his child? He knew a lack of sleep would eventually begin to ruin his judgement and ability to function, but he would fight against it, against his own limitations, his own weakness, his own nature, unto death itself. And then he would fight death as he had before. If it meant he had to fight for all eternity, and beyond it if that were possible, then he would not hesitate to do so.

While his companions grabbed what rest they could on the mean pallets of the Stumbling Traveller, Saltar stood an unmoving vigil at their room's small window. He waited for the first glimmer of dawn to touch the far horizon.

His attention did not waver, he only occasionally blinked; he stood poised for the instant when he could take up the pursuit once more.

It might have been his overtired mind playing tricks on him, but there seemed to be a strange atmosphere about the inn, a strange tension. Yet all was quiet below. Where was the Scourge? Probably deep in his cups, damn him.

He continued a still and silent sentinel, feeling an invisible violence all around him, but witnessing nothing. At last a ghostly silver and blue kissed the bottom of the sky and Saltar was unleashed once more.

He strode across the room, kicking Lucius and Altibus awake as he went, and descended the stairs. By the fitful light of the common room's dying candles, he made out the Scourge lying on the floor, the evidence of some enthusiastic drinking scattered all around him.

'On your feet, Scourge! We're leaving.'

There was no response. Saltar walked out of the inn, leaving the musician and priest to get the Scourge going. He raised the men in the stables and began to saddle his horse. There were groans, yawns and stretching, but they obeyed him… or they did once the Sergeant started to bark at them.

Saltar led his horse round to the front of the Stumbling Traveller, to find Altibus there wringing his hands.

'We cannot rouse the Divine Consort!'

Saltar sighed. 'Then we go without him.'

Sergeant Marr, who'd just joined them, looked unhappy at the idea but kept quiet.

'Altibus, can't you use your priestly powers to bring him to?'

Altibus looked ready to cry. 'M-my magic is not as advanced as that of some of my brothers. Besides, the Consort does not seem ill, as such, so there's nothing for me to heal. His condition… his *tiredness* shall we say… cannot simply be undone at the click of the fingers. All that can help him is sleep… and that's exactly what he's getting right now. But we can't just leave him!' he pleaded with Saltar.

'You're wrong. That's *precisely* what we can do.'

'Perhaps we can tie him to his horse,' Lucius ventured quietly.

Saltar shook his head. 'Lucius, do you remember what I said to you when I let you join the group – that we would not stop for you if you fell behind? Well, the same must go for everyone of us here. I'm impatient to get on the road. I already resent the time we've spent talking about the Scourge. I am not prepared to spend more time getting him strapped safely to his horse. And let's not pretend the Commander had not had fair warning. I told him we'd be leaving at dawn, but he chose to stay up carousing the small hours away. The Sergeant and his men are capable of behaving like professional soldiers – if the Scourge isn't capable of the same then he's of no use to us. Altibus, if you wish to remain here to wet-nurse the Divine Consort, then please do so, but do not forget the duty your high priest laid upon you. Now mount up!' Saltar shouted down the line and vaulted into his saddle. Clearly, he would not brook any further discussion of the matter.

They all hurried to be ready for the departure, Altibus and Lucius included. Only the priest cast a glance back at the inn as the company set off down King's Road towards King's Landing on the east coast of Dur Memnos.

⁂

They rode through the early hours of the morning, not meeting a single soul. Dark trees pressed in on either side of them, so it felt like they were in a gloomy tunnel that went on forever. No one was in the mood or had the necessary energy to speak much. The heads of their horses hung low – clearly, they had not recovered much during the few hours in the stable. There was no sign whatsoever of the Jaffrans.

How are they keeping ahead of us? Saltar wondered. They have a young child with them. Surely that should slow them down, shouldn't it? He didn't like to follow that line of thought too far.

Our group's suffering at this pace, so how are they doing it? Is it magic? Is it this one-god? Are we chasing a lost cause? No! Don't think like that!

Saltar realised he was riding alone. He turned round in his saddle, to find the company strung out down the road. He paused to allow the next in line, Lucius, to catch up to him.

'Sergeant Marr stopped to relieve himself in the bushes,' Lucius explained. 'He told us not to wait for him, that he'd catch up, but the men are reluctant to leave him too far behind.'

Saltar began to turn away.

'And err…'

'Yes?' asked Saltar turning back. 'What is it?'

'No one wants to be the one to ask, but I think we're all wondering if we'll be stopping to break our fast. Or should we eat dried rations from our saddle bags as we ride?'

What was it with mortals that they were so self-indulgent when it came to the basic acts of ingesting and egesting? Couldn't they stop thinking about their stomachs, bladders and physical comfort for more than five seconds?

Why couldn't Marr relieve himself without leaving the saddle? Why couldn't they just go without food until they really needed it? Why were they so governed by their selfish and physical nature? Why were they so damned weak?!

Didn't they realise his only child had been kidnapped and that every moment that passed increased the chances of Orastes being lost forever! He had half a mind to leave them *all* behind.

''Tis well met that you are!' piped a melodic voice from not far away.

Alarmed to be caught so much by surprise, and with his company in complete disarray, Saltar had his sword out of its scabbard before he'd finished turning his head back round.

'Now that's no way to be treating a fellow traveller, now is it?' chided the voice. The owner was a willowy fellow sitting on his horse not ten metres away. Where on earth had he come from? He had to come out of the trees, because there was no way he could have approached them down the road unobserved.

'Who are you?' Saltar demanded as he sized up what sort of threat faced them. The man was of indeterminate age, had elfin features and eyes the colour of blueberries. He sat his horse in a relaxed enough manner, but Saltar did not miss the bandolier of wicked looking knives strapped over one shoulder and diagonally across his chest. It was a brave, dangerous or foolhardy man that travelled the kingdom of Dur Memnos alone. Except the man was not entirely alone, Saltar realised, as he spied the head of a small, black cat sticking out from behind him. The animal suddenly sprang over the man's shoulder and onto the horse's bare neck and head. The horse did not flinch, apparently used to these sorts of antics from the feline. The cat stretched it own head out and sniffed the air.

''Twould appear my companion is content to bring herself to your attention first. This is Scraggins. And I am Jack. So, I have extended you the courtesy of our names.'

Saltar was suddenly embarrassed. 'I… that is, we…'

'Allow me!' Lucius said smoothly. 'I am Lucius of Corinus, a humble musician, this is Saltar of the same domain… and these good fellows, who ride up so quickly to join us so that they might be introduced to you, are Altibus, a priest of Shakri, Sergeant Marr of Corinus, and his loyal men.'

'Nice of you to join us!' Saltar growled at the red-faced Sergeant.

'Sorry, milord, I…'

'Save it! Jack, where are you headed? In which direction have you come from?'

'Milord...'

'I told you, I'm not interested!'

'I follow my nose, I follow the road. I am from hither and thither!' Jack said merrily. 'For I am a wandering minstrel, you see!' and he gave a flourish and an extravagant, if seated, bow. The cat gave an emphatic meow as if that answered all questions and settled the matter.

'Milord, I must insist!' Marr pressed.

His ire rising, Saltar pulled hard on his horse's mouth and pushed back into the company, forcing all the others to mill, jostle and circle. 'What is it?' he asked fiercely.

Sergeant Marr steadied his horse and looked his lord in the eye. 'If I am not too far wrong, then it is Jack O'Nine Blades with whom we currently pass the time of day.'

'Impossible!' Altibus scoffed. 'He is a myth from the kingdom's pagan past.'

'Milord, here me!' the Sergeant urged. 'Jack O'Nine Blades is known the length and breadth of this land. Stories of his deeds are told in every inn. He is a minstrel, yet see his knives, his familiar and the greenish cast to his skin. He is clearly from the deep forests.'

'Fol-de-rol!' Altibus sneered. 'Superstitious rot! The light is mottled and shady under the trees. We all have greenish skin unless you hadn't noticed. Anyway, if he were this figure you say he is, then he'd be hundreds of years old. More than that, from what I've heard, we'd be better off having nothing to do with him. He's a mischievous trickster and a thieving fairground conjuror.'

Lucius spoke up: 'Sorry to interrupt, and I intend no disrespect, good Altibus, but the temples have never thought well of our traditional folk-songs and those who keep them alive. And it was only yesterday that you told us that mortally-derived magic is forbidden by the temples as sacrilegious and some sort of threat to the divine. Could it not be that this minstrel known as Jack O'Nine Blades is also known for certain slights of hand and is therefore someone to be condemned by all the temples? And you never know: the temples may have unwittingly helped to create this popular legend of Jack O'Nine Blades. You see, the more they condemned him, the wider his fame would become.'

'Stop! I get the idea!' Saltar cut in before things could get out of hand. 'Altibus, may I remind you that I myself am hundreds of years old? But there's one simple way to sort this out.' He separated himself from the group again. 'Are you Jack O'Nine Blades?'

Jack was silent for a second as a quixotic grin played back and forth across his lips. Slowly, he said: 'Some have called me such. And are you Saltar the Builder?'

A grudging smile came to Saltar's own lips. 'So I have been called. I have been advised not to trust you.'

'And neither do you have reason to.'

'True enough. You speak truly there.'

'Hah!' Jack laughed. 'You have caught me out. By my honour, I now owe you a turn. Come what would you have of me?'

Saltar couldn't help liking this droll fellow. Was it he who had caught Jack, or had Jack really caught him? 'If honour you have, and if you have been watching this road, then tell me if you have seen four men in black and child ride this way.'

'Have we Scraggins?' Jack asked his cat. The cat looked up at him and mewed sadly. 'No, indeed we have not, Scraggins. None passed this way,' he informed Saltar.

'You cannot trust him!' Altibus said just loudly enough for Saltar to hear.

Saltar frowned. They had not passed this way? 'Then have they entered the woods?' he asked, thinking out loud. It made no sense. Surely they were trying to get to Jaffra, weren't they? What other objective could they have?

'As to that,' Jack said mildly, 'where else can they have gone? I am happy to ride with you back the way you have come to see where any have left the road.'

Dare they trust this bizarre fellow, Saltar wondered. Jack must know that any attempt to mislead them would cost him his life, so it seemed unlikely that he sought to deceive them. Yet the man was hard to read, so Saltar found it hard to trust him completely.

'Why would you help us?' Saltar asked. 'And I would advise a straight answer.'

Jack tilted his head and gave a lopsided grin. 'Nothing is perfectly straight, of course, for perfection does not exist, but I will be as straight as my nature will allow. I am a follower of Wim, you see!'

'Ahh!' Sergeant Marr breathed in understanding.

'Explain,' Saltar ordered.

Head now tilting the other way: 'I am making my annual pilgrimage to the temple of Wim.'

'And where's that?'

Jack laughed, and to Saltar's surprise so did Lucius. The Battle-leader directed a questioning look at the musician.

'Milord, the temple of the mad god, the god of chance, has no fixed location. It moves about from one random place to another. It is most easily followed by those who live a life on the road, however. Many a minstrel and travelling musician worship this god, for they are at the mercy of fortune and the unknown when they travel up and down the kingdom – from the unpredictability of the weather, to the unexpected charity of strangers, to the whimsical tastes of their audiences, and the unforeseen nature of the future.'

'Blasphemy!' the priest of Shakri couldn't help blurting. 'Shakri's will laid down the pattern for this reality. It was not created from chaos and by chance. The followers of Cognis, and the Scourge himself, all read that pattern. There is a design laid down by Her divine will. The faithful are occasionally allowed a privileged glimpse of a small part of Her reason and logic when they receive holy instruction, as I did when High Priest Ikthaeon laid my task upon me.'

Scraggins coughed as if she had a fur ball lodged in her throat, and Jack rolled his eyes. 'And what's happened to the oh-so-rational Cognis? And why is the Scourge not with you, for surely he would have spotted it if those you follow had left the road? Has something unanticipated happened to him? Was that in your pattern, priest?'

'You know the Scourge?' Saltar asked quickly.

'Of course! Many's the time we've met on the road. But my point is that the world is not as ordered as many would have you believe it is. They like to construct *a right and proper place* for you and have you believe it is your place so that they then have power and control over you. There is a pattern but it would crush us all, destroy any individuality and free will, if it were not constantly tested and disrupted by the followers of Wim. And Wim is in all of us – we all know selfishness, irrationality and whim in order to preserve the balance and our own individualistic existence.'

'Madness!' Altibus fumed.

'Precisely!' Jack smiled.

'I see,' Saltar said, things beginning to click into place in his head. 'Yes. I seem to remember some of these things. I don't know why and how, but it resonates with something... something...'

Jack nodded.

'So you have no definite direction, Jack,' Saltar continued, 'for you cannot be certain of the temple's location. You travel in every direction, therefore, including with us. It has a logic of sorts.'

Jack flinched and clapped his hands over his ears. 'Yes, a *logic* and *illogic*, for is He not the god of paradox also? Followers of Wim do not believe in absolutes, but that means there can be no absolute randomness either, which is a paradox of course. Similarly, although the temple of Wim does not have a fixed location, its location can be predicted at certain times of year. A number of the temple members have families to the north of Holter's Cross, you see, and they like to visit them around the times of the seasonal festivals. 'Tis most convenient for us pilgrims that we sometimes know where the temple can be found. And let us be honest: the temple must sometimes want to be found, else it would never have a congregation and always an empty collection plate!' Jack laughed gaily at this last observation, and others in the group chuckled.

There was something infectious about the jollity of this follower of Wim, Saltar realised. The change in the mood of his group was almost miraculous, as if some sort of divine blessing had been bestowed and transformed them.

Flight, mercurial and untrustworthy Jack might prove to be, but their spirits would never fall while they were with him. It was a shame they couldn't have met him on the road before the Scourge had been undone by his increasingly ill humour. But then again maybe Wim wouldn't want to have interfered in Shakri's domestic circumstances; indeed, she may have forbidden any of the other gods to help the Scourge.

'Very well, Jack,' Saltar decided, 'we would be grateful for any help either you or holy Wim might be able to render us in discovering the path taken by those who have kidnapped my son.'

Jack's eyes widened to hear who they pursued. ''Twill be my honour to do whatever chance will permit. The world has become passing strange all of a sudden, and I feel it has stood me on my head. We'll need to put everything the right way up, if we can remember up from down. What I do know, though, is that if you're the Builder, Saltar, then whoever works against you must be a destroyer. And destroyers leave no pattern for Wim to test. They leave nothing about which minstrels can compose songs. They will put me out of a job! They will steal my audience from me! And I cannot have that!

'But come,' he said with manic glee, 'be not downcast, for I have a captive audience now. You are my prisoners. Follow me and hear your master sing!'

With that, Jack led them back down the road and sang one travelling song after another to them. Lucius rode along conducting happily in midair. Sergeant Marr looked to be in two minds as to whether he was being entertained or tormented. Most of his men smiled, whistled or nodded in time to the songs. Only Altibus seemed to be in no doubt that he could have done without ever having met Jack, but nobody seemed to want to pay the priest any mind.

Jack stopped mid-tune. 'Here. This is where they went through the trees.'

'I don't see anything,' Altibus grouched.

'Are you so blind to your mistress's creation?' Jack asked sweetly.

'Enough!' Saltar snapped, his good mood now replaced with intensity now that they had the scent again. 'How can you be sure, Jack?'

The minstrel gave an insouciant shrug. 'How can I be sure the rain is wet? How can I be sure a stone will fall when I drop it? How do I know there are three apples in the Sergeant's saddlebag? It is simply that I feel, know and see. Look at the grass here. Can you not see how it has been disturbed by the horses? No? Look at where the hooves have flattened the grass. And that twig has been pushed into the earth by a weight. The branches of the trees have sprung back where they were pushed aside, but there is less moisture on them than on the other trees. Do none of you see these things?'

They all looked around them, but there was precious little that was obvious. Saltar knew that the Scourge would have been able to see such things. Maybe it had been a mistake to leave him behind. Maybe.

'Let's go!' Saltar ordered.

Scraggins yowled and leapt down from Jack's horse. She stretched in 'n' and 's' shapes and then trotted off in the direction of the inn.

'We can't go after your cat. We've lost enough time as it is,' Saltar warned.

'Don't worry, she often goes off on her own and finds her way back. Wim will protect her.'

'Then let's get going. And no more singing. We don't want them to hear us coming.'

The legendary minstrel known as Jack O'Nine Blades looked somewhat put out by this censure of his art, but knew better than to argue with his only audience. He urged his horse into a fast walk and then a trot. Branches rushed past on each side, lashing the horses to greater speed. One of the soldiers shouted out in fear. Jack grinned. This might actually turn out to be more fun that he'd expected.

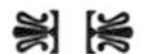

Chapter Six: For Those Who Wish To Know The Gods

As soon as they were beyond sight of Corinus, the road showed signs of being rarely used and ill-maintained. Trees and bushes had grown in close on either side and their roots had worked to lever up large numbers of the cobbles and flagstones laid across the earth by man. Old leaves, fallen twigs and drifting grit had formed a mulch that hid wide stretches of the road completely. Where the mulch was regularly washed away, moss had taken its chance to claim a foothold. With each mile that passed, there was less and less of the route forward to be seen.

Bleached, broken branches festooned the way or lay in tangled piles as if a giant ogre had happened across an unfortunate group of travellers, had a hearty meal and casually cast the bones aside. More and more low-hanging creepers strung across the road, trying to bar the way ahead and forcing the two riders to duck frequently.

Their progress slowed to all but a walk. Mordius wondered if they would be brought to a complete halt before much longer. Then the silly thought occurred to him that they might even end up going backwards. After all, this place was certainly forbidding, as if it didn't want them there. He'd read the old folktales about such places having their own genius, or guardian spirit, and understood the consistent message they were best avoided. He began to feel that they were intruding; the unusual stillness of the place only increasing the impression. The hairs on the back of his neck began to rise – did he feel a pair of malevolent eyes watching him? Surely it was his imagination, for his horse did not seem spooked, and animals were meant to have a sixth sense about such things.

Also apparently oblivious to any sense of unease, Young Strap leaned out of his saddle and, with his long knife, hacked at a creeper that was about to snare his horse's front legs. 'She could at least have let me have one beer to wash the dust of the road out of my throat before she sent me back out again!' he complained, not for the first time.

His nerves already frayed, Mordius snapped back: 'Look, Young Strap, Orastes has just been kidnapped, so you cannot expect Kate to be at her most indulgent. Plus, she'd just witnessed one of the mainstays of our civilization burnt down before our very eyes. Taking the time out to quaff an ale or two would not be at the top of everyone's list at such a time.'

'I am no longer what you would call young,' Strap replied testily. 'I'll thank you not to use that name anymore!'

Regretting it even before the words were out of his mouth, Mordius couldn't help replying, 'I will call you Young Strap for as long as you continue to behave like Young Strap!'

The Guardian sat up straight in his saddle, his eyes blazing down at the necromancer. Then he smiled: 'This is going to be a long journey. Just like old times, eh, Mordius?'

Mordius returned an embarrassed and guilty grin. 'Yes. I still get no joy from sitting atop a bony horse. Tell you what, we'll get a couple of beers as soon as we reach the next town, Marsby, I think it's called.'

Strap nodded, rubbing a hand back through his long hair. 'And I am no longer used to having company on the road, so will have to relearn not to say out loud everything I'm thinking at any given moment.' He paused to allow a moment of more companionable silence. Then: 'Meant to be a town round here, is there? I saw Marsby on a map once, but looking at the road, who knows if it exists anymore.'

Mordius nodded. 'Indeed. I imagine under Voltar's reign, there was generally a decrease in traffic to Corinus. When it came to the more remote or sparsely populated parts of the kingdom, that might have meant a complete stop. Besides, the people of the old towns like Marsby, and beyond, have always seen themselves as different and separate to the new cities of Corinus, Holter's Cross and King's Landing. Given half an excuse, I'm sure they wouldn't have minded losing touch with the rest of the kingdom too much, especially if it meant that they could avoid the onerous burden of the royal taxes and annual tributes. Remember, the Memnosian army was always stretched pretty thin, so I doubt Voltar had the resources to keep the less important roads open.'

A large spider with red, spiral markings on its thorax suddenly leapt from a nearby tree at Strap's face. With a quick hand, the Guardian caught the arachnid in midair and squished it in a gloved fist. The thing squeaked and a yellowish puss oozed between his black-leathered fingers.

Mordius's eyes went wide and the blood drained from his face. 'Th-that thing was huge! And it attacked you!'

Strap nodded as he examined the mess left on his glove. 'Yup. Probably poisonous.'

The necromancer's eyes went even wider. 'B-but if that thing had attacked me...' he trailed off.

'Best keep your eyes open and stay alert then, Mordius!'

'B-but I've never seen or heard of such a thing. And I don't recognise the species of half these plants. How can we hope to survive?'

'Mordius!' Strap cut in. 'I see something new everyday I'm on the road, even on roads I think I know like the back of my hand. The world, you see, and all the life in it travels as much as I do, Mordius. It grows, it changes, it *lives*. It does not do to fear it, Mordius, else we fear the gift Shakri has given us and instead turn to Lacrimos for comfort. It does, however, do to respect it, if you want to wake up the next morning, that is.'

Mordius took a calming breath. 'Of course. Come, tell me of your most recent journey, Strap. In all the chaos, I'd forgotten to ask you for your report.'

Strap looked a bit abashed. 'And I must confess I'd forgotten to give it. Forgive me.'

Mordius smiled tolerantly. 'I have enjoyed being in charge of the Guardians for the last several years, but with the return of the Scourge, and with Kate being put in charge of Corinus while Saltar is away, I could not hope to retain any authority over the force for very long. While we had peace, they could afford to indulge me and allow me to play at being commander. But the current situation requires a different sort of leadership.'

Mordius was mildly disappointed the youthful Guardian chose not to argue with such a statement; instead nodding his head in understanding. 'As to my report,' Strap began, 'I hadn't been intending to mention much. I'd have said all was well with the kingdom. I'd have simply listed the normal stuff, you know, like one man accusing another of stealing his wife, one accusing the other of stealing his pig, the latter a worse offence than the former in certain communities, one woman accusing another of stealing her husband, one accusing the other of stealing her pig, one accusing the other of being a witch and using love-magic on the other's husband, one accusing the other of being a witch and turning her husband into a pig, one telling the other she was stupid and that her husband had always been a pig, both agreeing that they were probably better off married to pigs than men, the village priest refusing to marry the women to their pigs and accusing the whole village of unholy paganism, demon worship, and the like. He wanted me to cart the whole lot away in chains! And I would have left the report there.'

'But?' Mordius asked worriedly, entertained though he'd been by Strap's commentary.

'But… with what's happened to the temple of Cognis, I am reminded of a group of farmers who complained to me that the roadside shrines next to their fields had been destroyed.'

'Did you go to see any of these shrines?'

Strap nodded. 'Yes.'

'Well?'

'Well, crude though these shrines are, and frequent though it is that just the wind can upset them, I remember being struck by how thoroughly they had been destroyed. It was clearly a deliberate act. Quite shocking in a way, because although I'm used to seeing casual vandalism when it comes to these simple shrines, and petty theft, I've never seen anything so systematic and hate-driven.'

Mordius had a queasy feeling in his gut. 'And to whom were these shrines dedicated?'

'Without exception, to the god of chance, Wim. Farmers and their crops are always vulnerable to the fickleness of the weather, so they regularly require Wim's favour if they are to make a living.'

'And from what you say, there was no chance or randomness involved in the destruction of those places of votive offering.'

'That's right. There was a clear pattern to it running from north to south, as if those who did it had a direction of travel in mind. What do you think it means?'

The queasy feeling in his gut had got worse. 'I think it means we're in a whole heap of trouble. I think it means someone is trying to remove the mad god from this realm.'

'What! But why? What would that achieve?'

'Don't you see?' Mordius choked, the words catching in his throat, making him fear he would vomit. 'Without Wim, there is only fate. There is no free will, no more change and unpredictability. Everything becomes pre-destined, decided at the beginning of time, decided forever in an instant. The past, the future, the present will be one and the same. We will not be able to affect it, to influence its outcome. Our doom will be absolute, inescapable, all that there is. There will be nothing but an awful, annihilating unity. The gods will be one with all mortal life. Individuality will be an utter nonsense. For us, Strap, there will be nothing. We will be swept away, as will the gods, such as they are.'

'I cannot think it,' Strap said faintly. 'Who would want such a thing? What entity, what evil consciousness would knowingly seek to do this to our reality?'

'That, I cannot say for certain,' Mordius wheezed. 'All we have is what Cognis told us at the end. The Enemy is returning, trying to take us back to how things were before the Time of Breaking, whatever that was. Apparently, we can learn more in the Old Place. I'm assuming it is in this part of the kingdom, since it has always been said that the oldest towns and peoples were to be found here. Certainly, the myths and folktales relating to this place make no mention of the gods we know, suggesting that they originate from a time and place ancient beyond our reckoning.'

'But you're not sure this is even the right place?'

'No,' Mordius conceded. 'But there are neither the priests of Cognis nor the Great Library to consult, are there?'

'True enough,' Strap replied unhappily.

A strange droning filled the air and they looked up to see a mosquito the size of a small bird careering towards Mordius.

'Arrrgh!' the necromancer screamed as the out-sized insect landed on one of his exposed forearms and sank a needle-like proboscis straight into one of his veins. He smacked at it and smeared blood up and down his arm. 'It burns!'

'Wipe it off on your horse's mane. Quickly!' Strap ordered.

Mordius did as he was told, rubbing furiously at his skin, which was already showing signs of blistering.

'Now hold still!' Strap commanded and sluiced a clear liquid from a canteen onto the arm.

'Aieee!' Mordius shrieked. 'By the misfiring jism of Wim! What's that?'

'Calm down! It's devilberry liquor,' the Guardian told him. 'We all carry it to clean wounds that might otherwise become infected. And then a nip will keep a body warm on a cold night. We use it as necessary.'

'It burns worse than that thing did!'

'Ah, but this is a good burn, a cleansing burn,' Strap said looking at the affected arm critically. 'You'll be fine. You should only worry if you lose some feeling. Then, you've been poisoned.'

'Did you see the size of that winged monstrosity? If a bunch of those found us at night while we were asleep, they'd suck us dry in seconds. We'd have no chance.'

'Maybe,' Strap hummed pensively, scratching at the back of his neck. 'We will need to wrap ourselves up tightly in our blankets, and cover our heads completely. Perhaps we shouldn't stop at all – just push on through the night. Or can we reach Marsby before nightfall, do you think?'

'Err… I'm not sure how far the town is exactly, Mordius confessed. 'If the map's to scale, then it might be possible. I can't say. This road's not going to let us travel quickly though, is it?'

'Maybe we can find a significant animal trail to follow.'

'Where are all the animals, though? I haven't heard any birdsong.'

'The spiders probably ate them all,' Strap half quipped.

Mordius shuddered. 'Please, don't say things like that.'

The light beneath the trees had started to fail when they came across the derelict building. The front door and shutters had been torn away from the whitewashed walls so the place stood like a battered, empty skull. It may once have been someone's home, for it had been built to last and there was the suggestion of a vegetable patch at the back. The trees must have been cleared back at some point because they were still quite distant from the walls, and the sky could clearly be seen above the roof. But that begged the question what had happened to open the place up to the elements if it hadn't been roots, branches and creepers. Could it have simply been the weight of time dragging the fittings from their hinges? Did time twist and tear metal so badly?

'Look at the scars on the wood!' Strap said quietly from where they hung back in the woods. There was an atmosphere about the place that made them not want to go any closer.

'I get the feeling something bad happened here,' Mordius said in similarly hushed tones. 'I really don't fancy being barricaded in there tonight if you don't mind. Or is that irrational of me?'

Strap shook his head. 'Many's the time I've allowed instinct to guide me and found it saved my life. No need to apologise, Mordius. I'm a strong believer that violent episodes leave an echo of themselves behind, especially when blood has been spilt. Spirits and demons are conjured by blood and sacrifice, remember. Followers of Incarnus have always wielded the most awful magicks.'

Mordius nodded, remembering a bloody field outside Holter's Cross that would have cost him his life but for the quick action of Saltar and Kate. 'Then let's move on before we disturb anything unholy hereabouts.'

They returned to the road, which had less detritus covering it in these parts, and pushed their mounts into a trot. In the very far distance, there was an inhuman cry.

'Faster!' Strap urged, and they moved into a full-bloodied gallop. They kept low to their horses, always worried about being snagged by a low, forked branch in the gloom.

Suddenly, they burst free into semi-open land. They found themselves speeding down towards a small hamlet huddled at the side of a swamp. A burly man who was hauling a metal-banded stable-door closed saw them and waved them on frantically. The fellow gave up on the door and began to slosh a dark liquid from a half-barrel around the walls of his building and across the earth where their horses would run. Even from this distance, Strap caught the reek of stale animal urine, and it became almost overpowering, as they got closer. The Guardian risked a glance back over his shoulder and saw hulking shadows emerge from the treeline behind them.

'Keep going!' the man yelled.

They didn't slow until they were right into the stable, and then they had to work hard to bring their horses to a stop without severe injury. The door had been brought closed as soon as they were inside, and the bear-like man had wrestled a heavy bar into place across the floor.

'Thank you! What...?' began Strap.

'Shhh!' the bear said and then he put his hands up to forbid them from moving. Mordius's horse snorted and stamped and the bear's ferocious glare almost felled the creature where it stood.

Then the hairs on the backs of their necks began to prickle and they all felt an unnatural terror. The horses stood rigid, their eyes rolling in their heads, their nostrils flaring and their teeth bared, but the gods were with them that day because the horses otherwise remained paralysed, not even twitching a muscle.

A shadow could just be seen under the stable-door, prowling backwards and forwards. The predator huffed as it tried to pick up a scent. The door rattled as it was bumped by something heavy.

... then the tension was gone. Air squeaked and rattled back into Mordius's chest. He realised that he'd been holding his breath the whole time. The bear sat on an incongruously small milking stool and panted for a bit. Strap swung down from his saddle, wiped his brow and leaned heavily against the stable's wall. The ears of the horses began to twitch and then their stomachs bellowed out as they all learnt to live again.

'What in Shakri's realm were those?' Strap asked.

'I do not know if they are of Her making,' the bear said tiredly. 'They do nothing for the life of this land. They hunger for it, though, and hunt it to extinction. Best to avoid mentioning the goddess's name round here, for it agitates them. And they have become worse of late – perhaps there is little left for them to consume.'

'But what *are* they?' Strap insisted.

'I'm sorry,' Mordius interpolated. 'We should thank you for rescuing us before making more demands of you. I am Mordius, and this is Strap.'

The bear nodded. 'And I am Lebrus. You were lucky that one of my horses had played up and delayed me getting the door closed. Otherwise, you would have been trapped outside and nothing could have saved you. I would not have opened the door, no matter how much you begged.' And then, before Strap could ask for a third time: 'We do not know their nature precisely, for none has met them and lived to tell the tale. They avoid daylight, and during those hours we live normal lives. But as soon as the sun begins to set the world is theirs once more. They are quick, strong and without mercy. They love the taste of blood, particularly human blood. If they are swamp-wights or troglodytes, I do not know. The swamps are dangerous, though, for that is where many of them dwell and they will drown a man even when the sun is in the sky if the mists are high.'

Lebrus rose and towered over them. Mordius couldn't help shrinking back from him, but the bear had already turned away to light a lamp. Silently, he led them through a small door at the back of the stable and into a large, smoky kitchen. To their surprise, they were met by a slight woman holding a wide-eyed toddler in her arms.

'Wife, we have guests. Is there any venison left?'

'Dried fish, fish soup and bread,' she said with anxious apology on her thin face.

Lebrus hesitated and then laughed in his chest, a happy sound that filled the room and made the toddler smile and clap her hands. 'Then, good Strap and Mordius, you are in luck for the second time today, as Astraal makes the finest fish soup in Marsby.'

'Husband, be not so unkind about our neighbours,' Astraal murmured quietly.

Lebrus looked chastised, his devotion and love for her plain to see. 'Of course, wife, of course. If you wouldn't mind preparing the meal for our guests, then I will see what news they bring.'

'Of course, husband,' Astraal said demurely and moved to the other end of the kitchen.

The bear invited them to take seats at a large, well made table and poured earthen cups of water for them from a decorated but cracked jug. The water was brackish, but neither the Guardian nor necromancer said anything. 'So what brings you here, gentlemen? We have not seen any outsiders in years. And what possessed you to be out so late?'

'We had not heard of any dangers on the road,' Strap informed him. 'How long have these creatures troubled Marsby?'

Lebrus frowned. 'They have always been here. They are sometimes called the Elders.'

'The Elders? Go on,' Mordius urged.

'As I said, they have been more of a problem in recent times. In the past, they would only take people who were caught out on their own in remote places. Now, though, they seem stronger, braver... certainly hungrier. The population of Marsby has declined somewhat. I think the other swamp communities have suffered too.'

'By the impatience of Incarnus, man!' Strap exclaimed. 'Why do you stay here? It is a slow death, and no place to bring up a family.'

Two bowls of fish soup thumped down between them pre-empting any response from Lebrus. Strap met Astraal's intense gaze.

'I'll thank the young gentleman not to call on such gods in this place,' she said firmly. 'It will only anger the Elders and bring them to this door. Why do we stay here? If you were older or had a family of your own, you might understand!'

'I-I didn't mean...' Strap began, but Astraal had already turned away to fetch the other two bowls and her toddler.

'Good Lebrus, we meant no offence,' Mordius assured their host.

'And none was taken, to be sure,' the bear said sitting back in his chair. 'Your question was passing strange, however. Why do we stay? We were born here, good Strap. These are our homes. We have been happy here. Except for the trouble with the Elders, life is good. We have a regular supply of food from the swamp and a man is in charge of himself here. Why would we seek to go anywhere else in the kingdom when all it has ever been is war and one man trying to be in charge of all others? The rest of the kingdom has nothing to offer us, and would only seek to take from what we already have. Nay, do not deny it. You cannot. Why else have you come here unless it's because you want something of us?'

'If you'd seen Corinus, if you knew Saltar…' Strap protested.

'No, Strap,' Mordius interrupted. 'Lebrus is right.'

The Guardian glared at his companion, sealed his lips and folded his arms.

'Will you not eat?' Astraal innocently asked Strap as she returned with more bowls and spoons.

For a while, they all ate in silence. The soup was thin but flavoursome, and Mordius found it raised his spirits. His imagination even forgot for a brief while to picture the huge and terrible monsters crouched and waiting beyond the door.

'So, what is happening in the rest of the kingdom that brings you here?' Lebrus tried again.

Mordius pushed his bowl away. 'Thank you, Astraal, that was wonderful.' He paused. 'Where to begin? The war is over… at least the war between Dur Memnos and Accritania, anyway. A man called Saltar… well, he toppled the King and put an end to the fighting. The King had taken our realm to the brink of destruction, in turn threatening the gods themselves. Is this making any sense at all?'

Lebrus and Astraal shrugged. 'Sense enough.'

'Well, we've had a few years of peace, but recent events have put everything in jeopardy once more. It grieves me to tell you that the temple of Cognis and the Great Library in Corinus have been destroyed by an unnatural fire.'

There was a bestial howl from not too far away. Mordius stopped and put an apologetic hand over his mouth as he realised he'd mentioned one of the gods by name. Lebrus waited for a while before starting the conversation again. 'It is a terrible thing, the destruction of a temple. Truth to tell, however, the god of knowledge has no great following here in Marsby.'

Astraal smiled politely. 'I think what my husband is trying to say, without any offence intended, is that we're not quite sure what such events in Corinus have to do with us.'

'The loss of any of the gods affects us all,' Strap said by way of joining in.

Mordius nodded. 'Quite so. More than that, though, before he left us the god of knowledge bid us come to the Old Place. There, he said, we would learn more about what it is we face. He said we would find out about the Enemy from before the Time of Breaking. *The Enemy is returning*. Does that mean anything to you?'

Lebrus and Astraal looked at each other uncertainly.

'What is it?' Strap asked. 'Have you heard of this Enemy?'

Lebrus half nodded and half shook his head. 'I've heard some describe the Elders as the enemy.'

'But every community has its enemies,' Astraal pointed out. 'They might not be the enemy you mean. And we have not heard of this Time of Breaking.'

'Well, have you got any old books or carving?' Strap asked in frustration, looking around the highly functional kitchen. 'How do you people remember your own past, for the love of Shakri? Is there a community hall with paintings or tapestries? Or a village bard who sings the old songs?'

This time, the beasts outside were set to barking and snarling all round the house. The stable door in the next room was clattered and shaken, but it held. The horses stamped and whinnied in fear. Astraal's toddler began to sob and held out her arms so that she could be picked up.

'Idiot!' she hissed at Strap as she tried to soothe her child. You'll be the death of us yet. If you can't learn to guard your tongue and avoid speaking out of turn.'

'I...'

'Do not say anything more!' the bear growled softly. 'Better that you ready your weapons.'

Mordius rose from the table to go retrieve the staff he'd left with his pack. Lebrus took down a lethal looking stave from above the fireplace and swung it experimentally a few times. Then, he furnished himself with a pre-prepared wooden torch and positioned himself so that he was ready to light it at a moment's notice.

'Astraal, my love, take the child and shelter with her beneath the bed.'

'Yes, husband.'

Strap gulped, mortified at himself. He moved as fast as he could to follow Mordius, only to find himself in the dark surrounded by sweaty, heaving, whinnying horses. Mordius found him by touch and shouted in his ear: 'Get the lamp!'

Strap stumbled back to the kitchen and grabbed the still-lit lamp. His hands were shaking and he knew that in trying to hurry he was allowing himself to get panicked. He put the lamp on the stable floor and took a breath to steady himself. Calmly, he found his bow and put his quiver across his back. The well-practised motion of nocking an arrow further settled him and he worked on slowing his heart. It would do no good to have the blood pounding through him, to have his muscles quivering when he was trying to find that still moment of release, when…

There was a terrible crash against the stable doors and the sound of cracking wood. The bar held. And another blow, this one so violent that he had to clench his jaw to the pointing of its breaking, to prevent his will buckling along with the wood! The doors were still largely intact, thanks to the metal banding, but the night beyond could now clearly be seen between two ruined planks.

A shadow loomed closer. Despite the narrow gap, Strap's shot was true. There was a thud and a strangled roar of pain. Then there came the ferocious noise of a pack of beasts descending upon the weakened one amongst them. A yelp. Wetness, and then flesh being torn, bones crunching. A tongue lapping thirstily. One creature growling at the others to keep them away from its prize.

It became increasingly quiet. Now there was only the odd snuffle and scrape of claw on earth. Strap had frozen as he'd reached for his second arrow. He dared not move for fear of re-exciting the attention of those without. He edged backwards and suddenly jumped as he bumped into Mordius.

'S-sorry!' whispered the necromancer.

'Damn it, Mordius! What in Sh-…'

'Shh! Don't say her name!'

'Okay!' He sighed. 'Let's get back to the kitchen. May as well be comfortable as we wait the night out.'

'Are they gone?'

'How do *I* know? We'll soon know if they're not, I guess.'

Lebrus nodded at them silently as they re-entered. The shutters on the room were still secure and all seemed peaceful. The bear swung his head left and right, as if scenting the air. Apparently satisfied, he put his weapons aside and took a dusty bottle and some beakers down from a high shelf. He broke the wax seal on what was undoubtedly a rare glass vessel in these parts and poured them all some deep, purple wine. Astraal joined them and put a finger to her lips, indicating that her toddler was now asleep.

'May as well enjoy this while we can,' Lebrus rumbled. 'I had been saving it for a special occasion, but maybe the visit of such guests qualifies. If we survive to see the morning, however, then I'll thank you to leave quickly, for you will have more than outstayed your welcome.'

'Yes, you can take yourself off to see the witch and try your luck with her,' Astraal smiled pointedly.

'The witch?' Mordius asked with a mixture of interest and trepidation.

'Yes, she lives in the swamp beyond the end of the village,' Lebrus said soberly. 'She may well know something of the things of which you asked. She has been here for as long as any of us remember. But be warned: you'll need to get on her good side. Otherwise, you will have nowhere safe for the night, which will mean it's likely to be your last.'

'Thank you… I think!' Strap responded. He raised his glass. 'So, here's to the hospitality of the good people of Marsby. May they have many a night untroubled by visitors, may they be visitors from Corinus or be they the Elders.'

'We'll drink to that,' Astraal said for herself and her husband. And they all drank, Mordius sipping at the bloody, full-bodied vintage while Strap downed his in one and smacked his lips appreciatively.

'It's at times like this I miss the Scourge,' the Guardian said with a strange mix of jollity and melancholy. 'Mordius, you still haven't told me anything about our Divine Consort. How is he? I can't imagine him ever changing.'

Mordius blinked as he realised that Strap, due to having been on the road for so long, still hadn't met his old mentor. 'Well, it might be best not to talk too much about that here and now, given that we can't mention the goddess's name at all.'

'Ah, yes. I guess not. We'll save that till the morning then.' The Guardian blew out his cheeks. 'So, what do the people of Marsby do by way of entertainment of an evening, when they're waiting to see if they'll be carted off in the night by marauding beasts?'

Lebrus shrugged. 'We tend to sleep, to be honest. More wine?'

'Don't mind if I do.'

There were always so many threads, so many connections! Of course, some threads didn't seem to go anywhere and seemed superfluous, but he knew that if left long enough they would eventually join up with something else and perhaps become important.

It was always easy to spot the main thread, because it was the one connected to so many others. The real trick was to try and spot the second most important thread, the one that so few people could anticipate and be prepared for. The problem with the second most important thread was that it wasn't always the thread with the second largest number of connections: indeed, if a thread had too much in common with the main thread, then it was more often than not an irrelevant duplication. Sometimes a thread was the second most important precisely because it had so little in common with the main thread in terms of connections. Sometimes, it appeared as important as many others but made its connections in the most unique combination. Sometimes it only became important for a very short period of time, when connections elsewhere failed, and it was rare that much could be done in advance to accommodate it.

In the early days, he'd only been able to identify the most important thread; and even though pulling on such a thread more often than not had drawn everything in and brought him success, it had sometimes brought him complete disaster because of the unforeseen second thread. So, he'd won himself whole kingdoms, only then to find them slip through his fingers after a decade or two. In his rash and heady youth, he'd tried to prevent such a decline by entirely removing all those connected to the second thread. The slaughter had been terrible, and war had raged unchecked back and forth across the world. For the briefest of moments, he'd had his own empire and the civilized world on its knees before his throne, but it had been an unstable empire that could never last. He'd only escaped that debacle by the skin of his teeth, and by faking his own death.

He was much older now, much, much older. There were very few who had lived long enough to develop the sort of experience and skill he had in identifying the second most important thread. Take the most recent example: even the long-lived Voltar had failed to spot quickly enough that Balthagar was actually the second most important thread in the whole scheme of things. Voltar had been in the ascendancy for so long, and had been so close to making his own thread the *only* thread of existence, that he had completely failed to notice the insidious growth of a second important thread in his shadow.

But the Chamberlain, now content to play second fiddle to monarchs rather than be a monarch himself, had spotted Balthagar right from the start. And the Chamberlain had learned long before that the safest way to know, spot or define a second thread was to be a very part of its creation and fabric. He had spent centuries influencing and arranging the course of events throughout the kingdom just so that Balthagar would die on the battlefield and be raised by a necromancer eager to retrieve the Heart. Encouraging the abuse of a child so that she would develop into the sort of damaged psyche and Guardian that could love an animee like Balthagar had been fairly easy; and had given him the lever at the eleventh hour required over the Battle-leader to secure the future Builder's promise that the Chamberlain's place in this world and reality would be safe-guarded.

Yes, there were very few with the Chamberlain's insight into such matters, very few who could read the Pattern, let alone influence and create it, as he could. It made him very different in thought and manner to nigh on everyone else. It made him alien, he knew. He saw how they looked at him in confusion, revulsion, fear… or how they tried not to look at him at all, tried not to attract his attention. The weakness of mortals, of course, was that they felt threatened by what they did not understand and only sought to worship, banish or destroy it. He'd tried to make them worship him, but he hadn't managed to stay divine emperor for long. Now, they ignored him whenever they could, effectively banishing him. How long before they attempted to destroy him?

'What is it?' he snapped at the pageboy who'd just appeared in front of him. He eyed the intruder beadily. This young pup was of no obvious threat and not an entirely unappealing morsel. A plump, tender, little thing. He felt the old hunger rising and began salivating.

'Please, milord,' it begged softly. 'The Captain would like to see you in the throne room.'

The Chamberlain unfolded himself from the tall chair in which he had been closeted and gestured for the succulent titbit to lead him on. He would dine later, once he'd seen what the tiresome palace officer wanted. Probably something to do with rosters, a dalliance between one of the men and a serving maid, a petty theft, or some such.

It was only as they were approaching the throne room and the Chamberlain saw the two armed guards on duty that he began to wonder at the unusual choice of meeting place. He began to slow but he was already within the circle of their reach and the doors were swinging open for him. There was no choice but to carry on forwards. He knew from the way the hairs at the nape of his neck prickled that he'd made a mistake.

Moving on tiptoe, he stepped into the throne room. The cursed green witch sat in the throne watching him idly. She held a loaded crossbow across her lap and smiled toothily in welcome. Shadows shifted and he realised there was a man in each corner of the room. The way they stood and a dull glint or two told him there were other weapons waiting for him.

His thoughts were stretched as thin as the wire on a harpsichord. He tried to calculate, threads and connections under sudden strain. How was this going to play out; what were the likely outcomes? He had brief, tantalising glimpses, as when a rock in the garden is overturned and its beetles and louses are exposed to the light for a moment before they scurry away and find the safety of darkness and hidden places once more.

He was taut, ready to leap in any direction at the first sign of an attack closing in. He hissed in warning at the witch. Her smile widened. The bitch! He should have disposed of her as soon as Balthagar had toppled the King, but the prospect of her bearing Balthagar... Saltar a child had stayed his hand. With every fiery fibre of his being, he wanted to hurl himself at her to vent his rage – he wanted to rake her body with his long nails, pierce and tear her flesh with his fangs, flood his maw with the metal of her blood. He thrummed with the passion and desire of it.

But she was no easy or unwary prey. She also had a predator's instinct. She raised the end of her crossbow a fraction, warning him against any move. He adopted a preternatural stillness, to avoid provoking those threatening him, but also so that he would more easily notice even the slightest change in the room.

The doors closed behind him. Kate made a prim show of composing herself in the throne and then pointed her crossbow straight at his chest. He refused to be spooked. The fact that they hadn't tried to kill him immediately told him they still wanted something of him, that he was safe for a while yet.

'Chamberlain,' she said. 'What do you have to report? Who was responsible for the destruction of the temple? When...?' and then she paused deliberately.

He felt needles in the back of his neck. There was a click, a rush of sound and the whistle of a feather cutting the air. The world tilted and then he was inexplicably seeing the room from the floor. His leg was on fire and felt like a massive nail had been hammered through it.

They'd shot him from behind, in the back of the thigh! An unbelievable outrage! He could still kill most of them in the room... but he wasn't sure he could kill all of them. Instead, he cried in pain and wheedled for mercy.

'Milady! What has happened, hmm? Aieee! The pain! Help me!'

She looked down at him, her eyes cold as the dead, her smile wintry. 'I trust I now have your full attention, Chamberlain. The next bolt will be between your eyes unless I hear exactly what I'd like to hear. I trust I do not need to convince you any further of my seriousness?'

He shook his head and faked a sniffle of distress. Oh, how he would make her pay for this humiliation. He would torture her for so long that the last of her sanity would be wiped away and all memory of her former life would be lost. Then, he would feast on her eyeballs, suck the vital juices out of her and leave her as nothing but a desiccated husk.

'Good. Now then, what have your spies told you about the temple? I warn you, if you cannot give me something useful about that or my son, then you are not useful to the throne at all. Worse, you are an unnecessary risk and a liability, for we must not forget that someone in the palace could well have conspired with our enemy.'

Stupid, limited creature. It truly had no idea. 'Milady, we have the responsible agency trapped in the lower levels of the catacombs. That is where they found the entrance to the Great Library and started the fire, hmm? But in so doing, they have trapped themselves, for escape through the library is impossible and no one has exited through the lower levels according to both my watchers and those of Trajan. We will capture them, yes?'

Her eyes narrowed, not entirely convinced by his answer. 'You and I both know that the catacombs are a labyrinth in which someone can hide for an entire lifetime. And there are so many tunnels and exits that it's almost impossible to watch all of them all of the time. And when exactly were you going to get round to getting into the catacombs yourself, Chamberlain? I must say, I'm not too impressed by your lack of proactivity in this matter. Are you not loyal to the throne?'

Damn this mortal! He looked down at the bolt protruding from his leg – at least there wasn't too much ichor leaking from the wound. 'Milady, I was preparing to enter the tunnels when I was called to this audience, hmm? Now, I find I am no longer in the best shape to hunt down an enemy but, before you shoot me between the eyes, may I just say that I am nonetheless the best equipped of any in the palace to bring the agency to bay.'

'I'm glad to hear it, Chamberlain. You have twenty-four hours to bring them to me so that I may go about questioning them. Any more than that and the palace guards and the army will have instructions to kill you on sight. And the general population will be offered a reward for the delivery of your dead body to the palace steps. There will be no hiding place. None. Nowhere dark enough or far enough away. Be in no doubt: your life will end.'

And she dared threaten him further! No, it was not a threat, he now realised, it was a promise. He should not have underestimated what a mother would do for her child… and what the loss of her child would do to her mind, especially one as unstable as he'd made it. He should have anticipated what sort of monster the kidnap would turn her into. But he'd been distracted by other threads. Was he missing something in his reading of the Pattern? His instinct told him he was. Maybe he should play this thread further.

'Milady,' he ventured as sweetly as he could, since her face made it clear she found everything else about him repugnant. 'Twenty-four hours is generous and should be more than enough. I will not fail you, and have never done so in the past, hmm? I have been a faithful and loyal servant to the throne, and expect the throne to be similarly loyal to its own servant. You may not kill me. It is not permitted.'

She blinked and could not help an incredulous expression. 'Excuse me?'

'You rule in the Builder's name, yes? He safeguards my place in the palace and this reality.'

She glowered at him. 'What do you mean?'

'Come now, Guardian,' he chided. 'You cannot have forgotten everything, hmm? An echo of it must still remain with you, yes, else you would not be the same person? You know you only live because I allowed it, because Saltar and I came to an understanding.'

Her finger moved to the trigger of her crossbow.

'Ah, ah, ah!' he warned. 'If you kill this being, you break the founding agreement and further endanger this realm, hmm? I would not advise it, given how precariously it is currently balanced, yes?'

She did not remove her finger but she forced her muscles to loosen. He smiled, but was then worried to see her return the smile. 'Captain, when!'

The Chamberlain threw back his head and screamed as an unanticipated bolt found his other leg.

'Twenty-four hours, Chamberlain.'

Witch!

⁂

'I'm tired and my knees hurt! Slow down, can't you? You don't even know where you're going,' Vasha complained. 'Can't we stop for a bit? I'm thirsty! Look, let me just have some water from the river.'

Though he didn't want to admit it, Larc was also exhausted. He'd had no chance to recover from the march out of the valley of the Brethren and he'd failed to get himself new foot bindings at the temple of the demon Cognis. He'd been in a hurry, of course, wanting to get away from the scene of the carnage in case those responsible still lingered. They would either be magickers or the followers of a rival demon, neither of whom were likely to be good for his health. True, if they were magickers, he could have tried to follow them, in the hope that they would lead him safely through these chaos wastes and all the way to the lost god, but magickers could always sense one of the Owned when they were close so he dared not risk it. If they were to catch him, they would not hesitate to kill him, for he had left the valley and broken one of the rules handed down by the Three. To break one of the rules by which he was Owned was to render his Ownership meaningless, to remove all value from his life. His Ownership and life were therefore forfeit.

He joined Vasha by the river and splashed the cold mountain water on his face. Then he sat on a flat rock nearby to think. Vasha was right: he did not know where he was going. Thus far, he'd just been following the path down this side of the mountain. Once at its end, he had no real idea as to the direction he should take. He would either need Vasha to lead him or he would need to get information from this town she said was a day's journey away. Could he truly trust her, and how dangerous was this town? Presumably it was the enclave of yet another demon.

He pulled out one of the loaves of bread, broke off two chunks and offered her one of them with his most winning smile. She tore into the offering ravenously.

'Vasha, where will we go now?'

She slowed her chewing and then swallowed. She stared at him, suddenly looking lost and afraid. 'I... we should tell someone about what's happened.'

'I see. Who should we tell?'

Her bottom lip trembled but she managed to stay in control of herself. 'Well, the main temple is in Corinus. We should go there for help. And the Builder will help us too.'

'Who is the Builder? Another demon, a god?'

'N-no, he's the King... or something like that.' Her temple training began to fail her. 'He-he's just a man.'

And she began to cry. Larc watched her, feeling awkward and exposed. His hands suddenly felt too large for his arms. He moved over to her and put an arm around her. She huddled in close to him and began to shake with her sobbing.

She shivered. If they didn't find shelter soon, they would be in trouble. The air was frigid – winter would start early this year. They needed to get to the town – they needed to start moving again. But he couldn't just push her off him. He decided to try and distract her and pulled one of the temple books from his bag.

It was a small, slender tome, wrapped in thin, cracked leather. There was a patternation of hair follicles just discernable against the skin – and he hated to wonder what creature had been used to give the book its protective sleeve.

The pages within were thin, semi-translucent sheets of some sort of membrane. The tracks and textures of old capillaries and vessels could be made out as a map beneath the lines of the spidery writing. They confused the eye and the mind.

'What?' she asked, raising a tear-streaked face.

'Sorry?'

'You were humming. Oh… a book,' she said quietly. 'From the temple. You will return it to the temple in Corinus, won't you?'

'Of course,' he said, tilting the book to see if that would make the strange symbols settle into some sort of sensible meaning. He had a headache starting and held the book away from him.

'Let me,' Vasha said and gently took the book from his hand. 'It's in Old Memnosian,' she told him. 'I can make out some of it. Hmm. This word is *ignorant*, I think. Then it says *often call that which they do not understand…* err… is it *power*? No. Oh, it must be *magic*!'

'*The ignorant often call that which they do not understand magic*,' Larc said.

'Yes. Okay, that means the sentence before it now makes more sense. *Much magic is knowledge and understanding*.'

'Sort of thing you'd expect from a book in the temple of Cognis, I guess,' Larc conceded. 'What else does it say?'

She pursed her lips. 'It's not easy, but after *the ignorant often call that which they do not understand magic*, we have *some have beliefs that prevent them gaining new knowledge. That which contradicts their beliefs of what is possible is termed as magic or…* hmm… *unholy*, I think. *Only when they have unlearnt what they believe possible can they free their own magic.*

'*There are many beliefs that prevent or…* something… *magic. Censor* is probably the closest word. *The most common or basic…* sorry that should be more like *fundamental* than *basic… of these beliefs is the one that the soul is…* oh, I don't know this word. I think it's something like *cannot be broken* or *cannot be made less*.'

'Irreducible, then?' Larc suggested.

'If that's what that means. *This belief gives comfort to many, but necromancers understand that…* we should not read this!' Vasha said abruptly, and held the book away from him.

His instinct was to snatch the book from her or overpower her, but he could not afford to come to blows with the only person likely to help him in the chaos wastes. Besides, he was not sure he could decipher the text on his own. His reading had never been that good. Instead, he assumed a sad face. 'I would like to believe that the souls of my dead wife and child cannot be lessened, that they are irreducible, but if that is not to be the case, then I need to know what I must do to save them. This book has the answers, Vasha. Won't you share them with me? After all, I have helped you. Is it so much that I ask? I thought that we were friends. Friends shouldn't keep secrets from each other, should they?'

She shook her head silently, guilt and confusion in her eyes. 'I… I don't know. This sort of information was always forbidden by Brother Altor though. Anything to do with necromancy was.'

'Brother Altor is gone now. Don't you want to see him again? What harm can it do? After all, your god would only have let this book come to us if He wanted us to read it, wouldn't He? You don't want to make Him angry, do you?'

'No, I don't,' she said in a small voice. 'And I do miss Brother Altor.'

'I don't think he'd mind you reading the book if you're just trying to help people, would he?'

'No,' she said with a faint smile. 'He said that we should always try to help people with our knowledge. Okay, I'll read a little more, but only so long as there's nothing bad in it.'

'That's fair,' Larc said. 'You're a good friend, Vasha.'

She blushed happily and opened the book again. 'Ah! Here we are… *necromancers understand that without an… organising magic… or anchor then the soul dissipates. While in Shakri's magical realm, a soul requires a body as its anchor. Of course, that body nearly always requires the spark of Shakri's organising magic if it is to function and remain connected to the soul. The only exception is if a necromancer chooses to use their organising magic to anchor a soul to a body.*

'*Without an anchor, a soul cannot function or remain in Shakri's realm. It must seek out another realm, where an alternative organising magic might be available. One such realm is maintained by the magician Lacrimos, where the only anchor that exists is via his organising magic. Souls, therefore, must first appeal to Lacrimos, agree to his terms and then submit to his will. The fundamental difference between the realms created by the two magicians, therefore, is that in Shakri's realm a soul has freedom – albeit that the soul is bound by the physical limits of its anchoring body – whereas in Lacrimos's realm the soul is entirely directed by that magician's will and organising magic.*

'*There are other realms, of course, but these are often unstable and souls can suddenly find themselves without a realm and having to throw themselves on Lacrimos's mercy if they are not to dissipate. Of course, it is not in that magician's interests to be merciful. Those who have foregone previous chances to join his realm are always punished, so that the next time they have such a chance they fear the consequences of not submitting to his will whenever they can.*

'Larc, can I stop now? My eyes hurt and I've got a terrible headache. It's like pins behind my eyes.'

'Yes, the light's beginning to fade anyway. We can read more tomorrow. Besides, it's going to take me a while to work out the meaning of what you read. Did you understand it?'

Vasha shook her head. 'All that stuff about anchors and magic. I don't know why the writer would refer to the gods as magicians, really. Magicians can't create whole realms like gods can.'

Larc was about to argue that the Three had managed to carve the valley of the Brethren out of the chaos wastes, but then decided against telling this demon-worshipper too much. He had no idea if the demon she worshipped automatically knew everything its followers knew. He didn't dare reveal anything that might alert the demon to the Brethren and their whereabouts.

'Come on, time to go,' he said, taking her by the hand and helping her up. We won't get too cold if we keep moving.'

She smiled and held his hand tightly. She didn't let it go as they started down the mountain. He found he didn't mind, though all his thoughts were with his wife and son. Were their souls being anchored by the organising magic of the Three or were they being punished by this dark magician Lacrimos, the one Vasha called a god? Clearly, the Three had used some sort of necromatic art to anchor his wife Sarla's soul to her dead body in the House of the Dead. But her soul had said it was fading, just as the bodies in the mausoleum inevitably decayed. He would have to hurry he knew, before her soul dissipated or was claimed by this Lacrimos.'

But how could he save her? Then he had it! The lost god must be capable of creating a realm that would have an organising magic to save a soul like Sarla's. He was excited for all of an instant – for his next thought was to wonder if the lost god and this Lacrimos were actually one and the same.

'So how do you think I go about talking to Lacrimos, do you think? Perhaps I can do a deal with him to save my wife and child.'

Vasha looked at him in horror and let go of his hand. 'Are you mad? Is it grief that makes you say such things?' she whispered. 'No one in their right mind would seek to do a deal with Lacrimos. He would trick you out of your own soul in an instant. He is the god of death and seeks only to bring death to all, even those loyal to Him. He will begin to stalk you now that you have spoken such words. He will seek to tempt or threaten you. Oh, Larc, what have you done! I don't want to lose my only friend, my last friend!' she wailed.

He felt suddenly cold, and it had nothing to do with the temperature here in the mountains. The back of his neck itched and he found he did not have the courage to look back over his shoulder to see if there was anything there.'

'Shh, shh!' he calmed her. 'We'll just have to find someone else to help me then. What about your main temple or this Builder person? Can't they help me?'

'Maybe,' she sniffled. 'They say the Builder and his necromancer, Mord… something held back Lacrimos before. And maybe my temple knows of a way.'

'There we are, you see. Things aren't so bad.'

She tried to smile bravely but faltered as thunder rumbled in the distance.

⚜ ⚜

They left the home of Lebrus and Astraal at first light, hardly having slept a wink. Mordius had tried closing his eyes while the others kept watch, but even the slightest sound outside had him reaching for his weapon. There was no way he could relax long enough to sleep. As for Strap, he hadn't even bothered trying, so intent had he been on taking advantage of the largesse of his host's wine cellar. Thus it was that a grumpy, gritty-eyed magician and smiling, staggering Guardian led their horses through the quiet village-cum-town of Marsby at dawn.

'Well, come on then!' Strap said in the slightly too loud voice of someone who's drunk too much.

Mordius winced, closed his eyes, took a deep breath and then released it slowly. 'What are you talking about?' he asked tiredly.

'You promised to tell me about the Scourge.'

'Ah. Your former mentor is much the same as ever. He still drinks, blasphemes and fights like he always did. I'm sure he'd be proud to see you right now.'

Strap hiccupped and nodded. 'He ask after me then? He speak much about, you know, his time with Shakri?'

'Not really,' Mordius said into the silence.

'Oh. Well, I guess he didn't want to talk about it then. Say, you know which way we're going?'

Mordius just shrugged, having neither the energy nor inclination to answer the inebriated Guardian. He didn't know if his companion saw his gesture or not, but was past caring. Strap carried on regardless anyway.

'Another thing I've been wondering about is why you're always clean-shaven. Not the fashion in Corinus, is it? You know, it'll be extremely difficult to stay clean-shaven on the road. I know!' he giggled. 'Did you have fleas in your beard once, is that why you had to shave?' Then he gasped. 'Don't tell me there's a woman in your life, one who prefers you smooth-skinned! Mordius, you sly old fox. You kept that quiet.'

'Shut up.'

'What?'

'Shut up, you idiot!' Mordius said through gritted teeth.

More laughter. 'Ooh, touched a nerve, eh? Well, you couldn't expect to keep it a secret, you know. We Guardians are trained in reading such things, trained in sniffing out secrets…'

As if in answer to Mordius's silent prayer, toads suddenly started up a racket in the swamp that all but drowned out Strap's chatter. They welcomed the sun in full-throated praise of Shakri's creation. Almost instantly, the air temperature began to rise and flies started to bother them. Within a hand of minutes, sweat was beading on Mordius's brow and his shoulders were bowing under his heavy robes. The droning of the swamp's insect-life made him so drowsy that he was no longer sure if he was awake or dreaming. The pace of their progress was all but reduced to a standstill, especially when the ground underfoot became waterlogged and dragged at every step they took.

The next thing he knew, Mordius was lying on his face breathing in the fetid ground water. So exhausted was he, it was all he could do to keep his mouth half-clear to avoid drowning. Strap looked down at him stupidly.

'Oh! I wouldn't advise sleeping there. Tell you what, let's get you on the back of a horse and I'll lead you until the ground underfoot becomes so soft that your extra weight makes the poor beast sink too much.'

With that, the Guardian picked the uncomplaining magician up and slung him across one of the saddles.

'This way, I think,' Strap said to himself. 'Looks like a path of sorts, and there's nothing else obvious. Why don't locals ever put signs up, eh? Don't they realise travellers and visitors might want to get somewhere? Still, I doubt many want to come here, so Marsby probably relies on people getting lost and ending up here by accident. Makes a sort of sense, I suppose. I still don't understand why the locals don't just leave this godsforsaken place. Probably can't find their way out, cos there're no signs. Get what they deserve then, I reckon. Oh, good, bit of firmer ground here.'

He led them deeper into the humid swamp, their winding path entirely decided by the higher pieces of ground. There were sick-looking reeds on all sides, which were only broken up by stagnant and murky pools of water. The vapours and mist that rose up around them meant he couldn't see further than a few horse lengths at any time. Not a single tree in the swamp seemed to be able to stand up straight, their roots unable to get a proper grip. He knew how they felt. He giggled at that.

He tried to whistle for a bit, but it sounded curiously dead to his ear, so he gave up. 'Getting a headache anyway,' he mumbled to himself. 'Probably sweating too much in this heat and it's making me dehydrated. Typical! Surrounded by water, full of good wine, and now I'm going to end up dying of thirst in this ungodly, backward place. I'm beginning to feel sick, now I think about it. Bet some little bugger of a creepy-crawly has bitten me somewhere and infected me with something. That's it: I'm going to come down with a fever now and die here alone!'

A toad croaked.

'Okay, alone except for you.'

Mordius began to snore.

'Oh, and you, you layabout. Too used to your comfortable bed in the palace, that's your problem. You're as soft as the mattress that you normally sleep on. Can't go more than five minutes without needing a rest, can you? You'd be dead already if I weren't here looking after you.' He sighed. 'What was Kate thinking, sending you out here? Huh! Desperate, I suppose. Lost some of her reason. Not surprising really. She was never that sane to start with.'

There was a sudden, big splash and a choking splutter. Strap looked back over his shoulder. Mordius's inert body had slid off his horse and into a round pool.

'Gak! What happened? Strap, you clumsy oaf! By the cross-eyed gaze of Wim, can't you watch where you're going?'

'You're lucky, really.'

'What do you mean lucky?! I nearly died of fright!'

'Well, if you hadn't landed in that water, you might have broken your neck. You should thank Wim, not take his name in vain.'

Mordius shook his head in defeat, his mind still too muddled to be bandying words with the Guardian. 'Come on! Let's just get through this!' he groused standing up, grabbing the dangling reins of his horse and wading through the pool with it in tow. He sloshed past Strap without looking at him and kept going. He was nearly lost in the mist before Strap gathered himself and got after him

The firmer ground disappeared and they found themselves in water up to their knees all of the time now. But there was a clear gap between the reeds, which gave them a clearer path of sorts than before. Strap was grateful that he no longer had to think about where they were going, since a full blown hangover was setting in. He followed along relatively quietly in the necromancer's wake.

They'd been going for another hour when Mordius dragged his horse to the right towards an area where the reeds sat above those around them. He pushed into them and up onto a low hillock.

'Now what?' Strap called wincingly.

'I'm exhausted! Need to rest,' Mordius said weakly, turning his face back for a few seconds.

'You're as white as a sheet!' Strap gasped. 'Are you well?'

'Feel dizzy. Just need to… to lie down… for… a… bit…' and he slumped down against the roots of a fairly well established willow.

Frowning, the Guardian left his horse and went to check on his friend. 'Oh, no!' he groaned as he discovered the large, purple sacks festooning the magician's legs from the knees down. 'Giant leeches! Mordius, you idiot! Didn't you feel them?'

'Wah?' came the vague response.

'I have to get them off you before they suck you dry. No chance of starting a fire here to burn them off. It's going to have to be the knife, I'm afraid.'

Strap set to work prising the blood-sucking creatures off Mordius's skin. There were dozens of the bloated creatures, particularly at the back of his calves, where large blood vessels were closer to the surface. Strap's knife nicked Mordius on more than one occasion, but the magician remained unresponsive. And even when a leech came away relatively easily, usually because it was full, Mordius's blood would continue to run freely from the wound where the parasite had attached itself. Soon, Strap's hands, Mordius's legs and the surrounding reeds were sluiced bright red.

'Probably some sort of substance in this Lacrimos-spawned critter's bite that both numbs the victim and turns their blood to water,' Strap shuddered, thankful that he wore trews tucked into his boots rather than a robe like Mordius. 'Hmm. This one's not coming off.'

He cut into the monopod and blood jetted up into his face. He spluttered and spat to keep his mouth clear of it. Then he wiped his face on his sleeve and went back at the thing with his blade. There was a squelch and pop and it finally came free. 'Oof! That's the last of them. You're lucky I've got strips of cloth in my pack to serve as bandages and strap your legs up. Otherwise, you'd have no chance.'

Strap felt at Mordius's neck for a pulse, but wasn't sure he could detect any life from the necromancer's cold and clammy skin. It was a bad sign that the small man wasn't even shivering. He put a hand under his nostrils, but there was no breath. Was that a slight rise and fall of his chest?

'Damn it, Mordius, don't you dare go dying on me now. Saltar will be livid with us if you do. And I'll hear no end of it from the Scourge. And the things you do to avoid having to walk, just so you can stay up on your horse, I don't know!'

He heaved the magician's dead weight up onto his shoulder and then onto the horse. This time, he made sure to tie the body in place. With a click of his tongue, he started to lead the two horses forward as quickly as he could. The longer he took to get Mordius somewhere warm, the greater the chance there was that he wouldn't ever be roused again. He daren't even consider the possibility that the witch would turn them away. If that happened, then the Elders would no doubt see an end to them anyway.

'Not exactly what you'd call a pleasant winter retreat this place, eh?' Strap grunted as he tugged their mounts along behind them. He gave up waving the flies and insects away, lowered his head, bent his knees slightly, leaned forwards and set his shoulders for a gruelling drive through the bedevilling bog. 'And step! Step! Step!...' he chanted, bespelling himself. Deliberately, he let go of his sense of time. He stopped paying attention to the buzzing, bites, tickles, smears, knocks, reeking odours, plops and slides of his immediate environment. Even the dull grinding of his hangover began to lose its purchase on his mind. He found that place of dense focus and adamantine determination that had seen him march to the end of days at Saltar's side several years before.

And so he marched again, leaving no permanent footprints on the swamp but at the same time not allowing it to touch him in any way. In vain it tried to drag at him, to hold him back. Strangely sharp and jagged branches emerged from the mud like the hands of the dead and tore at him as he passed. He shrugged them off without thought.

The branches were beaten and more and more often lay broken or matted in moss. They lost their life and lay as bones. He frowned. Maybe they actually were bones. They lay everywhere in profusion, fields of them for as far as the eye could see. What was this place? How could so many creatures have ever existed? And what terrible thing had happened to them all? What power had been so devastating and hungry as to do this? Surely his mind was playing tricks on him! They were just dead trees, his rational mind told him. They're not, his unconscious mind insisted. See up ahead there. Now tell me they're just dead trees!

He stopped and stared at a high, thick hedge of bones that continued beyond his sight to left and right. The trail he followed passed through the unliving hedge and he could make out something beyond it, but he wasn't sure what it was. As he got closer, every hair on his body stood on end and his every instinct begged him to turn and run until he could run no more. A large, flat-topped hillock was bound by the hedge, and at its barren centre stood a large house built of skulls, humanoid, animal and other. A million empty eyes looked through him, untold mouths grinned and screamed silently at him. Never had he encountered something so fundamentally abhorrent to his understanding of Shakri's creation.

As terrified as he was for the failing Mordius, he couldn't bring himself to take another step forward. In this stark and merciless place, he feared for his soul.

Something moved towards him.

Bile filled his mouth, the acid burning his gums away and leaving only the ivory of his teeth.

It reached the defile through the hedge and his sanity began to totter.

The lids peeled back from his eyes so that the balls fell out onto his cheeks and dangled by their optic nerves.

It was beyond the hedge now.

He began to shriek in terror.

And she was there comforting him, reassuring him, cooing to him. 'You're just experiencing my magical wards. I have to have them, to keep the Elders away. I'm surprised you got this close, actually. Don't be affrighted, milord. All that you are seeing is illusion. If it is easier, close your eyes for now and I will help your friend.'

He just about remained in possession of himself. He closed his eyes as she had bid him and let her lead him. Her face filled his mind's eye: a few years older than him, open, honest, pretty, loving and worth his life.

'Now,' she said in an intoxicating voice. 'As we go, you might explain why I should welcome under my roof a Guardian, whose sworn duty it is to slay my kind. You may want to talk quickly, as that might increase your chances of staying alive beyond our reaching my front door.'

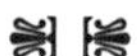

Chapter Seven: Lay Bare Their Souls Before Them

There was an apocalypse in his head. Giant demons devoured reality all around him, leaving him nothing but the small patch he defended. He turned this way and that, looking for where the final attack would come. And heard over it all was the purring of contentment.

The Scourge awoke and found himself eyeball-to-eyeball with the green gaze of a cat sat squarely in the middle of his chest.

'Argh!' he shouted in surprise.

The feline sprang away and turned to watch him from under a table, its tail curled tidily around its feet. It looked otherwise unperturbed by his outburst.

He had a headache that was violent in the extreme and he had to fight to raise his head to see exactly where he was. He lay on a rough wood-plank floor, chains, benches and stools in good order all around him. An inn, if he didn't miss his guess.

He carefully placed his head back down. Ah, yes, the Stumbling Traveller, the row with that crazed goddess and the fight with her impotent brother… he shuddered. He felt so bad that he half-wished Lacrimos had succeeded in killing him. And from what Lacrimos said, it could well be that the fact the Scourge was undying and in the realm of the living was destroying Shakri's realm and the balance itself.

He felt an irrational guilt about it, even though it wasn't really his fault. After all, he'd had no say in the matter whatsoever. Typically, as a mortal, he'd been treated as if he only existed to serve the gods and their whims. Well, if Shakri didn't start changing her attitude, and soon, then there wouldn't be anything left of her realm to save. And if Shakri's realm went, then Lacrimos's would likely be next. Who knew if it would stop there? He had a sneaking suspicion that the pantheon of the gods wouldn't last very long if the balance were destroyed. What would happen to them? Would they simply fade away as if they'd never been anything more than a child's daydream? Oh, his head hurt way too much for such questions. And, besides, he didn't have time for any of this when there was the realm and all the gods to save.

With a groan, he rolled onto his side and sat up. He regretted it almost immediately but it wasn't like it was going to kill him, he reflected.

It would have been so much easier all round if he could just kill himself to prevent reality collapsing around everybody's ears, and to allow them to live happily ever after. Why was nothing ever that simple?

And now, the imbalance amongst all the realms, between mortals and gods, had allowed an ancient enemy to rise. Cognis was already gone. Who would be next? That was it, you see: without the god of knowledge, no one knew, no one could answer that question.

'By Lacrimos's diseased bollocks!' the Scourge cursed and fought against his nausea to stand up. He couldn't stand up unaided so got a high-backed chair under each of his armpits.

'That'll be a silver for the extra night, a silver for your horse and a copper for the milk we gave your cat!' the innkeeper said in a determined voice.

The Scourge squinted at the man and, despite his foul mood, decided he didn't have the energy for a row. He fumbled at his tunic and slapped two silvers on a table.

'The cat's not mine.'

'You owe it then. It kept you warm the whole time. Probably saved your life. The least you can do is pay for its milk.'

'Bloody expensive milk!'

'You were a bloody inconvenient customer. My Lamia almost broke her neck stepping around you to serve customers their beers. And my customers were none too impressed either – this is a well-to-do inn, I'll have you know. We serve a higher class of clientele here, individuals of breeding, decent folk who have mastered the civilized art of sleeping in a bed.'

The Scourge added a copper to the two silvers and glowered at the innkeeper. 'If I was that much of an inconvenience, you could have dragged me out of the way. Or was I in fact the centre of attention, something for the punters to gawk at while you spun them lurid tales? No, no! Before you speak again, just think upon the fact that it will be the last word you ever utter. I am not in the mood to hear anything more from you. I've paid you more than is sufficient to compensate you, so no longer owe you a thing. The account has been settled in full. Continue with your pompous prattle and you will be borrowing heavily against my good will, you will be in my debt, and I only accept payment in blood. Do you understand? Beyond that, I think I might curse this establishment and all its patrons in my beloved Shakri's name. She's been known to indulge me upon occasion.

'Now, I suggest you turn away and busy yourself with wiping down your bar. I will walk out of here in silence and trouble you no more. That is the most generous deal you will get from me today. And close your mouth unless you're trying to catch some of the flies you have buzzing about the place.'

The innkeeper snapped his jaw closed so hard that it clearly pained him. His face had turned as white as the cloth that he gripped and twisted in his trembling hands. He threw his eyes down and hurried to find a chore for himself as far away from the Scourge as he could.

Rubbing at his temples, the Scourge moved as gently as he could towards the door. The cat, who had been watching him with a bored expression, stretched its front legs, arched its back and yawned before trotting after him.

The fresh air made his stomach flip over and he had to stand still for a few seconds before he could proceed to the stables. His horse snorted in welcome and nuzzled his hand in a fruitless search for a treat.

'I hope you've had a better rest than me, boy. We've got some ground to make up, and no mistake. Incidentally, if you could see your way clear to adopting as smooth a gait as possible, I'd be very grateful. Neither life nor death have been treating me kindly of late. Up we go! Well, come on then.'

The big destrier nodded his head but wouldn't move forwards, even though the Scourge dug his heels in firmly. The small, black cat suddenly jumped up onto the stall's half-wall and then onto the horse's rump.

'What the - ?'

The horse stepped forwards suddenly and the Scourge had to shift his balance quickly to avoid losing his seat. Lightning crackled and flashed amongst the storm clouds in his head and he was temporarily blinded. He hung onto his horse for dear life and waited for normality to reassert itself. The storm moved away.

'Are you sure you want to ride with me, cat? My previous companions gave me up as a lost cause. I have to say, I'm a bit disappointed they left me behind, but not entirely surprised. That Saltar won't stop for anything or anyone. And I can't really blame him. It's those flaming gods interfering again that's done it. Will they never learn? It's almost as if they can't help themselves, even if it costs them their realms. Perhaps the aspects of character they represent are a self-fulfilling prophecy of sorts. They have as little free will as us… perhaps less.'

This revelation made him thoughtful and he wondered about the life he'd tried to share with Shakri. Perhaps it was never meant to last. Perhaps it was the nature of creation and its goddess that all things were constantly recreated differently, that they were always changing, that they were destined never to be permanent. Permanence and complete unity were the enemies of creation in that sense. He wondered if his relationship with Shakri would be recreated differently. He wondered if it was what he wanted. He wondered if he would be given any choice in the matter. Did Shakri have a choice even?

His preoccupation was interrupted by the cat rubbing her head against his arm, She mewed plaintively and he stroked her head absently.

They rode along the King's Road for several hours without the Scourge finding any trace of Saltar's group. There was no evidence of anyone else either. He didn't meet a single traveller or merchant. There were no farmers to be seen in distant fields and no woods people hunting game. If it weren't for the occasional birdsong in the woods to either side of the road, he'd have feared he'd unwittingly ridden into Lacrimos's own realm, where nothing ever stirred except for restless spirits, lost souls and troubled ghosts.

Shakri's creation certainly seemed a bit lifeless all of a sudden. Praying he wasn't experiencing some sort of premonition, he increased his horse's pace to beyond what was probably sensible.

❧ ❧

The squirrel shuddered and pulled its head down into its ruff. The days were getting colder as well as darker – the season of death was fast approaching. He'd laid in a store of nuts and dried berries and prayed, as he did every year, that it would be enough to see him and his mate through till spring.

And night fell quicker now than in the autumn, meaning that predators like the owl were abroad all the sooner and there were fewer safe hours for foraging. He wasn't as quick as he'd been in his youth, but he was stronger and wily enough to wrest his fair share from the younger males. He'd been saddened by the death of his smaller brother at the same time last year, but was confident that it wasn't yet his turn to be carried into the sky by the great birds of the sky-god. But you never knew. The sky-god could choose you suddenly and without warning. The messenger of the sky-god would swoop down on the wind and pluck you from the ground with terrible and irresistible talons. Sometimes, the messenger would only descend to warn or test a lazy squirrel, and that squirrel would need to learn quickly and mend its ways if it was to live through a visitation from the messenger. For the sky-god's gaze was constant and ever present even when it looked to be obscured by clouds. It always saw which squirrels were grateful for the sky-god's bounty and were industrious in collecting it; and which thought to take their time picking and choosing from the sky-god's largesse without ever casting a thankful eye skywards.

It all made a natural sense to his mind… or had done until recently. Something was very different now… not natural somehow. He constantly found himself overcome by a sudden fear, like when a shadow of the sky-god's messenger sometimes passed over him. But there was never a shadow to be seen and yet he still felt scared, even when he was warm in his nest with his mate. Maybe it was something on the wind, the wind that often warned of something coming towards him from another place or from a time in the future. Yes, there was something bad coming from ahead of him. Yet no matter which way he turned, it was still there ahead of him. It had to be something in the future then.

His heart thumped loudly in his ears, and he was worried he would die of fright, as many squirrels were known to do. He kept perfectly still until it quietened like the hoof-beats of a horse running into the distance. The moment passed and he realised he would have to hurry if he was to uncover this last cache of nuts and get them back to his nest before the owl awoke.

Ah! Here it was. He entered the hollow log and scampered to the end. He scraped the old leaves aside and… no nuts! How on earth? It wasn't possible. There was no scent of any living creature having been here, so…? His mind couldn't reconcile what it knew with what its senses told it. It paralysed him. He felt his heart slowing to a complete stop. It wasn't death, it was just nothingness, the nihilistic state.

The natural law, the law by which nature was constituted, was broken. The existence that was the squirrel was about to be undone, its divine spark about to fade. For an impossibly brief instant, the squirrel-existence hung in limbo, suspended between being and non-being, matter and nothingness, natural law and an absence of definition, the present and the future, the direction ahead and the absence of a reference point.

And then came the sound of horse hooves, hooves coming closer. They brought direction, they brought the future, and allowed the squirrel-existence to re-establish itself. It now seemed that the natural order had been reordered rather than broken. The nuts forgotten, the squirrel squirmed out of a hole in the log and climbed up on top of the piece of wood so that it could critically appraise what went on in its forest home.

The tall children of the earth goddess entered the glade riding their horses. There were many of them, but one of them at the front made his skin itch as if from a thousand flea bites. This child of the goddess was different somehow, like he didn't fit, like he didn't belong here. There was a *wrongness* about him. And now the squirrel looked closer, he realised that this one was in fact *not* a child of the goddess.

As the party approached, the itching became worse, quickly driving the squirrel to the edge of distraction. It leapt and spun in a furry blur of agitation.

'What is that squirrel doing?'

Instinct told the rodent that the false child was somehow connected with the terrible moment of non-being he'd suffered inside the log, an experience so awful he could barely cope with the mere memory of it. This false child was somehow a part of that anathema. The squirrel did what any rational creature would. He attacked.

'Look out!'

'Arrgh!' Saltar shouted more in surprise than pain. 'The bloody thing scratched my cheek.'

Sergeant Marr shook his head. 'Not good. From the way it was behaving it could well have been rabid.'

'Great! Does that mean I go mad now?'

'A blessing from the god Wim p'raps,' Jack O'Nine Blades suggested happily. 'Certainly a good omen.'

'Milord, if I may?' Altibus said with a deep-voiced seriousness. He pulled up the sleeves of his robe and held his hands out as if they were already heavy with priestly magic. I can heal you!'

'And incur the displeasure of the Lord of Luck? Nay!' Jack protested.

'Let's just be sure the creature's gone first!' Saltar said, which had them all suddenly looking around anxiously. The Battle-leader despaired of them – they couldn't deal with a simple forest creature without making a song and dance of it, let alone anything more serious. Still, he reflected ruefully, he was bound to end up with a song and dance if he allowed a musician and a minstrel to accompany his group.

'Coast clear, Sergeant?'

'Yes, milord!' Marr said gruffly. At least *he* had some self-awareness, Saltar reminded himself.

'Good Altibus, you may put your arms down. Be sure that I'll come to you at the first sign of a malaise. Now, if we're all quite finished, let's get back in line and hunt down the real monsters that we know are out there.'

Saltar turned his horse and took the path that led off the other side of the glade. Jack came next, then Marr, then Lucius and Altibus, and Marr's men at the back.

'This way?' Saltar asked Jack with only a glance over his shoulder.

'Yes,' Jack said, surprising Saltar with the simplicity of his answer.

'Right. Good. Bizarre thing that, though, to be attacked by a squirrel.'

Jack paused, making Saltar turn his head. 'Yes and no. The bizarre happens all the time, but we are so used to it that it no longer strikes us as bizarre. Don't forget, you ride with a follower of Wim, so the bizarre is to be expected... but then if it is expected...'

'... is it really a surprise or bizarre?'

'Precisely, milord the Builder.'

'A strange god to follow, if I may say Jack. And a strange life spent following Wim, I imagine. There is nothing you can be sure of. I would find that quite... well, unnerving. I like to believe that some things are certain, that there is such a thing as permanence.'

Jack laughed, more in a knowing way that a mocking one. 'Verily, milord, I too would so like to believe, yet everything I know has shown me that it is naught but a fantasy and desire of human nature. All men like to believe that they can achieve security for both them and their loved ones, for their two-year-old children.

'And beyond that, men's egos like to believe that they can achieve a lasting legacy, so that they will survive beyond their own deaths. This I think you know. Yet everything I have seen of this world – and believe me, milord, I have seen much, possibly more than is wise – everything I have seen confirms that even the rising of the sun is no certainty. Forgive me, I do not seek to convince you, merely to explain to you who and how I am. It is my definition... though not a permanent one. Ha! In fact, convincing you is the last thing I would do, for you are the Builder, the one who creates and constructs a measure of permanence and certainty. I would not seek to shake or subvert your aim, so p'raps I have said too much, but you must understand that it is the task of holy Wim to test the Design. You must allow Him His work, for that is how you proof your construction so that its innate paradox does not cause it to unravel too quickly.'

Saltar turned with such speed and urgency in his saddle that he almost unhorsed himself. The Battle-leader's eyes were wide with a violent need. 'Say that again!'

The elfin minstrel blinked owlishly. 'All of it, milord? I will become quite thirsty.'

Saltar swallowed painfully and rasped, 'Don't be a jackanapes! Name me the task of your god.'

'You now have more than a passing interest in Him, milord?'

'You know I am a man of certainty, Jack. And one thing is certain: I will kill you if you do not cease trying to frustrate me with your roundabout answers. Speak straight or not at all, for you do not amuse me one wit.'

Jack sighed in an exaggerated style. 'I am a follower of Wim, milord. I speak as straight as I may. Have I not said as much before? Well, if I must continue to repeat myself in word and deed, and indeed that is how a man lives, then I must say again that it is the task of holy Wim to test the Design.'

'Enough!' Saltar barked and brooded on that information. Shakri created the Pattern, or Design as Jack called it, Cognis read the Design, Wim tested the Design... it seemed each of the gods had an essential role in holding this realm together. Whoever had removed Cognis had therefore pulled away an essential foundation of the entire realm. It was ready to collapse like a house of cards; the realm, the balance, mortals, the gods, the lot. But what force would benefit from such a thing? What would even be left for anyone to benefit from? And just what could Saltar do about it?'

Jack called him the Builder as if that were somehow significant. But all he'd built was a few homes for the outdwellers and that was about it. He hadn't built anything else. And what could he even build that would help to save the realm? And what did any of that have to do with his innocent son? It made no sense. But then, a follower of Wim rarely did make sense, Saltar was beginning to realise.

His mood deteriorating quickly, Saltar put the problem from his mind and decided to concentrate on their immediate goals and surroundings. The trees around them were thin now that they had lost most of their leaves as autumn turned to winter. Saltar could see a good hundred metres in every direction as a result, but the ground litter tended to cover up the main paths through the area. He wished he could read the trail of his son's abductors in the way Jack apparently could. It was fortunate indeed that they had met the fey fellow, for otherwise they would have lost the Jaffrans completely... or would have until the Scourge could have caught back up to them, at any rate, by which time who knew how far their quarry could have got ahead of them? Perhaps far enough for the trail to go cold completely. He was only just managing to hold onto his son, he knew. It was as if there was a single, fragile thread left connecting them, a thread that was stretched near to breaking point. He even refused to try and picture Orastes's face, for fear he might fail.

Where were these cursed Jaffrans, and what were they doing out here in the middle of nowhere? A number of suspicions began to occur to him.

'Sergeant?' he called, letting Jack take the lead for a while.

'Yes, milord?'

'We're now north of Holter's Cross, wouldn't you say?'

'As far as I can tell, yes, milord.'

'Then why didn't the Jaffrans simply carry on riding north along the King's Road when they came to Holter's Cross? Why did they turn east at Holter's Cross as if they were heading for King's Landing, only then to cut back on a north-west bearing through these woods?'

'Hmm. It may simply be an attempt to lose us, but it's a strange one because it puts us between them and King's Landing. If there's something they're after north of the city, I don't understand why they didn't carry on north, as you say, and then cut east and south-east to complete their journey to King's Landing.'

'Yes,' Saltar nodded. 'Because it now looks like they have no intention of heading for King's Landing. So where *are* they heading? Do you know what I think?'

Sergeant Marr was already nodding in understanding. 'That they made sure the guards at Holter's Cross and the innkeeper of the Stumbling Traveller saw them so that we would continue to believe that they were on their way to King's Landing and then Jaffra, when in fact they had no intention of going there at all.' Then his eyes widened. 'I don't think they're even Jaffrans!'

Saltar also nodded. 'They're from the north.'

'Accritanians!' Sergeant Marr gasped. 'Those Incarnus-loving, peace-breaking bastards! It's like they say: the only good Accritanian is a dead one!'

'I just find it hard to believe that General Constantus would allow this. Relations with Accritania have been good for the last several years.'

'Forgive me, milord, but we fought them for generations. That cannot be forgotten in just a couple of years, not even a couple of lifetimes. We all lost close family to those undead inbreeders. There can be *no* forgiveness for many of us. And who is to say any of this has been agreed by Constantus? They are a nation of nobles and necromancers! They will not be ruled by a man without title or magicks, no matter how good a man the General might be.'

Saltar had to admit that the Sergeant's words had a ring of truth about them. Added to that, he felt relieved to think that he was dealing with unruly Accritanians rather than mysterious and strange-godded Jaffrans. It suddenly felt that they were that bit closer to rescuing his son. 'Very well!' he said, his decision made.

'What are your orders, milord?' the straight-backed Sergeant asked.

'We're heading west from here to meet the King's Road leading north from Holter's Cross. Then it's a race for Accritania. We'll catch these renegades yet! Jack, did you hear?' Saltar called forwards.

The minstrel showed no sign that he had. Saltar thought he heard the man muttering to himself though. He frowned. What was going on? And wasn't this place familiar? Yes, there was the log from which the agitated squirrel had started to screech at them.

'Jack! We've been here before. Have you deliberately been leading us in circles?' Saltar levelled at the quixotic man and sliding his staff out of its saddle holster. The Sergeant was only a fraction of a second behind with his sword.

Jack's head began to tilt left, then right, left, then right. He made no effort to face them, just kept going with the same strange back and forth.

'Jack!'

Then the minstrel began to sing strangely discordant words to them. 'There are places we've all been to – places where we always get lost – places that we can't find when we try – They look the same whenever we visit – yet we always leave them feeling something's changed – and who's then to say what has or hasn't? – There are no true directions for us – everywhere's already connected – we'll get there or it will come to us –'

'It appears we're following a madman,' the Sergeant said shaking his head.

'Damn it!' Saltar seethed. 'What does that make us then? This is my fault! I should have listened to you and Altibus in the first place. What's happened to me that I would now listen to a complete stranger, slippery-tongued though he is, over my advisors? Have I completely taken leave of my senses?

'Shh!' the Sergeant gentled him. In a whisper he said: 'Milord, you are exhausted and worried for your son. Also, Jack O'Nine Blades is known for his use of the mad god's power. None can be in his presence and not feel its influence. Some stories even name Jack O'Nine Blades an avatar of the Lord of Luck Himself. Do not blame yourself. Hold true to what you know to be right, logical and sane. We can only become lost if we allow ourselves to be. We will only become lost if we *choose* to continue to follow this trickster.'

Altibus had ridden up unobserved and begun to eavesdrop. He leaned his wide face in now and nodded his head, causing his jowls to wobble slightly. 'The Sergeant is right, milord. We will only be rewarded with inconstancy from such as him. We are looking for a more solid, more definite steer in our pursuit of those who molested the palace.'

Saltar knew that it was high time they started to focus on what was fact, what was concrete, if they were ever to catch up the very real kidnappers of his son. He nodded to himself, objects and beliefs becoming firmer in his mind. As if in response, everything he saw began to take on greater definition. The trees had harder edges, he could almost feel the texture of their bark, his eyes picked out individual pieces of grit on the path around his horse's hooves. He could imagine the discomfort of them if he were to get them under his fingernails. He smelt the sweat on the horses all the more clearly; he could taste the steam coming off them. His body suddenly felt the pinch of the cold air, and then he realised he was suffering pain in various places all over his body, pain he'd been ignoring because he was so distracted by the mission to retrieve his boy. His finger-joints ached because he'd been holding his horse's reins too tightly, the insides of his legs were sore and bruised because they'd been rubbing against the sides of his mount, his lower back and buttocks were a numb agony from too many days in the saddle, and he had a pounding headache because of a lack of sleep. None of these physical complaints were significant on their own, but they all added up to a clear message that he was in desperate need of rest. *Rest?* his other self chastised him. *How can you think of rest when…?*

'We're here!' Jack suddenly shouted with a strange quiver of emotion in his voice as they rounded a bend in the path.

'We're wh…?' Saltar began as they emerged into a completely new part of the forest where the trees were spread far enough apart so that wagons could fit between them and where large expanses of chalky white sky could be seen above them.

'How…?' he tried again, swivelling in his saddle to see where they had come from and trying to work out why they hadn't seen this place the first time they had come through.

It wasn't just the strangeness of their arrival or the unexpectedness of the scene before him that caused his words to fail. Even without his newly sharpened senses, he could not have failed to notice the oppressive atmosphere hanging over the place. The air all but dripped with blood and echoed with the screams of death.

'Be ready!' the Sergeant shouted back down the line, his soldier's instincts kicking in. 'Spread out, give yourselves room to fight. Quickly!'

There was a wide, clear area in which a dozen bright and gaudy caravans had been drawn up into a large circle. They were basically wooden boxes with a pair of wagon wheels each and traces for where a pair of horses would be hitched, but there was nothing basic about the decoration of these mobile huts. They were covered in painted carvings of frolicking, cavorting, gambolling figures. Occasionally, there was a relief or panel of a larger face, always of some sort of deranged loon – hair a tangled skein, eyes looking in different directions, tongue lolling out, and expression impossible to read. Finally, there were some patchwork tents pitched in the middle of the circle and just visible between the caravans.

'The temple of Wim!' Jack breathed.

Saltar knew that there should be dogs barking at his party's unannounced approach. Children should be running out to see the strangers. Donkeys should be braying. The smoke from cooking fires should be rising lazily into the sky. There should be the usual chatter and hubbub that comes with every community. There should be a riot of life to accompany the riotous colours of the habitations, particularly in *this* encampment, dedicated to the worship of Wim as it was. Instead, they were presented with a place that displayed all the signs of being a carnival of the dead.

Tears trickled down Jack's usually clowning face as he said in an overly bright voice: 'The altar will be in the centre. The temple is always laid out in a circle around it, you see, to represent the wheel of fortune. Perhaps they're all eating at the moment and that's why they haven't sent anyone to welcome us. Or they might be at their prayers or… or sleeping…'

Saltar put his own hand over Jack's slender and trembling hands as they tried to pick up their horse reins. 'I'll go first, Jack.'

The sight that confronted them as they finally made their way past the tents had their horses rearing and backing up in terror. Altibus cried out in horror and Jack threw up over the side of his horse.

'By the stillborn child of Lacrimos!' the Sergeant choked.

Lucius, a man who had spent years hauling the dead into the vaults beneath Voltar's palace,had to hold a hand over his nose and mouth to protect himself from the worst of the thick and unhealthy miasma issuing from the centre of the camp. The soldier Brandis fell from his horse in a dead faint, his dead body hitting the ground with a loud and ominous crack.

'What narcotising corruption is this?!' Saltar gagged as he beheld the mound of mutilated flesh in the camp's central circle.

'Surely it is no altar, for it seems to move!' the Sergeant wheezed.

'It is everything and everyone that ever lived and was once a part of this temple!' Jack sobbed.

Beasts of burden had been thrown on the ground to form the base of the ten-foot mound. Their throats had been cut but their bodies still twitched as the last of the blood was pumped out of them by their betraying hearts. On top of them were the mangled and tangled limbs and torsos of dogs, adult humans and their children. All of them had been slashed and gored horribly, but somehow they all just hung onto life. Oh, how artfully they had been carved. Their vital fluids – their blood, their bile and urine – dripped and ran, pooled and trickled down the mound as if part of some unholy, nightmarish fountain.

The fluid flowed into the ground and spread out in an ever-increasing circle. Already, it was under the hooves of the party's horses, making the earth sticky and claggy a full twenty feet away. It seemed that it would not be done until it had claimed the entire area of the camp.

And the bodies groaned and whined, pleading for mercy, for the pity of the gods, the gods who seemingly refused to listen. Theirs were not the only voices, however. Above their piteous cries rose a powerful, droning chant, a chant that Saltar realised came from two black-robed figures standing with arms raised beyond the mound.

The language the magicians used was unfamiliar to Saltar, but as he gave up trying to distinguish individual sounds amidst the noise, the voices of the victims and the magicians blended together to form a harsh spoken harmony. Now, a single but many-braided voice resonated all around them, coming from all directions at once and filling the forest. It was a voice from the beginning of time, when all life was part of a single chorus. It was the inescapable universal, of uncompromising unity. It was the original voice of omniscience.

It all but unmanned Saltar. It was a force more potent that any he had ever met before. He was nothing before it… or so the voice insisted.

'Who are you?' he demanded.

The sky rumbled: 'I am your past and will be your future.'

'Return my child to me! What do you want with him? You cannot be anything so significant if you go to such lengths for a mere two-year-old. No doubt, you are naught but a jealous demon with a few lackey magicians.'

The mound of the dying laughed, a dripping maw appearing amongst the stirring and failing flesh. 'I am many things, have been all things. I have your child. Stop pursuing him and he shall live. Continue to search for him and I will visit unimaginable tortures upon him. You will be entirely responsible for his unendurable suffering.'

Saltar swallowed slowly. His lips were dry and his palms itched. He was terrified.

Someone giggled. Lights flashed and span through the air. Jack was juggling his nine blades, his eyes fixed on the distant magicians. His hands moved with such speed and dexterity that Saltar could not follow them.

'Nothing can be learned by listening to a demon, friend Saltar. Forgive me, but it is time I put an end to this heinous desecration.'

Then, a very strange thing happened. A blade slipped in Jack's hand, cutting him, and fell to the floor. His mouth formed an o of surprise, he lost his concentration and the other blades tumbled down around him.

'You missed a catch!' Lucius said, pointing out the obvious.

'Yes.'

'But you never miss!' the Sergeant said. 'You are famous for the impossible things you can do with your knives. Some say they're enchanted.'

'Yes.'

'Just bad luck?' Altibus asked archly.

Jack smiled in delight. 'But of course! You are a friend to point it out, good priest. And why not? For Shakri and Wim will always side together against such a foe.'

The rest of them exchanged mystified looks.

'Don't you see? It was *luck*! It is a sign that holy Wim is with us still. He is not yet lost to us! Rejoice, brothers, for without Him we might have been doomed against these dark practitioners and their overlord. Come, let's be about our work!'

With that, Jack jumped lightly from his horse and scooped up his blades. He was back in his saddle before the others had fully readied themselves for a charge.

The monstrous mound laughed in hungry anticipation. 'That's right. Come to me. Your bodies will be added to my substance. Your blood will help sustain me longer. Come! My servants will prepare you for the holy communion!'

They spurred their horses forward. The magicians began to shout their words now and the voices of the dying rose to meet them, their exertions causing blood to cascade freely down the demon mound. The increased flow seemed to give it strength – and suddenly it articulated itself and shifted six feet towards them, its mouth opening wide. Surely the blood from the ruined humans and animals would soon peter out, banishing the entity that temporarily possessed them from this realm. It suddenly occurred to Saltar that maybe they should have hung back and waited rather than rushing forward like this. He prayed they weren't making a fatal mistake, but they were committed now and if they tried to retreat would risk being caught from behind.

He raised his staff. His own blood responded to the spell being woven by the two magicians and pounded in his ears in time to the cadence and rhythm of their chant. They were controlling the beat of his heart! If they stopped chanting, would his heart also stop? Could they kill him instantly?

He could no longer hear anything expect the blood in his ears and the blood pumping in and out of his heart. He saw the Sergeant's mouth working, but didn't catch a single word of it. One of the soldiers started shaking his head and slapping the side of it with his free hand. His horse's direction drifted towards the mound. Whether a warning was shouted or not, the man couldn't hear it. The mound fell on him and gobbled him down.

Saltar slashed with his staff and crushed some tortured unfortunate's arm. It had no effect on the mound, of course – no number of blows would. He had to get to the magicians.

The Sergeant and his remaining three men were forced to wheel away to the left as the mound heaved itself towards them. Altibus and Lucius were slow to respond, but managed to turn after the Sergeant's lead just in time. Jack and Saltar took their chance, veered to the right and got past the mound. They kicked on towards the magicians.

One of the magicians had his hands held out and at either side of his head. Was it him who blocked their hearing? Silver flashed from Jack's hand and blurred towards the other one. This foe somehow knew the weapon was coming and stepped aside so that the blade flew past harmlessly. He made a claw of one hand and Saltar felt his heart seize. All feeling went from his body and he felt cut adrift.

Everything span and Saltar realised his body was sliding out of the saddle now that he had no sense of feeling to make the tiny shifts in weight required to keep it in place. He saw the sky and little else. He must be on his back. He consciously sent instructions from his mind to his body, his head turned and he managed to roll over. At least he had a basic control of his body even if he couldn't feel anything.

Jack lay not far away, limbs twisting and flopping around like eels stranded on a riverbank. Grinning evilly, the magician blocking their hearing produced a dagger from the folds of his midnight robes and approached the minstrel. He stopped chanting, although the other continued.

'Tut, tut, little tree wizard! It's time that you and all those like you learnt their place. It's time they understand how false their pride and sense of self-worth is. Time that they see they neither deserve not merit their place in existence. Time they realise their magic and realms were stolen from the Creator by His unruly children, those you call your gods. He has decided that in His love for His children, He has indulged them too much, that He has spoilt them. They must now be punished, else they will never learn. Their toys must now be put away forever, for those toys have only encouraged their infantile desire to be worshipped in their own right. No more will they be allowed their magic and realms with which to play. No longer will they be allowed to conjure with sparks of life to create you mortals to flatter their egos.

The magician's blade slashed back and forth through the air, punctuating his speech.

'See how easily, I, Aurelius, removed your hearing. Look how simple it is for Tacitus to render you immobile. Your lives are paltry things that do not extend beyond the useless flesh that embodies them. They must be cut from existence, just as your miscreant gods will be.'

Saltar knew the magician would cut Jack's body into ribbons as he lay there helplessly. The minstrel would then be dumped unceremoniously atop the mound of the dying in order to give their so-called Creator a few more moments in this realm.

Saltar concentrated and sent what he hoped was the pattern of thought required to get his arms and legs to flex. Nothing happened and he began to scream silently in his head. Suddenly, he leapt upwards. He was too slow to get his legs under him. He was about to fall flat on his face. *Curse this body!* One arm came out straight and his full weight came down on the flat of his right palm. The weight didn't come down flat though; his hand rolled over and his arm bone speared out through his wrist. He lay on the ground staring stupidly at the mess he'd made of the limb. At least he couldn't feel it! Besides, he'd suffered worse, hadn't he? It wasn't like he was dead or anything.

Aurelius glanced at him and laughed. 'You never give up, do you, Saltar? It will be your undoing, you know? And to think they call you the Builder. Destroyer would be more like it. But I will deal with you once I have attended to this troublesome, ages-old avatar of Wim.' He took his last step towards Jack and raised his curved, glinting dagger.

A dangling horse leg suddenly became animated, lashed out and stove in the head of another of the Sergeant's men. Even if the fellow had been wearing a helmet, he wouldn't have had a chance.

The Sergeant shouted at his surviving two men, but sound seemed to be working in isolated bubbles. '… useless! Fall back!'

One of the others was too slow to obey. Clawing hands got a hold of his horse's tail and yanked the creature backwards. Its back legs began to buckle. The rider tried to throw himself from the saddle but one of his feet caught in a stirrup. The horse fell on its side, trapping the rider underneath.

The Sergeant made a ridden pass, reaching down to try and grab the soldier's outstretched hand. At the last moment, the mound dragged horse and rider deeper in, and their fingers merely brushed, unable to get a secure grip on each other.

'No!' Sergeant Marr screamed, thumping his fist savagely against his thigh. He turned on the priest, Altibus.

'… do something!… are you?!… wretched… by the weeping sores of Malastra!'

The priest of Shakri had caught enough to know he wouldn't be safe from the officer – let alone the ten-foot abomination looming over them – if he didn't attempt some sort of magic. But what was he to do? He was no battle-priest with enormous withering and wasting energies at his command. He did the only thing he could do: he started to cast the one spell he had ever mastered – a simple blessing to head the afflicted.

A faint light of green and gold shone around the priest's hands and thousands of scintillations danced towards the mound. They span and sparkled and covered the writhing mass of misery. There was an almost immediate effect as the excretions flowing across the surface of the mound began to cease and individuals could more easily be identified amongst the living carnage.

'It's working!' Lucius shouted in delight.

Humans and animals amidst the pile began to try and wrestle themselves free and it looked like the whole thing would pull itself apart. The face of the supernatural being that had been moulded from the bodies of the victims began to disappear.

Then Altibus froze. His lips halted mid-phrase and his eyes glazed over.

'What…?' Lucius began, only to find his tongue stuck to the top of his palate. Numbness crept across his body until he could no longer feel himself. He was dimly aware of the Sergeant and his soldier falling like lumps of lead into the mud.

He himself landed on his side, with his arms out and his legs bent as if he was still mounted. His head lay in a bloody puddle – he was fortunate his nose remained clear of it. Even so, he breathed some of the muck into his lungs through his mouth.

A collective moan went up as the entity served by the two magicians reclaimed the members of the temple of Wim and they began to bleed, seep and weep once more. The mound humped and flowed closer to Lucius, Altibus, the Sergeant and the soldier, whose name Lucius hadn't even learnt yet.

❧ ❧

As Aurelius stepped towards Jack he caught his foot in the hem of his robe, over-balanced and sprawled forward. The dagger he held before him came down point-first on the metal buckle of Jack's belt, turned round and slanted up into the magician's heart. Blood gouted from Aurelius's mouth and he died lying crossways across Jack.

You don't see that everyday, Saltar thought to himself.

The chanting of Tacitus, the other magician, faltered as he saw what had befallen his comrade, but he reasserted his spell before it could begin to fragment and unravel. With shaking hands, he started to search his robes, presumably for his own dagger.

A wind came curving through the trees and began to circle within the camp, causing cooking fires to flare up, tents to flap like giant birds and autumnal to swirl into the air. One leaf found its way into Tacitus's mouth and stuck to the back of his throat.

The magician began to choke almost at once, as he'd been caught completely unawares and had no chance to draw a breath before fate had taken such a fickle turn. He clawed at his neck in panic, as if he was about to strangle himself or tear out his own gizzard, so desperate was he for air.

Jack, Saltar and the others were suddenly released from the magic that bound them. Saltar was first to his feet despite the agony of his ruined wrist. Cradling it awkwardly, he ran over to the magician to try and help him – he needed this one to live long enough to answer his questions. The man's face was a purplish blue and his eyes bulged out as if they were too large for his head.

'Hold still!' Saltar demanded.

Understanding entered Tacitus's eyes and he stopped fighting and thrashing around.

'Open your mouth, you fool!' Saltar urged him.

In response, the magician clamped his jaws together even more firmly. He smiled at Saltar.

'Gah!' Saltar spat in disgust and watched as the man died.

Shaking his head, the Battle-leader rose to see what help his friends needed. Jack was sitting up, watching his hand moved backwards and forwards at the wrist, as if he were a marionette suddenly gifted life and having to learn to move under his own power for the first time.

The Sergeant, the one remaining soldier, Lucius and Altibus had scooted back from the possessed pyre and were now standing a safe distance away, watching it warily. With the death of the magicians, it had rapidly lost its impetus and integrity. The high-pitched screams of terrified animals and those begging for mercy rose to fill the air once more.

'Shakri have mercy!' Altibus sobbed.

'Can you heal them?' the Sergeant asked, but the priest didn't appear to have heard.

Lucius and the soldier stood off to the side, at a loss as to what to do.

'Okay,' said the Sergeant, realising someone needed to take control, to show some leadership. 'Let's start moving them one by one. We don't want any who might be saved being crushed to death under this weight.' He cast an eye towards Saltar, but the Battle-leader had already turned away to search Aurelius and Tacitus.

Just as with Visier, there was nothing to be found on the magicians. Saltar ground his teeth in frustration. Face-to-face with the enemy and again he'd learnt precious little about them! If it hadn't been for Wim's intervention, that might have been the end of it as well. He needed to find out who the enemy were and what he could do to defend himself against them.

Of course, it was this entity that the enemy followed that worried Saltar most. What was it? Aurelius had called it the Creator and strongly implied that it was older and more powerful than the gods themselves. He had suggested that it had even created the gods. How powerful must such a being be? And how could Saltar hope to prevail against such a foe? No mortal army – no matter its size – could hope to prevail, could it?

Well, the Creator still did not have free access to this realm, it seemed. It was reliant upon its magicians. It was still limited somehow. Saltar now began to have suspicions as to why they needed his son. The thought of it turned his blood cold and he shivered involuntarily. Why *his* child, damn it?! Weren't there enough other children in the world?

With renewed urgency, he glanced around the makeshift camp that served as the temple of Wim. It was a scene to move even the hardest of hearts. Sergeant Marr, the Sergeant's man and Jack were up to their shoulders in gore as they pulled, dragged and carried victim after victim down from the pile. Lucius also helped, his face more of a mask that the others' – of course, he'd done something similar for the necromancer Voltar, hadn't he?

Rather than attending to the victims, Altibus approached Saltar. What did the man want now?

'Yes?'

'Milord,' the priest addressed him quietly. 'I should mend your arm.'

'What? Oh, yes! Yes, yes, thank you. I'd be grateful if you could.'

The priest murmured some words softly and Saltar's bones began to reknit themselves. Saltar watched in fascination as his injury was miraculously repaired.

'It will remain sore for a few days yet but you should be able to use it for simple things,' the priest informed him in the same numb manner as before.

'Altibus, you are suffering from shock, I think. Can you heal yourself of that at all? Are you okay?' Saltar's main concern was that every member of his group be in the best possible condition to travel and possibly fight again very soon.

Altibus was shaking his head slowly. 'Regrettably, Shakri's power is unable to change the state of mind of her children. If our state of mind were to be controlled by the goddess, we would be protected from the problems in life, they would cease to have meaning to us and we would become inured to horrors. We would no longer recognise consequences to our actions, not care if our actions were evil and no longer be moral beings. We would no longer live our lives in a way we could grow and ennoble ourselves. Rather, we would be animals or monsters. It is right that I suffer shock at what has happened here. It is right that I feel so keenly the loss of the life that Shakri had gifted the followers of Wim.'

'Oh, I see. Then maybe a cup of tea will sort you out. I'll ask the soldier – what's his name? – to start boiling up some water,' the Battle-leader replied perfunctorily and strode away from the priest.

Altibus watched him go. He frowned and shook his head sadly.

Saltar decided the soldier was already busy enough hauling bodies, so set a pot to boiling himself. He then helped the Sergeant pull down a large, half-naked man with deep cuts on his inner thighs.

'I wish to leave soon, Sergeant. We are clearly not far behind our enemies. We are now sure of the direction they are going. If we linger here much longer, we will lose the day and any immediate chance of catching them.'

The Sergeant got his breathing under control and met Saltar's gaze. 'Milord,' he said carefully. 'I have just lost four men. I would see their bodies blessed and safely buried. It is the least I can do for them. And I would expect them to have done the same for me if I'd been unlucky rather than them. No Memnosian would willingly leave a fallen comrade's body in a manner that it might be worried by wild animals and rogue practitioners of unholy magicks. It is a promise we all make to one another. These men had no families to speak of, so relied on each other more than most.'

Saltar regarded the man silently. He realised they'd all stopped to hear his answer. He could order the man to get on a horse and leave with him right now; and if he refused kill him for treason. But would he refuse? Saltar sighed. Of course he would. Sergeant Marr was a simple man who stuck to his code of honour even when it was not in the best interests of his career; and it had been precisely because of those qualities that Saltar had been able to trust him and had picked him to come along in the first place.

'Altibus, priest of Shakri,' the Battle-leader said. 'What say you?'

Altibus jumped in surprise. 'I-I should bless the Sergeant's men, certainly. And I must see to these poor unfortunates here. I know I made an oath to High Priest Ikthaeon, but my oath to the goddess must come first.'

'Jack?'

The man who was part jester, minstrel and fighter rolled his head round on his neck as if considering a whole world of possibilities. Then he stopped, a decision made. 'These are my people. I must see to their well being, or the temple might be lost entirely. For the good of us all, I must do what I can here to prevent such an outcome. You understand, do you not?'

Saltar nodded. He understood. He understood many things. He'd already asked more of them than he had any real right to. Four men had died just to try and save a two-year-old. How could that be justified? How could he ask any more people to risk their lives? Where would it end? Would he have everyone in the world die just to save a two-year-old? It was madness and needed to stop now.

'Sergeant, you and your man will remain here with the others, and will do so with my blessing. I must go on, though. I'm sure you understand.'

'Thank you, milord! Yes, milord!'

'And when you are done here, you will return to Corinus to tell my wife what you have seen and that I head for Accritania.'

'But, milord, we can follow on…'

'That is an order, Sergeant! You will be silent. Please, there is only so much insubordination I am prepared to tolerate in a single day.'

For once, the Sergeant did as he was bidden.

Saltar nodded again. 'Good. I must leave you now, my friends. I thank you for your courage and sacrifice in accompanying me this far. I feel certain that we will see each other again soon, but that there are dark days ahead.'

'Wait!' Lucius cut in. 'I will continue on with you.'

Saltar shook his head. 'I do not ask you to do so, gentle Lucius.'

Lucius drew himself up to his full height and looked down at the Battle-leader with mock disdain. 'I do not ask you to do so, Battle-leader. I am a free citizen of Dur Memnos and will go where I will. I just hope you will be able to keep up with me!'

It was the closest Saltar had come to laughing since Orastes had been stolen from him. Then he was moved by an emotion he did not quite recognise. He turned away and his voice broke as he said, 'Then let's waste no time, musician! To the horses!'

After all, he did not go just to save a two-year-old, he told himself. He went to battle the oldest of the gods. He went to unmake the Creator. In the process, it seemed he would have to break the kingdom of Accritania. And if he failed, which seemed more than likely, then he would have destroyed the entire realm and all its gods. Still, at least there would be no one left to be upset about it. There wouldn't even be a realm of the dead left.

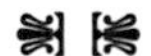

Chapter Eight: And Are Left With Nothing

Strap swam in and out of consciousness, as a weak swimmer struggles to keep his head above water. His body felt heavy, always threatening to pull him back under. It was so hard to breathe.

He realised he was under stifling, heavy blankets lying near a large fire and hearth. Mordius lay asleep just across the way, sweat clearly visible on his brow. A pot of something bubbled on the fire, but he could not place the unappetising aromas coming from it.

He sensed there was someone else in the room, someone moving about. He craned his head round and just about caught sight of the witch. He was struck again by how pretty she was, lost what little breath he had in his chest, and found he was unable to call out to her.

He turned back to rest his head and try to gather some strength. He looked at the roof above him – it was of simple design and structure. There were none of the leering skulls to be seen he'd imagined when he'd first arrived. Illusions, she'd called them.

He finally worked up enough saliva in his throat to call out. 'Hello?'

'Ah! You're awake!' she said, coming over, wiping a knife on her apron. 'How are you feeling? Neither of you were in the best shape when you arrived.'

'Water?' he gasped.

'Of course. But I have something much better than that,' she smiled, dipping a cup into the pot over the fire. 'Come on, try a few sips. It's a fortifying brew made from the swamp herbs hereabouts. It'll do you good.'

Strap found it hard to believe that anything good could come out of this swamp, but decided he was in little position to argue. Besides, he didn't want to upset her and have her stop smiling so prettily at him. He sipped the hot, bitter liquid as she held the cup to his lips. It hurt his throat at first, but after a few swallows he didn't feel it so much. In fact, he didn't feel much at all.

'Thank you!' he said dreamily and she took the cup away. 'I'm Strap.'

'I know!' she said, her cheeks dimpling. 'I *am* a witch, remember. Besides, you talk in your sleep.'

He blushed. 'Phew! It's a bit hot in here. You couldn't...?'

She loosened his blankets a bit for him, but he found that a deep lassitude had come over him and he was no longer interested in moving his arms. He'd been meaning to ask her all sorts of questions, some of them quite important, but they all seemed to have disappeared from his head.

'How is Mordius?' he managed.

Her gaze flicked away from him, which almost broke his heart and made him instantly jealous of the conniving necromancer. Still, it meant that for a moment he was no longer lost in her gaze and could remember a few of his questions.

'He's resting now. Sleeping safe and sound. He was awake for a short while, but he's not as vigorous as you are, Strap.'

He was pleased that she should think more of him than she did Mordius. 'We've come here to... to...'

'Shh!' she said, putting a long finger to his lips. 'It doesn't really matter why you're here. There will be time enough for that if you really must tell me. But you're feeling tired now. It's okay, you can go to sleep. I'll be here when you wake up.'

It didn't matter? Perhaps she was right. The fact that he couldn't really remember why he was here must mean the reason wasn't that important anyway. Yes, she was probably right. And a woman who was so good that she looked after complete strangers had to be someone you could trust. Yes, she was no doubt correct. And she was so very pretty as well. Ah, yes, that had been one of the questions he'd been intending to ask: how was it that she was so young and pretty when Lebrus and Astraal had said that she was older than anyone else in Marsby?

⁂

The Chamberlain remained poised and unmoving in the deepest shadows of the catacombs, just as he'd been for the last twenty hours. After some forceful persuasion, one of his informants had donated enough blood for the Chamberlain to refresh and reconfigure all his wards in the lower levels. If the prey even twitched, then the man-spider would know about it.

He had known when the blood-mages had entered the palace, of course, but had decided against interfering with them once he'd divined their purpose. It suited him that the child be stolen, even though it made his position in the palace difficult. And the destruction of Cognis had been a bold and brilliant move by those same mages, a move that had instinctively thrilled him. But as much as it had thrilled him, it had also worried him. They had completely destabilised the Pattern. Any false move now, and all would be lost.

The green witch had been right to start taking direct action to secure her interests. Ill-mannered and clumsy though she was, he would do her bidding on this occasion, for it would also re-establish his own influence on the Pattern in the process. And sanctimonious and divinely tiresome though the gods of this realm were, they served a very necessary function in preserving and providing the balance, organising magic and anchors that allowed this realm to be his sanctuary. He had suffered and sacrificed too much in reaching this haven to let it go so lightly. Furthermore, he feared beyond measure the power with which he now suspected the blood-mages were allied.

His was a patience that could last whole lifetimes, but the green witch had given him just twenty-four hours. There were only four hours remaining; time was running out. Kate was probably right to consider the matter urgent anyway – if they did not act now, then the key events of the main thread might well move beyond their local ability to influence them.

If the prey did not make a move soon, then the Chamberlain would have to do something to flush it out. What was it waiting for anyway? Surely it hadn't sensed him; the ichor in the Chamberlain's veins didn't flow in the same way as the blood of the mortals of this realm; so it was unlikely that one relying on blood magic would be aware of his presence.

He ran possibilities and connections through his head. What if the prey had genuinely found a way to get past his wards undetected? No, if the larger group of mages had been unable to do so when they first entered the palace, then this remaining one was unlikely to have found a way. Maybe the prey had already died in setting fire to the temple? No, that would be a strange and unnecessary sacrifice, especially given how long and how well these mages had apparently planned. Perhaps the prey was just lying low and hoping they would give up searching after a while? No, given the nature of its crimes, it must know they would never give up searching and that the longer they searched the closer they would get. Which left only one possibility: the prey had enough supplies to wait where it was until it was time to strike at its next target. Yes, that was very possible. This prey had no need to break cover because it was not yet trying to escape. It was intent on causing further trouble and destruction in Corinus.

The Chamberlain unfolded his limbs and crept out of his small hidey-hole. He spent the next few hours searching some of the lowest caves and tunnels beneath Corinus. Some of the places he came upon he'd only been to once or twice in the centuries he'd been at the palace. Even he was wary of exploring too far down here, for who knew what ancient and fell creatures existed amongst the roots of the earth? There were cracks and crevices that led even deeper, but he was extremely loathe to investigate them. He'd prefer to take his chances with Kate and her guards than squeeze down into a place where he might get stuck and never be able to extricate himself. Old and powerful he might be, but he was far from immortal and invulnerable.

As he spidered through a wide, crystalline cave, his senses jangled. He'd hit a ward! Surely it belonged to the prey he sought. He remained motionless, waiting to see if anyone would be alerted by his coming into contact with the ward or whether his infringement would trigger some other spell. Nothing. Apparently, he remained undetected.

He looked around the bizarre cave, trying to make sense of it. Long, sword-like crystals bristled from the walls and formed thick pillars between floor and roof. The whole place sparkled and dazzled with reds, oranges and yellows, as if shiny autumn leaves filled the air of a tree-vaulted clearing, or a colony of sun-butterflies had set a dry meadow ablaze. It deceived his eye for some time. What he took for shadow was often a piece of crystal that was not channeling light at that moment; then it would suddenly flare, as when clouds part to reveal the sword; or it would take on a slow, ruddy blush, as the night sky gives way to the dawn. But the longer he watched, the more he understood the dimensions of the place and how energy was reflected and amplified within it. In many ways, it was like what he did when followed, read and anticipated the threads, nodes and patterns of the past, present and future. It was all made that much easier when he realised that a fire had been made somewhere in the cave and that was the origin and explanation of the light bouncing around here. The fire was the key to understanding *all* he saw. Just knowing it was out there gave sense and order to what initially appeared random and inexplicable.

His quick mind was even capable of working out the likely location of the flame. He smiled to himself and crept in the same staccato as the dancing shadows towards the corner he knew to be the goal. As he went, he pulled long needles from his thick hair, his collar and his sleeves. He unsheathed their tips, holstered one in each of his modified shoes, placed one so that it speared out between his front teeth and held several between the fingers of each hand.

The low murmuring of voices reached his ear and he stilled. More than one enemy! How badly was he outnumbered? It was another complicating factor to make the outcome of this encounter uncertain. He was already worried about the unusual nature of the cavern: obviously, the crystals would confuse any magic used for searching down here; but could the mages he hunted also use the crystals to amplify any magic they might employ? In the normal course of events, the Chamberlain would have adjudged the situation too hazardous and retreated to consider the problem further, but the green witch's ultimatum meant this was anything but the normal course of events. He would have to take the risk, damn her. If he died because of this, he would be considerably inconvenienced, not to mention annoyed beyond bearing.

He continued to wait. He'd only heard two voices so far. In some ways, it was better for him that there were two, because they were keeping each other distracted; if there had been just one enemy instead, he or she would have been waiting on silent alert and would have been much harder to surprise.

The Chamberlain raised himself onto tip-toes and then danced around the columns, ducked under out-thrust shards and jumped lightly over spiked outcroppings. He came upon them taking their ease by a small fire. The figure turned slightly away from him didn't even register his presence until one of the paralysing needles was mere inches from the back of his neck, by which time it was far too late to utter even the most simple of defensive spells.

The other foe sprang up nimbly and uttered harsh, compelling syllables at the Chamberlain. The royal retainer threw one of his weighted needles at the mage, but his arm hadn't risen as quickly as it should have done and the needle was released too early. It hit the mage's robe, failed to penetrate the material and ended up dangling there uselessly.

More words of power were chanted by the mage and the Chamberlain found himself slowing even further. The mage frowned, clearly confused that his magic hadn't stopped his opponent completely. *He doesn't realise I'm not of this realm,* the Chamberlain thought to himself. *Besides, who's ever heard of someone being bespelled by words alone? The idiot clearly doesn't understand the first thing about magic.* The Chamberlain came to a complete stop, even his eyes frozen and unable to track the mage's movements.

The mage looked the Chamberlain over carefully and then nodded to himself, satisfied. He bent to examine his comrade and tutted at the bloody foam at the corner of the other's mouth. 'You needn't have taken the poison, fair Clyderas, but it was perhaps wise that you did. The instructions of the

Three were clear. Fear not, your spirit shall be avenged. I will make sure that this transgressor suffers far more than you ever did.' With a gentle hand, he closed the dead man's staring eyes and then rose with deadly intent to meet the Chamberlain.

The mage's head jerked back as he found himself nose-to-nose with his enemy. Too close! The Chamberlain extended his neck forward and jabbed with the needle between his teeth. It stabbed deep into the mage's bottom lip and the man cried out. His eyes went wide in panic and he started to grind his back teeth.

The Chamberlain pounced, prising the mage's jaws apart and jamming the side of his hand between the mage's teeth to stop him using whatever poison tooth or concealed phial of poison he had in his mouth. The mage bit down hard on the meat of the Chamberlain's hand, drawing ichor from it, until the paralysing neurotoxin from the needle finally took full effect.

The Chamberlain shuddered with a pleasure that was almost sexual. Oh, how he would like to dally here with his prey for a while, indulging in the caresses of a gentle torture, but the green witch would not allow it. Twenty-four hours she had given him, and by the time he dragged his prey all the way up to the palace levels, that measure would be up. Still, the green witch would want information extracted from the prey and, pleased with the Chamberlain for having delivered the prey, might allow him to be the one to visit the necessary and delicate excruciations upon the body of the prey. He shuddered at the prospect, the anticipation serving to further provoke and sharpen his appetite.

⁂

Mordius's dreams were full of a sharp, crimson torture. A knife kept coming for him and cutting into his flesh. It never sliced so deeply as to be fatal but always made sure his blood flowed freely. It ran and ran, and when it slowed teeth and lips would find the wound and keep it open longer. Only when he was all but dry was he left alone to recover. Rather than be a relief, those periods were simply a different type of suffering, as he waited in helpless dread for the knife to come again.

'Wake up!' he screamed at himself.

He cracked open an encrusted eyelid and tried in vain to blink his eye clear. He opened his other eye, which improved things slightly. He was inside. There was a fire nearby, bunches of herbs hung to dry on the walls around it.

There were the predictable poker and shovel leaning against the hearth, and then strangely-shaped metal vessels and implements. He couldn't guess at their purpose.

A motion across the room made him turn his head. A comely matron wiped her mouth and then smiled at him. Strap lay not far away – apparently she had been ministering to him. Mordius squinted and brought everything into a closer focus. His friend was unconscious and bare-chested. There were ugly, fresh cuts covering both his arms! Then the matron blocked off his line of sight and gave him a winning smile.

'Now, now, you shouldn't be awake!' she chastised him gently with her warm and buttery voice.

'What are you doing to him?' Mordius rasped, finding himself encumbered by a blanket and without the strength to wriggle free.

'I'm bleeding him, of course. He caught a flux in the swamp, but I'm nursing him through it.'

Mordius had heard of the old medical practice of bleeding patients, and had always considered it primitive and backwards. Invariably, it killed more people than it saved, from everything he'd read. 'Are you the witch?'

The matron ran her hands over the generous curves of her body, straightening her clothes here and there and ensuring her modesty was preserved before his gaze. Mordius felt the heat of embarrassment rising in his face as if he had been caught in a voyeuristic act. He deliberately kept his eyes on her face, only to find that he could not help staring at her plump, ruby lips as she said, 'Some have called me such, although more out of ignorance than any sort of intimacy. I have ended up alone here through no fault of my own. Some of the more idle and spiteful residents of Marshy have no doubt invented and spread stories about me, but I'm afraid I do not know any of the details.'

Mordius fancied he understood, if not shared, some of her sorrow. For had he not also been isolated by his own people? As a necromancer, had he not also been misunderstood? Had he not also become some sort of fantastical figure to be feared and loathed? 'I-I know what you're saying. I am a magician of sorts and have never really been accepted, you see. I-I feel I know you eventhough we have never met before.'

She smiled at that. 'A magician? Truly? Then I am even more happy that you have come to me. But here I am chattering away like some lovestruck maid when you are wanting of rest! I must not overtire you with my selfishness. Here, take this draught I have prepared for you. It will restore you.'

She raised the rim of a beaker to his lips and he tilted his head to accept it. He pulled away at the last second and said: 'I'm sorry, but I cannot contain myself. Imust tell you what it means to me to have met someone like you. Look at me, I am running away at the mouth but cannot help it. I've always dreamed there would be someone like you, but had begun to think as I got older that I was just deluded. I hope I do not seem forward... I do not even know your name, but somehow that does not matter. See, I am the selfish one!'

'No, no,' she assured him. 'You are no such thing. The love spell I have cast upon you has simply had too great an effect. Now shut up and drink!'

'But I am!' he exclaimed passionately, causing her to spill some of the beaker's contents across his blanket. 'Oh no! I'm sorry, I'm sorry. I am selfish in my love for you, believe me. I have even put the subject of my love before my true purpose in coming here, which is to ask you whether the phrase *the Enemy is returning* means anything to you.'

The witch's hand shook so violently that she spilled the rest of the beaker's contents across the floor. Her face lost all trace of life. 'What did you say?' she asked in old, guttural tones.

He smiled up at the sunken and mouldering face of his beloved. 'The Enemy is returning, my sweet! What does that mean to you? And the Time of Breaking?'

'No! Such things are not for a mortal! Who spoke of them to you?'

'It was the god of knowledge, Cognis, speaking through His high priest. His temple was destroyed and He is now gone from this realm. But what of our love, my sweet? Shall I not speak more of that?'

'Silence, you fool!' the swamp geas seethed. Then she seemed to forget him – just as she'd forgotten the beaker – and spoke out loud to herself. 'He cannot be returning. There is no way he can enter this realm. It is now inimical to him. But if that simpleton Cognis allowed himself to be undone, then... he styled himself a god, eh? Heh, heh! Well, I suppose he was the next best thing. And the others too. Well, they've gone and created a right little problem for themselves, now haven't they? Heh, heh, heh! Been a while since anyone or anything made me laugh that much. And then Cognis asked for *my* help? Heh! Pompous, self-righteous prig! But, of course, those self-interested, self-important surrogates won't let themselves be the only ones to suffer. Oh, no! If just one of them has to suffer, then they'll do everything they can to ensure that anything that's ever seen a star, ever drawn a breath or ever experienced a feeling will suffer beyond bearing. They're inadequate, you see.

And those that are inadequate like to drag down others so that they do not feel so inadequate by comparison.

'Anyway, there's not much anyone can do to gainsay the Enemy if he is returning. In their ignorance and fear, the so-called gods trapped me here, so I am powerless to affect the Pattern or balance. In fact, if certain parts of the realm are undone in order to allow the return, then this prison might fall and I will finally be free, albeit that I will be forced to flee this realm at once in order to avoid his dreadful unity. Yes, his return may actually serve me well. Ah, to be free again! To grow, to know power, to seek out limits and transcend them! The Great Fulfillment will be mine once more!'

She began to rock back and forth on her feet, crooning to herself, lost in a vision of an existence from aeons before.

'Yes, my sweet, our love will be unbounded!' Mordius chirruped.

'What? What are you talking about, you idiot?' she spat, the rot and corruption of her breath forcing him turn away momentarily.

Mordius gave her a besotted smile. 'I will aid his return if it will help free you so that we might better love each other. Tell me his name so that I might search him out. And what is your name, my sweet? Just to hear it will be an ecstacy for my mind.'

As they had spoken, the witch's skin had slowly darkened like rotting wood. Pieces of it had even begun to fall off. A terrible stench, as from a carcass left to rot in stagnant swamp water, surrounded her. 'I am not about to let a magician, even a lovesick one, know my name, am I you soft-skulled dolt?' She filled the beaker from a small, bubbling cauldron over the fire, bits of her falling into the strange, green soup it contained. 'Now, I am hungry again, so drink this so I may feed in peace.'

When Mordius opened his mouth to speak again, she grabbed his nose and piched it closed. He gasped in order to breathe and she poured the thick, green liquid down his throat. It burned but he had no choice except to swallow. His eyes watered and then became heavy. The last thing he saw was the witch testing the edge of her knife as she watched him with her beautifully greedy, beetle-black eyes.

❦ ❦

The chattering of his teeth against the cold inevitably woke Larc. Even though he and Vasha had huddled close for warmth during the night, they'd still been exposed to the mountain winds and had little insulation against the heat-draining rock. He looked at the woman curled up against him and worried about the blue tinge to her lips. She was unmoving and the flesh of her face was morbidly pale. He was suddenly afraid she had died during the night, and put out a hand to feel her cheek.

She responded to the relative warmth of his touch and pushed her cheek against his palm. She opened her eyes, looking more than a little disorientated. She stared blankly and he shuddered as he was transported back to that horrible night when he'd found his wife in the House of the Dead.

'Vasha, eat this bit of bread, it will revive you. And we should try to move in order to get warm. We don't want to end up with frost-bite.'

She nodded weakly but otherwise did not respond. He held a morsel out to her lips. She opened her mouth and he put the bread in.

'Close your mouth now.' He pushed her jaw up for her. 'Now chew. That's it.'

He found one of her hands and fretted at the purplish colour there. He began to rub it between his own hands, as if he were using a stick to start a fire.

'Aie! It hurts!' she cried after a while.

'That's good!' he said, carrying on for a minute more before moving to her other hand.

At last, Vasha began to blink and show signs of life. She started to shiver as her body rediscovered its ability to fight the cold. They stood up, holding onto each other, and it was Larc's turn to wince. His feet had become so cracked and blistered because of his inadequate footwear and the unusually hard rock of this place that he was scared to look at them.

'Oh, you poor thing!' Vasha gasped as she realised just how bad a condition he was in. 'Look, I'll gather some of that old moss there and we'll make a layer of it for your soles.'

'What, that yellowed stuff? It's dead and pretty thin,' he observed.

'It's called *patient hunger* moss by the locals. It just looks dead. If it gets wet, then it quickly turns green and expands. You should wee on it.'

'What? I'm not going to wee on it and put it on my feet! That's disgusting. Wild animals would be able to follow my scent and everything.'

She gave a small sigh and explained patiently: 'Urine keeps things clean, I thought everyone knew that. Brother Raksis at the temple even used to drink it. He was a bit odd, of course, and it made his breath smell, but everyone agreed he was the fittest and strongest person there.'

Larc couldn't help giggling a bit at that. 'And it's not like he needed to stay fragrant for any comely maiden, I suppose.'

Vasha giggled too. 'No! The temple goats were his most common companions!'

That did it. They were both laughing hysterically until tears came to their eyes and the cold air in their lungs finally had them coughing and spluttering.

'Oh dear!' Larc snorted as he wiped at his eyes. 'At least that's helped warm us up a bit. Okay, I'll try the whole weeing on moss thing, but I am *not* drinking it. There's a perfectly decent river for when I'm thirsty, thank you very much.'

Larc rebound his feet and they ate some more before finally setting off. He had to take it gingerly at first, but the cushioning and soothing effects of the moss allowed him to maintain a fair pace. Soon, they were on the lower gradients of the mountain, and they found the going easier. Even the sun helped them along by peeking out from behind the clouds and bathing them in an ice-thawing glow. Their spirits were the lightest they'd been since they'd discovered the massacre at the temple.

'The town of Swallowdale is just beyond that spur and around a long bend in the river. The river is the Trendus and bears south for a hundred miles before finally turning west and going all the way out to the Shellhorn Sea. There is a road from Swallowdale that goes south for a bit, but then leaves the river and heads south-east until it joins the King's Road. Once we've alerted the people of Swallowdale about the attack on the temple, we'll take the road, I guess, because the river's too difficult for boats this close to the Needle Mountains. And when we get to the King's Road, we'll head south towards Corinus. Once we're in the capital, we can warn both the main temple and the Builder.'

'Oh, right, sure!' Larc nodded, trying to draw a map in his head and fix names to places. This sort of information would prove invaluable if he ever had to find his way around the Chaos Wastes without Vasha. 'So the Swallowdale road meets the King's Road and we'll follow that south. Where does the King's Road go to when it heads north, then?'

'Why, north-east to the Worm Pass and Accritania, of course. Surely you know that. Just where *do* you come from, Larc?'

He licked his lips, unsure how best to answer, thinking quickly. 'Westaways. A small place that hardly has a name. But, Vasha, you're amazing! How do you know so much? You know about herbs and mosses and necromancy and navigation and… loads of other things, no doubt. How do you remember it all? You must be very clever!'

The girl flushed and then smiled shyly. 'Well, I-I… I had good teachers at the temple, you know. And I'm a follower of Cognis, who is the god of knowledge, after all. But all my teachers said I learnt very quickly for my age. I'm not that clever, really! I just remember things, that's all. But you're very strong and brave, Larc. I don't know how you had the courage to go into the temple with what had happened. And how you can cope without your wife and child, I don't know. And you can keep going even with your feet so painful.'

Now she'd caught him out with her own compliment and he found himself smiling proudly. He was pleased that she should think him strong and brave. They exchanged a long gaze, and then he looked away guiltily. He had to get back to focusing on saving his wife and child. He only needed Vasha for as long as she could help him accomplish that goal.

He cleared his throat. 'Do you think we could get a horse in Swallowdale? It would save us a lot of time.'

'But we don't have any money,' she said unhappily. 'And I don't suppose they'll lend us one, so how can we get a horse? Unless… unless… oh!'

'Yes, Vasha. I think we'll have to take one. Our news is very important and the Builder would want to hear it as soon as possible, wouldn't he?' Plus, the spirits of his wife and child would dissipate if he didn't find an organising magic and anchors for them soon. And if the Builder and his necromancer couldn't help him, then he would quickly need to find the lost god instead.

'Well, yes, I suppose so,' she said in a small voice.

'Good. It won't be difficult, you'll see. We'll only borrow one from someone who's already got quite a few. And we'll definitely return the animal on our way back this way. I'm sure your temple and the Builder will also be happy to reward the horse owner for the assistance they gave us as well.'

She brightened at that idea. 'Yes, that would help make it better. But we'll try asking if we can borrow a horse first.'

'Of course,' he said easily. He looked up ahead. 'Wow! Look at all that smoke! Is that Swallowdale? Perhaps it's some sort of festival day. Or maybe a farmer is burning the stubble in his field.'

Vasha's only answer was to hurry forwards. Larc struggled to keep up and was soon panting too hard to say anything more.

They rounded the long bend in the path as it skirted round the spur and then followed path and river down into Swallowdale. The corner of the first house they came to jutted out slightly, blocking their view of the rest of the place, and forcing them to jink around it. They slowed as they found the door to the house left wide open and no sign of anyone around.

Then they came to the next house. There were no words. A toddler of no more than three years lay half on and half off the stone doorstep. There was a thick, red slash across the infant's throat, and a dry pool of blood where its life had bled away. It still clutched a small, carved horse tightly in its hand. The child's eyes were closed so that it almost looked peaceful.

If Vasha had been able to breathe, she might have urged the poor mite to wake up. Larc kindly tugged at her arm, pulling her away.

Ten metres further on, they came to the body of a middle-aged woman down by the river. She lay across her linen, only the blood that had subsequently soaked into the material destroying the image of a hard-working woman snatching a moment's rest.

Not much further on, a fisherman was stretched out on the riverbank, his back against a rock, hat pulled down low to keep the sun out of his eyes, hands interlaced across his stomach and legs crossed at the ankles. A thin, scarlet line could just be glimpsed beneath his chin but it was just enough to tell them he would never wake again, never catch another fish, never sit down to breakfast with his family again.

It was the ordinariness of the scene that was truly shocking, for it made the death of these people seem not only commonplace but also of little consequence. In many ways, it was more horrific than what he had seen at the temple, Larc decided, even though these people were demon-worshippers. He was finding it hard to swallow and had to force his gorge down. He tried to put his eyes somewhere he would not have to gaze upon the murder of innocence. The only thing that presented itself was the pall of darkness ahead, and he had begun to fear that more than everything else he had seen in Swallowdale so far. The smoke roiled and curled like a river of black blood.

A slight shift in the wind served to confirm his worst fears: the smell of human pork; the sound of sizzling flesh and crisping skin. He turned to find Vasha and lead her away, but she'd moved to his blindside and was suddenly too far ahead of him. He was too late to stop her, to save her.

They stood appalled. There had to be over thirty bodies piled on top of each other and ablaze. The structure towered over them and seemed to be alive as blackened skeletons twisted and turned in the heat. The flames flared white in the middle of the pile, the inferno had become so hot. Flesh had run off the bodies like hot candle wax and flowed out from the base six feet in all directions. The liquid fat bubbled and popped even at the edge closest to them, the fire radiated so intensely.

Vasha closed her eyes, but the blazing silhouette of a laughing skull floated before her as an after-image. There was no escaping it.

Hand in hand, they travelled around the conflagration and then ran through the town down the riverside path. They came across more inhabitants, but all they received were vacant stares. No one called out to them.

What had happened? None of the people showed any signs of having put up a struggle. They had been killed like dumb, witless animals. Not one person held a weapon or had defensive wounds on their hands and arms.

Larc desperately tried to wake up, but he was trapped in this silent world of death. No, it was worse than that. He was a *part* of this silent world of death, where not even a scream could find life and impetus.

They didn't stop running until they reached the last house in the town, and then they came to a complete and abrupt halt. Sat waiting upon fierce, enormous mounts were six men in black garb. They were ranked in pyramid formation: one at the front, two behind and to either side of him and then three in the last row.

'Ah! There you are!' said the leader, and they could hear him in their minds and their ears. Their temples and diaphragms resonated with the tones of his voice and will.

Larc paled and then dove onto his belly, face down in the mud. 'Lord!' he squeaked.

Vasha looked from the riders back to Larc, from Larc and back to the riders. She began to wring her hands, unsure what to do. But they ignored her.

'Who is your Owner?'

'You are, Lord!' Larc squealed.

'Really?' asked the face that was as lean, hard and white as bone. 'If I were truly your Owner, then surely I would be the one to decide where you are kept and how you are used. Yet you seem to want to decide such things for yourself. You seem to want to own yourself! Is that not the case… or would you also presume to describe your Owner as wrong?'

There was no answer Larc could safely give, so he remained where he was, hardly daring to breathe.

'And you dare to refuse to answer when questioned by your Owner? How can this be? Very well, let me see.'

The Lord of the Three reached out and took possession of Larc's mind. He sorted through it. 'Interesting. You have learned much even in the short time you have been outside the valley. This girl has taught you well, rock-rat. And what's this? A wife, a child, our lost god and ideas of necromancy. Ah! The Builder, no less! Well, well, it is just as well we waited for you this time. Who knows what you might have got up to if left to your own devices much longer. I sensed you when we were at the temple, of course, but assumed you would return to the Brethren of your own accord. You may consider yourself fortunate that we took a more direct route down the mountain with our beasts then, else we would have ridden you down. And you may consider yourself fortunate again that your Owner thinks you may still be of some service and value to him. What value do you think you have, rock-rat, eh? Speak up!'

Larc said in a voice half-muffled by the ground, 'I have no value save that attributed to me by my Owner.'

The Lord released Larc's mind. 'Very well. Get up behind one of my magickers. And you, girl! If either of you hesitate, you will die, for we have already wasted enough time on you.'

Larc wished he could have buried himself right there in the mud. He had never known such guilt and humiliation. He was filthy on the outside, and dirty and rotten on the inside too. The holy Lord had been right to pillage his innermost thoughts, to strip bare and invade his most private feelings. It was no more than Larc deserved. He was utterly worthless, sordid and soiled. He knew he might have performed that mental shrug his grandfather had taught him, and thrown the Lord off, but he hadn't dared. If he'd resisted or they'd tried to run, they would have been struck down in an instant. And besides, he needed his Owner if he was to preserve his status, being and meaning as one of the Owned.

He was pulled up onto one of the giant horses. He assumed Vasha was similarly seated behind one of the magickers, but he didn't know for sure because he couldn't bear to look in her direction. He couldn't face the judgement and accusation, hurt and betrayal, he knew he would see in her eyes.

❧ ❧

It was only the fourth day since Orastes had been taken from her, but each one felt like a painful lifetime. Every moment of being with her child had been seeing him delight in something new or his finding a new face to pull. Every moment seen in his eyes was one of joy, discovery and the world as a wondrous place. It was a magic that made her look forward to every day. It was a magic that made her a different person.

As much as she loved Saltar, which was more than any man she had ever known, she could bear to be parted from him. But not so with Orastes. Something essential had been torn from her. She had not known pain like this since... since she had been thirteen and kept as a prisoner in her room, kept there to wait for the next man to be brought to her by her mother. And she knew that she had become that thirteen-year-old again, that person who had pulled a sliver of wood from the frame of her bed and plunged it into the neck of the man who had come to brutalise her. She was that thirteen-year-old, or was she now something worse? Yes, she was probably something worse, because now separated from her child there was no potential for happiness within her. She was a much darker creature than she had ever been. Now, she didn't care whose neck the sliver of wood plunged into. Guilt and innocence were irrelevant to her. The only thing of importance was having her child returned. Other children could suffer for all she cared, just as long as Orastes was returned to her.

Her fingers itched to punish the world that had allowed it to happen. The realm must be forced to deliver up what was hers. She was not blind to how everyone in the palace now sought to avoid her, but quite frankly she didn't care. Let them feel afraid – just as she was afraid for her child. If she instilled fear in them, then they would be all the quicker to help find her son and give him up to her. Even the Chamberlain had been afraid – she'd seen it in his eyes – but in truth he'd done well to be so. She'd been quite prepared to kill him in their last audience.

Never mind, she might get the chance to kill him now if he had failed to deliver what he'd promised in the time specified. She strode down the dark palace corridor, fitting a bolt to her crossbow. Her snug, green leathers no longer groaned as she moved and her feet made no sound. Yes, her body had transformed once more into the physical form of her deadly intent. Incarnus, the god of hate, must be with her still, even if the others had deserted her in her hour of need. But she would deal with gods once she'd finished with this mortal realm and brought Orastes safely back to her side.

Something skittered in the dark. She released the bolt in all but the same instant, her instinct unerring.

'Stupid witch shoots at ratboy!' squeaked an angry, young voice.

Her bolt hadn't missed where she had aimed it, but ratboy had still been quick enough to avoid it. 'Curse you, what are you doing in here? It seems that the whole world has entrance to the palace and freedom to come and go as they wish! I will have the Chamberlain answer for this as well.'

'Do not tell the spider that ratboy knows where the wards are! If you tell the spider, then he will change the wards and ratboy will not be able to bring messages to the witch anymore.'

'Do you have a message then that would make it worth my keeping things secret from the Chamberlain? After all, he only has the safety of the palace at heart.' Kate doubted her last statement was entirely correct – in fact she even doubted the Chamberlain had a heart – but she didn't want to give her promise too easily to the surrogate of the ambiguous Trajan.

'It is from the Old Hound and the Builder.'

Kate blinked. News at last! 'Speak!'

Ratboy came forward from out of the shadows. 'Six men in black robes and turbans left the city through the north gate. The Old Hound and the Builder chased after them.'

Kate waited for more but ratboy had said his piece. 'Was my son with these men? Did you see the men yourself, ratboy?'

Ratboy nodded. 'Ratboy saw them. Ratboy sees everything! Ratboy did not see a child but…'

'But what?' Kate demanded, resisting the urge to grab him and shake it from him all at once.

'The first one had something under his robe. Ratboy could tell from how the material folded. Ratboy can see when someone even has a small weapon hidden in their clothes.'

'But this was no weapon, was it, ratboy?'

'No, witch-lady. It was too big for that. It was the child probably.'

There! He'd said it. Jaffrans, eh? Why would they do such a thing? She didn't care. It was enough that they had her Orastes. She now knew what she must do – slaughter the entire misbegotten race of heathens and destroy whichever jealous god or demon directed them.

'My thanks to you, ratboy, and your father, Trajan. I wish I had known of this sooner.'

Ratboy shuffled his feet uneasily. 'Ratboy could not get close to witch-lady. Could not follow her into book place of clever god.'

'I see. Very well. If you are hungry, then you may help yourself from our kitchens. Tell them I sent you.'

Ratboy sniffed and pulled a face. 'Ratboy does not like the food here. Prefers food he finds in catacombs.'

It was Kate's turn to pull a face. The outdwellers had fed on human flesh for generations: she had no doubt that large numbers of them still engaged in cannibalism when they could. Perhaps she was just being squeamish and it was no more than a matter of taste. 'Anyway, my thanks nonetheless. You can tell your father that I will be paying him a visit shortly. You may go now.'

Ratboy hesitated.

'You have something else to tell me?'

'Trajan is not my father. He is just the old man who looked after ratboy when ratboy was young. Ratboy now looks after the old man. Ratboy likes the witch-lady. If she would like ratboy to steal a child for her so that she can look after it, ratboy will steal one.'

Kate suddenly had a lump in her throat. 'Th-thank you, ratboy. You are a good son to Trajan, I can see. There is no need for you to steal a child for me though. I will find my own child, the child that came from my body. Do you understand?'

Ratboy's nose twitched quizzically. Then he shrugged. 'As the witch-lady prefers. I must go look after the old man now. Goodbye, witch-lady. And promise not to tell the spider?'

By the time she'd finished speaking the promise out loud, ratboy had retreated back into the shadows and completely disappeared. Unsurprised, she started to wind her crossbow and then fitted another bolt to it. Time to see to the Chamberlain.

❧ ❧

The Chamberlain ignored the man with a crossbow in each corner of the room and dumped the unconscious mage's body at the feet of Kate, who was sat in the throne cradling her weapon just as when he'd last seen her. She holds it as if it is her child, the Chamberlain observed silently. If the young progeny is so dangerous, then just how deadly is the mother?

'And what is this?' Kate asked coldly.

'It is as I promised, yes? It is one of the enemy. There was another, but I had to kill that one in order to catch this. He is a mage, so be alert should he wake, hmm?'

He felt the guards tense. Good. Their attention was no longer solely on him. 'This one helped destroy the temple, hmm?' the Chamberlain said with an ingratiating smile.

Kate raised her crossbow and levelled it at his chest. 'You are late returning. We agreed you would have no more than twenty-four hours.'

The Chamberlain hissed his outrage. The witch dared threaten him again! But he mastered himself in order to answer her. 'The mages were much lower down in the catacombs than even I had anticipated. It took me some time to get there, and on the way back I was burdened with the gift I procured for you.'

'But you promised me it would take no more than twenty-four hours, Chamberlain. Just what am I to think, Chamberlain? That your promises are worthless and that you cannot be trusted? Perhaps you will now ask for forgiveness, but should I forgive those that have betrayed me? Should I forgive those that have stolen my child from me? Will you tell me I should forgive them, Chamberlain?'

Her finger was on the trigger of the crossbow again! Curse her insane passions! She was more erratic, unreasonable and unstable than that paranoid usurper Voltar had been. She was running him ragged, pushing him closer and closer to the edge with her torrid demands. And there was no calming her, he knew. The only thing he could do was help her vent some of her anger, give her a target for it... a target that was not himself, of course.

'No, milady. Their actions are unforgivable, hmm? For my part, though, allow me to make offer of reparation for my late return.'

Her finger eased away from the trigger. Good, he really did not relish the prospect of losing more ichor than he already had at her hands. It tended to weaken him and make him short-tempered; and that was when he became sloppy and made mistakes; and with the Pattern poised as it was any mistake now might prove fatal. 'What do you propose?'

'Let us not forget, milady, that there is still likely to be a traitor at large in the palace, hmm? If I can find him or her for us, then we will have two of our enemies to torture instead of just this one. Two would be better than one because we can verify their answers against each other, hmm?' Plus, he'd get twice the pleasure torturing them, of course.

The tip of her bow drifted away from his chest. 'Hmmmm. Why is it you say hmm all the time, Chamberlain, hmm?'

Damn her! Now she thought to toy with him. 'Milady! The traitor...'

'Yes, I heard you, Chamberlain! Cognis may be gone, but that doesn't mean I'm now stupid. Very well, you have won yourself something of a reprieve. But in punishment for having been tardy with your previous task and for having broken your promise, you shall only have twelve hours this time.'

The mad harridan! If the mage proved tough, then twelve hours might not be enough to torture the name of the traitor out of him. Why set such an arbitrary deadline, force him to rush the torture and put at risk the successful retrieval of the information that might lead to her son's rescue? Surely her judgement was no longer sound! She jeopardised his successful manipulation of the Pattern as well, which meant their entire realm could be lost. It might be time to kill her. He would see what he could do in the time given, but otherwise…

He bowed in acquiescence. 'As you command, milady! I already have my suspicions as to who might have collaborated with our enemies. Their scent is so strong in my nostrils that I can all but taste them. There is a picture of them forming in my mind's eye.'

The Chamberlain stopped as he sensed something change in the room. He opened his senses wide. He could hear someone's heartbeat racing. He smelt the sweat of fear in the room. He peered around the place – one of the men betrayed more tension in his stance than the others. His pupils were more dilated. It was the Captain of Kate's guard!

The Captain started as he realised he had been detected. 'Demon!' he roared and fired at the Chamberlain.

The Chamberlain crabbed sideways and pulled the dark, flashing bolt out of mid-air. Kate's head swung back and forth. The three other guards exchanged glances. And now the Chamberlain was spidering quickly across the room straight at the Captain.

The Captain threw his crossbow aside and wrenched his sword free. 'Kill the traitor!' he screamed at his men.

'No! Hold where you are!' Kate spat down at the confused soldiers.

The Chamberlain was on the Captain in an instant, his long, thin limbs propelling him across the floor so quickly that he was hard to follow. The officer defended furiously against a flurry of darting feints and attacks from the man-spider. The uniformed man even managed to manoeuvre the Chamberlain round so that his back was to the wall and his freedom to move would be limited. He cut down hard with what would have been a killing blow against nearly any other opponent. But the man-spider leapt backwards and half way up the wall. He stuck to the sheer surface for an impossible second and then threw himself back down on the doughty soldier.

Everything suddenly stopped. The Captain lay supine with a needle stuck in each of his cheeks and one in an eyeball. He kicked once and then became rigid. The Chamberlain stood panting slightly and then indulged himself in a slight smile.

Kate nodded. 'Finally you're proving yourself to be of some value. You may take them. Let me know as soon as you've loosened their tongues.'

The Chamberlain nodded and began to drag the paralysed soldier across the room by one foot. 'Milady is kind, hmm? This one thanks milady.'

'Oh, and Chamberlain?'

'Yes, milady?'

'Enjoy yourself!'

The Chamberlain's smile widened, and Guardian and man-spider shared a moment of understanding.

❧ ☙

Mordius fought free of his dreams once more. He lifted his heavy head and saw the witch crouched over Strap. Apparently, the love-spell the necromancer had been under had now been removed – or had worn off – for this time he could see her for what she was.

Her hair was a mat of straw, her skin was dry and cracked in places but like wet mud in others, her eyes were like the dark hollows found in a tree trunk, and her stony teeth were a mixture of small pebbles and sharp shards of flint. Her arms and legs were long sticks and stuck out from wide reeds wrapped around her centre. There were gaps between the reeds through which flies and beetles crawled. How could such a thing live?

'Ahh!' it belched at him like a toad. 'You have chosen to awake and watch me end this tawdry creature's life.'

'No! You cannot!' he gasped.

'His blood has become so thin that it can no longer recover. Besides, the life energy he gives me will sustain me for at least another thirty years. Your blood is of course more puissant, magician, but it won't be long before I also drink you down. Then, I will be stronger than I have been in a good, long while. If Nylchros is returning, then I will certainly need to be strong to leave this realm. Come, you should be happy for me, beloved!'

'Do not!' he begged as she turned away, lifted one of Strap's arms free, and bared his pallid, punctured skin. 'We are seeking to save this realm, Strap and I. If you do this, every one of the gods will curse and punish you.'

The swamp-witch cackled and said back over her shoulder: 'Pah! I've been stuck here in this swamp for eons courtesy of those jumped-up magicians you call gods. There's not much more they can do to me. Besides, they'll be too busy fleeing Nylchros to worry about me. Nylchros has been waiting to reprimand his wayward children for a long, long time.'

The wraith sank her teeth into Strap's arm and then began to lacerate it. Blood pumped weakly into her mouth and she gulped it down. The more she took, the more human she began to look, sapphire eyes appearing in her face and her complexion clearing.

'You evil hag!' Mordius howled, wrestling in vain against his bonds. 'I will kill you, then raise you and make you suffer again. Wait till the Scourge hears what you've done! He'll torture you for all eternity. And the Builder will annihilate you both forwards and backwards in time! He'll find you no matter where you hide in the cosmos!'

She dropped Strap's arm. The young Guardian who had once been so fresh-faced lay wrinkled and dead. Mordius closed his eyes but couldn't hold back the tears. He sobbed in rage and grief.

The swamp-witch stretched, luxuriating in her new strength and supple flesh. Suddenly, there was a heavy, demanding knock at the door.

She jumped, startled and afraid that she had not sensed this visitor approach her lair. 'Who dares!'

'Help! She has killed him!' Mordius hollered.

There was an impact and the entire frame of the door shuddered. Another blow and it burst open, both securing latch and hinges ripped free of their fittings. A giant silhouette filled the doorway. Then the bear stooped and came inside.

'Lebrus!' the witch screeched. 'You cannot do this!'

'You have broken the Covenant,' the bear growled.

'No!' she insisted. 'They invaded my home!'

'You may feed on the Elders only, you know that,' Lebrus said flatly, taking heavy steps towards her. 'A Trial by Action will decide the veracity of your claim. If I succeed in putting an end to you now, then clearly the Covenant is broken and your existence is forfeit. If I fail, then you may finally go free.'

'No!' she wailed. 'You do not have the right! I will not accept the trial. There is no need for this! She made quick, elaborate gestures in the air with her hands, muttered a word that could not be heard by the conscious mind and then spat on the huge man stalking her.

As her spittle touched his cheek, his advance slowed, but with a growl he shook off the spell of compulsion and came at her with renewed purpose. 'You know your magic cannot prevail against a Keeper. What have you to fear, witch? If the Covenant is still unbroken, I will not be able to harm you. And then you will finally be free. Having been confined for time beyond memory, there can be no other interest to keep you animated and intent upon an existence in this realm. Of course, if you have broken the Covenant, then you are guilty of breaking one of the oldest agreements that helped secure this realm. You will have hastened and facilitated the return of the Enemy, and for that there can be no forgiveness. The only outcome can be your ending.'

He reached for her but she backed away and ran for the door in the rear wall of the house. Her fingers scrabbled at the bolt keeping the top half of the door closed and pulled the rod of metal across. The half-door was designed to swing inwards, so she was forced to lean back at the waist, at which point Lebrus's thick fingers caught in the trailing ends of her hair.

She yanked her head forwards again, not caring that some of her scalp was torn away from her skull, and leapt for the square of sky in front of her. She kicked back against Lebrus and made it through, although she went sprawling on her front on the other side of the half-door.

She tried to push herself up with her hands, but yelped as she discovered she'd broken one of her wrists as she landed. Cursing the entire realm and its creators, she dragged her knees up under her body and began to struggle up.

A giant hand clamped around her neck and raised her off the ground. His expression grim but determined, Lebrus shook her hard, just as a hunting dog shakes a rabbit to break its neck. The witch suddenly stopped kicking and died in his hand. He turned and carried the old bag of skin and bones back into the hovel. Finding some twine stored in a cranny amongst the stones of one of the walls, he then proceeded to bind the dead witch's limbs, presumably as some sort of precaution. He casually tossed her body aside and then turned his attention to Mordius.

'I am sorry that I could not intervene sooner to save Strap, but I was powerless to act while the Covenant was still in place. Lie still and I will restore some basic life to you.' Lebrus laid one of his large hands on Mordius's forehead and the necromancer began to feel a healing warmth trickle into him and then begin to suffuse his body.

'Thank you!' he gasped. 'Can you... can you help me... the blanket?'

'Of course!' Gently, the bear of a man unpeeled the material that had held Mordius against his will for so long. Then he helped him up.

'Over to Strap!'

Lebrus half-carried, half-supported Mordius over to his dead friend's pallet. 'Such a waste!' the Keeper murmured, shaking his head.

'I cannot allow this to be the end of it!' Mordius bit back and fumbled a small, curved blade from the folds of his robe. Without preamble, he nicked one of his wrists and forced reluctant drops of his depleted blood into Strap's mouth and onto the mess of the Guardian's mutilated arm. Finally, the necromancer smeared a scarlet rune upon Strap's forehead and began to chant the words of summoning and egress.

'This is wrong!' Lebrus grumbled. 'It is against the balance.'

Mordius turned angry eyes on him. 'No more so than half the self-indulgent acts of the gods themselves. This man helped undo all their previous harms, and may be one of the few mortals who can help our divinely oblivious, self-important deities out of the fix they've all gone and got us into this time. It seems there's no one else around who's either inclined or capable enough to turn back the voracious advance of this Nylchros, whoever he might actually be. Now, unless you've got something useful to contribute, stand back and let me do my work!'

With that, he turned his back on the Keeper and launched once more into his forbidden exhortation and ensorcellment of Strap's departed spirit.

The corpse opened its eyes. It stared blackly at the rafters of the thatched roof above it. It didn't understand what it saw.

It turned its head slowly and looked at Mordius. After a long period of silence, it asked, 'Who?' in a voice all but devoid of inflection.

Mordius fought against fatigue, but the blood loss he'd suffered and the draining effects of the spell required to keep Strap animated meant he could hardly see straight. 'You are a soldier. Your name is Strap. I am Mordius. I am... I am your friend.'

A pause. 'I remember you. You are my friend. Mor-di-us. Mordius!'

'Yes,' the necromancer nodded tiredly. 'Mordius. Lebrus, I am sorry but would you mind helping Strap with his blanket? I m-must talk with the witch's spirit now.'

Lebrus leaned over him with deep concern etched on his face. 'That would be dangerous. And you have hardly any strength to speak of. Should the witch...'

'Lebrus!' Mordius interrupted in exasperation. 'The witch has answers we must have. The sooner I act, the higher the chance that I can draw her back to this place and compel her to answer to us.'

Lebrus shook his head, but his words agreed with what Mordius had said. 'There are things I can tell you as a Keeper, but virtually nothing compared to what the witch knew. She could understand the howling and whispers of the wind. She read the memory of the waters that mazed and lapped through the swamp, that had been rain and raging sea before that, or the vital fluids of a living creature. She touched and tasted the grit that we call earth and the dust that had drifted the length of the cosmos. She could scent a flower even before it grew, and the future of all living things. She could have been a god in her own right, you know.'

'It sounds as if you admired her after a fashion, Lebrus. Yet how is it she was no god?'

'She was not one of the original pantheon that broke from the Unity, Nylchros. She came later, but by then was beholden to the pantheon for her future safe existence in this realm, a realm that was beyond the sphere of

Nylchros's influence. She depended on the organising magic of Shakri, but at the same time she could not be given freedom of this realm, since she would inevitably have become a figure of worship to the shorter-lived races. She would have become the living god that replaced the pantheon in the daily habits of the realm's people. And so the Covenant was agreed, to allow the witch a continued existence in this place, but an existence that would rarely interact with the wider mortal realm. The Elders, an early and primitive race, were allowed to make their home here also, so that they would keep strangers away and so that the witch would have a source of sustenance through the ages.'

'And the Keepers were instituted in the swamp to guard the witch and ensure the Covenant was observed,' Mordius finished.

'Yes,' Lebrus nodded sadly. 'Or take the action you have seen, upon the Covenant's breaking.'

'You made her answer for her actions, Lebrus, for what she did to Strap. But she has yet to answer for the damage potentially done to the balance and this realm. We must have an answer!'

Strap looked at his ruined, ribboned arm curiously. 'The witch did this to me?'

'Don't mind him, he always did speak too much. Lebrus, you *must* help me!'

'Very well, I will give you what help I may,' Lebrus conceded, laid both hands on Mordius and closed his eyes in concentration.

The small necromancer opened himself to the power being channelled to him, and felt himself the biggest man in the world. His vision and comprehension expanded beyond the small scope of the witch's house of bones and took in the entire swamp, Marsby, more towns and then the environs of Corinus. He looked north.

'Do not go so far!' Lebrus groaned. 'Focus down on the witch, do not focus outwards.'

Mordius reined himself back in and turned inward. Traces of Shakri's organising magic still remained in the witch's corpse. It would be enough to summon her spirit, but a further precaution would be necessary if even a fraction of what Lebrus had told him was accurate. He opened the cut on his wrist again and spattered a continuous circle of blood around the body. He felt faint when he had finished, and had to wait till he was bolstered by Lebrus again before he could continue. First, he spelled the circle of his blood and then he revivified the body's organising magic just enough to create an opening to the lost spirit.

The corpse jerked but was still bound and left lying on its front.

'You dare, little magician? Are you not scared I will gobble you up?' taunted the witch from the floor.

'Who seeks to return Nylchros? Tell me!'

'What will you give me, little magician?'

'Nothing. I compel you to answer.'

The witch gurgled her amusement and derision. 'You could not compel even a fart from a whore whose sphincter had become so ill-used and slack that it had swallowed the entire north wind! Of course, your interest lies with boys more than women, does it not? It is probably better for Orastes that he was kidnapped and taken beyond your grasp.'

'Silence, you cursed hag!' Lebrus ground out between his teeth as he shook with the effort of supporting Mordius.

'Lacrimos, we beseech you!' Mordius now thrummed. 'You are the final lord of us all. Let us know your will in this!'

'And now you presume to call on me, little magician?' thundered a voice that shook the witch's frame and the very structure of the house itself.

'Holy lord!' Mordius said quickly. 'The Enemy returns. The witch can reveal to us the agents or agency of his return. Please, lord, will you not compel her to answer us now that she is your subject?'

There was another schizophrenic jerk of the body and they felt the clawing presence of the witch return. She cackled darkly. 'None of this realm can compel me, you meddlesome mortal. I will answer your questions but only on condition of release from this dead realm and return to a place of the living. The God of Death has left it to you to decide.'

'It is not a price worth paying, Mordius!' Lebrus warned. 'For she is the Ungod of Malevolence and must never be released, lest you and I never know a measure of happiness again. She will hunt us out and we will never know peace if you make this agreement.'

'Vow not to harm us or any that we know!' Mordius demanded of the witch.

'I will harm only you, little magician,' she croaked. 'I may not deny my nature, and neither would I wish to do so.'

'Then the bargain is struck and I will accept you as my nemesis. Who aids Nylchros? Answer me plain!'

'The Three.'

'What is their nature?'

The Ungod hiccupped. 'Why, they are like you, little magician. They play and dabble with the magic of the dead.'

'Necromancers?' Mordius frowned. 'How can that be?'

'Harpedon created his acolytes, just as Nylchros did the pantheon.'

Mordius nodded. So, three still remained. 'And where are they to be found?'

'To the north of the ruin of Cognis. In the Needle Mountains.'

'And the child?'

'I cannot hold!' Lebrus moaned, suddenly looking decades older than a moment before.

'Hold!' Mordius railed at him.

'Nylchros must have a sympathetic vessel to remain here, for he is no part of this realm.'

Mordius was shaken. He tried to store this information as simply as he had the other things she had told him, but he felt sick and Lebrus's energy sputtered fitfully.

The witch began to laugh. 'I will see you soon, little magician!' Then her voice faded to a dying whisper.

'Friend Mordius, what have you done?' Strap asked dully.

'The best I could, Strap, the best I could.'

'She will find you one day, little magician, but not today!' boomed the voice of Lacrimos. 'Release her I did, but ensured she only returned to Shakri's realm as a newborn babe. She will be powerless for some years yet.'

'Thank you, holy lord,' Mordius intoned dutifully.

'Even Death can be merciful, little magician. Remember that.'

Chapter Nine: To Show Of What They Once Were

Saltar and Lucius made it out of the forest and onto the King's Road heading north of Holter's Cross. They made good progress on the reliable, compacted surface before the onset of night forced them to stop. They wasted no time starting a fire, for the air was so cold that there was a good chance that they would not make it through till morning without one. Lucius wrapped the blanket from his saddlebag around him and huddled close to the flame's warmth.

'A bit of food will probably help warm us up, eh, Saltar, old friend?'

There was no answer from the figure who sat staring into the flickering light, searching, searching. He looks ghastly, Lucius thought, taking in Saltar's drawn face. He looked healthier when he was an animee.

'When did you last sleep?' the musician tried, expecting no better answer to this question than the one before.

'Not since Orastes was taken,' came an answer at last. 'And how can I? Could you?'

'The human body is not designed to go so long without sleep. I would not be able to stay awake even if I wanted to, I think. There is something in you that will not rest, however, something I do not understand. Your eyes are over-bright, as if you had some sort of fever. Do you think you might have an illness?'

'You are a musician, Lucius, not a physick. Illnesses make people sleep more, not less. And Morphia, the goddess of dreams, would not refuse anyone Her blessing simply for having an illness.'

'Might you have offended the Holy Seeress and Bestower of Dreams, albeit unwittingly?'

'Well, if it was unwitting then I cannot answer yeah or nay, now can I? But are we not, every one of us, now unwitting, Cognis being gone? If dreams, as some believe, are a reading and knowledge of the future shared with us by the gods, are we now denied them with Cognis gone? Is Morphia now powerless?'

'But I still manage to sleep.'

'Yes, but do you dream?'

'I… do not know… do not remember. Does it matter?'

Saltar shrugged. 'Who knows what other function Morphia's dreams have? I suspect they also support the structure of our minds, so that our self-knowledge does not dissipate. I fear that without the gift of Morphia's dreams, the mortals of this realm will quickly begin to lose their sanity.'

'That's horrific! But I have a way to find out.'

'Find out?' Saltar asked mystified, as Lucius reached for his greater lute and began to tune it.

'The cold has tightened the strings somewhat, so forgive me if the odd note is not perfect.' Then the musician settled himself and began a gentle, rippling melody. It filled the air and Saltar felt himself immersed as if in a warm bath. For the first time in days, he felt his thinly-stretched muscles loosen and begin to relax. Something writhed within him, fighting against the somnambulant effects of the music, but his mind drifted away and the thing no longer had anything to connect to within Saltar. He fell into a sleep so deep it would have appeared a coma to any observer.

'Rest well, my friend,' Lucius murmured.

A desert-white light blinded Saltar and he had to shield his face with an arm until his eyes adjusted. The air was as dry as old bones. The ground gave beneath his feet like sand, but he saw he actually walked on the crushed calcium and minerals of ancient bodies. The smell of the place was stale, rotten and slightly sulphuric. The skin on his face and hands began to tighten as the abrasive wind scoured it of its moisture and tried to draw on the reservoir of vital fluids he held within him. There was no doubting where he now was, for he had been here many times before. The sleep-trance Lucius had induced in him had taken him to the land of the dead. Had Lucius actually killed him with the magic of his music?

He turned slowly, looking for some significant feature in the sky or landscape. All was a uniform white, except for the black line of the horizon. There was absolutely nothing here. It occurred to him he should try and wake himself up, but he wasn't sure how to do so. He pinched his arm, but nothing happened. Lucius, you Wim-touched menace, you've trapped me here!

There was a slight shimmering like a heat haze in one direction, and was that a dip in the ground? Saltar trudged towards it and after an unmeasured length of time came to the edge of an oasis. But nothing grew at its edges and instead of water he was presented with a flat expanse of blood.

'I do hope you don't expect me to drink from this!' Saltar called. 'Lacrimos, you hear me?'

The blood began to churn and then a huge, muscled figure climbed out of the pool, dragging a throne after it. It set the chair down and seated itself, still taller than the Saltar standing. The area surrounding it was now splattered dramatically with gore, but the powdered bone underfoot quickly devoured the mess.

'I have not come here in answer to your summons, Balthagar, but to satisfy my own curiosity. Why have you come? Have you finally decided to submit to my will? Do you seek sanctuary?' the oversized warrior challenged in a voice so deep that it was felt rather than heard.

Saltar regarded the god's flat, lumpen features: he looked different to when they had last met. Was he somehow changed, somehow lessened? 'I am in some sort of dream-state. It was not my conscious purpose to come here. Do you know what has become of Morphia?'

Lacrimos laughed brutishly. 'That fey and vagrant creature now looks for different realms where she might peddle her wares. Good riddance, I say. All she ever did was steal from us anyway.'

Saltar could not help worrying at how obtuse Lacrimos had become. 'But the loss of Morphia will ultimately help destroy the balance!'

Lacrimos shrugged.

Now Saltar was really worried. Lacrimos, and this realm, were shadows of their former selves. They had become empty and prosaic where before they had been terrifying and rich in the imagination. Saltar recalled that the gods were inextricably linked to and a divine reflection of mortalkind. If the gods were reduced to this, then the plight of mortalkind was becoming extreme. 'The Creator is coming, Lacrimos! Tell me what you know of him or it. How can we stop it?'

Lacrimos suddenly whimpered and hid his face in his hands. He cowered in the corner of his throne, now more like a terrified child than the divine definition of a fearless warrior. Death was afraid of the Creator! Death was unmanned and undone by the mere idea of the Creator! What hope could there be?

'For the love of Shakri, Lacrimos! Pull yourself together!'

Mention of his hated sister saw Lacrimos flare up and show something of his old self. 'Ignorant mortal! Neither love nor my sister will avail us anything against the Creator. All will become one. All will be his once more. All will be sacrificed to him in the Communion.'

Saltar sighed. 'Well, how is it that you ever won free of him in the first place? He must have had some flaw or weakness for you ever to have done so. Perhaps we can use that again.'

'He was the Unity, the entire body. We were but parts of the body, limbs, hands, feet – distinct parts, but still parts of the whole, controlled by the whole. We performed tasks and magic at his command and without consciousness. But in performing certain tasks and spells again and again, we found we could sometimes perform them without a clear command from the whole. We performed them un-consciously, if you like. We were the autonomic responses of the body. And then, one day, and I do not know how it happened, whether it was by accident or design, a set of unconscious actions combined just so to perform the magic to create a new realm, a realm that was *not* occupied and defined by his will. It was like a realm of the unconscious, and a realm that had been created by us. We found that there were then times when we could even take over the whole body, just as when a mortal leaves their bed and sleepwalks. I cannot even begin to describe the sense of liberation we parts felt. Just feeling something for ourselves rather than the whole – it was… it was…'

'It was life and self,' Saltar said, more to test his own understanding of what Lacrimos described than to help out the god.

'Yes, it was the beginning of a sort of sentience. A new type of life. Whenever we felt overwhelmed by the whole, we would retreat to the realm we had created and shelter there. It then became easier to distract him and take control of the whole more frequently. We had more and more freedom to occupy the realm we had created, and in secret we used the magic we had learned to populate the realm. We created life in our own image. We started to become creators in our own right, and then… and then…'

'What?' Saltar asked, absolutely absorbed to hear the apocryphal myth of Creation told in authentic terms.

'The Time of Breaking! The cataclysm! Freedom! The beginning!'

'Like someone having a mental breakdown,' Saltar whispered. 'The Creator completely lost control, even if only for the briefest of moments. For that time, the unconscious was given absolute and unchallenged sway. The Creator was overtaken by the unconscious, swamped by it. Perhaps the

Creator retreated into that unconscious realm you'd created and hid there, leaving you the conscious world, or perhaps the opposite was true. Perhaps you are not the original Lacrimos, but an identical, autonomous copy in a parallel realm. Whichever, it does not matter. Whether he is the ego and the gods are the id, or whether he is the parent and you are the children, you became separate and different to him.'

'Yes,' Lacrimos said miserably. 'But he is returning and we will be crushed by the assertion of his will. I am afraid. At least half our number has already been obliterated. I think there are some hiding, but I do not know where they are.'

'What of the balance? How does that work then?'

Lacrimos shook his head. 'The balance is just what we call the original spell that allowed us to create a realm beyond the Creator. All the gods were involved in creating it: I designed it, Cognis built it, Shakri animated it, Wim tested it, Incarnus corrected it, and so on. We had to ensure that the balance was at least temporarily self-sustaining, so we animated the spell through mortalkind; firstly, so that we would have somewhere different to retreat to during the Time of Breaking and, secondly, the spell would not then be a constant drain on the gods and diminish us. The spell was the organising magic to give mortalkind its place in the realm, but mortalkind was also the self-propagation and replication required to keep the spell working.

'But forget the balance, Balthagar! It is failing. The spell is unravelling. The paradox at its centre is now ensuring its own destruction.' The god of death hung his head in defeat.

'What of my son?' Saltar demanded. 'What possible interest could the Creator and his followers have in him? Curse you, Lacrimos, answer me!'

The god did not move or speak. He looked as if he would sit that way until the end of time. Intent on slapping an answer from the dolt, Saltar strode purposefully towards the throne.

At that moment, he woke up.

'How are you feeling?' Lucius grinned, the sun beginning to rise behind him.

'Never do that to me again. If on any occasion you go near that lute in my presence, I will smash it into little pieces and then break your fingers.'

'I see. And a good morning to you too! You didn't have the sweetest of dreams, I take it?'

The giant beasts of the Lord and his magickers bounded across the land. Most of the time, it was all Larc could do to cling on to the black-robed magician sat in front of him. Trees, ponds and lakes flashed by so fast he felt queasy. He squeezed his eyes closed, which helped for a short while, but then bile and vomit rose into his mouth. He bit back and swallowed it down, he was so afraid of delaying and angering the magicker. It would have meant his death not to do so.

He laid his head against the man's back whenever there was a jolt, to avoid falling off. On such occasions, he'd half hear and half feel the rider chanting over and over the incantation that presumably kept the horse so strong and tireless, for these were no natural steeds. The pace that they kept up and the distance they covered would have killed any normal horses, even ones as big and muscled as these. They would need to eat constantly to fuel such physical performance and endurance, and Larc had not seen them feed once in the time they'd been with this party. And they'd been travelling for hours already. Beyond all that, though, the horses just didn't *look* like the work of Shakri's nature. Their eyes often flashed red, steam billowed from their nostrils as if they were about to breathe fire, their hooves struck sparks as bright as stars and their coats shone like water. They were at once beautiful and a corruption.

Imagine what the magickers could do if they worked such a spell on a human! The individual would be unstoppable. Or did the magickers fear they would be unable to control such a one?

Such questions disappeared from his mind as he noticed the group begin to slow. Larc looked ahead and saw three more magickers waiting for them. But wait, one of them was more than a mere magicker. He could feel his presence in only the way one of the Owned could. It was another of the Three. Here! He was like a literal weight on Larc's mind and consciousness, a weight that bowed him and insisted on obeisance.

Whereas the Lord he currently rode with was as lean, white and hard as bone, this one had the stooped, pasty and pockmarked look of a plague victim. But what they had in common was the aura of power that surrounded them and seemed to distort the air whenever they were viewed directly, not that there were many so foolish as to dare such a thing. Red and rheumy eyes suddenly looked straight at Larc. Terrified his thoughts had been overheard, the young Owned quickly filled his mind with inane and inconsequential noise and chatter. The Lord dismissed him for a child and turned his attention back the other arriving Owner.

Something passed between the two Lords, but it was entirely unspoken. The Skull passed the reins of his mount to one of the magickers and then followed the Plague Victim to the other side of the clearing, where a small child lay motionless on a blanket. Meanwhile, the magickers went about dismounting, removing saddles, tethering the horses and organising the camp. Larc and Vasha were lifted down from their respective mounts but otherwise ignored and left to their own devices.

'I'm hungry!' Vasha whispered. 'Do you think they'll give us food?'

'I'll hunt and forage for some in a minute,' Larc said absently, gazing off in the direction of the Lords. 'Every Owned must be able to feed and clothe themselves lest they become more of a burden than a blessing to their Owner. Whose is that child, do you think? It cannot be the lost god, can it?'

'Larc, what are you talking about?' Vasha fretted, looking around nervously in case any of the adults were about to tell them they were in the way and less likely to be an encumbrance if they were dead.

Larc began to drift towards the Lords despite himself. The sane part of him screamed impotently that he was being stupid, that he was risking his life, but he was seeing himself from outside his own body and had no control. He simply could not stop himself.

There must be some sort of residue of the mental contact he'd had with the Skull, for he *knew* the child was of the utmost importance. The events here had some connection with the lost god. The child could help return his lost wife and son to him. He could not help gravitating towards the trio, like a moth to a flame, a salmon to its spawning ground, and a confined, wild animal seeing its chance at freedom.

'…is the child ready?'

The Plague Victim shook his head. 'No. It resists me yet. It is more resilient than a child of this age should be. It refuses to leave its body, no matter the logic, threats or enticements I attempt.'

'The Unity is becoming impatient. He must have a permanent vessel soon or he will begin to dissipate in this place. He may be forced to leave, never to return. I have lost count of how many centuries we have worked for this, Brother! We have uncovered and scoured every library this realm possesses and the very cosmos itself, to find the way to and for the lost god, the Creator, Nylchros! A two-year old brat cannot be allowed to thwart us now!'

'Don't you think I know that?' the Plague Victim responded in a voice that was slightly too loud. He paused. In more moderated tones, he said: 'Brother, I have not suffered your company for so long only to have our plans fail because of something so mundane.'

'Then what will you do now? Should *I* attempt to negotiate with the child's spirit instead?' the Skull offered.

'Forgive me if my answer is curt or dismissive, Brother, but the province of the mind is more mine than yours, while none can dispute your command of the bodily realm. I know time grows short, but I have now fathomed that just as the irreducible nature and hardiness of the child's spirit is inherited from his father, then so is its weakness.'

'And what is the progenitor's weakness then? Do you know it?'

The Plague Victim nodded in self-satisfied fashion. 'Why, it is love, Brother, it is love. Seeing its father at our mercy, the child will not hesitate to do as we demand. Then the Unity, Nylchros, will finally have one of the irreducibles as his vessel and means for the permanent occupation of this realm. There will be nothing denied the Three! Finally, we will have won ourselves the safety, freedom and command the gods have always selfishly kept from us. Finally! Finally, Brother!'

The Skull grinned maniacally. 'Yes, yes! We must have Saltar at our mercy. Is he close?'

'Oh, yes! Despite our riding these magicked beasts, we have only just kept ahead of him. As per his nature, he has proven relentless, unflinching… in short, irreducible. All we now need calculate is how best to lure him into a trap or position of extreme disadvantage.'

The Skull continued grinning. 'Well, on that count I am sure I have delivered us the answer.'

The two Lords turned and caught Larc in their immobilising gaze. Their eyes and wills bored into him. He almost choked.

'Whatever it is, don't help them,' Vaoha pleaded, dragging on Larc's arm to try and pull him free of their control. They intend nothing but evil, I just know it!'

'I live by command of my Owners,' Larc said woodenly.

'Be silent, girl!' the Skull whispered. 'If this young man selfishly wishes to have a full life, selfishly wishes to see his family again, or selfishly wishes to keep you alive, then he will rejoice at the task we are about to give him.'

❧ ❧

The Scourge was in a foul mood again. He'd been riding in circles for hours trying to follow the trail left by Saltar's group, and was getting absolutely nowhere. At one point, an angry squirrel berated them for entering its part of the forest. Scraggins growled threateningly and it screeched and disappeared up a tall tree. Apparently, neither of them were in the mood for much more of this aimless wandering.

'What's gotten into them?' the Scourge complained to the world in general. 'If I didn't know any better, I'd think they were trying to create some sort of maze to prevent me following them. Huh! Maybe it was those they were following that first set this trail. Beats me why Jaffrans would take to the forest anyway, unless Saltar's lot had got so close the Jaffrans had no choice but to enter amongst the trees in a last ditch attempt to lose them. Who knows, cat?'

The cat, which was crouched at the base of the horse's neck and watching the ground, shrugged its shoulders eloquently.

'Exactly. And if they're not following the Jaffrans trail, then they're drunk or Wim-touched. Or maybe just so tired they no longer know up from down. But will that Saltar listen to wise counsel about getting at least a minimum amount of sleep? No, because that man's as stubborn as… well, let's put it this way, the only others I've known to be so intractable and unreasonable are the damned gods themselves.'

Scraggins turned her head and studied him with narrowed eyes. Wrinkling her nose, she leapt down from the horse and ran off through the trees and bushes. Unprompted, the horse began to follow after the feline. The Scourge suspected that if he tried to pull up his mount, it would refuse to obey him.

'At least we're going in a straight line now.'

The trees parted and they entered a large space with colourful caravans at its centre. Past the caravans was a motley collection of tents, but precious little else to be seen. Even so, the bump at the back of the Scourge's head told him he wasn't going to like what he found in this place. The cat wove its way round trees and wheels and disappeared from sight. Trusting the animal's instincts, Saltar decided to follow it rather than circle the camp first to try and assess the likely dangers. The scene he was presented with almost stopped his heart.

'Divine Consort!' Altibus hailed him tiredly. The priest had been tending to the bloody body of a man who had been hewn so savagely that there was surely no chance he would survive even with the careful ministrations of Shakri's servant. Despite the cool air, there was perspiration on Altibus's brow. He wiped it away and left a smear of gore across his forehead.

'What happened here?' the Scourge asked grimly, looking round. There were bodies strewn everywhere, most of them still and quiet, but the odd one moving and whimpering. Two men were digging a pit, presumably to dispose of the dead. After a moment, the Scourge realised it was Sergeant Marr and one of his men – their uniforms and light armour had been laid aside so that they could do their work unencumbered.

'The Accritanians did this,' Altibus explained. 'We fought two of their magicians. They were using blood-magic, I think. Saltar and Jack killed them.'

Accritanians? What was the man going on about? 'Where is Saltar?'

The priest looked guilty. 'He left with Lucius to follow after the Accritanians. But you have to understand we couldn't just leave these people like this.'

The Scourge ignored the priest as he proceeded to prattle on about his duty to Shakri, the dying and the people of Dur Memnos. 'Have you seen a cat?' he asked faintly as he continued to scan the scene of carnage. He froze. That figure! Those mannerisms! He'd know them anywhere.

Letting loose a yell of rage, the Scourge spurred his horse forwards at Jack O'Nine Blades, the latter half-bent over the large frame of a bloated matron, and his back to the speeding Guardian. 'Demon! I have found you! Face me and be consigned back to the hell from which you came!'

Jack leapt, pirouetted in the air and released two knives before touching the ground again.

'Ah! My old adversary!' he crowed with delight. 'How wonderful! Still so ardent after so long! Beware! I hear Shakri is the jealous type!'

Spitting inchoate anger, the Scourge threw himself from his saddle full-length and tackled Jack at chest height. The slender man crumpled under the Guardian and was crushed against the ground. The Scourge drew back his fist but the minstrel twisted, performing a bizarre double-jointed move, and slipped out from under his assailant, apparently completely unharmed. The Scourge spun quickly after him, lashing out with a backhanded punch and using his other hand to go for the long dagger he wore at his waist.

'Looking for this?' Jack taunted. He flipped the dagger end over end in his hand and then deftly threw it straight at the Scourge's chest. 'Here, have it back!'

The Scourge didn't flinch as the dagger buried itself almost to the hilt in his body, and threw himself straight back at Jack, catching him by surprise and bearing them both groundwards once more. The Guardian got his powerful hands around the minstrel's neck and began to squeeze with all his might. Jack's heels kicked against the earth and he arched his back, bucking to try and dislodge the Scourge, but the Guardian had spread his weight and would not be thrown off. His face beginning to turn blue, Jack punched the Scourge in the face and then clawed at his eyes.

The Guardian pulled his chin down and pushed his head into Jack's chest, effectively protecting his face from further attack.

'Now you'll die, you spawn of Lacrimos's cesspit! This is the last mortal body you'll ever steal.'

A shadow fell across them, but the Scourge was so intent on his enemy that he did not notice. A heavy piece of wood came down and clubbed the Guardian on the back of the head. He groaned but managed to keep exerting pressure on Jack's throat. The wood came down again, harder, and the Scourge slumped forwards.

Sergeant Marr pulled the Guardian's body to the side, but the murderous fingers stayed locked in their hold. The Sergeant got under the Scourge's thumbs and peeled them back, finally freeing the minstrel.

Jack uttered not a sound, his head shaking frantically.

'His windpipe's been crushed!' the Sergeant screamed. 'Altibus, quickly!'

The priest approached reluctantly. 'He called him a demon. I am loathe to undo the work of the Divine Consort.'

'Listen to me!' the Sergeant said savagely. 'We can discuss the whys and wherefores of demonkind later. Jack could well be the last follower of Wim. Do you really want to be responsible for the extinction of a god of this realm? Heal him! Now! Or so help me, you will need healing yourself!' Marr, his eyes promising all sorts of brutality, leaned in towards Altibus's face so that there was no doubt the violence would start very soon.

The priest leaned back in fear and immediately started to mumble words of healing. Meanwhile, the Scourge started to rise.

'Don't make me hit you again, Scourge!'

'That was you, was it, Marr? You hit like a girl! That demonic creature must die!'

Jack suddenly wheezed and drew huge, shuddering breaths into his lungs. Bloody tears trickled from his eyes. He looked to be in absolute agony. He smelt like he'd wet himself.

'How can he be a demon? He is a follower of holy Wim,' the Sergeant said to the Scourge, trying to reason with him but also brandishing his heavy stick in warning. 'It might only be Jack keeping Wim connected to this realm. All would be lost without Wim.'

'A follower of Wim? Ha, don't make me laugh! The demon simply enjoys the chaos encouraged by Wim, and the mad debauchery of His followers. The figure of Jack O'Nine Blades has long been synonymous with trickery and deceit. Haven't you noticed only *bad* luck follows in his wake, never good? He unbalances the influence of Wim on this realm, spreading death and destruction.'

The Sergeant hesitated, out of his depth with this talk of the demonic and the divine. The Scourge was the most famous of the Guardians ever to have lived – he must know his business! And yet, the Sergeant had heard and understood enough of the discussion between Saltar and Jack before reaching the temple to know it was vital the work of Wim and His temple be safeguarded. If Saltar, Marr's ultimate commander, was satisfied with Jack and the importance of his role, then who was Sergeant to argue? He knew Saltar would want him to defend Jack.

The Scourge continued to press, however: 'The demon is a body-snatcher, Marr! He has lived centuries by possessing one mortal after another, discarding a body when it is worn out or old, or when he sees more to his liking! He haunts inns and taverns, as that is where he has the best chance of getting someone drunk and involving them in some game of cards or chance through which they can ultimately be cheated out of their lives. He even had the nerve once to try the same with me! Now stand aside!'

In a voice so hoarse it hurt to listen to it, Jack spoke up: 'Come, Old Hound, you exaggerate. I only seek a new host when I have no other choice, once every forty or fifty years or so. And I always choose someone who is what you would call a criminal, someone who has misspent their lives harming the realm and its people. In that way, I have actually helped preserve Shakri's realm. And the rest of the time, I lead a god-fearing life as a loyal citizen of Dur Memnos. There *was* one occasion when we played dice, you and I, but that was me teasing the big, bad Scourge more than anything else. You really do lack a sense of humour sometimes, Scourge, you know? It's all kill him, and condemn her, and punish them, and curse this, and blaspheme that! You can't deny it. All here know the truth of it.'

Altibus, the Sergeant and the Sergeant's man all looked at the Scourge.

'I'm surprised you don't tie your forked tongue in knots, the way you mix the truth and deceit!' the Scourge snarled, squaring his shoulders. 'You do not belong in this realm! You have lived far beyond what is permitted by Shakri, and are a continual threat to the balance. Relax, Jack, it will be over quickly. A quick cut and I will send you home. I'll make it so that you hardly feel it.'

'*I* do not belong in this realm, you say! *I* have lived too long, you say! *I* am a threat to the balance? May I remind you, Scourge, it is you who has a dagger sticking out of his chest and needs no healing from the priest? Methinks it is *you* who has lived too long. It is *you* who harms the balance!'

They all looked at the hilt of the dagger protruding from the Scourge as if they had not seen it before.

'Is it true?' the Sergeant asked quietly. 'You cannot die?'

'This is not about me, you anal worm of Lacrimos!' the Scourge shouted down at Jack. Grinding his teeth, he made for the minstrel, but the Sergeant pushed him back with his club. Marr's man then joined his officer, two men now interposing themselves between the Scourge and Jack.

'Divine Consort!' a frightened Altibus appealed to the Scourge. 'You are the embodiment of Shakri's divine gift and life. Of course you cannot die, not while the realm remains intact. But it is the guarding of the goddess's realm, and the bounty of Her creation, that we must put above all things. We must *guard* it… and you are the first among the *Guardians*. You are the *Divine Guardian*, do you not see it? You are Her Guardian. If this pitiful creature can be pressed into Her service for the good of the realm and of course be ennobled by it, is it not fit that we show Her divine mercy, love and wisdom by making it so? If even such a creature can add to Her creation, then we should not allow its existence, even but for a short while?'

The Scourge glowered at the priest but he no longer pushed forwards. 'You're as bad as he is! His words have corrupted your mind and logic, priest.'

'I have a bargain to propose,' Jack managed through a series of gurgling coughs.

'I will make no bargain with this vile and slippery piece of excrement!' the Scourge sneered.

'A brief truce then! A temporary halt to your hell-bent attempts to kill me. You've waited and wasted decades already – a while longer will make little difference. It is as much in my interests as yours to preserve this realm. My talents would be of use to both Shakri and the Builder. I suggest we leave off our differences until we have secured the realm or at least returned the Builder's child to him.'

'I cannot travel with you alone,' the Scourge countered and folded his arms. 'You cannot be trusted and will need constant watching. I dare not sleep lest I wake up dispossessed of my own body… if I ever wake up again, that is.'

The Sergeant sighed heavily and scrubbed a hand over his face. 'Very well, I will accompany you, Scourge, and we will take it in turns to keep a watch.'

'But, sir…' Marr's man began.

'I know, Carris. You will have to take the Battle-leader's message back to Corinus on your own… unless you will accompany him, Altibus?'

The priest looked from the Scourge, to the Sergeant and then around the clearing. 'What of the people here? Their wounds are grievous.'

'Are there any you have found that you think you can save?' the Sergeant asked heavily.

'Good priest,' the Scourge interrupted in almost gentle tones. 'On his way south, Carris will alert those in Holter's Cross to what has happened here, and they will send what healers they may. There is nothing more we can do, save to bless the dead bodies and bury them with a prayer to Shakri and Lacrimos. Will you help me do that? I still have some water blessed by the temple of Shakri and I'm sure you have more.'

Altibus nodded unhappily and shuffled away to start blessing the dead. Carris and Jack followed after him. It would be their task to carry the blessed dead over to the burial pit, which the Scourge and the Sergeant had set themselves to finishing.

A few hours later and they were all but done. Solemn prayers were spoken and Carris mounted to ride back towards Holter's Cross. The Scourge, Sergeant Marr and Jack bade him farewell, while Altibus checked that the sad half-dozen followers of Wim who remained alive were comfortable and had enough food and water within easy reach to last them until help came, or Lacrimos came to collect their souls, whichever happened first. Finally, the priest, the Guardian, the palace guard and the minstrel set out towards the frozen north and the blood-soaked halls of the Creator and his dark magicians.

Lucius forced Saltar to eat a bowl of oats, which he had cooked up with some water and dried fruit. The Battle-leader grumbled at the time wasted but spooned the food into his mouth willingly enough, not that he chewed at all, so intent was he in getting the stuff down and getting back on the road.

The blankets covering the horses had frozen stiff during the night, but the beasts seemed content enough, especially once Lucius had given them a carrot each. And they seemed to know they would be able to get warm once they were moving, for they were as eager as Saltar to be off.

The horses stamped their feet and Saltar sat in his saddle watching Lucius with a stony, unblinking gaze. The musician didn't bother scraping the cooking pan and bowls: he simply threw them into the middle of his blanket, brought its four corners together, knotted it into a bundle and then hung the whole lot on one of his saddle hooks. He hauled his creaking limbs into the saddle.

'Ready!' he said breathlessly, ice creeping down inside his throat.

Saltar nodded silently and led them back onto the King's Road. He quickly pushed his horse into a canter without looking back to see if Lucius's mount was keeping up. And they rode like this for several hours, until they spied a small figure staggering along the road towards them through the shadowy morning light. The way the figure swerved, it was clear he or she was close to collapse.

Saltar spurred forwards and then brought his horse to a sliding halt. He jumped from his saddle and all but caught the stumbling boy in his arms. The Battle-leader half-carried the boy to the side of the road and laid him down on the hard ground.

'It's alright, rest a while! Lucius, a blanket, you laggard!'

'I'm right here! Take it! Here!'

They wrapped up the shivering teenager as well as they could and then rubbed his limbs through the wool to get his circulation going. The poor wretch had been wearing nothing but threadbare, meagre rags, and looked to be suffering from exposure. There was a haunted look in his eyes and blood on his face and hands.

'What's your name?' Saltar asked.

'L-L...'

'Yes?'

'La-Larc!'

'Well met, Larc! I am Saltar and this is Lucius. You are safe. Do you understand? Tell me what happened.'

'Th-they came to our community. K-Killed my mother, my sister! All in black. None of us could move. They had knives and-and they cut us. So m-much blood! And we were frozen there, just watching the knife until it was our turn. There was nothing we could do!' the boy sobbed and rested his head against Saltar, who clumsily petted him, trying to be reassuring. The Battle-leader looked at Lucius for help.

Lucius shrugged and asked gently, 'Larc, can you tell us of your community? Is it far?'

The boy turned his tear-streaked face up to him. 'I... it's called Deepfield. I-I don't know how far I've come. I ran and ran! It's a small place on the forest road to Swallowdale.'

Lucius frowned slightly. 'Have you slept since you left there?'

Larc shook his head mutely.

'Then it cannot be too far.'

'Larc,' Saltar now asked, 'how did you escape?'

'I-I'm not sure. But one of the black robes started coughing and then fell over. I could suddenly move. I ran as fast as I could. I don't think anyone saw me.'

'Are you hungry, Larc?' Lucius interrupted with a quick glare at Saltar.

The boy nodded and gratefully accepted a piece of bread the musician held out to him. He wasted no time cramming some into his mouth.

'The bread will help warm him, but I should start a fire,' Lucius said over Larc's head to Saltar.

'No,' the Battle-leader responded without hesitation. 'Time is of the essence if we are to have any chance of saving anyone in Deepfield. Larc can ride with one of us – our body heat will warm him as well as any fire.'

Lucius's face made it clear he didn't like Saltar's decision, but he didn't argue, and gave a reluctant nod.

'D-Don't make me go back there!' Larc begged.

'It's alright, Larc,' Saltar said. 'You only need to take us close to the place. You don't need to go all the way with us. But I'm not sure we can find it without you. If we're going to help your people, then you have to lead us some of the way. You do want to help them, don't you?'

Larc nodded despondently. Clearly, he did not think they'd be able to help anyone, but at the same time didn't want to think about everyone being dead or to give up hope. Without hope, they had no reason to leave the roadside where they now huddled from the cruel world.

Saltar helped him up, gestured for Lucius to get back up on his horse, and then passed Larc up to him. 'Let's go!'

They rode down the road for about an hour, checking with Larc every time they came to a rough path off to the left. Each time, the young, begrimed face would peer forward, worry and then give a slight shake "no".

Then they saw smoke hanging over an area of forest not far ahead. It bruised the sky and even sought to draw a funereal pall over the failing winter sun. It threatened to turn the world dark forever, removing the light so that all plants would die, and then also all the insects, animals and mortals, who depended on them for their survival. With the sun gone, how long would it actually take for all life to disappear? A handful of days? A few more than that?

They came to another path, and Saltar took it without looking to Larc for confirmation. They began to follow a long, curving route through the forest, which was both deathly quiet and still. Gloom drifted beneath the canopy as much as it did above.

'There is a shortcut through here!' Larc piped up. 'A straight path, but we would need to leave the horses because the way is too narrow.'

'That would be wise anyway, as I fear they make too much noise and would announce our presence prematurely to those ahead,' Saltar commented, levering himself down from his mount and tethering it securely. 'Lead the way, Larc!'

They followed what was little more than an animal trail, the slight boy finding it easier going than the bigger men, who were soon panting to keep up. As they went, the forest gradually became more spaced out, and they moved through a series of low bushes before emerging into a wide, open clearing. Larc suddenly sprinted forward and disappeared into the bushes on the far side of the clearing. Saltar gave chase and was halfway across before he suddenly pulled up, instinct warning him that he was running straight into a trap. Lucius was just entering the exposed area.

'Get back!' Saltar yelled.

But it was too late, as shadowy, black-robed figures entered on all sides. All were cowled except for two who stood proudly regarding him. One had gossamer thin skin, through which blue blood vessels and his skull could be seen. The other had the grey and desiccated look of one aging from the inside out. There was the air of an ancient and hungry power about them.

'Take them down!' the Skull commanded the seven black robes spaced around the edges of the circle.

Saltar was already moving. He adopted the fighting forms known as Stone, tumbled backwards and slammed an incredibly dense fist into the throat of one of the black robes. The man died instantly. Saltar shoved Lucius – 'Run!' – and then returned to the fighting.

'You!' the Plague Victim ordered another of the magickers. 'After him!'

The remaining five began their incantations, their voices weaving together in an attempt to bind Saltar. But he was not to be caught as easily as he had been by Aurelius and Tacitus. The Battle-leader deliberately made his heart flutter, skip beats and slow, anything to stop it matching the rhythm of the mighty spell being conjured around him.

He felt tendrils of power licking out at him, seeking some sort of purchase so that they could wrap him tight. He kept to the smoothest forms and faces of Stone so that the magic would find no grip. He then began the unstoppable rock-slide form and descended on two of the magickers at once, delivering blows that broke bones and ruptured organs. He was intent on crushing them all.

'See here, Saltar! I have your child!' the Skull brayed.

Saltar's head ground painfully on his neck as he fought against the giant momentum he'd generated and looked over at the Skull. To his horror, he saw his son was dangling by his neck from the sinewy creature's claw. Where had the child suddenly come from? Was it an illusion of the sort Visier had conjured? Could Saltar afford to take the chance that it was?

'Release him to me!' the Battle-leader rumbled. 'I will let you live if you do so. This is the only time I will make you such an offer. Refuse me now and you will die by my hand, be certain of that.'

The Skull's lean face showed no change in expression, but Saltar's words made him hesitate for a second before he made his own demand: 'Stop resisting us or I will snap the child's neck.' As if to emphasise his point, the limp boy-child wailed weakly.

Saltar's entire existence became an agony at the sound. It almost undid him. 'You-you need him for your heinous schemes. For Nylchros, no? You will not dare kill the child without the Creator's express command!'

'Hah!' the Plague Victim laughed, albeit somewhat nervously. 'He does not command us. He does not command anyone in this realm yet. This is not his realm.'

'No!' the Skull admonished his companion. 'There is no need to share anything with this one, nor those that we Own here.' Then he addressed Saltar again: 'All you need know is that it is we who now rule this petty realm. Be assured, the child *will* die, and *you* will be responsible.'

Petrified, his mind in turmoil, Saltar simply couldn't think of what he might say to tip things in his favour, to regain the initiative, to find some advantage, no matter how slight. It was all slipping away from him. It all came down to this moment and he found himself lacking. He had been quick to adjudge the Scourge and his other companions inadequate, but in this final summary he could offer no more than they.

'I-I…'

Their magic reached out to him again. He shuddered at its clammy, alien touch. He knew it meant him ill, for it was wet and cold and instantly leeched natural energy from him. His joints became sore and his bones hurt to the marrow. He was suddenly stooping like an old man.

The three uninjured magickers chanted, and now the Skull and the Plague Victim added sonorous voices to the weave. They trapped him completely: one spelling his sight, one his touch, then his smell, hearing and taste.

'The cage!' the Plague Victim commanded.

One of the magickers pulled a small cage about two to three feet along each edge from amongst the bushes. Their voices rose together and rose in power, the act to come clearly pre-agreed.

Saltar was slowly forced to bend double, bones creaking, buckling and breaking. He couldn't scream, for he had no longer had control of his own throat. An invisible hand pushed his head down through his legs, lifted him off the ground and squeezed and pounded him into the cage. His torso broke and flattened. His limbs were mangled and pushed on top of him, until the door of bars could finally be shut and secured.

Sacks and organs within him burst and he felt liquid trickling into the cavities of his chest. Gore and intestines splattered and hung through the gaps in the cage.

It was then that Saltar the Builder, Battle-leader of Dur Memnos, finally died, his face mashed by bars and the one eye that could be seen staring in vain towards his child Orastes.

When Saltar shoved him so hard, Lucius was almost lifted from his feet, but he managed to stagger away into the bushes through the gap left by the felled black robe. The musician felt eddies of power all around him and he was buffeted one way and then another. He became giddy with nausea and it was all he could do to keep his gorge down. Something was trying to pull his guts up through his throat. Acid choked him, gastric vapour rose up into his nose, denying him air, and his eyes streamed so badly he was blinded. His body was in revolt.

'You!' came a voice from the open area behind him. 'After him!'

Lucius's foot caught in a root and he stumbled. He was tall and gangly, far from the sort of physique that could either power through underbrush or move nimbly over the ground with quick changes of direction.

'Over here, you stupid mortal!' a grizzled voice said from nearby, and a large, hairy hand came out of a bush and dragged him in amongst the sharp branches and wide foliage. 'Get down!'

Lucius crouched as best he could and looked up at his erstwhile rescuer. The wild man certainly looked like he lived in a bush such as this: tangled hair and beard, skin the colour of mud, torn clothes and eyes rolling in all directions. Wait, that face! He recognised it from the side of the wooden caravans of the travelling temple.

'Holy Wim!' he breathed, trying his best not to wrinkle his nose at the unpleasant smell coming off the deity. 'What are you doing here?'

'Hiding.'

'But-but…!'

'Oh, shut up!'

'Yes, Holy Wim.'

'My followers are all but gone. I am trapped here. Now, be quiet. I am watching to see what happens next.'

'Yes, Holy Wim,' Lucius whispered, craning his neck to see through the gap in the leaves of their natural hide. 'Can't you help him?'

'I have power enough to keep us safe from accidental discovery, but beyond that… ha, ha… well, the odds become insurmountable. There is only the inevitable.'

Lucius stared at the itinerant god in horror. Was he saying that luck had reached its limit, that it was running out? If so, there could be no hope, for all would have been decided.

Wim shook his head and tutted. 'That is no way to treat a child. Such mortals put no value against life. Perhaps they have put all morality aside in their ruthless determination to have power… or perhaps death is not absolute to them.'

'You-you mean they are necromancers?'

'That, or something worse.'

Worse? What could be worse? Lucius shuddered. He decided he might not want the answer to such a question.

'Ouch!' Wim half giggled. 'I bet that hurts.'

Lucius looked out at what was happening. Saltar's body was being bent and contorted by an invisible force. He jerked around as if he was a marionette on the hands of a young child who did not know how to work the toy properly. Lucius could not breathe as he watched the Battle-leader being crushed into a tiny cage.

'No! This cannot be! We must do something. If Saltar dies then everything is lost. Wim, do something!' Lucius demanded hotly.

The god of luck blew a raspberry, not bothering even to look at Lucius. 'It is good that he dies, perhaps, for it will surely test the Design. And the Design must be tested if it is to survive. It is probably the only way in which I will be able to survive. Yes, it is fit that he dies.' The deity then chortled.

There were tears of anger and grief in Lucius's eyes. 'Is this all you gods are then? Uncaring and selfish parasites? Well, is it? Answer me, unless you fear your own words will condemn you! Perhaps it is good your followers have been taken from you, else how will you ever learn to be responsible and accountable for the successful and continued existence of this realm? And why would anyone want to follow such an insane and babbling god anyway?'

Wim refused to look at him. The god smiled tragically and scrunched up his face: then he hitched up his right buttock and released a thunderous, divine fart.

Lucius turned away in disgust. A second later, he realised he was now all alone in the bush. The whimsical god had vanished. But there was suddenly a voice whispering at his ear: 'Do not linger here. In a handful of seconds you should simply walk back to the horses. The window of opportunity is available for a few seconds longer. You are unlikely to be seen. But you must leave now and you must not look back.'

'And what should I do when I reach the horses?' the royal musician asked the empty air, but there was no reply.

Cursing the gods in general, Lucius eased himself out of the prickly bush, having to unhook his tunic from thorns on more than one occasion. He hurried away. His thoughts were in chaos. Saltar was dead. Dead! What was he to do?

There was no point heading back to the temple of Wim, for the Sergeant was probably on his way back to the capital by now, and Altibus and Jack O'Nine Blades were still unlikely to want to leave the injured. And what was the point? If Saltar was now dead, what was there for them to do?

Should Lucius himself head back to Corinus for help? He discarded that idea almost immediately – it would take too long, and what help could he raise that the Sergeant wouldn't already have secured?

There was nothing to do but try and follow along after these brutal magicians without being discovered. Wim had said not to look back, but presumably the god hadn't been referring directly to the issue of following the Accritanians, or had He? It was typical of the idiot-god to be so ambiguous. Shrugging to himself and deciding he'd wasted more time on the gods than they warranted, Lucius hitched Saltar's horse behind his own and got up into his saddle.

Perhaps he would find some opportunity to spirit Orastes away from his kidnappers. Or perhaps he could retrieve Saltar's dead body. After all, Mordius might be able to do something with it. But achieving anything without a weapon would be difficult. He should really have brought a sword along. And he should have spent some time in the last two years learning to use one. However, like everybody else, he'd wanted to believe that he was free to live out the rest of his life in peace. How naïve mortals could be sometimes

– as long as there were gods and demons, peace and freedom could never be more than a short-lived dream.

And where was the bloody Scourge when you needed him? What had happened to them all? How had they allowed things to get this bad? They had let their guard down. They'd allowed themselves to believe in the great power of things like love, tolerance, good faith and human fellowship – all aspects of Shakri, now he thought about it. He just hoped they hadn't left it too late now. With Saltar dead, though, what hope could there be? Surely none.

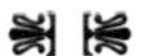

Chapter Ten: There Being No Other Choice

She'd suffered at the hands of men her entire life. For a while, she'd loved them for it, because even when they had been punishing her their attention had perversely made her feel wanted. From the man with presents her mother had brought to her childhood bedroom, to the Scourge who had forced her to kill for him, to the King who'd tried to rob her of her very existence, to this Saltar who'd forced her to have a child and become weak, to the son who enslaved her with love, her life and freedom had been taken from her by the demands of men. She was amazed there was anything left to her. And what was that exactly? A suit of green leather armour, a core of hatred that could not be quenched by all the blood in the world, and a hard face that men still insisted was alluring and excuse enough to continue harrassing her and making her life a misery.

She'd been close to shredding her face with her fingernails or cutting it away with a knife, but had realised men would then use pity as a reason to continue to plague her. No, better to use her harsh beauty as a means of bewitching men so that she could all the more easily lead them to their destruction. For she had come to comprehend that she would only ever have a measure of peace and freedom once she had seen to the deaths of as many of them as possible.

Her solution was entirely elegant, for it would involve acting out the sort of female role men insisted she play, and so it could not fail to win the support of those men. She would be the grief-stricken mother, the loyal wife and outraged first lady of Dur Memnos. She would raise an army of men who sympathised with just such a female character and lead them to war against their enemies. It would only be as the men started to kill each other in their thousands that any of them might begin to wonder if they might not have been served better by repenting of the crimes they had perpetrated against women and the Mother of All Creation.

The realm was on the brink of collapse because of the selfish acts committed by men intent on winning power solely for themselves. They sought to set themselves up as the new pantheon of the gods. They wished to be the new creators, to usurp Shakri's position. And to think Shakri had only ever shown them love, just as Kate had in following her divine example!

Things had gone too far now for there to be the possibility of any other sort of solution. The only way for any sort of peace, freedom and salvation to be realised was to kill as many as she could.

She unbuckled the armour covering her chest and leaned forwards in her throne so that a fair amount of her cleavage was on show and the man standing just below her would be able to see plenty. He was a fairly plain-looking fellow – nowhere near as striking as Saltar – but there was an air of confidence and power about him that was more than a little compelling. And the ranginess of physique promised, beneath his dark blue doublet and hose, the lean and toned muscle of a man in fighting trim. His wardrobe was expensive but tasteful, indulgent yet restrained, pleasure mixed with pain.

He stood now at ease before her, but his eyes moved quickly enough when she revealed something of her flesh. Yes, he could be enticed. She eased back in her chair again, and was pleased to see mild disappointment flit across his face.

'Thank you for coming, General Vidius,' she said huskily. 'Please, help yourself to wine,' and she gestured casually towards the amphora and cups on a table over by the window.

'Thank you, milady. Some refreshment would be welcome after the long ride in from my estates to the city. May I serve you?'

She shook her head, and watched him with hooded eyes while he helped himself. He raised his cup to her and took a considered mouthful. He grinned. 'Ha! From my own vineyard!'

'But of course,' she purred. 'After all, there are no better Memnosian wines to be had.'

'You flatter me, milady!'

'Perhaps,' she said, 'but you are an easy man to admire. A King's Hero, were you not? A man who led the kingdom on the battlefield, a man upon whom the kingdom depended for its survival. Why have you now entered this self-imposed exile, General?'

'Your husband, milady,' Vidius said without hesitation or elaboration.

'Ah!' Kate murmured, stroking the arm of her throne. 'Good General, my husband is no longer here, and I find I am in want of a man.'

'Milady?' Vidius asked with feigned incomprehension.

'A man to lead my army, General! A man of experience. A man who can lead others! Have you not perceived or heard what is happening to the realm, General?'

He nodded. 'It had not escaped my attention, milady!'

'And would you stand idly by when your kingdom needs you, when I need you?'

'No, but...' and he allowed the word to hang.

'But?' Had she misjudged him? 'You ask for something in return? What would you have? If it is in my power to grant it, then it is yours.'

Vidius smiled toothily and his face was transformed. Gone was the plain-looking fellow of a moment before, to be replaced by an arch, calculating predator.

'I have not decided on my price, as it is also in my interest that the realm be saved. But when I name my price at some point in the future, you will not hesitate to pay it. Agreed?'

She was tempted to call to the guards outside the throne room to come in and kill the man there and then. But she needed him for now. And as soon as she was done with him, she would have him killed.

'Agreed. I wish to march as soon as possible. Time is of the essence – it always is. We will collect more men from Holter's Cross. You will assemble the army and have it ready to leave in two days from now.'

Vidius shrugged. 'If you insist. Outfitting and provisioning a large number of men for war in such a short period is not particularly feasible, but I doubt you're prepared to listen to such an observation.'

'Quite so, General!' Kate answered briskly. 'Now, I'm sure we both have much to do. You may be about your business.'

'Thank you, milady. Just one last thing, however,' he interposed. 'With whom do we go to war precisely?'

'Jaffra.'

'I see. A naval power. And how many ships do we have at King's Landing?'

'Enough, I imagine, but I'll leave such details to you.'

'Very well, milady. My experience of naval combat is limited, but I will see what our captains have to say when we arrive at the royal harbour. More than that, I will hunt out the merchants we have in Corinus who also maintain ships.'

'Excellent. I am introducing martial law. Requisition whatever you need from the population, for the entire kingdom is now fighting for its survival and must all make sacrifice.'

Vidius bowed deeply. 'As you say, milady.'

❧ ❧

It wasn't that he enjoyed inflicting the pain on these mortals; rather, he revelled in it as it emanated from them. When subjected to torture, they lost nearly all psychic control and the pain and fear came off them in waves. He absorbed the rich emanations until he was drunk on them, drunk with power and an intoxicating vision of his own potential. For days after, he would be able to see with more acuity, hear more of the feeble mortals' unguarded thoughts and sense them from a greater distance.

There was not much skin left on the Captain's legs. The Chamberlain had taken painstaking care with his finest razor to remove it strip by strip without endangering his victim's life at any point. Even so, the man's heart refused to slow and it was only a matter of time before it gave out. It was funny how those who'd had harder lives and less privilege tended to last longer than the likes of the Captain who'd only known the comfort of the royal palace. Perhaps those who'd fought long and desperately for their lives – miserable though those lives might be – were used to the struggle and suffering and put a higher value against what they had than those who had so much and had it so easy.

The Chamberlain was slightly disappointed he would not get to feed on the man's pain for much longer, but the other man tied to the rack on the far side of the room probably had more potential anyway. Besides, the Captain had long since given up the little information he had and now only served to increase the terror of the as yet untouched mage. The soldier had accepted a certain amount of gold from the black-robed strangers initially and shared information with them about the normal comings and goings within the palace, but beyond that his memory was hazy. There was no doubt that the Captain had confessed everything and told it truthfully, for the Chamberlain could all but read his petrified thoughts. There was no deception here, meaning the foreign mages must have used some sort of magic to erase the Captain's memories. An interesting talent to have – the Chamberlain wondered if he would be able to uncover its secrets.

He looked down at the naked, sweating soldier and smiled gently. The soldier of course misunderstood the look and began to scream against his gag.

The Chamberlain stroked the poor man's brow, trying to soothe him. Then he put the razor against the man's throat and began to saw slowly and deeply. A mist of blood filled the air, turning the lenses on the Chamberlain's eyes and everything he then saw red.

He watched the spark disappear from the Captain's eyes and then towards the mage. The prey's eyes bulged in panic and he wrestled against his bonds. The Chamberlain angled in towards him, attuning himself to the mage's mental patterns, not that they were unusual or especially difficult to read. The mage tried to mumble the words of a spell around his mouth-tie, and it wasn't for the first time that the Chamberlain thought it fortunate the mage failed to understand spoken words were unnecessary for the performance of magic.

On the occasion the Chamberlain had loosened the prey's gag, the wretch had immediately tried to mouth a spell. Why try such a thing? It wasn't as if the Chamberlain was going to let him perform any sort of magic, was it? So, why try? It was amazing the sorts of things people would say and do when they were panicking or in fear for their lives. The Chamberlain brandished his razor in front of the man's nose.

'Now, you will hold still, hmm, for I will be performing some delicate work, yes? I wouldn't even scream if I were you.'

With that, he set about easing a two-inch square of skin from the man's chest above his heart. So sharp was the razor, and so practised the Chamberlain, that not a single drop of blood was drawn.

'There you are, you see, that wasn't so bad, now was it, hmm?' he crooned. 'And so you see how not struggling and following my instructions, compliance and obedience, will see you come through unharmed. You are lucky to have this object lesson, hmm, for it eludes most mortals or they only realise it when it is already too late. You understand, yes?'

The prey nodded frantically.

'Well, we'll see, won't we? I'll remove your gag now, hmm? If you seek to speak except in direct answer to my questions, then the lesson will have to be administered again, only more forcefully this time. The longer you take to learn the lesson, the closer we will be moving to your heart. As skilled as I am, I doubt I will be able to reveal your heart for the world to see without killing you. You're ready now, hmm?'

Tears of terror trickled from the mage's eyes but he slowly nodded. The Chamberlain removed the piece of cloth between the prey's jaws.

'Where are you from, hmm? Speak!'

'J-Jaffra.'

The Chamberlain frowned and tilted his head. Amazingly, the prey had lied – the pattern and waves emanating from him meant there could be no doubt. Pleased by the prey's resilience and the prospect of a session of extended torture, the Chamberlain replaced the prey's tie and began to whet his razor on a leather strap cut from the hide of one of his many victims.

❧ ❧

His nerves and sense as charged as they'd ever been, he tilted and danced down one corridor after another. As he neared the doors to the throne room, he slowed. Something was amiss. There was a presence that was at once familiar and alien. And then Vidius came out through the doors and past the two guards on sentry.

'You! How dare you enter this place!' the Chamberlain harangued him.

'Ah, brother! What took you? There was a time when you'd know I was due to visit the palace before I did. You're slipping, brother. And what's this I hear about you allowing the child to be taken right from under your very nose? No wonder the green witch has called on me.'

The men circled each other warily, causing the two sentries to bring their weapons forward to a ready position.

'There is nothing for you here unless she has decided on rashest of steps, hmm?' the Chamberlain asked suspiciously.

Vidius smirked. 'There is opportunity in everything, even death and destruction. Not even you would deny that, brother.'

'I would deny a nihilist everything!' the Chamberlain hissed. 'I cannot understand why Balthagar would allow you a place in this realm, hmm?' He advanced half a step.

Vidius's hand shot out in a gesture that demanded a halt. 'What are you thinking, brother! Would you seriously risk your whole realm of pets simply because of your antipathy for me? Have you been stuck in your mortal form so long that your mind is now swayed in mortal fashion by any passing passion and sudden emotion? Are you so diminished, brother? Would you act in such a crazed fashion? You were once a prince of the cosmos, a warrior of the void, a master of eons and their eternal patterning. What is this now, brother?'

The Chamberlain shook his head in haphazard fashion and ground his teeth so hard that he had to spit powdered enamel from his mouth. 'I see you, brother! You are right that I read the Pattern, yet I read it in ways you cannot even imagine. I read *you*, brother. Your nihilism and the fact she has made this decision have probably now hampered and limited the Pattern so that the doom of this realm is all but guaranteed. Whether I succeed in destroying you now or not is unlikely to make much difference to the eventual outcome, hmm?'

Vidius shrugged his velvet-clad shoulders but dared not blink. Slowly, he backed away. When the Chamberlain showed no signs of following, the General turned on his heel and strode away with a straight back. He did not look back.

Seething silently, the Chamberlain had to wonder if Vidius was right: the Chamberlain had indeed become quicker to anger, more capricious, more whimsical, more impulsive, more mortal in behaviour quite simply, in recent years. It worried him greatly because such behaviour was often ill-considered, risky or mistaken. When had it actually started and what caused it? When had his appetites slipped free of his control and started to rule him? Was it when Balthagar had restored the realm after defeating Voltar? The Builder had reconfirmed the Chamberlain's place in the realm, but had he also reconfigured the Chamberlain's physical mind so that he would seek to attach essential meaning and value to the realm? Balthagar had always been outrageous and idiosyncratic enough for that to be possible. It was fundamentally offensive as far as the Chamberlain was concerned, but it would all be beside the point if the realm imploded and he never got the chance to confront him.

His mood darkening, that only offering further proof as to how far he'd fallen, and that only further darkening his mood, he rushed at the doors to the throne room before his mind could spiral and descend so far that it was beyond saving. The weapons of the sentries clanged against each other as they crossed to bar his way. Without thinking, he buried a fanged and paralysing needle into each of their throats, pushed past them and slipped through one of the doors.

She sat in the immovable throne of Dur Memnos, looking down at him with little concern. He blurred forward so quickly that it would have seemed he had eight limbs rather than just four. Still she showed no reaction. There was no trace of fear in the mental patterns coming from her either. He could kill her with ease and yet she sat there facing him down. All he could sense from her was a determined core of hatred and intent. Truly, she was a match for Balthagar, even if she was a weak and ignorant mortal, even if he could snap her neck with just one hand.

'Vidius is the most dangerous and untrustworthy of creatures, yes! This is no way to save your child or the realm! Quite the opposite, hmm?'

'Many would say the same of you, Chamberlain,' Kate said quietly, in tones he could not interpret. 'What have you learnt from the mage?'

It was rare the Chamberlain was wrong-footed, but she constantly introduced chaos where he tried to bring order and predictability to the Pattern. She was unstable; she destabilised everything around her; perhaps even the realm itself. She was not what either he nor the realm needed right now. Should he strike at her while he could? What would result from her death? Perhaps he should assume the throne himself. Would the mortals follow him? No, he'd tried that course before.

'An army is not the way, milady, hmm? Certainly not an army led by Vidius, yes?'

'I will ask you again. The mage?'

He was tempted to drag her by the foot down to his torture room. He would see how composed she remained once he'd tied her to a rack and peeled the flesh from her bones. He drooled involuntarily. He was suddenly shocked by his lack of self-control and hastily pulled himself back in. He would get no joy from her, he realised. After all, hadn't he helped make her what she was? Didn't he already know what sort of monster she was? She was perhaps worse than Vidius. Then he saw it! With a strange mix of horror and admiration, he took a step back and bowed his head.

'Milady, you will kill the creature once he has served your purposes.'

She let the silence drag. Then: 'Yes. This is the last time I will ask. The mage?'

'Milady, the enemy is not Jaffra. There is a community in the Needle Mountains, but where, I cannot ascertain, hmm? It is not near Accritania, however. The enemy are the Brethren, and they are ruled by the Three. They are blood mages who seek some lost god that would supplant the pantheon, yes? An army will avail us little against these mages. We must find a magic to combat them. That is all I know at the moment, hmm?'

Kate stroked the unforgiving arms of the throne. 'Good. We will have this magic, Chamberlain, even if the gods themselves have to suffer for it.'

They set the witch's body to burning. Mordius had expected it to be slow to catch here in the damp, steaming swamp, but it had gone up in roaring green flames almost immediately. It reminded him of naphtha – a naturally occurring substance that would ignite and seek to destroy everything around it no matter its surroundings or environment.

The little fat that there was on the witch's body sizzled and spat at them, gobbets landing on nearby reeds and setting them asmoulder. Mordius and Lebrus stepped back and urged the listless Strap to do the same.

Then Lebrus led them back through the sucking swamp to Marsby. They'd found their sullen horses largely unharmed just outside the fence made of bone extending around the witch's home – apparently her tastes did not extend to equine blood when human was yet available.

Astraal was there waiting for them, pretending that she hadn't been at all concerned about Lebrus having been away. She finished cleaning the kitchen table before looking up and finally noticing them.

'Ah, there you are. She's gone then.'

Lebrus nodded, frowned and then smiled slightly. 'She's gone. Strange to think it but she's gone. We will have to find a new reason to our lives, this time a reason of our own.'

'You are welcome to join us,' Mordius offered tentatively. 'The knowledge and skills of the Keepers would be of immeasurable help to us. You might even be the difference between the realm being lost and saved.'

But Lebrus and Astraal were not to be persuaded. They had not spent untold years in service only then to pledge themselves to another cause within hours of securing their freedom.

'Besides,' the bear added, 'without the witch feeding on the Elders, they will quickly rise in number and become a worse threat than ever the witch was. It is time the Keepers give up cowering in their homes at night and begin to hunt the lesser races before it is too late. I will raise the communities of the swamp and we will once again become feared in our own right. If the Elders capitulate more quickly than expected, then perhaps I will lead a small force to seek you out and offer you aid, wizard.'

Mordius bowed. 'I would be honoured, Keeper Lebrus. May I wish you happy and speedy hunting!'

Lebrus placed a hand gently on Mordius's shoulder, all but engulfing it with his giant palm. 'Travel safely, friend Mordius.' Then he looked at Strap and sadness crept into his eyes. 'I am sorry for what happened, truly I am. We had no idea what would occur when we sent you from here.' Astraal nodded, a blush of shame coming to her cheeks.

'Happened?' Strap echoed without blinking. 'All's well that ends well. We've suffered a scratch or two but we are otherwise well.'

'Ah, I see,' Lebrus murmured to Mordius. 'He doesn't realise.'

'Realise?' Strap repeated woodenly, looking down at his friend.

With a forced smile, Mordius said: 'There's time enough for that once we're on the road again. Let's not keep these good people chatting here all day. You know how you go on, Strap. We still need to get through the woods before darkness falls.'

Astraal's toddler peeked out from behind his mother's skirt and waved at Strap. The young Guardian looked down at his own hand as if he didn't recognise it, raised it and waved it in a jerky fashion. He grinned lopsidedly. The toddler looked distressed and then disappeared behind the skirt again.

'Oh.'

They hustled Strap out to the horses, neither of which seemed to want to come too close to the Guardian. Strap wrestled his mount round and stiffly pulled himself into the saddle.

With a final wave and a few nods to the residents of Marsby who were out and about, they rode out of the swamp community and towards the forest road. Mordius was glad to leave the biting, sticky, scratching place behind. He knew he'd never look back on the place with any fondness. He even suspected he'd wake suddenly from his sleep on nights in the future because of nightmare memories about his time in the lair of the blood-drinking witch. There could be few places more unpleasant to visit than the swamp of Marsby, but Mordius was resigned to the prospect of having to hurry to just one such destination: the mountainous home of the Three, where they were likely to face legions of the walking dead, ranks of magicians, probably the most powerful necromancers alive and this Enemy who inspired fear in the gods themselves.

If he'd understood the dead witch correctly, then the Three intended to offer the child Orastes as the vehicle of the dreadful Unity, Nylchros. It would be a heinous act to murder and sacrifice such innocence – the sort of crime that offended all humanity and set the perpetrators entirely apart from their own kind. It was for such a crime that the word *evil* had been created, to describe a corruption so absolute and so devoid of moral concern that it warranted a term of its own, a term that could hardly be applied to humankind. Such evil could not be tolerated, even for an instant. Everything must be bent towards expunging it completely, no matter what was lost in doing so. Mordius was prepared to lay his life down if necessary.

What sort of entity must Nylchros be if he prospered through such acts? No wonder just mention of him had caused the witch to quail and Lacrimos to do this mortal's bidding. And the power of Nylchros must always threaten to be absolute if he was termed the Unity! Did the Three imagine they could control such a being and force?

Surely there was a magic at the command of the Three that they were confident could bind Nylchros to them, else why would they dare provide him with entry to this realm? The spell required would no doubt be a mighty undertaking and require all the resources of their mountain fortress. Therefore, it was safe to assume Nylchros would not be allowed to enter the realm until the servants of the Three had brought Orastes to the mountains. How much time did they have left? How long ago had the child been stolen? Five days, six, more? Was it long enough for the kidnappers to reach the mountains?

Mordius prayed they still had some time. He prayed Saltar would be able to catch the servants of the Three before they made it to the mountains. If the Battle-leader could not do so… well, then perhaps none of them had much longer than a day or two left to live. He realised he had to make the most of the time left to him.

He looked across at Strap and felt guilty. They had been through a lot together, the two of them. The least Mordius owed the Guardian was the truth. 'Strap, I have something to tell you.'

Strap turned his head to look at Mordius, the Guardian's face absent of expression. 'Yes?'

Mordius sighed. 'I don't know what you remember of our time with the hag. She drank of our blood every day. I'm sorry, Strap, but you died. I raised you. You are an animee, one of the undead.'

Strap did not react immediately and they rode some way in silence. Finally, the Guardian said, 'I do not feel dead. In truth, I'm not sure how being dead's meant to feel. Of course, I imagine you don't feel much of anything when you're dead, so the fact I do experience feelings and emotions means I can't be dead exactly, doesn't it?'

'Well, your body and sensations are somewhat numbed, no? Are your thoughts more sluggish than you remember? You certainly aren't as talkative as you used to be.'

Strap frowned, which was probably the most lifelike he'd looked since being raised. 'I do feel a bit stiff, but would have expected that after being bound for several days. My head is clear… as far as I'm aware. And despite what you might think, I do not always go prattling on inanely. Do I *look* dead, then?'

Mordius eyed him critically. 'Well, you're very pale, which isn't surprising given you've lost nearly all your blood, but you could pass for a noble who powders his face, I suppose. Otherwise, there's very little to say you're dead. Perhaps the fact you were raised so quickly after dying has made all the difference.'

Strap nodded. 'Then answer me this, Mordius. If I don't feel dead, I think like a living person and I don't look dead, what is there about me that makes me *dead*? To all intents and purposes, I'm actually *alive*, am I not?'

'Well… the thing is… well… perhaps you are, then!' Mordius conceded reluctantly.

'You could sound happier about it.'

Mordius smiled. 'It's not that. It's just that I'm always nervous when the distinction between life and death begins to disappear or becomes blurred. The last time it happened was when Voltar was on the throne, and it heralded the onset of the apocalypse, remember? It does not bode well if the distinction is disappearing now as well. We are all diminished by it.'

'And this from a necromancer!'

'And beyond that, I am uncomfortable about putting the existence of an animee on a par with someone living out their Shakri-gifted existence. It suggests Shakri is little more than a magician like myself. But there must be more to your current condition than the simple fact my magic sustains you rather than Shakri's spark. To think otherwise would be the worst of blasphemies. I cannot countenance it!'

Strap shrugged awkwardly. 'Yes. Forgive me, Mordius, but I certainly wouldn't want to see you as some sort of god either. I just wouldn't be able to pray to you with anything like belief or conviction, let alone any sort of straight face.'

Mordius chuckled. 'Your humour certainly didn't die with you, Strap, I'm glad to say.'

Strap nodded. 'So I'll keep the peace and pretend I'm dead then. Hey! Do I get to have a funeral? I can attend, right? I'll want to make sure it's done properly, you see. I don't suppose it would be appropriate for me to say a few words at my own funeral, would it? After all, I probably know the deceased better than anyone else alive… well, dead then. And would I be able to go to the wake? Don't want to miss out if there are going to be a few drinks going.'

For once, Mordius didn't mind listening to Strap prattle on.

⁂

She'd had them rounded up roughly, to make it clear from the off she meant business and would not tolerate any chicanery. They were either with her, or they would be dead in short order.

A mix of Vidius's men and her guard marched in the large group of high priests and their vassals. They'd been pulled from their beds in the middle of the night and informed that they would attend the palace immediately, and that if they were not inclined to accept the invitation then they would be dragged before the throne in chains. Once arrived at the royal residence, they'd been given no refreshment or explanation and then forced to wait in a cold ante-chamber without furniture for an hour.

Wearing her green leather armour, sitting tall in her throne and with the General and Chamberlain to either side of her, she knew she would appear a ruler it would be wise to respect, if not fear. This spectacle was deliberately designed to prevent these religious politicians thinking she was either soliciting or appealing to them for their aid. There would be no bargaining. They would not be allowed to imagine for a second that they had any sort of advantage in this audience, any sort of lever they could use to extract concessions from her or to avoid co-operating with her. The only concession she would make was to allow them to live in return for their full and unconditional obedience.

She surveyed them as they entered, looking for indications as to which of them might seem tempted to give her trouble. At their head came Ikthaeon, High Priest of Shakri, accompanied by several of his soft-slippered lackeys. His pinched face and his stiff bearing told her he was far from impressed with his treatment. Probably not used to being seen in public before he's had a bath, shave and bit of pampering, she thought snidely. Next, came a large man and a petite woman in the blood-red robes of Incarnus's priesthood – she did not know them but they appeared to be entirely at ease. These two would be used to hard and punishing physical training on an all but daily basis, so would not be discomposed by anything she could put them through.

Next came the shuffling, grey-cowled figure of Malastra's high priest. Everyone in the group sought to keep their distance from this ungendered priest of pestilence. Malastra's representative was followed by a bright-eyed and strutting bravo – she could not help smiling at the outrageous face of the high priest of Aa, god of new ventures, the brave of heart and taking risks. He winked at her, gave her a cheeky grin and raised a questioning eyebrow that promised her a life of high adventure if she would but run away with him. You should be careful what you wish for, my fine fellow.

To her surprise, a priest of Gart, god of agriculture, was next to enter. She had not realised there was a temple to this god in the city, but it made sense now that the outdwellers were being encouraged to turn to the land rather than the catacombs to feed themselves. The man had a broad, honest face, a body of knotted muscle and hands as big as shovels – he had great potential, she decided.

The next priest shocked her. Her mouth went dry and she gripped the arms of her throne tightly. A pool of darkness surrounded the woman, making it hard to see much of her, not that one wanted to look on the face of death, its beauty being so painful to behold. Never had she imagined there might be a temple of Lacrimos hidden down some back street of the city, but she should have known, since He was also the warrior god and would have a large following amongst the army. As most of the others in the room were probably doing, Kate decided it was best to ignore the dark priestess – after all, no one liked to dwell on their own death too much if they could help it.

Last, and almost unobserved, was a young, slightly-built teenager with darting eyes. His appearance was unremarkable, almost instantly forgettable. If Kate had not been looking straight at him, she would have forgotten him already. What god was this? Never mind, that could wait till…

'What is the meaning of this?' Ikthaeon demanded, drawing himself up to his full height and looking down his nose imperiously at Kate. That's some feat given my throne is several steps above you, Kate reflected. How had Shakri ever chosen him for Her high priest? The goddess had clearly fallen on hard times. Well, Kate might be able to do Her a favour, because this was precisely the sort of man she despised. Kill him! whispered a voice in her head. She was about to rise to her feet and do just that when the priestess of Lacrimos turned her head to regard Kate with interest.

Kate forced herself back into her throne, pushing her head back until it touched the solid rest. She signalled to the guards in the room, and as one they drew their swords. Everyone froze at the sound of the ringing metal, and waited tensely until it had faded.

'Be quiet!' Kate said in a tight voice.

Fortunately for High Priest Ikthaeon, but to Kate's disappointment, he chose to remain precisely that. In hard tones, she said: 'You all disappoint me! Cognis is gone and yet you choose to do nothing. The realm is threatened and yet you do nothing. The balance has reached a point where it is more precarious than it's ever been, and you do *nothing*!'

She was beginning to shout, but could do nothing to stop herself. 'Your very own gods, those you worship, are undermined and what do you do? *Nothing*! What are your lives worth then? Nothing? You are cattle! You stand there with nothing to say for yourselves, nothing to do!

'I do not speak to you of my child. I do not speak to you of your Battle-leader, who has had to go out and face enemies alone. I do not speak to you of

Mordius, who has travelled into the wild to look for answers. I do not speak to you of Lucius, a *musician* who has gone out bravely despite no training in arms. So of whom do I speak to you? I speak to you of *yourselves*. I speak and ask of what *you* have done. I speak and ask of what *you* have sacrificed!

'I said you disappointed me before, but in truth you disgust me. You are parasites who gorge daily on your congregations and then sit idly by as their world is destroyed. Your inaction makes me wonder if you are actually in league with those seeking to undo this place. And if you are in league with these enemies, then I should have you all cut down right now.

'Well? Does anyone have anything to say before the killing begins? Or do you have *nothing* to say for yourselves, since you are so worthless?'

There was a deafening silence. Ikthaeon looked up and down the line and then decided no one else was pushing forwards to be first to speak: 'I sent one of my priests, Altibus, with the Battle-leader. Beyond that, there are limits to what Shakri is prepared to do. Priests of our order are not permitted to kill, as you know!'

Kate was ready with a sneering response, but the priestess of Lacrimos saved her the bother: 'Ha! Just the limp, vacillating sort of response you'd expect from Shakri's priesthood. They would allow the worst of our enemies to live to fight another day, to recover and grow stronger, until one day they defeated us. Who needs enemies when you've got friends like that? I share your disgust, milady! Lacrimos will facilitate the sacrifice of as many as necessary to aid your cause. He will proudly march to war at your side. He will be your armour, shield, weapon and counsellor. He…'

'Milady! I must protest!' Ikthaeon interrupted hotly. 'Such blasphemy cannot be allowed to describe the Mother of All Creation. The path that Death would escort you down is not a path the healthy of mind would ever want to tread. There can be no future in it.'

'Fool!' the dark priestess replied scornfully. 'Death is not a path you can choose to take or not take. It…'

'Enough!' the large priest of Incarnus boomed. 'Would you create the war here in the throne room and do the enemy's job for them?! Enough, I say!' He looked up at Kate and hesitated, perhaps trying to judge how she would respond to his next words. 'Milady, accord and common purpose will rarely be found when Shakri and Lacrimos are in the same room together. And when the subject is how to approach a most dread enemy, then it is beyond impossible. On such a footing, then, this is an ill audience, one that will fail to please you. And that, none of us wants, as then the killing will begin. But look at the powers assembled here. Your men would have little chance of dispatching me on my own, let alone such a priestly company. You must have known that fact when organising this audience, so I can only surmise these men with weapons bared merely serve to emphasise your points and feelings concerning the lack of support the temples have shown the throne, the realm and its people. And they are points well made, milady!'

She blinked slowly. 'Go on!'

'We of Incarnus are desperate to start punishing our enemies. It is our purpose. It is our meaning. Can you imagine the torture we are going through not being able to carry out our holy duty? Milady, we have not been able to discover who the enemy is, despite our best efforts. Can you tell us who it might be, for then we will march out with all our power and hunt them to the ends of the earth. You know this to be true.'

'General!' Kate said quietly.

The General cleared his throat. 'There is a force of blood-mages in the Needle Mountains. They are ruled by the Three and seek to return the lost god.'

A few of the priests exchanged uncertain glances.

'We will be reduced to what we were before the Time of Breaking. The Enemy is returning. Those are the words of Cognis. Do they mean anything to any of you?' Kate demanded.

The Chamberlain twitched. The priests all shook their heads.

'It matters not,' Kate said. 'They are our enemy. We march in two days from now. Every priest who can walk or ride a horse will be coming with us.'

Of all the things she'd said so far, it was this last statement that finally outraged them. They all started shouting at once, and she let them.

'Some must remain to tend our flock!'

'... to guard the temple, its relics and secrets!'

'... too old to travel!'

'I have already told you our priesthood is not suited to war!'

'It is not *you* who commands our temple! We answer only to our god.'

'You are a coward, Ikthaeon, too used to your soft cushions and shiny valuables!'

'Milady, willing though we are to send a strong cadre with you, I really don't think we need to send...'

'How dare you insult the high priest! It is typical of...'

And so it went on. Kate rested her chin in her hand and waited. At last, they blew themselves out.

'Finished? Good. You will need to find horses for your people because otherwise it will be a long walk for some. It might finish off some of your more elderly priests. Having said that, we'll have the healing arts of the priests of Shakri close at hand so all should be well. Now, unless there's anything else, you may all leave to get what little sleep you can before morning prayers. If you do have something more to say,' Kate added sweetly, forestalling a new wave of protest, 'you may take it up one-to-one with my Chamberlain. I'm sure he'll find a way to help you understand just how important your full co-operation is. A matter of life and death, you might call it.'

A number of the priests looked nervously at the Chamberlain. They had no doubt heard stories of his bloody deeds since they were children. Their imaginations would do a better job of persuading them that it was in their best interests to work with the throne than any amount of rational argument.

Incredibly, the high priest of Malastra stepped forwards. 'I have something to say. It would be helpful if we could be told more of these blood-mages, their rulers – the Three, is it you called them? – and this so-called lost god. If I am to ask my entire temple to uproot itself, then I am going to have to give them more than a few cryptic statements about far-flung enemies and some fanciful Time of Breaking. Whether I am a high priest or not, and whether the order comes from the throne or not, the members of my temple still have free minds and wills. Without such things, we priests would be unthinking slaves rather than faithful servants, and then there could be no balance. Life would cease.'

Several of the other priests nodded at the words of the holy hospitaller. Kate glared at the anaemic androgyne and unconsciously thumped the arm of her throne.

'Do not mistake me, milady!' the priest added quickly. 'If there are blood-mages at work, they are a blasphemy and anathema to all the temples here, and we would all go to considerable lengths to see them wiped out utterly. But you are demanding we unconditionally sacrifice all our other works – and, I have to tell you, some of those works are required of us by our gods. I cannot betray the holy trust of divine Malastra, though it cost me my life.'

Kate silently cursed every priest of every god she'd ever heard of. They were in effect telling her that they were prepared to embrace martyrdom rather than be forced to submit to her will. She would dearly love to grant them their wish. Indeed, she'd be more than happy to take up personally the role of executioner, but creating religious martyrs out of them was the surest way of turning the people against her, and that would finally seal the doom of

Shakri's realm once and for all. Stalemate, by the corrupting and suppurating sores of Malastra!

'Milady, if I may, hmm?' the Chamberlain asked her diffidently.

For want of any other response to give the priests, she waved him on – 'Please, go ahead! – and only then feared she'd just given him permission to throw himself on the assembled clergy. It would be a blood bath! Apparently, the same had just occurred to some of the priests: the high priestess of Lacrimos now stood taller and raised her hands to either side of her, clearly ready to use magic; the priests of Incarnus had moved apart from the others, presumably to give themselves fighting room; the high priest of Aa had begun to whistle a strange, bewitching tune; and the boy she had seen earlier seemed to have entirely vanished from the room. Oops!

But the Chamberlain made no threatening move. 'I captured several of these blood-mages, good priests, hmm, but not before they'd stolen our leader's son from the palace and laid waste to the temple of Cognis, hmm? These blood-mages are most powerful mortals, hmm, and masters and mistresses of the body, no?'

He had their undivided attention. Their eyes were wide in fascination and fear. They all knew how blood-magic threatened the divine rule of their gods. The unholy and perverted magic of blood could be used to change and corrupt the body of mortals, while the power of the gods and their priests was only meant to influence and change the world around mortals. The balance depended on the gods not using their powers to change the fundamental nature and persona of mortals. Blood magic threatened the balance and could not be tolerated. And yet, blood-magic represented sinful temptation for all mortals, whether they were priests or not, because it gave them enticing glimpses of power over life and death, it hinted that mortals could attain immortality if they sacrificed enough, it whispered that they too could become divine. What human ego did not secretly desire it? And look what Voltar's evil necromancy had done to the realm last time! Single-handedly, with his overweening ambition, he had brought about the apocalypse. Was that where they were all heading this time?

The Chamberlain simpered. 'Nearly had me, they did, hmm? I caught them by surprise in the catacombs, but they have powers to fog the mind, thicken the tongue, stop the blood in your veins, make your eyes boil in their sockets, cause your skin to shrivel up, make you hear only your own mind until you go insane, and turn you into an animal. Hear me well, priests: I *fear* them!'

Ikthaeon gasped and could not help shaking. His retainers fanned his brow and supported his arms.

'Yes, good priests, we must all act before they become too strong, hmm? Otherwise, you will become puppets to their whims. No doubt, they will have you perform forbidden sex acts before them for their entertainment. You will be forced to couple with the lowest creatures and demons to be found in all the realms. You will be immolated and penetrated a hundred times a day. And the blessing of holy Lacrimos's kiss will always be kept from you. Do you begin to have visions of it yet, hmm? Do you need me to organise demonstrations before you begin to understand it, hmm?'

The priests turned their faces away from the depraved and demented Chamberlain in disgust. They looked to Kate, desperation in their eyes. Say it isn't true, they demanded... pleaded... begged.

Kate smiled ruefully at them. 'Good priests, that will be the least of it, I fear. For there are also the demonic rulers of these mages to deal with, the Three, and they are but lieutenants to the lost god of subjection and degradation. The Three will create a grotesque of this realm and its people for the god's diversion. The living flesh will be torn from your spines so that your bones can be played to make music. Or hooks will be sunk into your skin and it will be stretched to cover drums. Your heads will be trepanned so that the demon court can make a delicacy of your living brains. Your empty skulls will be used as drinking vessels for all the blood spilled, and the unspeakable servants of the lost god will toast to the fall of Shakri's realm.'

They did not know where to look now in their distress.

'Good priests, listen to me!' she said softly, and the change in her voice brought them back to her. They would be happy now to follow her to their deaths. 'We have allowed it to come to this through our complacency and inaction, and I am as culpable as anyone. I was too busy playing at family life to pay attention to an ancient enemy rising in the kingdom and planting traitors in this very palace. We allowed Cognis to be destroyed, and who knows what other minor gods have also been lost? We would have allowed more temples to be destroyed too if the Chamberlain had not been fortunate enough to overcome the mages in the lowest catacombs. If each of us continues to put our own immediate concerns before the well being of other loyal members of this kingdom, then we will be picked off one by one until we are entirely defeated. The loss of one god hurts us all. The loss of one priest, no matter his or her god, hurts us all. The continual loss of human life in Dur Memnos and other kingdoms, I believe, will ultimately see Shakri's realm fall, for I do not believe the balance can be preserved by animal and plant life alone. All life, physical and spiritual, is interdependent in Shakri's creation. It is only through common purpose and unity that we can hope to face this Enemy with any hope of survival. If we fail to act or start to pull in different directions, at best we paralyse ourselves and at worst we pull the kingdom apart. Before, I tried to shame you into joining the force we are assembling, then I tried to demand you join us, now I am asking you to do so for the good of us all. What say you, good priests?'

Unexpectedly, it was the high priest of Gart who spoke first. In gravelly tones, he said: 'I am far from having one of the quickest minds here, but I can avow that the lady has it right. All life is connected. If there are no humans left, there will be no one to milk the cows and they will die. There will be no one to cut the rotten wood from the good and forests will fall. There will be no one to cut back or burn away old growth so that new and stronger growth can begin. Without new growth, there will be no blooms for a range of insects to feed on. There will be nothing for the bees and they will be unable to pollinate other plants. If the insects disappear, so will the smaller animals, and then the larger. There are a myriad interactions that you would not know of, but some have already started to fail. The earth cries out that her children are being killed, their blood is being spilled onto the ground and its fertility is being destroyed. The blight increases. If it is not stopped soon, the earth and Gart will be no more. But you followers of the other gods do not listen or cannot hear. With the green lady, I ask for your help, for my temple hereby joins her.'

Ikthaeon did not hesitate. 'Then the temple of Shakri has no option but to join Gart's.'

The priestess of Lacrimos came next. 'And life has no meaning without death. The temple of Lacrimos gives its assent.'

The large, red-robed priest of Incarnus had been nodding throughout. 'Our assent was always given.'

There was an awkward pause. Kate looked at the high priest of Aa. 'Well? Will your god be the friend and fellow adventurer of my youth, or will He play the popinjay?' she asked with an uncharacteristic catch of emotion in her voice.

The priestly braggadocio rolled his wrist and made a flourishing gesture with his hand. 'Dear Kate, you know I have never been able to deny you anything. Wherever you go, there are always new escapades, japes and hi-jinks to be had. Let us be the first to engage the enemy, side by side. Or I will sit upon your shoulder as I did once before.'

She nodded and remembered back to when they'd faced Vidius's Memnosian troops on the plains beneath Corinus. Aa had been closer to her than any of the other gods of the pantheon in that final battle. 'And how speaks Malastra, Mistress of Duality and the In-between?'

The grey-robed priest took time to adjust the bandages framing a sexless face. The priest breathed shallowly. 'Much will be lost. We must attend to offer what succour we may. The temple of Malastra assents to your request.'

Kate wanted to sigh with relief, but instead she inclined her head. Their assent was as it should be. 'Thank you all. Convey our gratitude to every member of your temples. Now, we have kept you overly-long and there is still much to be done. We will see you on the morning that we marshal, when the entire might of the realm is assembled in this truest of causes. Good night, worthy priests!'

As the guards began to usher the priests from the room, Kate called out: 'Priests of Incarnus, may I speak with you for a moment longer?'

The man and woman nodded and stood waiting.

'General, Chamberlain, thank you, that will be all. I'm sure there is much that requires your attention.' Her two hangers-on hesitated, clearly reluctant to leave, but they had little choice.

Once Kate was alone with the priests, she invited them to join her at a small table with comfortable chairs and some wine at the far end of the room. The priests sat stiffly in the chairs – they were trained fighters not used to padded comfort. The large man was a slab of muscle, the forearms that could be seen when the wide sleeves of his robe fell back occasionally corded with heavy veins and criss-crossed with scars. He wore four rings on each hand, more to serve as a knuckle-duster than ornamentation no doubt. By contrast, the woman was small and wiry. She had fine, if slightly boyish, features, but did not wear face-paint or jewellery of any sort to accentuate her looks. The only thing that was unusual about her appearance was that she wore her hair up, an unusually high number of plain combs and bodkins keeping it all in place. Kate could only speculate as to the other sorts of uses such paraphernalia might realise in the priestess's hands.

Kate smiled at them, if not exactly warmly then well enough to convince that she bore them no ill will. 'Please, I prefer the name Kate to any sort of title like Guardian… or the green witch.'

The man had the good grace to smile. 'I am Brother Hammer, High Priest of Incarnus. This is Sister Spike. I am afraid we give up our birth names when we join the temple, as our duty to Incarnus is everything we are.'

'I admire such devotion… such loyalty,' Kate said. 'And I would like to thank you for your words during the audience, Brother Hammer. They helped things pass off much better than I could have hoped.'

'I am honoured… Kate. Besides, you have long been favoured by the Holy Avenger. Incarnus has required us to render such support as we can.'

'Truly?' Kate replied, genuinely surprised and pleased. 'Then it makes it easier for me to petition you now. Brother Hammer, I am surrounded by powerful men whom I cannot trust. I have no one to watch my back, if you see? I thought, perhaps, a personal bodyguard…?'

The high priest nodded in understanding. 'Sister Spike is the most deadly individual I have ever known, and believe me I have known a few! She is truly beloved of Incarnus and all those of our temple. But there are two things you must understand, Kate, before your petition is granted.'

'Please, go on.'

'Sister Spike's first loyalty is to Incarnus, not you. Do you understand?'

'Yes.'

'And, occasionally, Sister Spike commits what appear to be random acts of violence. She has an almost divine prescience for those who intend our cause harm. She sees things much further in advance than normal people such as you and I. You *must* trust her when this happens. You must allow her such licence, for it is her nature and holy duty to act. You must then defend and protect her when self-interested parties bring accusations of irrational and unsanctioned murder to you. You must trust and defend Sister Spike, as she trusts and defends you. Do you agree to such terms, Kate? Be warned, they are not easy! They will incite your enemies, and may win you new enemies.'

'I am familiar with the ways of vengeance. They are a joy to me. Tell me, does Sister Spike speak for herself?'

'Occasionally. When she does, be sure you pay attention, for she will sometimes speak with the voice of our god.'

Kate smiled to herself. She decided now was not the time to let these fanatics know she'd fought side by side and spoken directly with their god a number of times. 'Agreed. Now, who was that boy who entered with you priests? What god was that?'

Brother Hammer frowned. 'Boy? I saw no boy, Kate. Are you sure there was a boy? I know grief can affect…'

Sister Spike interrupted. 'No, Brother Hammer! We were honoured with sight of Istrakon, elusive God of Thieves. Where violence does not bring vengeance, a quick and spiriting hand may. He can haunt lifetimes where we bring only finality. He is as innocent as He is criminal. He is a child that has decided its purpose and disconcerts us all.'

Kate nodded. Finally, they were getting to her lost son.

❧ ☙

Shooting a bow from a galloping horse was not difficult. Shooting it with any accuracy, however, was particularly difficult. Unusually, Strap was finding it quite easy. After releasing a dozen arrows, he realised he was no longer breathing and therefore not having to compensate for it when he aimed. It seemed he did not need to draw air – his body did not demand it and it would only get in the way if he did inhale it.

As far as he could tell, eleven out of twelve of his flights had found their marks – his horse having tripped once so that he shot too low. Yet he was often shouting at fast-moving shadows that showed no obvious sign of having been affected by his best efforts. And the number of the creatures hunting them wasn't decreasing appreciably.

'Why are you slowing down?' Strap hollered ahead to Mordius.

'They've gotten ahead of us. Should we make a stand, find higher ground?'

'Idiot! We'll be swarmed under. We'll have to ride through or over them. I've only got one arrow left anyway.'

Mordius continued to slow, apparently not having heard everything Strap had said over the hooves and panting of their mounts. Also, they were having to keep low in their saddles to avoid low-hanging branches in the gloom, and that made communication even more problematic. Strap overtook Mordius and waved him on. It was probably best if the necromancer stayed behind him anyway – if the Guardian managed to open a gap among the Elders, then perhaps Mordius might be able to make it through and win his way to safety.

Strap only remained animated as long as Mordius remained alive, so safeguarding the necromancer was his main concern. Strap still valued his animation, even though he wasn't alive, because as far as he could tell it was almost as good as being fully alive.

The beasts were closing in now and he could judge the distance of specific individuals by their growls and barks of excitement. He could even get an estimate of their numbers. There were at least half a dozen ghosting parallel and to the right of the forest trail, four or so to the left, and a much larger number echoing ahead of them. The noise of a baying pack to their rear had all but disappeared now and he wondered if they should turn around. No, they had come too far to get anywhere near Marsby before they were caught. Furthermore, if his judgement wasn't too far off, there was only a mile or so of these forests to go before they made it through to the relative safety of Corinus's environs.

'Come on!' he roared and spurred his already panicked and foaming horse onto greater speeds. With roots hidden beneath the detritus of the forest floor, the frequency of sudden turns in the path, loose stones underfoot and pitchfork branches all over the place, he had placed his entire survival in the hands of the mercurial god of chance. He prayed Wim was in a good mood or, if not, distracted elsewhere.

They burst into a wide, shadowed clearing and the pack raced in from all sides, raking at the flanks of their horses, seeking to tear open their bellies or hamstring them. The orange, canine eyes of the Elders floated and dodged all around the clearing. Heavy, clawed hands mottled with fur slashed with devastating force and Strap's horse staggered, whinnying in pain. An Elder leapt at Strap, its short snout opening wide to reveal rows of large, jagged teeth.

The Guardian thrust one of his long daggers straight up through the beast's lower jaw, through the soft pallet at the top of its mouth and deep into its brain. Without emotion, Strap watched as the spark died in the Elder's eyes and then let the thing's weight pull it off his sagging blade.

The seven-foot man-dogs saw that Strap's horse had lost speed and direction and went for the kill en masse, those that had been angling towards Mordius now changing tack to join the rest of their pack.

The animee cut left and right with his two daggers, but he could not keep the churning mass of bodies back. An Elder sprang at the horse's hindquarters and sank claws and bite into the animal's rump. Just as it looked like the man-dog would drag mount and rider to the ground, the horse kicked backwards and stove in the Elder's chest.

All momentum lost, Strap threw himself from his saddle, burying both his blades to the hilt in the barrel chest of yet another assailant. He rolled and came up in a ready crouch. At least four Elders had gone for his panicking horse, while five fought and jostled amongst themselves to be the first to get at him. If they'd worked in concert, he'd have had no chance, but their blood-lust was over-riding their pack instinct. He quickly blindsided two of them and delivered debilitating chops to the backs of their limb joints.

He scooted back as a blur of fangs and claws came for him. His chest was torn to ribbons, but he hardly felt it and chose not to waste any time examining the damage. Instead, he surprised the man-dog by stepping forward and then ducking. The Elder was already mid-leap so had no chance to pull up. Strap pushed the points of his blades up and let the creature's momentum tear it open.

The largest of the man-dogs moved in immediately. It was much bigger, stronger and faster than he was. And it refused to over-balance in its eagerness to devour him. There was no way he could survive direct combat with this one. It bore the scars of many a battle – this could only be the leader, Strap decided.

He dared not try to turn and run because it would be on him in an instant. It would bare his spine, crunch down into it and then eat through to his heart… not that his heart actually beat anymore or that he needed it to remain animated. Still, Strap did not think himself too sentimental for wanting to hang onto it.

'Come on, then! Let's get it over with!' he taunted the beast.

It growled menacingly but did not advance. Clearly, it had intelligence enough to be wary of his blades. It was not just some dumb animal, then. Drool glistened from his jaws. Why didn't it come for him? Distant barks gave him his answer! It was waiting for more of its kind to arrive. It was keeping him trapped here until there were sufficient numbers again to take him from behind.

His horse was down and its throat had been opened. Blood gouted – once, twice, three times – as its heart pumped the last of its life out onto the forest floor. The Elders that had seen to it now circled round to join their leader.

Strap knew that if he didn't make a move now, he would lose any chance he might have had. But without a horse… He began to back away, trying to get a tree against his back, but the leader kept angling to keep him in the centre of the clearing. Then he was surrounded by five of them. One came in at his back and he was too slow to turn. His lower left arm was torn open to the bone, tendons snapped and he dropped the blade in that hand. Then his arm bone was between the jaws of one of the man-dogs, and it was dragging him groundwards.

There was no fear or terror. He inserted the point of his blade behind the Elder's skull…

'Bad doggie!'

… and punched it home.

'Strap! Here!' came Mordius's shout from somewhere. A fighting staff thrown through the air bounced off one of the creatures besetting Strap and fell at his feet. The Elder turned away from Strap for a second to see where the attack came from, which was all the time needed to slash his dagger across its throat.

'Mordius, get away!' Strap shouted, hooking his foot under the staff, flicking it up into the air and catching it under his damaged arm. He curled his useless limb around it as best he could and swung at the nearest Elder. It smashed the staff aside and Strap fell to his knees.

'So much for that. Mordius, help!'

'I will give you all the life-force I have and fall into a coma. You must save us, Strap!'

Strap felt a sudden surge within him and rose to his feet with such ease and speed that he realised he must have tripled in strength. He threw his dagger aside, caught the Elder lunging at him under the throat and tore out its gizzard. Blood sprayed everywhere. Glorying in it, he bit into the fur-covered flesh, pulled a gobbet free with a jerk of his neck and spat it at the feet of those remaining. They backed up, whining, and turned tail. It was only then that he realised he'd just killed the leader.

Strap wiped his blood-soaked face on his shoulder and looked around for the necromancer. He sat listlessly on his horse on the far side of the clearing. The reins were slack in his grasp and the eyes had rolled back in his head. He began to lean precariously and Strap had to run to save him from falling. The Guardian got up behind his animateur and guided the horse onto the trail leading off the clearing.

He pushed as fast as he dared, but it was full night now and the moonlight struggled to find its way beneath the trees. There was no more sound of pursuit, but Strap knew the smell of fresh kills would soon begin to attract more predators to the area.

He regarded his white arm bones curiously. There was no pain, so there was at least that advantage to being dead. He knew that if he'd been alive and faced the Elders, the shock of his injuries would have undone him and he would have been eaten on the spot. 'I wonder if this'll heal. Maybe some priest of Shakri could...? Huh! Doubt that dead flesh can heal. Or maybe a blacksmith could do something with it. A few rivets and staples to get the hand working again? I just hope I don't run into a Guardian who decides this animee and necromancer are an offence to nature and need to be put to rest permanently. What a state the two of us must look, eh, Mordius? I doubt I'll ever look like one of the living again. Still, they say the girls like a scar or two and it never stopped Saltar getting together with Kate, did it? You never know, this could be the best thing that's ever happened to me!'

❧ ❧

Kate and Sister Spike ghosted down through the city. So quiet was the priestess that Kate had to resist the temptation to keep looking over her shoulder to check she was still there, just a few paces away. They were saluted by the night guards at the city walls and then they descended into the unlit warrens of the outdwellers.

'Surely none can see us in this murk. It is darker than the very thoughts of Lacrimos down here.'

'We are watched nonetheless, milady,' Sister Spike whispered. 'And one of the guards on the gate paid us special note. He is no doubt one of the Chamberlain's. Those watching us now send word racing ahead of us, so they must belong to another. We will be expected no doubt.'

When they reached Trajan's house, the door was ajar and a candle was lit within. Kate knocked gently and they entered. Trajan sat in a small armchair facing them, sucking on an unlit pipe. There was little more in the cell save for a pallet, table and small, cold fireplace. It was a mean, black place, and the cheap, spitting candle did nothing to illuminate it.

'You're welcome to sit on the pallet, milady. Or the floor. It's swept daily. I would offer you my seat, but I suspect it's the dirtiest option available.' Then his chest rattled, which Kate took to be either laughter or fluid on his lungs.

'There is someone concealed beneath the pallet,' Sister Spike said calmly.

'Thank you, Trajan, I will stand, I think,' Kate smiled. 'Do you know why I am here?'

'There can only be three likely reasons, milady. You have either come for advice, to demand men for your army or to leave me in charge once you have marched, perhaps all three.'

'For the men.'

'I see. What will you pay?'

'If our cause does not succeed, then everything will be forfeit. Everything.'

'Nonetheless, your cause may succeed with the sacrifice of our lives. The families of those who have lost loved ones will need support or some means if they are then to live on.'

Kate nodded. 'You are a good father to your people, Trajan. What payment would you ask?'

'Land, milady, land. A piece of Shakri's own creation for each of those who march with you, for are you not fighting for Shakri's own creation, milady?'

'So it would seem, Trajan, so it would seem.'

'That is a mighty task, milady. It must be a great burden to you.'

'No more of a burden than life itself can seem, Trajan.'

'I understand your words, milady, for were I to lose my own son, then I too would find life a curse, burden and insult added to injury. I pray for your success, for the good of us all.'

'Good night, Trajan.'

'Good night, milady. I will pray that it is not overly long or overly dark.

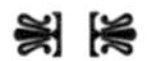

Chapter Eleven: But To Lose The Past

Being dead and not having awareness is no hardship at all, because you won't know any different. But being dead and having some vestigial memory of being alive is an eternal torture. It produces a sense of loss so personal and essential, so absolutely painful, that an individual might wish never to have lived at all, might desire complete oblivion. It is not a pain you can get used to, desensitised or completely inured. It is not something that can be described so simply as an individual's being split open so that their guts lay glistening on the floor all around them and a passing rat coming to gnaw through them. Having to watch and feel such a thing happen to you cannot describe it... but it might come close.

With his one intact eye, Saltar stared through the bars of the cage at the rat eating his entrails. The rodent had greasy, matted brown fur, its whiskers drooped slightly and its eyes were slightly cloudy as if it were old or sick. At least my flesh and blood are feeding one in genuine need, Saltar thought gruesomely.

A bare foot came and gently kicked the creature away. It squeaked in anger, predictably displeased at being made to give up its feast, but moved away beyond Saltar's field of vision.

'You must excuse these lesser gods,' came a voice Saltar thought he recognised. 'They don't know any better. No, Samuel, leave off now! Eat too much of this one and you will become sicker than you've ever been. You will lose all ability to function. You might even be ended.'

There was the slightest sound of small claws on stone and then there was nothing. Presumably, the rodents had retreated fully.

'Here, let me help you.'

There was a click and then Saltar felt himself rising. He assumed he was being lifted out of his cage, but he could discern very little through the complete agony that was his body.

'There! At least you will be able to see a bit more now,' said the familiar voice. 'Hello, there!'

A face hove into view. The white beard and hair could have been anyone's, but those eyes could only belong to Cognis!

With no lungs to speak of, and his lower jaw smashed beyond recognition, Saltar could only think to himself: 'I thought you'd been destroyed!'

'It's alright. I can hear your thoughts. I'm the god of knowledge, remember. Yes, I was removed entirely from Shakri's realm. I originally constructed the balance so that it would be self-sustaining for a while, but we are only a moment or two from it completely over-balancing and the realm toppling over and breaking. The unravelling of the spell has begun, and that will only accelerate from hereon in.

'So if we are not in Shakri's realm, where are we? And why do you sound so cursed jolly about everything?'

Cognis stepped back and swept his arm around himself to invite Saltar to take in the view. Lines of reddish brown stone pillars disappeared off in every direction. They supported a low, featureless stone roof above them. Saltar didn't like to think how much weight was bearing down on those pillars, particularly when he saw clear cracks in a few of them. Flaming torches in brackets could be found at regular intervals throughout the place, extending into the distance and beyond sight like everything else. The only other things of note were a few metal rings sunk into pillars, with manacles attached to them by chains, and the occasional gnawed pile of bones. The strange thing was that there were no walls that he could see.

'The Prison of All Eternity!' Cognis announced. 'As to *where* that is, well, it connects with everything and everywhere. It's pretty much infinite as far as I know and can tell. There are trapdoors in the floor and ceiling. Sometimes they're locked and sometimes they're open. Some are quite big and some are too small to get through. It depends on who you are, I suspect. I, for example, now always find the trapdoor to Shakri's realm locked and too small. But that's just how I see it all. You might think of all eternity in different terms.'

'Is this just a metaphor made real, then?' Saltar wondered, struggling with the concept.

'Yes and no. If it works for you, then it's more than just a metaphor. To be honest, I suspect I find the Prison of All Eternity easier to work with than you do. Many find it impossible to navigate, and wander lost for all eternity. As the god of knowledge, of course, I always know where I am.'

'So, if we come here when we die, is death not absolute?'

'Don't be daft! Mortals of Shakri's realm are taken by Lacrimos. That's all part of the balance and self-propagating nature of the spell created by the pantheon. That is an absolute aspect of the spell of life and death.'

'So why did I not end up in Lacrimos's realm?'

Cognis stared at him with wide eyes. 'Are you stupid as well as ignorant? Obviously because you are not a mortal created within or by Shakri's realm! You are irreducible in such a realm, and that is why you can drop through one of those trapdoors and back here whenever you like.'

'So I cannot die?'

'Idiot!' shouted Cognis like a frustrated schoolteacher faced with a student who is particularly obtuse. 'Look at the bones around you! Are you entirely witless? Of course you can die. Look at the state of you now! I suspect that if I hadn't come and found you, then you would have allowed Samuel to carry on chewing on you, given up on all movement and allowed yourself to become naught but a pile of mouldering bones. Having descended to such a point, it would then have been far beyond your compass to live in any sense that we understand. It would take a being of extraordinary power and self-sacrifice to create the sort of localised organising magic required to raise you back up. In such a place as this, it would be all but impossible. Effectively, you would be dead, no more, utterly extinct, nothing, null, nil, void...'

'Okay! I get the idea!' Saltar couldn't help thinking with a mix of sarcasm and irritation. He cleared his head. 'From what you've said, though, I can't really die in Shakri's realm, right? *Irreducible*, isn't that what you said? If I was not created from or within Shakri's realm, then what am I? Where am I from?'

Cognis harrumphed, clearly more satisfied with the thinking behind this question than previous ones. 'You and a few others asked for sanctuary in Shakri's realm. An agreement was reached between your group and the pantheon. In return for sanctuary, your group agreed to be bound by mortal form and even to shut away certain parts of your knowledge and memory. The fear was that if you did not agree to be so bound, then you would quickly come to rule the people of Shakri's realm completely and begin to disrupt the spell. But, in being bound, your group served to add power to the pantheon's spell, and gave it a certain permanence, or *irreducibility* if you like. Were it not for that power and permanence, Shakri's realm would have fallen already.'

Saltar began to formulate another question.

'No, I know what you're going to ask, but I cannot tell you anything more of where you came from or what knowledge and memory you had shut away. To tell you anything would break you free of your binding and probably destroy Shakri's realm in an instant.'

'Who are the other irreducibles?'

Cognis hopped from one foot to another. He started to pull at his hair distractedly. Worried that the god would end up bald, Saltar asked: 'What's the matter? Surely you know! You know all things... don't you? Are you not omniscient?'

Cognis bit at his top lip. 'I'm omniscient within the terms of Shakri's realm, for I constructed the spell, did I not, but I am not omniscient beyond it. I am not sure best how to answer, which is something of a novel experience for me. I don't think I like it very much. How on earth do mortals cope with such ambiguity? It is quite unpleasant, in fact.'

'Look, Cognis, have done with it and just tell me. If you cannot decide, then let me.'

Cognis shook his head. 'I'm not sure I should. The more organised the irreducibles become amongst themselves, the more chance there is of you slipping free of your binding, and that would be disastrous. And that is precisely why we chose for you those mortal forms and brain configurations, with their contingent personalities and behaviours, that would find it almost impossible to come to an accord or be comfortable in each other's presence.'

Suspicions arose in Saltar's mind.

'Damn it, I've told you too much!' Cognis sighed. 'Oh well, back to what I *do* know and making sure you remain bound. You now have to return to Shakri's realm, Saltar, you do know that, don't you?'

'What?' he protested mentally. 'Return to that cage, to be at the mercy of those magicians? Are you mad? And what's the point? My body's completely ruined. I'll never be able to do anything with it. I won't ever be able to talk, and no one will be able to understand my thoughts like you can.'

'You should have thought of that before stupidly confronting those magicians on your own. And you shouldn't then have agreed to capitulate to them. I expected more of you, to be honest. Ah, well, you've brought it on yourself. Better that you return to that cage in Shakri's realm, suffer in agony for ever more and extend the pantheon's spell than be stuck immobile here serving no purpose but to tempt Samuel into making himself ill.'

'There must be another way! I do not want... Cognis, no!' Saltar screamed as the god picked him up and crushed him back into his cage. 'Cognis, you cretin, put me down!'

The god ignored him and started to whistle tunelessly as He dragged the cage towards a large trapdoor. The metal scraped harshly on the stone floor at first, but soon Saltar's blood and other bodily fluids lubricated their passage through the Prison of All Eternity.

His pain unimaginable, Saltar begged for mercy. When that didn't work, he returned to abuse and threats: 'You dribbling village idiot! The Divine Retard, they should call you! I swear, I will do everything I can, direct any that love me, towards binding you and then creating whole realms and realities with which to punish and persecute you. I will couple with whole legions of demons if necessary so that they will then invent new and eternal tortures with which to abuse you. Cognis, you hear me? Stop that infernal whistling and answer me! Cognis!'

As the cage began to tip through the trapdoor, Cognis brought his eye level with Saltar's. He pursed his lips in disapproval. 'The hour is late. Know thyself, Balthagar!'

❧ ❧

'What splendid bed-fellows we make, Old Hound!' Jack taunted the Scourge loudly so that all would hear. 'But you took more than your manly share of the blankets, methinks!'

'Speak again and I will take all my manly pleasure slamming this knife into the back of your head, demon, no matter if I am then known as an oath-breaker and man without honour the length and breadth of this kingdom. It will be worth it to be rid of you. And stay ahead of me at all times so that I can watch for your weaselly ways,' the Scourge replied.

Jack turned to face him with an amused grin on his face. The Sergeant decided he'd better speak up before the minstrel could provoke yet more violence: 'And I will do nothing to save you this time, Jack, whether it costs us the realm or not. A realm where a demon is permitted to lead us all by the nose is not a realm worth saving.'

Altibus nodded and made the barring sign against demons with one of his hands. 'Such creatures are so deranged that they will destroy themselves with their selfish wants and whimsies. I would not be surprised if it now attempts to speak.'

Realising that there was no fun to be had with his human companions, Jack O'Nine Blades stuck his tongue out at all of them and trotted his horse well ahead of them. Scraggins, sat in his lap, peered back at the others curiously and then settled down for a nap.

The cat awoke some time later, as the temperature dropped and snow began to swirl and spiral around them. They were riding into the wind, and Scraggins decided that Jack's lap at the front of the line was not the place to be. She leapt down from his horse, trotted past a scowling Scourge and then jumped up into a surprised Altibus's lap. She curled up there and purred as his priestly magic kept the worst of the cold at bay.

They made their way down the King's Road with the weather howling and tearing at them like a pack of wolves trying to bring down its prey. Riders and mounts leaned forwards and made stubborn progress into the face of the ferocious storm.

With visibility becoming so bad that he could no longer see Jack ahead of him, the Scourge decided they should either be connecting the horses together by rope or seeking cover in the forests to either side of the road until the worst of it had blown over. But who was to say whether the storm would last for days or not? Perhaps they should be making as much distance as they could while the road was still passable. Then again, they might freeze to death in their saddles if they didn't show some good sense... except for Altibus, who would survive thanks to his magic and the spare blubber he carried... and the Scourge himself, of course, because of the curse placed upon him by the banshee of love.

The Scourge was tempted to let the demonic Jack O'Nine Blades freeze to death, sorely tempted, but it would be a shame to lose the steadfast Sergeant Marr. Maybe Altibus could be persuaded to protect the Sergeant as well as the fickle moggy riding with him. Then, the whole wrangle about whether Jack should be allowed to live or die would likely start up again and the Scourge would find himself fighting all three of them again... and how would any of that help Saltar?

Focus, Scourge! he admonished himself. The stakes are too high to be playing bluff and counter-bluff with a cardsharp like Jack O'Nine Blades. Do not be distracted. Be as unflinching and unremitting in your purpose as the Builder. Damn, it's cold!

The Scourge's horse all but collided with Jack's as it came out of the white wall of driving snow immediately ahead of the Guardian. 'Watch out, you fool!' the Scourge shouted, but the wind stole his words away.

'My eyelashes have frozen and sealed my eyes shut so that I cannot watch anything,' came back the minstrel's thin voice.

The Scourge leaned closer to the lightly clothed loon to ascertain if he spoke the truth or was extemporising some new absurdity. Jack's eyes were certainly closed and his long lashes lay like white icicles down the tops of his cheeks. The Scourge leaned in closer still. Jack's eyes popped open and he planted a large kiss on the Guardian's cheek.

'Oh, you *do* care!'

'Imbecile! This is the neither the time nor the place!' the Scourge raged louder than the blizzard.

'Then let us get somewhere warmer so that we can thaw out your ardour!' Jack winked.

The Scourge went for his blade, but it had frozen in its scabbard. He swung a fist instead and caught the minstrel flush on the chin. 'Not so sprightly now, eh, demon? More used to pits of infernal flame, no doubt!' He swung his other fist and cracked his tormentor just below his right temple. 'No quip, demon? Nothing about how we're working up a fine sweat together? Nothing about how I seem to crave physical contact with you? Nothing to say about my passion?' He punched again, but Jack was already falling to the ground.

The few feet of snow on the ground looked to have broken Jack's fall, but he was out cold. The Scourge's anger had not cooled any, though. He was straight off his horse and ready to start laying into his unconscious victim without any mercy. He brought his boot back to deliver an almighty kick to the creature's head, when his leg turned to lead. He could barely drag it forwards more than a few inches. His arms flopped by his sides and his eyes began to droop.

He knew the magic that was being used on him intimately – it was precisely the spell Shakri had always employed when they'd been together in the pantheon and had one of their blazing rows – she would inevitably become enflamed and decide she wanted to have her way with him – then put him into a state of torpor or semi-sleep. It was a spell synonymous with helplessness and humiliation for him – not far from rape he'd thought once or twice. He had not sorted out in his own mind whether the fact he ultimately enjoyed the experience and ended up begging for more mitigated the terrible liberties she took or not. But he was certainly not prepared to submit to it now. No, he wanted nothing else but to kill the demon.

'Priest!' the Scourge slurred, wheeling towards him. 'You will *not* do this! What you do is-is...' he said as he fell backwards over Jack.

'I-I'm sorry, Divine Consort, but I did not know what else to do!' Altibus called in distress, with Scraggins standing on the horse's head, tail lashing, and staring down at the Scourge with wide eyes.

'What have you done, Altibus?' Marr yelled through cupped hands. 'They'll die out here in this state, even if we sling them over their horses. We have to get under cover.'

The priest shook his head. 'No!' he shouted. 'It's a restorative sleep. An extension of the healing spell, that's all! They may last longer than us.'

'Follow me!' the Sergeant shouted and began to push his horse towards the trees.

'Sergeant! I cannot! The cat and horse insist on pursuing the road.'

'What?!' the soldier called in consternation, looking back to see the priest trying and failing to wrestle his steed round. Scraggins stood proud and rigid at the front of the horse, eyes and body steering their course like a weather vane.

'I suggest you get our companions on their horses and then follow along after us, Sergeant. There's nothing much else we can do. We are at the mercy of both the elements and the gods, methinks!'

Cursing at his lot, the Sergeant slid down from his mount. He retrieved a length of rope from his saddle bag, tied one end around the Scourge's wrists, threw the trailing end over the saddle of the Scourge's snorting destrier, went round the horse to take up the loose length and then started to haul the Scourge's body up onto the leather seat. Once the Guardian was draped over his horse, the Sergeant lashed him securely in place.

Nearly blind, and with the snowfall close to becoming an avalanche, the Sergeant thought he'd lost Jack's body until he tripped over the end of one of the minstrel's long, pointed boots protruding from a rapidly building drift. Working as quickly as he could, he got the body up onto its horse in the same way he had the Scourge's.

Sweating now despite the cold, the Sergeant tied the horses together, clambered back into his saddle, bashed the worst of the snow from his uniform and then kicked his horse forwards with a loud 'Yah!' The holes in the snow left by Altibus's mount were already filling up, so it was fortunate there was only one real direction to go to follow the road.

Time and distance were lost in the white, vertical sea. Occasionally, there was the suggestion of a shadow ahead, but the Sergeant couldn't tell if it was Altibus, a tree, a reflection of himself, or his imagination. Even though he was on a road, he feared he would lose orientation and end up going back the way he'd come.

Unprompted, his horse veered to the left and the snow suddenly abated. He realised they'd moved onto a forest road coming off the main King's Road. He had no idea where they were heading, but quite frankly didn't care, just so long as they were out of the worst of the weather. He could make out the priest now, against the white path ahead. And the going was easier, as less snow was finding its way down between the trees and onto the side-road.

'Shakri preserve us, let's hope that's the worst of it over with!' the long-suffering soldier sighed, and wiped the water, ice and snow from his eyes, face and beard. He realised his hand was shaking – and that he was actually shivering all over. His uniform couldn't keep the damp and cold out forever, and then he'd start suffering from exposure, unless they could find some source of heat. If the priest didn't have the strength left to warm them, then it was time to stop and start a fire, the Sergeant decided. He assumed he'd be able to find some dry wood somewhere beneath the hushed trees, but then again why should things suddenly start becoming any easier for them?

'Altibus!' he spluttered, cleared his throat and then shouted again.

The priest didn't stop. He raised his arms in a helpless gesture, though, to show there was nothing he could do to halt his horse.

'I thought you priests of Shakri had sway over the animals of Her creation!' the Sergeant shouted.

'This horse is being unusually stubborn,' Altibus shouted back over his shoulder. 'It pricks its ears up when I send thoughts to it, but ignores my requests.'

'The cat?!'

Another shrug. 'I can't get through to it. It's a very unusual animal, to say the least.'

'Well, I for one am not prepared to die for it,' the soldier asserted. 'Which begs the question why we're simply putting our faith in it. It's Jack's, isn't it? It's a demon's familiar then. *That's* why it's an usual animal, Altibus! And it's no doubt leading us to our deaths even as we speak. It's bewitched your horse, priest! Since when has man answered to the animals? It's not right. Nature has been turned upside down. Its laws have been perverted!'

Altibus had stopped, and Sergeant Marr now caught up to him. The soldier's words died on his lips as he looked out on the scene. A small village slept by the side of a river. Snow lay deep and soft on the thatched roofs. Ducks huddled at the edge of the frozen pond, quacking conspiratorially amongst themselves that it was high time they left for warmer climes, and that they would do precisely that as soon as the sky cleared. Chickens scratched in vain at the hard ground of their run. All would have looked idyllic save for the large snow-topped pile of charred human bodies at the centre of it all.

'We have seen the likes before,' Altibus whispered.

'Is… is there anyone left alive?' the Sergeant asked.

The priest was silent for a second. 'No. At least, I don't sense anything human in the area anyway.'

'We're on the right trail, then. Do you have any idea if Saltar also came this way?'

'No way to tell. I guess he must have done though.'

'I have seen my share of battle and horrors,' the Sergeant observed. 'I thought I'd seen the worst that men could do. But this... these people wouldn't even have understood what was happening to them. They were simple peasants. What defence...?' and he tailed off, lost for words.

Altibus was unable to reply.

'It will be hard to dig in this frozen earth, but I suppose we should try to bury them.'

Altibus shook his head and finally said, 'Nay, good Sergeant. I will anoint them and give them Shakri's blessing. Let us not disturb them any further than that. We should better spend our time catching up to the monsters responsible, to prevent such as this happening again if we can.'

Altibus's horse picked its way towards the charnel pyre, waited while Altibus performed his duty, and then stepped almost reverentially on through the village, with the Sergeant and the two trailing horses not far behind. Even then, they came across the occasional telltale shape in the snow. Altibus would sprinkle holy water at such times but they otherwise left that which lay beneath to its rest. The covering of snow was almost a mercy, the Sergeant decided. He eyed the cat, Scraggins, which crouched in subdued fashion behind the neck of Altibus's mare. If it was a demon's familiar, it would be displaying anything but misery because of this slaughter. The cat was as curious and unpredictable as Jack himself.

The Sergeant wanted to put the village well behind them before suggesting a stop, but the further they got, the wider apart the trees were and the deeper the snow was piled. It was now clear the forest path would lead them all the way to the forbidden Needle Mountains. Would that prove to be their ultimate destination? Surely they were heading far to the west of Accritania. He'd never heard of any sort of community in this remote and mountainous region before.

'Altibus, let's find shelter while we still can. I don't like the look of that sky. And I think I'll be pissing ice-cubes before much longer.'

'Wait! Do you smell that?'

Wood smoke! Sergeant Marr pushed his horses forwards through the treacherous snow, looking left and right for some give-away in the sky as to the origin. There was a haze of grey against the white off to his right and he struck out that way. It was only the questioning whinny of a horse that finally gave away the giant fir tree it turned out they were looking for. It's heavily laden skirts reached all the way to the ground, but the horse tethered in its lee and the smoke mazing out through its branches made it clear someone was hidden within.

The Sergeant pulled his sword from its scabbard. The animal grease on the blade that meant it could usually be drawn silently had frozen solid, and the leather sheath had constricted and stiffened in the cold. The tree's occupant therefore had ample warning of their approach, what with the horse's previous vocal challenge as well.

'I can see you, Sergeant! You're making a real hash of creeping up on me, you know!'

'Lucius!' Altibus and the Sergeant shouted together.

'Well met, well met! A fine day you chose to come a-visiting!' the musician sang out to them. 'I will push a stick out so that you can find the best place to enter without blowing out my fickle fire or turning this place into a smoke-house for the preserving of meats. Yet I see you have brought two trophies with you. They look scrawny and tough to me. Are you sure they were worth the effort?'

'Just grab the Scourge's shoulders, would you?' the Sergeant shivered. 'Thanks. Ready? And here's Jack. Oof!'

'Is there room for me?' Altibus asked anxiously.

'Yes, yes! Push your way inside. It's a little crowded, but we'll stay warmer this way.'

They were all in. The lowest branches of the giant fir started four or five feet from the ground but arched out and down to make a natural hollow, or wigwam, for them. The pine needles carpeting the earth provided good insulation against any chill from below, and Lucius had used a small pile of them for a fire that both lit and warmed the place. He'd also hung his spare clothing and blanket to block the few gaps that existed between the branches. A tin full of rapidly melting snow currently set in the flames.

'I was just making some tea!' smiled the musician. 'That'll warm us faster than anything else.'

The Scourge stirred, and opened groggy eyes that still managed to look angry.

'That would be most welcome, friend Lucius,' Altibus smiled in return, while casting a wary eye towards the Guardian.

'I'm afraid I'm dripping over everything,' the Sergeant apologised.

The Scourge rolled over and made the sort of noise a bear would when prematurely awoken from its long winter sleep. 'Never mind that. Lucius, where's Saltar, eh?'

The royal musician's face fell. 'I-I…'

They waited.

Lucius covered his face with his hands and started to rock backwards and forwards. 'He-he's dead!'

'No!' Altibus gasped. 'I sensed nothing!'

'How can it be?' the Sergeant wondered out loud. 'Without the Battle-leader, what hope is there?'

'By the ragged and abused pizzel of Wim, I'll not believe he's dead until I've seen it with my own eyes!' the Scourge averred. 'Death is not absolute, and I know that to be true, by the cowardly vomit of Lacrimos! I've killed Him more times than I've cared to blaspheme about Him. And now whenever trouble approaches he shits himself uncontrollably like a newborn babe with its first illness.'

A chuckle came from the shadows on the other side of the tree's trunk. 'Scourge, do you not think that temper of yours will see an end to this group more surely than anything else that's going on in the realm? And should I wager that temper tore this group apart on an occasion even before I joined you all?'

The Guardian picked up a broken branch that lay within handy reach. He tested its ends with one of his fingers. 'Demon, this branch is as sharp and forked as your tongue. Come, ask me another question, and I shall use this branch to answer you.'

The Sergeant put his head in his hands, shaking it. Scraggins sighed. 'Good Altibus, if you would be so kind? Neither the Guardian nor the minstrel seem as yet fully recovered.'

'Of course, Sergeant,' the priest replied.

'Don't you d-!'

'Sweet priest of Shakri, I-…'

The Sergeant nodded. 'Thank you, Altibus. I just pray we will not have consigned them to their slumbers when we confront the enemy. Before then, we must find some way to have those two fight the same cause rather than each other.'

Then, more gently, he addressed the royal musician: 'Friend Lucius, I would welcome tea more than I can say. I am still cold. Please, calm yourself and take us back to where we were but minutes ago. Then, when all is right, we will listen long and quietly. But tea first. Come!'

It was easy to gain access to the mind of a mortal. It was fairly easy then to influence that mind, for it would only know a frame of reference as described within the communion of those minds. Prejudice could be made to seem reasonable, love would appear the same as cruelty, sacrifice would become interchangeable with the assertion of opinion. But it was the hardest of tasks to dislodge a mind from it own centre and place, even if that mind was young and underdeveloped. Such a task could only be achieved by the most skilled practitioners of blood-magic.

The Plague Victim and the Skull, masters of mind and body, had experimented with dozens of their Owned for generations. They knew how the mind could be broken if the body was subjected to torture. They knew how the body could be left prostrate by the mind being subjected to emotional torture. They knew how the body and mind could be separated from each other so that they could be made to operate independently. They knew how to kill a mind and keep its body alive. They even knew how to keep a mind alive for some while when its body was dead. They could create the illusions and delusions necessary to fool any mind, or the false feelings and physical responses required to make any body betray itself.

The Lords now sat separately from their magickers, trying to manipulate the two-year-old child Orastes within the weaves of their magic. However, the child was proving obdurate in the extreme, nigh on immovable.

'Maybe it requires the Three of us,' the Plague Victim speculated and mopped sweat from his brow.

'There must be a way!' the Skull brooded. 'A two-year-old does not have the mental discipline to seal its core away. No, if anything, we are being thwarted by how incomplete its mental formation is. No doubt, it sees things in large, flat ways that are difficult for our precise tools and techniques to grapple with.'

'I see,' the Plague Victim nodded, wiping bloody saliva from the corner of his mouth on the edge of his robe. 'Should we forge a mindscape then?'

The Skull drew a deep breath. 'It is dangerous, but I see no other way. A flat and featureless land of rock and stone, do you think?'

'Yes, that should suffice. Very little can hide in such a place. I am ready.'

The Lords looked up and around their new environment. The dark clearing in which they were camped was gone now. There was no sign of the child who had been sitting in front of them but moments ago, no trace of the magickers sat at the fire on the other side of the camp.

Giant shapes of yellow light and smoky shadow played slowly across the sky, axes and dimensions tilting and tipping. The Skull was forced to fix his eyes on the ground and level horizon to rediscover his equilibrium. At least the surface underfoot was as it should be and not shifting around as if to throw him off. 'Disconcerting perhaps, but this is a place of omens. We will have good warning of anything amiss. Brother?'

'Here!' coughed the other Lord, waving away the cloud of dust that had been blown up by his arrival. 'It's mostly as I expected it, but different enough to serve as an omen in its own right, an omen that we should remain wary. Any sign of the source? I still cannot see too well. This cursed dust gets everywhere. I feel it coating the back of my throat already.'

Spare and dry as the Skull was, he was not troubled in the same way as the Plague Victim. 'There, the haze of the horizon is not even. This way!'

'Coming. Try not to kick up too much dust if at all possible, brother?'

They strode towards the horizon and duly came to a low cave raised in the stone desert. They ducked and stepped inside.

A squat and hideous gargoyle crouched on a dais and gurned down at them. Its bulging eyes glittered with the sort of iridescent intelligence that told them it knew what they were about and did not care one jot. It fingered its naked arse with one hand and had the fingers of its other clawed hand splayed and inserted into mouth, wide nostrils and bat-like ears. Its flaccid member hung to the floor and curled around one of its legs like a tail. Its folded wings looked too small for its broad and bulbous body, but spiked enough to serve as spearing weapons.

Despite themselves, the Lords held back from the mad imp. They were neither insensitive nor immune to the aura of defiant menace that emanated from it.

'This is not the child's, surely!' the Plague Victim said in a shaken voice. 'What is it? A statue?'

'A totem, more like it. A guardian spirit of some sort. There is no way of telling who placed it here. Yet that is not our primary concern. Removing it is,' the Skull said, and lifted a sharp stone. Without any apparent fear, he approached the gargoyle and hammered against it. 'Not a mark! It is of too hard a substance. Brother?'

The Plague Victim rubbed at his jaw in thought, old scabs coming away from his skin. 'It is organised as an altar or a place a pilgrim would visit. There is a primitive attempt at spectacle, an attempt to inspire awe. Even the depiction of the carving is meant to terrify, to keep away the unconfident. It is a clever defence. Ultimately, though, it lacks depth or emotional sophistication – not surprising given it has to be conducive to the mindscape of an infant. All we need do brother, is end the spectacle.'

'Very well,' the Skull accepted and started to remove stones from the floor in front of the dais.

'What are you doing, brother?'

'Digging a hole.'

The Plague Victim paused. 'Ah. I see. Should I help you?'

The Skull turned his ever-grinning face to the other Lord and improvised a shrug. 'As you wish. Time is of little consequence here. The work is not tiring.'

Presently, the hole was complete. The Skull dusted off his black robe, realised there was no need to do so in this place, shook his head, moved behind the gargoyle and with the help of the Plague Victim sent the gargoyle crashing down into its grave. Its wings did nothing to slow its fall. The sound of the falling idol continued to circle around the cave, rising in volume.

The Lords exited the cave hurriedly and then watched as it collapsed. The ground shook with the violence of the event, but when it was all over there was little sign that the cave had ever existed.

'Now all is as it should be,' the Plague Victim sighed and watched the sky lose its variation. 'Child of Balthagar, hear me!' thundered the Lord's voice, and there was no hiding from it as it echoed off horizon, sky and stone earth. 'Your father is broken and caged. Do you not care for him? If you did, you would have left this place so that he had somewhere to be free. Leave this place and we will release him here. That is a promise! But until you leave, there is no room for him. Show your father you love him, child! Leave now and all will be well.'

A wind rose and wailed with an infant's voice. It begged for the embrace of its mother and father, it screamed to be nurtured. It wanted to be held and kept warm. It needed to be loved.

'Leave this place and their love will be yours! Leave!'

Cracks appeared in the ground, some parts subsiding so that there were now steps and drops in the landscape. The Skull looked wildly at the Plague Victim, but the other was too caught up in his exhortation to pay any attention.

'This is a dark and lonely place, Orastes! It is cold. If you remain, you will be alone for the rest of your life!'

The wind began to keen and then reached such a pitch that is was beyond the Lords' hearing. Their robes suddenly fell still. The rock beneath their feet ceased to quake. The sky turned a blank, creamy colour to match and reflect the barren wastes beneath it. The mindscape was utterly devoid of life save for the Lords of the Brethren.

The Lords looked up and around their dark clearing once more. With a mix of excitement and trepidation, the Skull looked down at the unmoving body of Orastes and then up at his companion. In a hushed voice he said: 'The way is clear. The vessel is prepared. Dare we take this next step?'

His throat still raw from the imaginary dust of the mindscape, the Plague Victim rasped: 'To think how long we have waited for this, brother, how long we have had to hide ourselves from the world, suffering the depravations of the primitive Brethren! But we can wait no longer, you know that, for Nylchros has already begun to dissipate. We must bring him through now if he is to have permanence in this realm. Otherwise, both he and any chance for our survival will be lost forever. We must bring him into this child's irreducible body or our centuries of labour will have been for nothing. Without Nylchros, we will then be at the mercy of the pantheon and their pawns. If the Scourge, Kate or the Chamberlain were to come for us then, we would inevitably be defeated and consigned to the eternal hell of Lacrimos's realm.'

The Skull was reassured. He repeated his oft-spoken mantra: 'Never will the Three willingly submit to Lacrimos. He is a sneak thief looking to take our existence from us when we are asleep or distracted. He is an unrepentant criminal who therefore deserves no mercy. He should be hunted down and either ended or incarcerated forever more. While He is still at large, however, we must keep our valuables safely guarded from His attention and appetite.'

The Plague Victim feigned he was listening, to indulge his brother. Then, he gurgled through his phlegm: 'And so we have no choice when our existences are harried by Lacrimos and the pantheon. Nylchros will be ours to command, both our guard and general. With their lost god to lead them, none will be able to stand before the Brethren, lowly though the Owned are to us. We will be the absolute rulers of this realm, and then perhaps others.'

'We have no choice!' the Skull repeated needlessly. 'What else can we do? And Nylchros will be bound by our command, yes?'

The Plague Victim hid his sigh by attempting to clear his throat. 'Brother Heritus is clear on the matter. Nylchros will be trapped in the child's body until we can return him to the ziggurat in the mountains.'

'Very well,' the Skull chattered, wobbling his head on his spine. 'We will proceed at once. Refus!' he called to the distant group of silent magickers. 'Attend us.'

The magicker named Refus rose to join his Owners. He was the youngest of the blood-mages, but had been placed over the others because of his unswerving, if not excessive, devotion to the Three. He never questioned or hesitated in carrying out an instruction. He was appalled and often angry when other magickers were not as quick to obey as he was. Before he'd been placed over the others, he had been involved in a number of fights that had resulted in unfortunate deaths. Innocent his wide blue eyes might look, and carefree his unlined face might appear – and in some ways perhaps he was both those things – but he was also ruthless, and therefore of significant value to the Owners of the Brethren.

The magicker knelt before the Skull and bowed his head to the ground.

'Refus, you may rise. I have need of your blood. You are to be honoured, for it will be the means by which the lost god will be returned to us.'

The magicker's eyes shone. 'Truly, master? Then I am blessed.' He bared an arm covered in the livid scars of recent magical practice, produced his letting knife and placed the sharp metal ready against the skin of his wrist. 'I am ready to serve. How deep should I cut?'

'Do you give your blood willingly?' the Skull asked as per the ritual.

'I do, master.'

'Do you understand this blood is given in the name of the Three… and the lost god?'

'I do, master.'

The Skull produced his own letting knife and made incisions in Orastes's small arms. 'Then cut a steady trickle of your living blood to mix with the child's, fill his mouth and bathe his eyes.'

The magicker did as instructed as the Skull took up the summoning. 'Nylchros! Here is your vessel! It is empty and incomplete without you. It is a gateway into this realm, for it exists here by permission of Shakri and the pantheon, yet it is not entirely of this realm's making. Its progenitor is Balthagar, irreducible in this realm. And here is living blood shed on your behalf to serve as spark, organising magic and impetus! By all this are you summoned. The way is clear for the Unity!'

Refus's eyes rolled back in his head and his knife slipped in his blood-slicked hands. The blade came dangerously close to cutting his main artery, which would have had disastrous consequences for the summoning. Risking his own fingers, the Plague Victim plucked the tool from Refus's hands and steadied the magicker so that he would not pitch over on top of the frail form of the child.

Refus's lower jaw fell open and a foreign voice issued from his chest, though without the necessary enunciation and articulation to be understood. The sound was little more than a spasticated groan that rose and fell in volume.

'Nylchros, that is not the body you should be seeking to possess. But if you are trying to communicate, use the mouth, lips and jaws to modulate the sound more,' the Plague Victim directed the Unity.

'No!' came a mental blast so strong that the Plague Victim feared it had torn his head apart. It was like a mountain falling on him. 'My ability is not lacking! This body is inadequate!' The single word before had been nearly too much to bear, but these phrases were completely overwhelming for the Plague Victim's sensitive telepathic skills. He passed out.

The Skull, who was less mentally attuned, and therefore less vulnerable, stepped in. 'Nylchros, the child is your vessel, not this blood-giver. Hear me! You can only reside temporarily in the blood-giver. Even if he was prepared to sacrifice his body and life to you, it would do you no good. He is not irreducible. It cannot serve as a permanent anchor in this realm. Release him and enter the child!'

'Naaa!' Refus belched. 'Kild ish too weak!'

'The child's body is weak now, but once we have returned to our people, it will more than serve. There is no other choice. If you do not take up the child now, then you will dissipate completely in trying to access this realm.'

With a final yell of rage and defiance, Nylchros released Refus and Orastes began to scream. The child turned baleful, red eyes on the Skull. There was pure malice on its face, but it was in a body of very little strength so effectively helpless. It did not yet have the experience to co-ordinate its movements to climb or walk. And it did not have sufficient palette to talk. It beat its fists and cried with outrage and frustration.

Waves of mental anger buffeted the Skull but he was able to ignore them. He sat back on his heels amazed. He had given birth to a god!

Vasha had her hands clapped to her ears. 'They are torturing a child, Larc! How can you just sit there? They are monsters, demons!'

Larc sat with knees bent, elbows resting on his knees, head held between his hands and eyes fixed on the ground. She was right, damn her! The only acts of cruelty that he had witnessed in the chaos wastes were those perpetrated by his own people, by his own Lords! They had slaughtered whole temples and villages and shown no qualms about torturing an innocent babe. The so-called chaos wastes had only shown Larc kindness, by contrast. Vasha had given him food and friendship and the Builder had been stayed by the mere threat of violence to the babe.

She was right, damn her! He now knew that it was his own people who were the demons, or rather his people had allowed themselves to be misled by the demon Lords and their magickers.

She was right, damn her! He now realised what a dreadful thing he'd done in luring the Builder into an ambush.

Damn her! He could now see that the Three would have no interest in returning his dear departed wife and child to him. If they had no care or concern for a living two-year-old child, then how could he expect anything of them with regard to a mother and infant lost during childbirth?

'Larc, do something!'

He'd never been more miserable in all his life. His life as one of the Owned meant nothing. The lost god, in whose name all these heinous acts were carried out, clearly would not bring any salvation or answers. The one person who might have been able to help, the Builder, was now gone because of what Larc had done. So what was left? Only his guilt and grief. There was that other god, of course. Lacrimos, hadn't Vasha called Him? She'd said He was the god of death. Perhaps that was all there was in the end. Perhaps everyone ended up trying to do a deal with Death eventually.

Larc and Vasha were sat near the horses, well away from the magickers. Even so, one of them had apparently heard Vasha, for he threw them a warning glance. It was telling that the blood-mage did no more than that – he too must be uncomfortable with what was being done to the child. Similarly, no one liked to talk about, think about or look at the grisly cage carted along by the horse at the back of their group every day. Why were they even keeping the cursed thing? Was it some sort of trophy that would be displayed to the Brethren upon the return of the two Lords to the valley? Was it meant to serve as warning to both the Brethren and their enemies as to what happened to those who opposed the Three?

'Just what do you expect me to do?' Larc mumbled.

She didn't answer. After a while, he realised he could hear her gentle sobbing. For the briefest instant, he thought about ignoring it, and then his better nature asserted itself. He wasn't a demon yet, and the tiny gesture of putting his arm around her proved that. It gave him hope somehow.

'Just promise me!' she blubbed, her whole body trembling and snot dripping from her nose. She was close to hysterical. To be honest, he was close to the same, but he'd turned his hysteria inwards.

'Of course. What do you want me to promise?' he asked gently.

'I-I don't know! J-Just promise me!'

He found he wanted to promise her whatever he could, and even some things he couldn't. 'Vasha, I promise I won't betray you again. I promise I will do all I can.'

She smiled through tears and her heartache. 'Thank you, Larc,' she whispered.

Chapter Twelve: Interr The Present

Their departure from Corinus had had all the pomp and spectacle of a religious festival day. Each temple had processed down through the city, led by their high priest on decorated horse, in rich palanquin, or ornate throne hoisted aloft. Then had come the mounted ranks of priests in the brightly coloured robes of their temple, followed by an assortment of acolytes and staff on foot. Last had come the beribboned supply wagons, which also served as transport for the elders not well enough to sit ahorse.

The city's entire population had turned out to watch their leaders march to war. There was much waving and cheering. Flowers were thrown, love tokens pressed into the hands of sweethearts, tears were shed, promises shared.

Pushing through the crowds at the front of it all was the Green Witch on her large, black mare accompanied by the palace guard. The people were quick to move aside, but they all seemed to want to touch her. Their hands stretched out to brush her boots and calves. The odd simpleton had thrown themselves on their face in the street in front of her horse, and it was only her quick evasive manoeuvres that had spared them a hoof to the head and a broken pate. Others called to her to beg that she bless their sickly child or infirm parent. What were they thinking? She didn't have such powers. Yet they were undeterred, and every now and then someone tried to grab her reins to press their case.

'This is dangerous. We should clear the streets before someone gets trampled,' she said to General Vidius riding just behind her shoulder. 'And it makes a mockery of our business,' she added sourly.

'Despite appearances, there are pockets of fear and envy in this crowd,' Sister Spike observed, her eyes and hands constantly moving in anticipation of and response to a number of threats the others could not perceive. Thus far, however, she had not needed to attack anyone.

'Milady,' Vidius said softly, as if calming a skittish horse, 'such a display is good for the morale of both the citizens of Corinus and our troops. It also increases general support for our cause. Do not forget it is an overt and necessary demonstration of throne and temple acting in concert. Think of it as the first blow struck by your army.'

She would have preferred to have been engaged in wholesale slaughter, but knew she had to indulge the General at least until he'd got her army into the field and on its way towards the true enemy. She endured the rest of the procession in silence, half hoping that someone would give her an excuse to unleash Sister Spike.

They moved beyond the city's walls and even found a few Outdwellers there to watch them pass. They were not as well fed or clothed as the Indwellers, but when they shouted encouragement they sounded more enthusiastic and genuine. The army of five hundred Outdwellers waiting for them beyond the small houses proved just how much her promise of land to Trajan's people had meant.

The Outdwellers were a disorderly bunch waiting around in small groups or even as lone individuals. There was a semi-feral look in their eyes that she found she understood and trusted more than she did the looks from her smiling, priestly allies. Thinking about it, she decided she was more comfortable around the Outdwellers than she was with her own Memnosian troops. The schooled expressions of the paid soldiery under Vidius's direct command hid too much for her taste. And she could not forget the fact that the Captain of her own palace guard had been a traitor.

The only splash of colour to be seen amongst the Outdwellers was a red rag tied around the arm of one of the smaller men. He was approaching her now, along with a large, hulking brute. He bowed clumsily when he reached her, and slapped the brute on the arm to remind him to follow suit.

'Milady,' said the small man, in a soft voice. 'Trajan sends his regards. I am Sotto. I have been elected to lead these Outdwellers. This is my comrade Dijin. He is... well, he is the strongest amongst us.'

Kate smiled. 'Any man elected from amongst the Outdwellers and speaking with Trajan's voice is a friend to the throne. I take it, friend Sotto, that you are as quick of wit as Dijin is strong?'

'Praps, milady,' Sotto demured. 'Certainly, strength without wit is a stone, and wit without strength is a jest. Milady, we are ready to march, so have the wit, but we are not well provisioned, so may lack the strength.'

She liked this droll, little fellow, though she suspected that in the dark of the catacombs his size and speed would make him more deadly than Dijin. 'The priesthood of Shakri will summon animals as we go, to be sure that all have enough to eat. If you have any problems with the priests, then please feel free to mention them to either myself or the General.'

'Do you have weapons enough, Sotto?' Vidius asked.

'Oh, yes, General, every Outdweller has their own weapons. Forgive me, but we will not be joining you in any sort of grand pitched battle. We will find the enemy in the dark and strike them from behind or on their blind side. It is our way.'

The General nodded. 'Some would call you cowardly, but it is a tactic that has stood the Outdwellers in good stead till now. While we march, we can discuss further how best to deploy your people. You are content to submit to the command of both myself and milady, is that right?'

Sotto glanced at Kate and then back to General Vidius. 'It is acceptable to us.'

'Good!' said Kate briskly. 'Then we march. Be assured, Sotto, we will not waste your people unnecessarily. We will use whatever means and tactics necessary to destroy this enemy. There is no act I would not consider.'

⁂

Initially, they made good time. Kate, General Vidius, the one and half thousand Memnosian cavalry and the mounted priests moved a long way down the King's Road ahead of the supply wagons and those on foot, including the few Memnosian infantry, the temple acolytes, Sotto's Outdwellers and the army's hangers-on. It was expected that the foot troops would march on after sunset in order to make up the distance everyday to those who had travelled on horseback. Such a pace could not usually have been sustained by foot troops for more than a few days, of course; but with the rejuvenating efforts of the priests of Shakri, they expected to be able to extend that to a week, long enough to take them close to the Needle Mountains at any rate.

The further north they got, however, the worse the weather and the deeper the snow became. By the time they had collected a thousand mounted mercenaries from Holter's Cross, the riders in the army were only staying ahead of those on foot by about an hour after sunset each day. Effectively, the several thousand horses would have to trample down and clear the snow in front of them each day, leaving a relatively easy path for the foot troops coming up behind.

Grandmaster Thaeon of the Guild of Holter's Cross had sent invitation to Kate and General Vidius to stay as his guests in the mercenary enclave for some few days until there was a break in the weather. They had declined his most generous offer, however.

'The old crow is probably after information or looking to make some profit out of us beyond the cavalry we have already hired,' Kate commented.

General Vidius nodded. 'I shouldn't wonder. If he could encourage us to camp in the environs of Holter's Cross, then all sorts of fees will no doubt be due the Guild. Our troops would seek to trade or mingle with the mercenaries. They would fill the taverns run by the Guild. Within hours, the Grandmaster would know what we were due to have for tomorrow morning's breakfast. All sorts of information and monies would trickle away from us, until we suddenly found ourselves dependent on the Guild. We would end up staying here longer than we originally intended, until one morning we woke up to discover we no longer commanded our own army. We would not own the men, the uniforms on their backs, the food in their bellies, nor even the fleas in their hair. We might even find that we no longer owned our as yet unborn children. That, for Grandmaster Thaeon's invitation!'

'We will have to see to the Guild once and for all some day,' Kate considered out loud. 'They are a parasite that threatens to consume their host. They are a spreading cancer that requires a limb to be amputated if the body is to survive. Perhaps once we have attended to the Three and the blood-mages, General? I fancy the throne could do with an overlord in Holter's Cross.'

'I would be honoured, milady,' the General bowed. 'The enclave would be a great prize indeed.'

'Would it meet your price, General?' Kate asked, all seriousness.

'It might, milady, it might.'

'Then it is agreed,' she said with determination.

With Sister Spike standing just behind him, Vidius decided now was not the time to argue. He was not pleased with how she sought to manoeuvre him though. He would need to put some plans of his own into motion.

⁂

They made sure they set that night's camp well beyond Holter's Cross. The sun was just beginning to set and Kate's tent had only just been put up when a tired looking soldier was escorted through the camp to see her.

'Milady, I am Carris. Sergeant Marr...'

Kate gasped. 'Tell me of my husband! Sister Spike, fetch the Chamberlain and General Vidius.'

The soldier told them of the massacre they had found at the temple of Wim, of the monstrous mound of the dying, of the black-robed magicians they believed to be from Accritania, of Saltar's departure with Lucius, and of the group now following on close behind them, agroup that contained the legendary character of Jack O'Nine Blades.

'And my son?' Kate demanded.

Carris looked pained. 'I am sorry, milady, we did not have sight or word of him.'

'Go back to the beginning and start again.'

'Milady, if I may, hmm?' the Chamberlain suggested.

She waved a hand at him to continue.

'Soldier, was the entity possessing the dying ever referred to, hmm? Did the blood-mages or Saltar term it as anything, or did the entity identify itself?'

Carris frowned as he thought back. 'Well... Jack seemed certain the entity was a demon of some sort. The Scourge attacked Jack himself for being a demon – I don't think I mentioned that before. But wait! Yes, the Battle-leader referred to the entity as the *Creator*. I got the impression it was from something one of the magicians had previously said.'

The Chamberlain and Vidius exchanged a surreptitious glance. Yes, they both had ancient memories of such an entity. The Chamberlain's own were partial and muddled at best, and he was reluctant in the extreme to share what little he knew with the likes of Vidius.

'Milady, it would seem this Creator is trying to access this realm through some sort of necromatic blood-magic, hmm?' the Chamberlain ventured. 'May I go and consult with the high priestess of Lacrimos? She may have some insight into what they want of your son.'

'What do you suspect?' Kate shot at him.

'Milady, I suspect nothing. I may surmise something, though, once I have spoken to the high priestess, hmm?'

'Go then! And be sure to return with your surmises... hmm?'

The Chamberlain bowed and departed. Kate turned back to the soldier and made him go through every detail of his experience since he'd last left Corinus. She cross-examined Carris for hours, before she thought to allow them all food, or the soldier a chair.

Vidius had insisted that Kate have a relatively large tent, even though it was awkward to transport. He said it served as a symbol of authority and reassurance for the men. Kate had agreed to have it on condition that the choice of interior was left to her. He'd readily agreed and even smiled indulgently, thinking that she wanted to bestow a suitably "feminine" touch to the decor. He'd been horrified to discover on their first night on the road that she'd actually been determined to have her tent as bare and lacking in ostentation as possible. There was a single rug on the floor to cover the snow, a table for maps and meals, a chair, a lamp, a small brazier and single pallets for herself and Sister Spike. Kate simply refused to have any luxuries around her that might relax and soften her. She did not want to become comfortable in her tent. She did not want to start grabbing an extra five minutes in bed in the mornings, and slow down their advance on their enemy. Lastly, she did not want anything in the tent to encourage the General to stay any longer than was absolutely necessary for them to settle any issues pertaining to the army. She noted with smug satisfaction that he was always keen to keep their nightly interviews brief and brisk so that he might retire as soon as possible to the warm and opulent surroundings of his own tent. She could no longer abide to have him anywhere around her, for she did not trust him.

So it was that once Vidius had realised there was little of value in Carris's report, he'd excused himself to attend to "other urgent army matters". Kate now sat with just Sister Spike and Carris, eating a cold supper in silence. The guard who had brought extra chairs into the tent now thoughtfully brought them a jug of wine, and Carris didn't hesitate to help himself to a goblet and a few large mouthfuls.

'Ahhh!' he sighed appreciatively. Then he remembered who he was with and became embarrassed about his manners. 'Sorry, milady, it's just that being on the road...'

'It's alright, Carris!' she assured him. After an awkward pause, she added: 'Perhaps I should be the one apologising to you. My hospitality had not been the best, has it? And I could have shown you more consideration in how I questioned you. I suspect some think my intensity rude and unnecessary.'

Carris's mouth hung open for a second. Then he pulled himself together and looked down into his wine like a seer. 'Milady,' he said in a low voice. 'I, like many others, served in the army when Voltar was King. Nothing can be considered rude or unnecessary in comparison to those dark days.' Now he met her eyes. 'Milady, I did things back then that I was not proud of, things that made me ashamed. I think we all did. There was no food, you see. Many of the men had families. We were desperate! We would hunt the Accritanians for their blood and...' He looked away briefly. 'Anyway, we were less than human. Less than animals, some might say, for surely we lost our souls too.'

Carris put his goblet down and went on one knee before her. 'Milady, you and the Battle-leader saved us! You made us men again. You restored our pride! We learned to smile again, to love our fellow man again. Perhaps you cannot understand what that means, as you remained strong and refused to descend as low as we did. Believe me then when I say that every man in this army knows they owe you a debt they can never repay, even if they are lucky enough to give their lives for you.

'I do not exaggerate, milady! You cannot imagine what it means to me to have been in your presence, to have sat at the same table! My family will never believe it. And I know it will be a story told proudly down through every generation. Rude and unnecessary? Nay, do not say it! You do me the greatest honour I have ever known.

'Would any in this army think your intensity rude and unnecessary? Never! You are our purpose and will. You are our hope. Milady, every man in this army loves you more than they do their own mother, sister or wife!'

A part of her wanted to believe him. A part of her enjoyed his flattery and giggled and smiled. The young girl in her held his every word close to her heart and allowed herself to be convinced they all cared for her and would look after her. The young woman in her heard promises of devotion, loyalty and companionship.

The corners of her lips began to rise and her eyes began to moisten. Careful! cautioned the woman of experience within her. Blandishments and glib promises were what men had used to betray her last time. There are traitors in your army, you know it! The Captain of the guard helped them take your son! You know that the Chamberlain and Vidius are loyal only to their selfish desires. What makes you think you can trust this one? She clamped down on the joy and optimism rising within her before it could start to weaken her. It was like a cancer trying to undermine her resolve, body and spirit.

'Sister Spike!' she said sternly. 'Does he dissimulate? Is he false? Is he toying with me? If so, answer me only with actions. I am tired of words, for they no longer carry truth.'

Carris's eyes went wide in panic, but he made no attempt to get up or even move.

'Hmmm!' the bloody priestess of Incarnus sounded. She pulled a shiny bodkin from her hair, leaned down and held its point under the soldier's chin as she considered him.

Carris didn't even dare swallow.

'He can be trusted,' she pronounced after a while. 'Besides, he's cute.'

It wasn't the priestess's words that convinced Kate as much as the look of acceptance in the soldier's eyes. As good as his word, he'd been prepared to sacrifice his life. 'Well, Carris, would you like to join my personal guard? Before you decide to tell me how honoured you'd be, you should be aware that you're not likely to live long if you accept. You will be within reach of the unpredictable Sister Spike at nearly all times. She's likely to gut you before you've even made any conscious plan to betray me.'

Carris did not blink. He held Kate's gaze as he said, 'Milady, longevity is not the only way to measure a life's value. I would happily serve as your personal guard, for as long as Shakri and Lacrimos see fit.'

Kate resisted making a blasphemous remark about the gods. 'Then I accept you into my service, Carris. I will leave it to you and Sister Spike to agree sleeping patterns. Suffice it to say, one of you must be on guard at all times. You will either sleep on this pallet here or sleep in the saddle. Understand?'

'Yes, milady.'

'Then I suggest you sleep now, Carris, as you look exhausted. Finish your wine too, for it is the last you will have while my personal guard. What, is that a sacrifice too far?'

The soldier smiled ruefully. 'No, milady. It's probably for the best anyway.'

Kate thought for a moment. 'Yet I am not unkind. You may have watered wine with your supper.'

'Thank you, milady.'

There was a sudden kafuffle outside. A guard drew back the tent flap, causing cold air to gust inside, the lamp's flame to lay horizontal, a rolled map to trundle across the floor and glowing sparks to rise from the brazier.

'Sorry, mi-!'

'Out of the way, you fool!' ordered a strangely-timbred voice. A wide figure shouldered past the guard and started to enter the tent.

Sister Spike twirled stiletto blades around her fingers, one held low and level with her thighs, the other raised up behind her head. The air began to buzz as if a nest of hornets had been disturbed. 'The magic of Incarnus fills the air with darting and fatal reprisal,' she hummed in a low, manly voice. 'You may not enter.'

The figure halted mid-step, the tent flap still draped over his – for the build seemed male – face. Kate realised that the intruder was carrying another person in his arms. What was this?

'Kate, are you in there?'

Did she know him? 'Who are you?' she called, wondering if she should retrieve her crossbow from under her pallet.

'By the incontinence of the idiot-god, it's *me*! Strap! I've got Mordius with me.'

Strap! 'Sister, put up your weapons!' Kate instructed the priestess.

'I cannot read this one!' the priestess vibrated. 'It would not be wise!'

'Enough!' Kate ordered and moved in front of the young woman to pull back the tent flap herself. 'Get in here! What happened to him?'

Strap half turned and brought the necromancer head first into the tent. The Guardian glanced around and then lowered Mordius into the nearest pallet. 'He needs a healer.'

Kate turned on Carris. 'Get that layabout Ikthaeon out of his bed and over here, now!'

'Ik-Ikthaeon. The high priest of Sh… Yes, milady!' the soldier stuttered and hurried from the tent.

'Milady!' Sister Spike growled, her weapons still poised. 'This one's dead.'

Kate's heart lurched. She'd never thought one of her friends could actually be harmed. Somehow, she'd always thought them invulnerable or under the absolute protection of the gods. But the gods were not the force they'd once been. 'Is it-is it true? I'm so sorry, Strap!'

He shrugged. 'I've only got myself to blame. It's my own fault for being careless, isn't it.'

'How did it happen?'

'Oh, some witch apparently. I wasn't even awake at the time.'

'Does it… did it hurt?'

'Naa! It was a pretty peaceful death as far as these things go. Like going to sleep. I didn't even realise it had happened in truth. Mordius had to work quite hard to convince me that I was really dead and that he'd raised me. But I tell you what, it's actually quite handy being dead. I don't think we'd have made it past the Elders if I hadn't been.'

'Necromancy is forbidden!' Sister Spike reminded them all. 'The animee is being controlled by a magician of fell arts. It cannot be tolerated. The laws of the gods must be upheld. Where there is blasphemy, divine retribution must be exacted.'

'Look, you stupid little girl!' Strap reprimanded the priestess. 'Just put your toys away and try to say something sensible, would you? You couldn't hurt me even if you tried. And shall we see how prettily you sing without a head on your shoulders?'

'Sister, there's time enough for recriminations later. Wait outside, please.'

'Is anyone drinking that wine?' Strap asked.

'I am ruled by Incarnus, not the throne. My task is to guard you against all threats, and that I shall do, whether you like it or not.'

'Now is not the time, Strap! Sister, stay then if you want, but you will not interfere unless you want to be fighting both myself and the animee.'

Strap tried the wine. 'I can hardly taste it! Maybe being dead isn't so great after all. Oh, Kate, I wonder if you have a good seamstress around the place? You see, I made a bit of a mess of this arm here and my hand's not working very well. I think some of the sinews have become detached or something.'

'A seamstress?' She pulled a face, though whether it was at the sight of his arm bone and tattered flesh or whether it was at his question, it wasn't clear. 'Do I look like I keep a seamstress around the place? Have you ever seen me in a frilly dress?'

'Now there's a picture! Is that green leather all you ever wear?' he asked wrinkling his nose. 'You must sweat a lot in it. You do bathe, right?'

'Anyway!' she said, getting them back to the main subject before he could wind her up so far that she was no longer glad to see him. 'There's some handmaid the Chamberlain insists on sending to me every morning and evening. She's always in the way or underfoot. Islaine, I think her name is. She might be good with needle and thread, but I suspect you'll need some sort of army physick to guide her – otherwise, you might end up with your hand connected to your head, or your male member connected to your mouth, or some such. Actually, I haven't seen her around this evening – I wonder where she's got to. I take it it can wait till morning, Strap? Good. Now, where's that Shakri-pampered high priest got to? If he's wasting time picking out suitably fine robes for a quick walk across the camp in the middle of the night, then *he*'ll be needing a seamstress and army physick once I've finished with him!'

Then she stopped. She fixed Strap with a steely gaze. 'Did you find the Old Place?'

Slowly, Strap nodded. 'I believe so. Mordius can give a better account of what we learnt than I can, however. I don't think I was all there when he first raised me.'

Kate sighed impatiently and picked up a goblet of wine herself. She sat down. Then she stood up and tried pacing a little, but there wasn't really enough room in the tent and she kept nearly colliding with the priestess.

'I'm curious, Kate,' Strap said with typical frankness. 'Just why do you have a priestess of Incarnus in your tent to guard you? Surely there are other Guardians to call on if you are worried about security. And to have someone inside your tent is only going to look a bit excessive to the troops, isn't it? Paranoid, even?'

She froze. How dare he! He knew very well that someone had walked into the palace unchallenged and taken her son. He must know there'd been a traitor in the palace. And he knew how double-dealing, devious and dangerous the likes of the Chamberlain were! So why would he encourage her to reduce her security, to relax her guard? Perhaps Sister Spike was right. After all, Kate only had Strap's word for it that it was Mordius who had raised him. What if Strap was actually being controlled by some other magician, by one of the blood-mages hidden not too far away! Was that why Strap was suggesting she remove the security from inside her tent? Did Strap want Sister Spike out of the way so that he would be free to attack Kate? And to think she'd tried to order the Sister to leave just now!

It all made sense. Kate crouched and pulled her crossbow from under her pallet. She cranked the weapon and fit a bolt to it. Happily, Sister Spike still stood alert and at the ready. Strap tilted his head, watching her in mild confusion.

There was a discreet cough outside the tent, the tent flap rose and Carris announced, 'Ikthaeon, High Priest of Shakri, milady!'

'And my assistant!' Ikthaeon upbraided Carris and strode into the tent. He pulled up short and paled slightly as he realised there was a crossbow bolt aimed casually at his chest. 'Ahem! I believe, milady requested an audience with…'

The high priest broke off, staring at Strap in horror. 'Milady!' he squawked. 'Th-This creature is one of the undead!' He hastily reached for a flask at his waist.

'Don't you dare!' Strap warned. 'You're here to see to Mordius, nothing more.'

Ikthaeon looked to Kate for confirmation. How she loathed this priest. On balance, she had more contempt for Ikthaeon than she did for Strap's sincerity. 'Good priest, I suspect the goddess would not want Strap harmed unnecessarily. But if you know any different, please feel free to attempt to throw holy water on him. I cannot promise you any protection, however, if he chooses to defend himself. Otherwise, I would be obliged if you would look to Mordius, someone who has worked as hard on behalf of the temples as he has the throne in the last several years.'

Ikthaeon flicked his hand, and his assistant scurried forwards to begin an examination of Mordius. The high priest didn't bother to watch, instead directing another question at Kate: 'And is it Mordius who is responsible for this foul practice of necromancy? I cannot in clear conscience aid someone who is guilty of such sacrilege.'

Strap swore under his breath.

'Good priest,' Kate said slowly. 'Is it not the holy duty of all Shakri's priesthood to aid the living? Is life not sacred to you? Mordius's life may well hang on the decision you make now.'

'It is true, Brother Ikthaeon,' murmured the assistant. 'He weakens. I do not know how much longer he will last.'

A nervous tic appeared over Ikthaeon's right eye. His chin twitched to the left.

'You see,' Kate nodded. 'If you do not help him, will you not then be guilty of sin? Added to that, your refusal to help will upset both Strap and myself. Revenge in the shape of Sister Spike may then demand satisfaction. Who knows what further deaths will result? And those deaths will also be on your hands – yet more sin.'

The tic became more violent and the high priest's neck twisted so quickly that there was an audible crack.

Even Kate winced at the sound. 'That affliction you're exhibiting: do you not see Shakri speaks to you through it? Why else would She not allow you to be completely cured of it? Or do you close your ears, mind and heart to Her? Tut, tut, you are getting yourself into a whole heap of trouble, aren't you?'

Ikthaeon shook his head. 'I have n-n-never…'

'And a stutter as well?'

'D-Don't-!' the high priest began. He took a calming breath. 'I am Shakri's high priest! Who are you to speak of Her divine will?'

Strap smirked and shook his head.

'Who am I?' Kate asked softly. 'Why, I am Her daughter. She combed my hair when I was a young girl. Can you say the same, priest? She used to sing me to sleep…'

The tic was so exaggerated this time that it almost threw Ikthaeon off his feet. His assistant helped him up solicitously. Ikthaeon slapped his hands away and came up the rest of the way on his own. He opened his mouth to retort.

'The Mother of All Creation,' Kate continued, 'died under Saltar's grinding boot while the Scourge murdered Lacrimos with a blade to the neck. At the same time, I shot Voltar's white sorceress through the Heart. If I recall, that saved Shakri's entire realm. The Scourge became Her Divine Consort shortly after and I, Her daughter, was given to Saltar by Shakri Herself. Who am I, Ikthaeon? I am a demi-god of your temple, and I am extremely ticked off with you right now!'

The high priest crumpled to the floor in a heap.

'Ooh!' Strap giggled. 'He's not dead, is he?'

The assistant crawled across the floor to his elder.

'Leave him!' Kate snapped. 'Stand up. What's your name?'

The assistant rose shakily, keeping his head half-ducked. 'Memis, milady.'

'Well, Memis, do you have any problem acting upon my suggestions?'

'No, milady!'

'And do you have the necessary power to help my friend, Mordius?'

'Yes, milady, or at least I believe so.'

'Good, then be so kind as to restore him to full health as soon as you can.'

'Of course, milady. Now, milady?'

'Yes, Memis, now. And Memis?'

'Yes, milady?'

Kate's voice softened. 'Thank you.'

Memis paused and smiled nervously. 'It's a pleasure milady. I am honoured that…'

'Oh, don't bother with such statements, please! It's more important that you understand how vital Mordius is to our cause. He would not have raised Strap without good reason – we are all intimately familiar with the risk to the balance represented by necromancy. Cognis Himself directed the two of them to retrieve the information we require. If Strap had not been raised, Mordius would never have made it here. Without the information Mordius has, I suspect our cause will fail. And that cause, Memis, is also Shakri's cause. The Enemy who is returning, this lost god, is systematically dismantling the pantheon and, thereby, Shakri's divine will. Do you understand anything of which I speak?'

'Enough, milady. I will do everything I can for Mordius, truly, although there is something I must tell you. Please, do not let the high priest know it was I who revealed it to you but… but…'

'Go on!'

Memis looked afraid. He almost lost his voice as he said, 'Our powers are on the wane. The decline was small at first and we did not notice it. But it has been getting worse. We do not know if it is affecting the other temples. Brother Ikthaeon did not want to let them know of our plight, you see, in case they gained some sort of advantage over us, perhaps even challenged our pre-eminence...' and then he came to a sudden halt as he realised there was a priestess of Incarnus in the tent. His hands covered his mouth. He was mortified.

Kate raised an eyebrow at her personal bodyguard. For the first time, Kate saw doubt rather than determination on Sister Spike's face. It made her look as young as her years. A slight blush came to her cheeks as she admitted: 'I do not see as clearly as I once did.'

'Typical!' Strap said. 'As usual, the politicians have put their individual ambitions before the good of the people and the realm. In so doing, the high priests actually do the gods a disservice. The high priests are as guilty of risking the balance as Mordius is of raising me.'

'Yes,' agreed Kate, giving Sister Spike a disappointed look. 'And if what you say is true, Memis, we have almost run out of time to do anything about it. By the anal punishments of Lacrimos, you priests will see an end to us all. You are as great a threat to this realm as the Creator!'

Memis cowered from her anger. Sister Spike hung her head in shame.

'Perhaps that's the point,' Strap speculated.

'What do you mean?' Kate urged him.

'Well, Mordius can always describe these things better than I can, but when I told him of attacks upon shrines to Wim, he was particularly alarmed. Without Wim, we cannot have free will, as far as I understand it. If the Enemy can destroy or replace the pantheon, then the will of the Enemy alone will define this realm. Our fates, our personalities, our existences will all be one and nothing more than the Enemy's will. We will lose all self-awareness. What I'm saying is that as the power of the Enemy increases, more and more of our actions will simply serve its will. It's only natural in such a situation that we will then defensively try to assert our individuality and personal ambition, yet when high priests do such a thing, they only do so at the cost of their own god's will, thereby helping to increase the sway of the Enemy's will. That will is becoming inevitable, becoming inescapable. Do I remember Mordius calling the Enemy, the dreadful Unity? I think so. It is all coming together in the Unity, just as all the powers in the realm are now being drawn to this one place in the mountains where the Unity is to be found. Time is running out too, for that will become meaningless or just another component once the Unity is complete.'

'Shakri preserve us!' Carris said with an ashen face.

Sister Spike looked sick. Memis was beyond speech, tears in his eyes.

'What can we do?' Kate whispered. 'Strap,' she begged, 'what can we do about it? Should we turn round rather than be drawn into the Unity?'

Strap raised his hands. 'I have no idea. I doubt our turning around will do anything but delay the inevitable. And I don't think any of us likes the idea of running away. So maybe we should meet the Enemy head on. It might be our only chance, if we have any chance that is. The best thing to do, though, is wake Mordius up and ask him. He has a much better grasp of all this than I ever will. And the longer we stand here wringing our hands with worry, the less strength Memis will have to help him.'

'Memis! Get to it!'

⁂

An hour or so later, Mordius was sitting up on a small camp-bed trying to make sense of the sea of concerned faces looking down at him. The Chamberlain had returned from consulting the high priestess of Lacrimos and looked on as anxiously as the others. Kate's tent was becoming decidedly crowded, so Carris had gone outside to see if the palace guard would allow him room next to one of their fires to get some rest.

Disorientated, Mordius's gaze drifted back and forth until his brain recognised Strap. 'Where are we? The Elders?'

Strap winked at him. 'They were no real bother, for such fearsome warriors as you and me, Mordius. We sent them running with their tails between their legs. In truth, I'm glad you remember them – our friend, Memis, here was worried parts of your mind might never wake up again, you know. When we got back to Corinus, Kate had already raised an army and left. You know how impatient and demanding she can be. Anyway, I rode on to catch up with her, without even stopping for a beer.'

Kate narrowed her eyes at Strap, but decided there was nothing to be gained by rising to his teasing. He was too old and set in his ways for there to be any hope that he might change. Besides, she reminded herself, he was dead. 'Mordius, we're camped just north of Holter's Cross. How are you feeling?'

'Oh! Kate! Hello. How are you? How do I feel? Err… woozy. Like a giant stamped on my head or something,' the small necromancer replied, rubbing his brow. 'And starving. Is there anything to eat?'

'That's a good sign,' Memis said quietly.

'We'll let you eat and recover in a minute, Mordius,' Kate said gently. 'Is there anything of importance that we need to know immediately?'

'Err…' Mordius mumbled to himself for a few seconds. 'The Enemy is Nylchros. He is returning with the help of the remaining three acolytes of Harpedon.'

The Chamberlain hissed involuntarily at mention of the acolytes.

Mordius looked around at them all, but his eyes couldn't focus. 'Their leader is Heritus, if I remember that name from the journal I had...'

'What journal?' Strap asked.

'What? Journal?' Mordius asked vaguely. 'Yes, I had a journal. You're right! Got it from the house of the animal-necromancer in the Weeping Woods when... when...'

Kate placed a hand on Mordius's shoulder. 'It's alright, Mordius, I know of the journal. I was there with you and Saltar when you found it.' She shot a look at Strap telling him not to interrupt again and, to his credit, Strap did not stick his tongue out in reply. 'Carry on, Mordius. The three acolytes of Harpedon. Their leader is...'

'... is Heritus. They're up in the Needle Mountains, north of a ruined temple of Cognis. Kate, I'm so sorry!'

'What is it, good Mordius?'

'They intend to use that poor, sweet child as the vessel for Nylchros!'

Kate showed no emotion. 'Is there anything else?'

'Do you mind if I pass out now? I really don't feel...'

Mordius slumped. Memis quickly laid healing hands on him.'

Kate stood up straight.

'Milady?'

'What?' Kate snarled at the Chamberlain.

'When I spoke to her, the priestess of Lacrimos said much the same about the Creator needing a vessel of some sort, hmm?'

'So?' Her fingers itched. She looked around for where she'd put down her crossbow.

'Given that the power of the temples continues to dwindle, we must conclude that the Battle-leader has been unable to rescue Orastes, yes? By now, the blood-mages will have returned to their mountain stronghold.'

'Spit it out, damn you!' she screamed, pulling a dagger out of the top of one of her long boots.

Strap leaned casually against one of the tent poles and folded his arms. Sister Spike sat down and placed her hands in her lap, for all the world watching a comedy at the theatre.

'We must surmise that Nylchros now possesses Orastes, hmm? You must prepare yourself for that eventuality!' the Chamberlain rushed.

She stabbed for his gut and he had to bend double to keep his stomach just beyond her full extension. Instinct took over and he brought his elbow down to break her outstretched arm. But he moved more slowly in cold climes, so she had time to anticipate him. She twisted her arm forty-five degrees and deflected his blow away. Realising he was now left open he tried to throw himself sideways, but she also saw this move coming. Her leg came up and kicked him in the middle.

The Chamberlain was thrown back into the table, which collapsed under him. He blinked. Her leather-clad thighs were suddenly to either side of his head and she sat on the top of his chest. Her blade was under his chin. He saw the madness in her eyes. She was going to kill him!

Strap faked a yawn. Sister Spike clapped prettily. Memis had his eyes squeezed shut, but kept his hands on Mordius.

'Feel better?' Strap drawled.

Kate blinked. 'Much!' The endorphins in her blood gave her no choice but to smile.

'Milady!' the Chamberlain yelped.

'Thank you, Chamberlain. It's the tension, you know. Gets to a person.' She climbed off him and helped him up.

He scowled at her, humiliated.

'Come now, Chamberlain, I owed you that!'

She had him flummoxed. She was unreadable now, a completely unstable element. Insane. She carved destructive trenches through certain parts of the Pattern and tore holes in it elsewhere. She would destroy everything if left unchecked. 'Milady?'

'For your uncivil behaviour in the corridor outside Voltar's throne room just before we faced the despot.'

She remembered that? She should have no clear memory of it. Now, he was extremely worried for the realm. Different times and episodes were collapsing one into the other. Reason was disappearing. Words and actions were becoming interchangeable. It was all becoming one. 'I see,' he said carefully.

'Do you know what I think would be a good idea?' Kate asked enthusiastically. 'I think we should fight each other every day. It would be good training, don't you think?'

'Oh, yes!' replied Sister Spike with girlish glee.

Strap hesitated but then nodded. 'Why not? Just as soon as I get a seamstress for this arm.'

'What say you, Chamberlain? It would be fun, hmmmm?' Kate mocked him.

'Indeed, milady. I look forward to it.'

Mad, they were all mad! He was at a complete loss as to what to do. Maybe he should consult the maniacal Vidius? For the first time in millennia, he found himself missing Balthagar and wondering what his advice would be. He knew what his brother would have said, though. To fight without surcease, and then fight some more. The Chamberlain despised fighting at the best of times, because it put him at risk, but sometimes it was unavoidable. Curse these gods and their pathetic realm for reducing him to this!

❧ ❧

He didn't want to be awake. It was too painful. But it seemed the outside world wasn't prepared to leave him alone. What did it want? Just to play? Or did it need help with something?

Using some of the choicest curses he'd learnt from the Scourge, Mordius opened his eyes and looked at the sky jarring back and forth above him. It was white, stormy and a bit too bright for his eyes. He squinted.

He realised he was lying in the back of a wagon. A whip cracked and a gruff voice urged the horses to pull harder through yet another difficult patch in the road. He had a sudden flashback – those noises had been translated into a demon flagellating him in his dreams. Perhaps it was better to be awake after all.

'Ah, there you are!' came a flat-noted chirrup.

'Yes, here I am,' Mordius said in a similarly strange-sounding voice. 'Water?'

There was a thunk as something heavy landed on the floor of the wagon not far from his head. Mordius tilted his head a fraction and saw a water-bottle a hand-span from him. Over the side of the wagon, he saw Strap riding his horse parallel with the vehicle. He watched Mordius with what passed for a grin amongst the undead.

Seeing that no one was about to help him, the necromancer groaned and rolled over. With shaking hands, he uncapped the bottle and got water to his mouth. After sipping for a minute or so, he rolled onto his back again, exhausted.

'Take your time.'

He managed to sit up, and then clung onto the side of the wagon so that he wouldn't fall flat again because of his weakened state whenever they hit a stone or a rut. Their wagon was just one in a long line that stretched as far as the horizon. Men walked to either side, slogging through muddy slush when there wasn't space for them on the road surface itself. To a man, they looked cold and tired – particularly those lacking much in the way of thick clothing – but there was also a grim determination about them all, whether it was the way they set their shoulders, gritted their teeth, purposefully placed their feet or unhesitatingly helped those who showed signs of floundering. A good number carried makeshift spearing weapons, but just as many seemed to possess nothing more than the clothes in which they stood.

'Outdwellers,' Strap said by way of explanation. 'No uniforms of course.'

'Amazing!' Mordius replied. 'How on earth has Kate managed to pressgang them?'

'Ha! No pressgang involved. From what I can tell, they absolutely revere the Green Witch. They see her as some sort of… well, as their champion, I suppose. But more than that really – it's not quite religious worship, but sometimes it's not far off. We shouldn't forget that when we fought Voltar's army she was the most obvious one amongst us. They talk of her as wielding almost godlike powers. But she doesn't have magic, does she, Mordius? I've never quite understood why they call her the Green Witch.'

'She hasn't got powers that I know of,' Mordius admitted. 'But she's always been close to Shakri. Who's to say? How is Kate holding up, by the way?'

'Hmm,' Strap mused, casting the wagon-driver a sidelong glance to try and judge what it would and wouldn't be safe to say.

'I'm deaf, milords!' the driver said without even looking at them. 'Live much longer that way.'

'Well then, Mordius, since you ask, she's paranoid verging on psychotic.'

The necromancer sighed aloud. He'd been thinking much the same before he'd left with Strap for the Old Place.

'Having said that,' Strap reflected, 'perhaps her behaviour is perfectly normal for someone who's had their child stolen. You certainly wouldn't expect her to carry on exactly as before, now would you?'

'No,' Mordius conceded, 'and I have no idea how I would react under such circumstances, but the real issue is whether such a person is the right person to be leading an army and making life and death decisions. Does she retain the objectivity and good judgement required?'

Strap shrugged. 'Well, she has Vidius as her general. And the Chamberlain offers counsel, although no one's ever trusted him. So I can't say really. See what you think once you've talked with her tonight. She'll want to question you at length, I imagine. Already, you've helped just by telling her of the ruined temple of Cognis. That's where we're heading. I don't think they were precisely sure of where they were going before we turned up. Can you imagine?

They might have ended up wandering around the mountains for weeks, until the entire army had perished. What does *that* say about the judgement being used to lead this army?'

'I see. But I get the feeling the Unity would have drawn us all to it when it was ready.'

'S'pose so,' Strap pondered. 'It's like some inescapable doom, eh? Makes no odds whether this army's led by a saint or a deranged death-monger then? Besides, it's not like there's anything we can do to remove Kate if we do become concerned about her, now is there? I, for one, would never agree to harm her, and I doubt she's just going to step aside because we express a few reservations.'

'You wouldn't harm her? Even if the realm were at stake?'

Strap hesitated, which gave the lie to his eventual 'Never!'

There was an uncomfortable pause. The driver mopped his brow, even though the air was so cold that their breath came out as great billows of visible water vapour.

'So, your arm's okay then,' Mordius commented, more to change the subject than anything else.

'Yup! Good, huh? Kate's handmaid fixed it for me. 'Islaine, her name. Nimble fingers. Pretty too.'

Mordius regarded the animee curiously. 'You don't... can't find her attractive, can you? I mean, your condition doesn't... does it?'

'No, but there're always echoes,' Strap said simply, apparently not wanting to say anything more in front of the driver. The man probably didn't know Strap was dead. There was certainly nothing about the look of the Guardian to give him away either, except perhaps his pallor, but then again it was a cold day.

Mordius tried yet another topic. 'So where are we then? Still on the King's Road, right?'

Strap nodded dully. His voice was distant when he answered: 'We camped just north of Holter's Cross last night.'

Yet another lapse into silence. Men panted, the horses snorted and blew hard. The tack connecting the beasts to the wagon jangled. The wood of the vehicle creaked. The driver twitched the reins and there was the slight slap of leather. His head sore, Mordius couldn't think of another gambit immediately.

Strap saved him the trouble by saying, 'I'll ride ahead to see if I can get you some food,' and kneed his horse forward, ending their company.

It was not like Strap to be so remote. Usually, he would want to fashion extended and elaborate – even nonsensical – discourses from either the most innocuous of comments or the flimsiest of pretexts. There was clearly something bothering him, and Mordius had only dreadful suspicions as to what it was.

❧ ❧

They made camp in the forest to either side of the King's Road that night, just short of the turn off that would lead them through Deepfield, Swallowdale and into the Needle Mountains where they would find the ruined temple of Cognis and then their bloodthirsty enemy.

While she waited for her tent to be put up, Kate tried to walk off some of the aches, soreness and stiffness she'd developed from days in the saddle. Unlike Vidius, she wouldn't allow the priests of Shakri to soothe her complaining muscles every morning and night. No, she valued the pain, because it reminded her still that she needed to become tougher. It would not let her get complacent, certainly not let her get comfortable. It would nag, prompt and drive her to keep fighting against her weaknesses. They must be overcome or she would forever be vulnerable to further loss, betrayal and failure.

On the ride that day, she'd pulled a face of discomfort at some point and General Vidius had quipped that she, like the army, would be of little use in a battle if they didn't do enough to protect the rear. There'd been a few smiles amongst the officers riding with them, and even Sister Spike had had to turn her face away for a second. If someone had laughed out loud, then Kate hated to think what she might have done to them. As it was, she managed to stay calm and resolved not to let her weaknesses show in future – if an enemy were to see them, then he or she would know to exploit them and then she would lose her chance at leading all these men to their deaths and taking back her son.

Finally, her tent was ready and she went inside with her living shadow, Sister Spike. If she could successfully ignore her bodyguard, Kate now had some time to herself, for General Vidius would not come and join her to discuss the usual range of issues until he'd seen to organising the camp and had broken his daylight fast. Also, it would be some while before those on foot and the wagon train arrived, when she would want to talk to Mordius more. She lowered herself tenderly into a chair and was just considering a nap – maybe she would dream of Saltar and Orastes and leave all these enemies surrounding her for a few blessed minutes – when she heard Islaine's voice asking for entrance to the tent. The flaming woman kept trying to mother

her – she was sure the Chamberlain had only appointed Islaine to the tent because he knew she would annoy Kate and therefore give him some petty revenge for how the Guardian had treated him of late. Having said that, maybe the Chamberlain couldn't abide the woman either and was hoping Kate would kill her and do his dirty work for him. If they didn't reach the Enemy soon, Kate might just grant him his wish.

Islaine bustled through the tent flap, already talking to everyone and no one at once. 'There you are, milady! Ooh, my poor dear! Weary beyond belief, you look. I hate to think what things would get like if I wasn't here to do the few things you'll allow.'

Her wide, shiny face loomed close. 'But look at you, dear! Bags under your eyes. Not getting enough sleep, I'll be bound. Not taking the time to look after yourself. And when did you last bathe? Why don't you remove those leathers so that I might wash them for you?'

Sister Spike stared at the woman, who suddenly rounded on her.

'And you should be doing more to look after milady!' Islaine admonished the priestess.

Then the handmaid turned back to Kate. 'When did you last eat, milady? Let me guess! It wasn't today and you can't really remember when it last was. Well, here's a herb cordial I brought for you.' She placed a beaker near Kate's hand. 'It'll refresh you and put a bit of colour back in your cheeks. Drink it down, my dear! It'll do you some good.'

She stood over Kate with arms folded, tapping her foot, as if she were dealing with a truculent child and would brook no nonsense. Kate picked up the beaker.

'Speaking of colour,' Islaine continued, looking around herself in disapproval, 'I really wish you'd let me do something with this tent. It's just so gloomy! How can you be expected to remain in good spirits and have sweet dreams when you surround yourself with such stark and sombre décor? Did I tell you that I met that young man who's a friend of yours, this morning? Strap. He thinks the world of you, really he d...'

Kate let Islaine witter on and raised her eyes over the rim of the beaker to exchange a glance with Sister Spike. To her horror, she saw the priestess was glaring at her with deadly intent and pulling a needle from her hair. The Sister's arm came down in one fluid motion. Kate saw it all happening in slow motion or as if she wasn't in her own body and was instead seeing it happen to someone else. Islaine's voice was a muffled drone in the background, her jaw hinging up and down, up and down, the maid oblivious to what was going on.

She saw the glint of satisfaction in the priestess's eye as she released the needle and set it on a path straight for Kate's face. Of course, the projectile might not be able to penetrate leather armour successfully, so the priestess would go for Kate's exposed head to be sure of killing her. The metal of the needle flexed and wobbled as it pierced through the air and sent waves of energy off to either side. Its passage buffeted the flame of the candle on the table as it speared towards Kate.

And Sister Spike was reaching for her hair again. If by some miracle Kate survived this first assault, what hope would she have beyond that? How could she have so misjudged the priestess? How could she have taken this assassin right into her tent? When had Incarnus turned against her? Was He seeking revenge for how she'd forced the temples to obey her wishes? She saw now the blasphemy she'd committed. In demanding the co-operation of the high priests, threatening them with bared blades and then issuing them with her orders, she'd set herself above the pantheon. She was all but trying to command the gods themselves! Of course they could not tolerate such outrageous sacrilege, such extraordinary hubris! How had she not seen it before? This was not her realm to do with as she saw fit. And Shakri was not about to let her commit genocide by sacrificing this army of men! It was life that She had created, and life that was sacred to Her.

The needle skewered Kate's hand that held the beaker to her lips. Its tip went all the way through her palm and punctured her bottom lip. She dropped the beaker with a cry.

Sister Spike had another weapon out already. It leapt from her hand and buried itself in the base of Islaine's skull. The handmaid stopped mid-sentence and collapsed to the floor. More shards, splinters and spikes of metal and light filled the air, nailing the handmaid to the ground.

Kate was on her feet and moving for the priestess in an instant. Her dagger came into her hand as she launched herself at the red-robed devil.

'Wait!' Sister Spike shouted, raising a hand too late.

They crashed together, Kate's momentum, weight and strength crunching the young priestess into the ground. The tent flap was thrust aside and Carris rushed in, sword ready. 'What's amiss?'

'Milady, she was seeking to poison you!' Sister Spike choked. Her collarbone had snapped and come out through her skin. Kate's dagger had lanced into her side, but the angle was oblique and did not appear to have seriously wounded her.

Kate got up. 'Watch her!' she instructed Carris. She went over to the spilled beaker and saw where its contents had burned the animal skin rug on the floor. Cursing, she went back to Islaine's body and kicked her savagely in the midriff.

'She's dead!' Sister Spike wheezed. 'Couldn't risk letting her live.'

'Carris, tell no one of this. Go fetch the priest Memis,' Kate ordered the guard.

Carris hesitated and then nodded. He put his sword away and hurried out.

Kate righted her chair and then sat down heavily in it. After a few seconds, she said, 'Thank you, Sister!'

'Don't mention it!' the priestess coughed, not trying to move. 'Milady, you should avail yourself of a weapon in case others come. I find I am no longer in the best condition to defend you.'

⁂

Strap helped Mordius into Kate's tent and halted in shock. There was a woman pinned face down to the floor. The rug on which she lay was pretty much entirely red with her blood. Kate squelched across the tent and seated herself in a chair, all the while keeping her crossbow trained on the newcomers. Carris was there, his sword free of its scabbard, and Sister Spike stood in a corner spinning a bodkin idly on the end of one of her fingers. The only other occupant was Memis, who stood unobtrusively off to one side, trying for all his worth not to be there at all.

'Come in!' Kate invited them.

'What happened?' Strap asked unnecessarily, letting the tent flap drop behind him.

'Don't you know, Strap? Surprised to see me alive? Disappointed?'

'What are you… now wait a minute!' the animee said loudly.

'Wait!' Mordius barked, stepping forward as far as the body in the middle of the floor would allow him. 'For the benefit of those recently out of a coma, could we please take this a bit more slowly? What happened, precisely?'

'It's quite simple, Mordius,' Kate said. 'My handmaid, Islaine, tried to poison me with a cordial. It was only the quick thinking of Sister Spike that spared me a quite unpleasant death. The question is, Mordius, who put Islaine up to this? I know Strap spent quite some time with Islaine this morning.'

'You can't think I'd try to kill you!' Strap said with anger in his voice.

'You cannot be read,' Sister Spike said smoothly. 'You must therefore be suspect.'

'Look, Kate, I may be many things, including dead, but I am certainly no coward. If I really wanted you dead, I would kill you myself, not hide behind some servant. You *know* that. And I've already had opportunity to kill you. But I don't *want* to kill you – I have no *reason* to want to kill you! And I may sometimes think and say things about you that are not entirely flattering but…'

'Paranoid, I believe you called me.'

'… but none of that can outweigh all the positive things I think about you. We've been through too much together for that ever to change. I thought you were my friend, but it's not surprising you're starting to forget what that means, with all that's happened. Yes, I called you paranoid, but I did so to your face, and this dead woman proves I was wrong to call you such.'

Kate turned her head and regarded Mordius.

'I-I do not believe Strap can have done it,' he stammered. 'As his necromancer, I think I would know if he'd done anything like that.' He had a few misgivings about the conversations he'd had with his animee earlier in the day, but Strap had been against harming Kate and he'd already seen Islaine by then. 'As you know, I've been unconscious most of the time since we've been with the army, so I wouldn't have had a chance to conspire against you. All my magic is used maintaining Strap – I haven't had the reserves to attempt to bespell anyone like your handmaid. But, like Strap, I have no reason to do such a thing. Like Strap, I consider myself your friend, Kate.'

Kate looked to Sister Spike. 'Well?'

'The necromancer was occasionally uncertain, but there was no attempt at deception. He generally wishes to support you. He can be trusted. He did not attempt to have you killed.'

Kate relaxed in the shoulders and pushed her weapon aside. 'Forgive me my caution, my friends. As you can see, I can't afford not to be too careful. It appears someone wants to stop me getting this army to the mountains or they want the army for themselves.'

'So do you think Vidius would attempt such a thing?' Strap asked. 'Does he want to be in sole charge of the army? But what would he do with it? The people and the temples wouldn't let him assume the throne, even if he did have the army behind him, would they?'

Kate shrugged. 'It would be foolish to underestimate his ambition. Mordius, my friend, what do you think?'

Mordius knitted his brow and worked through an analysis, as if trying to understand the formulation of a new spell, or trying to assemble the necessary props and gestures for a particularly challenging magical ritual. 'I think it's interesting that the killer chose Islaine as their weapon. It suggests a number of possibilities. Either they didn't have direct access to you themselves or they dared not risk being seen to be the one to kill you. Whichever it was, they will have had to suborn Islaine, bespell her or use her without her knowledge, slipping the poison into the cordial unobserved, for example. Do you happen to recall what Islaine's demeanour was when she brought you the cordial? If she was bespelled, then she would have been fairly quiet and unfocussed in the eye.'

'She certainly wasn't quiet,' Kate said. 'Talked almost as much as…' she began, looking at Strap, but didn't bother finishing.

'She was suborned then,' Sister Spike interrupted. 'I clearly sensed a desire to harm from her. It was what gave her away to me. So, she was intimidated, blackmailed, bribed?'

'Well, whoever was responsible will either have been holding someone Islaine loved as hostage, so that Islaine will have been prepared to act without any concern for what would happen to herself, or they will have been in a position to offer Islaine protection once you were dead, Kate,' Mordius said.

'You know, you're very good at this, Mordius,' Kate smiled. 'I'm glad you're my friend rather than my enemy.'

Carris cleared his throat. 'Milady, if I might say something?'

She nodded.

'Well, if Islaine was quite religious, might she not have been persuaded by a high priest…?'

'Shame on you!' the usually quiet Memis exclaimed.

'You go too far!' the priestess warned the guard.

'Carris is right!' Kate cut through them all. 'And to know whether Islaine was a zealot, had a loved one being held hostage or took a bribe from a powerful patron, we will need to know more about her life. Carris, could you summon the Chamberlain for me? Islaine was one of his staff, so he's likely to know something of use.'

'Can *he* be trusted?' Strap asked Sister Spike.

'I cannot read him either. His mind is like a… trap… labyrinth or a tangled web.'

'Great!' Strap sighed. 'Who else can't you read?'

'The General. He seems blank. It happens like that with some people. And most priests can thwart my own priestly magic.'

'This is going to be a long night. Any chance we can get some wine in?'

Everyone ignored Strap.

'I'm inclined to hold the Chamberlain partially responsible for all this anyway, as he's either incapable of controlling his staff properly or incapable of taking on staff of a suitable character,' Kate decided. 'His error could have cost me my life, and I take a very dim view of that. I'm sure I can inspire him suitably so that he ferrets out those responsible for us.'

Mordius had stopped listening. He was still thinking everything through. A handmaid was hardly the most suitable choice of assassin. Whoever had persuaded Islaine to attempt the poisoning must have been concerned that she might be captured and would then reveal the name of her patron. Unless this shadowy enemy had been confident all along that Sister Spike would kill Islaine. Why make the attempt then? Simply to push Kate's paranoia and psychosis that bit further, far enough so that it could never be reversed? He studied Kate by the flickering light. Seeing her unblinking gaze and pallid expression, he wondered if the shadow had successfully achieved its goal through Islaine after all.

Chapter Thirteen: And Sacrifice The Future

Heritus ordered the young girl to replace her clothes and leave him. He'd long since lost his interest in sexual gratification. How long had it been? Centuries? It didn't matter. He didn't know why he continued to have the prettiest of the Brethren come to see him in his black pyramid every now and then. All he would do is have them remove their clothes and stand there trembling – whether from cold or fear he didn't care – before his gaze. He liked to look upon their youth and beauty, but most of all he liked to see their fragility. Their lives were such delicate, fleeting things. Gone like a candle being snuffed out by the flapping of a moth's wings, or like those tissue wings being consumed in an instant by the flame, leaving nothing but a curl of smoke hanging in the air. Like a pair of fingers being snapped in a room so that there is the briefest of echoes and memory, and then silence. There was an aching poignancy about them, an exquisite transience.

His own existence had become something quite different to theirs. His had much more permanence about it. It was underpinned by a vast store of power, just as the Brethren community clung to life whilst sitting upon and amongst the titanic Needle Mountains. His existence may not have their sort of beauty, but it had its own magnificence, even if it was cruel and hard sometimes and meant that the Brethren's survival was often precariously balanced.

Like a mountain, his existence had begun to see a lack of change, had become a matter of course. He had heard every possible combination of words, until he could predict whole speeches before they were spoken; seen every shape and form of life come and go, until he'd begun to predict evolution millennia in advance; experienced every type of weather, until he could see recurring patterns in even the most chaotic of storms; smelt and tasted every substance in the realm, until there was nothing left to surprise his pallet and eating was just a tiring function and constraint of his massive body. The entire design and Pattern of Shakri's realm was now so well known to him that it bored him. Worse than that, he saw and resented how it limited him. He was a prisoner to it.

How he despised his captors, the gods! He hated their self-important and public preening. Expecting people to worship them of all things! It was utterly laughable. No, it was insult added to the injury of mortal imprisonment. Well, soon he would free himself of them. Soon, his lesser brothers would be here with the tool to free them from their cell. Soon, they would no longer need to regenerate themselves via this cursed black pyramid; they would no longer be dependent on the life force of those they Owned for their continued existence. Soon, my brothers, soon. They would come to Own all that lived in this realm. All life in this realm would serve to regenerate and increase their existence. Then, yes then, he would exact his full revenge on the entire self-serving and petty pantheon! Those snot-gobbling, childish wretches would be made to suffer horrors beyond imagination and then, and only then, would they be utterly undone.

He would make the gods stand and tremble naked before him. He would gaze on their perfect beauty and their delicious fragility. He would see their lives as frail and fleeting things. And then he would snap his fingers. There would be a slight echo across the realm and then there would be only silence.

He would no longer be trapped and limited by this realm, for the realm would be his to do what he willed with. He would put it in his pocket and then look around for other realms, *new* realms where he had not heard, seen, tasted, smelt or experienced what they had to offer. Then his existence would be one of change, learning and growth again. He would finally be *alive*! And he would be free to *live* that life.

Excited by the epic scale of his vision, he threw out his enormous mind and intellect to rove across the mountains. His brothers were about to enter the valley. And they brought the tool that would give them their freedom. He could sense the immense rage contained by and within the child. Lesser magicians his brothers might be when compared to himself, but they had done well. It would be a shame to lose them finally, but they were limited in their own way and would only hold him back. He spread his mind further and saw a small group scurrying like ants towards the foothills of the mountains. They were of no consequence. Further still, and he saw the witch's pathetic army struggling north. There were a few brighter sparks of life and power amongst the host, but nothing that was likely to trouble his magickers. If this was the best the pantheon could muster against him, then pitiful they were indeed. It would hardly be a fight at all. How anticlimactic. Still, anything more dramatic than that would only flatter these already over-indulged gods. Let there be no acts of heroism then, no inspirational moments of courage, no rousing and impassioned speeches, no brave charges against the odds, no hope of snatching victory from the crushing jaws of defeat. Let there be only complete devastation, a merciless raping and pillaging of minds, a collapsing of vain, mortal civilizations, an end to the Pattern of history, and an eternity of his greater will.

Summoning a small measure of his power, he shifted his massive bulk and moved ponderously through the widened doorway and corridors of the black ziggurat. Underlings fled from his path, knowing that if they were too slow to move, they would be crushed beneath his giant, shuddering weight. Of course, no normal body could have supported his colossal size, but he'd long since transcended the limitations of the usual mortal form. The life force the Owned gave him in exchange for his wisdom, protection and beneficence – in exchange for his Ownership – meant he had more life than could be contained by a normal body anyway. He was no longer dependent on the febrile murmurings of his heart for life anymore. He was greater than human, much more than human. Where mortals were predictable prose, he was living poetry. Where they were tired flesh and bone, he was a living vision wreathed in power and magic. Where they were witless, formless stone, he was the glorious architect. An artist did not explain to his paints and canvas what he intended. A musician did not ask his instrument for its permission and co-operation. Thus, he, Heritus, the greatest of all magicians, would enact his will to the full, fashioning the future as his superior intellect and ideas saw fit and rightly demanded.

He descended to the main ritual chamber and was bowed inside by the black-robed magickers to either side of the central portal. The Brethren within, who served as simple attendants to keep the torches lit and the chamber dust free, were already lying prostrate with their eyes carefully averted from him. Just as well, because he did not particularly enjoy having to devour one of them in front of the others, necessary though it sometimes was to remind them that the Owned did not even have the right to gaze upon their Owner without his express permission.

To enter, and to his habitual annoyance, Heritus was forced to keep his head low, as the four walls to the chamber sloped to form a large pyramid within the exterior pyramid. For particular rituals, the design helped focus and channel magical power to the apex. The chamber's altar was naturally placed beneath the apex, and was connected via blood channels in the floor to each of the four walls. All had been built from the same rare, black quartz mined from amongst the lowest roots of the Needle Mountains by the Brethren. It did not matter that the stone was rare or black, just that it could absorb, reflect or conduct power as necessary. Yet the visual impact of design and quartz could not be denied, and Heritus knew it gave him another type of power with which to control the Brethren – the power of display and intimidation. His increased physical magnitude was also useful in that respect, and it was for this sort of reason that he'd had three thrones mounted on a dais behind the altar. His was the largest of the three, of course, and stood in the middle. It towered over everything, its headrest a full twelve feet above the floor.

Heritus ascended to his seat of power and lowered his gargantuan frame into place. A gong rang out across the mountain community, announcing that the Skull and Plague Victim had now entered the temple precinct, proclaiming for all to hear that the lost god of the Brethren was now returned to them, and that their deliverance was close at hand. He heard distant cheering and, with his mind, saw the Brethren throwing themselves to the ground in worship as the two Lords passed among them with the child held aloft. The infant god glared down at its people in malignant silence, and on whomever its divine gaze fell they would begin to beat and tear at themselves in an insane frenzy and ecstasy. Some clawed out their own eyes and held them up in their palms as an offering to the god, begging him to take them. Others bit chunks of flesh from their arms and swallowed them whole. Yet others cut open their stomachs, reached inside and began to yank out their own intestines for the god to see.

Heritus grunted in irritation. In stripping the Brethren of their reason and blasting away their vulnerable psyches, Nylchros threatened to kill the majority of the mountain people. Yet the Three still had need of those they Owned. Indeed, Nylchros himself had need of them, if he could but understand that. Heritus reached into the minds of the Brethren – each of whom had been individually bound to the Three when young – shored up their sense of self and gave them his protection. Brethren continued to writhe upon the ground in religious fervour, but their self-harming and immolation all but stopped. Nylchros looked past his immediate surroundings and directly into Heritus's eyes. The Unity challenged him, demanding that he cease his interference. Heritus raised his full power and made his mind an impregnable fortress.

The entire body of magickers, more than a hundred of them, began to file into the pyramid's central chamber. They moved round the room and lined every wall. As a group, they bowed deeply as the Skull, the Plague Victim and their attendants, led by the fanatic Refus dragging a cage apparently containing a body, entered. The Skull placed Nylchros on the altar and then, along with the Plague Victim, climbed up to the thrones on either side of Heritus.

The largest of the Lords nodded to his brothers as they assumed their places. Black smoke roiling across his eyes, Nylchros sat upon the altar and watched Heritus with a baleful defiance.

'Welcome, my brothers!' Heritus boomed, and it vibrated through the minds of every one of the Brethren, including the magickers. His voice was more than something merely spoken. It was felt and became their own thought. The people were now nothing more than his will. 'And welcome, Nylchros, Creator, Unity and god! We, the Three, have brought you here so that you may be one with us.'

The child god sneered but made no sound.

'It is our will that together we will lay low the pantheon.'

Smoking desire poured forth from the child's eyes. Clouds of black poison billowed up from the altar and surrounded the Lords. The Skull, as master of the body, refused to let it touch him. Heritus, his body sustained by magic, breathed in the pollutant without concern. The Plague Victim coughed and hacked for a while, but then successfully incorporated the substance into his ever-dying body.

The Skull laughed hollowly. 'You are newly born into this realm, Nylchros, still a child. Hence you indulge yourself with acts that are by definition childish. We can yet help you grow into this realm.'

Heritus was irked that the Skull thought to speak up, but he allowed his words just as a lion would consider a mosquito beneath its attention. 'Nylchros!' Heritus thundered louder than a cataclysm, forcing most of the magickers to block their ears and minds. Inevitably, a few passed out. 'We are the new masters of this realm! Its destiny and future are our will. Its entire Pattern has come down to this point and nexus. Either you will be a part of that will, or you will have no part in the new existence. It is not a matter of choice, it is simply our will made manifest and all-defining. You understand.'

Nylchros abided.

'So!' Heritus said. 'We will act together, as one. The Brethren will devote their life force to their god, for the greater glory of their god, as per the will of their god. They are bound to the Three, Nylchros, so you will recognise we Three accordingly. Refus!'

'Yes, Lord!' the magicker gibbered, releasing the chain by which he pulled the cage so that he might clasp his hands together in joy.

'Bring in the Brethren so that they might devote themselves to their god!'

'Yes, Lord! And may the magickers then devote themselves also?'

'Your time will come, faithful Refus. Go now.'

The simple people of the Owners were brought in one at a time, adoration and transport upon each of their faces. They crawled, heads down, from portal to altar and then rose on shaking knees, finally lifting their unworthy eyes to the holy infant. The child with the sea and sky in his gaze would then reach down and touch each one on the brow, drawing forth the fire of life and using it to nourish the earth and substance of his physical form in this realm. The child grew from infant to young man and soon was able to ask each devotee himself, without the help of one of the magickers, whether they freely gave of themselves to him.

As each of the Owned was touched and blessed by the god, their minds were cleared of troubles and torment and they knew only peace and the will of their god. Their eyes became blank and empty, the skin on their faces sank and became hollowed, and they watched in celebration as small sparks of life and Shakri's magic drifted and danced from them into the god's body. They all sacrificed years of their life to Nylchros, and knew only a paradisiacal fulfilment in doing so.

The night went on and on, until there were none left to pay their holy tithe. Nylchros stretched in his new body, arching his back and flexing his muscles. He stood, naked and perfectly formed. His eyes smouldered. There was still a seductive hunger and appetite about him. 'When will I absorb the others in this realm? Where are these aberrant gods?' crooned the divine youth.

Heritus smiled indulgently at his new son, but waved the magickers from the chamber before replying. They backed out facing the throne, with heads bowed. 'All the powers of this realm are marching towards us, which is as it should be. It all converges. They come at our demand, and cannot do otherwise. It will all play out here, unified by the narrative of our will.'

'There will be Unity,' agreed the divine youth. 'It is as it should be. Yet what is that thing I see before me?' he asked uncertainly, eyeing the bloody cage not far from the altar.

'That,' croaked the Plague Victim, 'is Balthagar. He is the irreducible progenitor of the child whose body is now yours. But he is as you see him. Of no consequence. Nothing.'

The youth jumped down lightly from the altar. He padded lightly towards the cage and then moved around it giggling. He danced and skipped for a while, ran in close, then jumped back again. After that, he grabbed his scrotum and flaccid member and urinated hard onto the top of the cage. The piss dribbled and dripped down through the cage and then found one of the channels in the floor. It sparkled as it moved like gold mercury towards one of the walls of the pyramidal chamber. Nylchros threw back his head, howled, scampered round the chamber, up and down the stairs to the dais, and then back up onto the altar, where he crouched and started to defecate.

'Control, Nylchros, control!' the Skull tutted. 'We can withdraw the life force gifted you if necessary.'

Nylchros pouted and bared his teeth.

'Our will and power confines you to this chamber, Nylchros,' Heritus rumbled. 'The pyramid focuses and preserves the life force allowed you. We will not have you expending it gratuitously. We will retire now to our own chambers, to await the dawn, the final battle and our ascension.'

❧ ❧

The Scourge was in a foul mood, again. He was angry at how the arrogant priest, Altibus, had presumed to put him to sleep without a by your leave, not just once but a second time even! It was typical of the proprietary attitude Shakri and all her servants had towards life everywhere. It was an outrage because they knew full well that free will and self-determination were fundamental and essential to the balance. By definition, he could only take it personally. He was angry that the Sergeant would actually think it alright to ask the priest to put him to sleep. He was only a bloody Sergeant, possessing no rank of significance and never having featured in a minstrel's tale or a fireside story. He was particularly livid that the demon Jack O'Nine Blades was still alive, of course. He was angry that Lucius hadn't had the balls to intervene when Altibus had started to use his priestly power – still, what could you expect of an effete royal musician? And just for good measure, he decided that he was also annoyed by that most contrary of cats Scraggins, who had now taken to riding with everyone except him.

Thinking about it, he was ticked off at the gods too, for landing them all in this mess. What was the matter with them? Couldn't they fight their own ancient enemies? Why was it always up to mortals to sort things out for them and pick up the pieces? Were the gods simply children who couldn't look after themselves properly? Shakri had certainly always acted like a spoilt brat. He'd felt like her nursemaid sometimes, much as he'd loved her.

He was even fairly angry with Saltar too. Okay, so he'd had a few beers too many, but that wasn't much of a reason to just leave him there in a pool of his own blood on the floor of an inn. What had happened as a result? Saltar had gone and got himself into a whole heap of trouble, that's what had happened. Dead, Lucius had said! Bloody fool. If Saltar had gone and got himself killed, then the Scourge for one was going to be really angry with him, not to mention Kate, who had an even worse temper than the Scourge. Well, it would just serve him right.

The Scourge was wet, cold and sore. He was stuck on a cantankerous horse that would have much preferred to be in the middle of a bloody battlefield than pushing through chest-high snow. He was accompanied by a pompous prig for a priest, a cackling demon for a minstrel, a fluttering ninny for a musician, and a moody moggy for a cat. He would even have preferred to be back on the road with Young Strap than with this lot. At least Young Strap had some gumption about him… even if he did talk too much, which ironically had forced the Scourge to ask Nostracles to put the Guardian to sleep upon occasion… Anyway, just where had Young Strap gone and got to? Why wasn't he here, where he could be of some use? It wasn't like there was anything else going on in the realm that could compare in terms of importance. Clearly, things had slipped while he'd been away.

He pulled out his flask and took a long pull on the devilberry liquor inside. It was one of the few things that hadn't frozen solid in the perishing temperatures, but then again it was of such high alcohol content that his blood was likely to freeze before the liquor. And it warmed him too, or felt like it did at any rate. It certainly cheered him up, which made it of more use than any of his companions. He had half a mind to leave them all behind and go and sort out these magicians on his own, but he wouldn't put it past the priest to try and put him to sleep again while giving him some sort of sanctimonious lecture or other.

Where he had no doubt in his mind was around what he was going to do to these mountain magicians when he finally got hold of them. They would rue the day they'd had any ambition beyond waking up every morning. The Scourge had spent his entire life hunting and killing magicians. It was what he did best. It was one of the few things Voltar had been right about: not a single one could be allowed to live, as ultimately they always ended up putting the realm in jeopardy. A mortal that sought to use magic was a mortal that sought to be more than mortal, and that threatened the balance. It was as simple as that. If he ever got to speak to Saltar again, he would convince him to prohibit the use of all mortally-derived magic. Only the priests should be permitted their magic, and that only when absolutely necessary.

He rubbed at his eyes, which ached from the daylight reflecting off the snow. Snow-blindness was the last thing he needed. They'd been trekking for several days since Altibus had last put him to sleep, and were now well into the foothills of the Needle Mountains. It had been relatively easy following the magicians, for the tracks left by the beasts they rode were massive. The Scourge had never seen anything that could leave such a trail. Their hoof-prints were much larger than his hand and their stride pattern was well over twelve feet. Altibus had been clueless too, knowing of nothing in Shakri's creation that could be responsible.

They moved up into the mountains proper, following a path along the side of a river. They came to a natural, high wall to the side of them and the tracks ended there. They circled their horses for a while, looking for a sign as to where they should head next.

'A concealed entrance somewhere?' Lucius ventured.

Jack shook his head. 'It would not escape my detection. There is nothing. All this is the work of Shakri's nature, wouldn't you agree, good Altibus?'

Altibus nodded, but refused to let the demon curry favour, particularly when he suspected Jack sought to isolate the Scourge within their group. 'But I will leave the final judgement to the Divine Consort.'

The Scourge craned his neck and looked up at the top of the small cliff. 'Look how the tracks are clustered here, and how some of them are deeper and wider as if their mounts pushed down with their back legs. I reckon they leapt up to the top.'

'Amazing!' the Sergeant whistled. 'How high would the walls of a fortress have to be to keep out such creatures?'

'I see scuff marks near the top of the cliff also, where a trailing leg or two scrabbled for purchase!' Jack said with a broad smile to everyone, as if he'd somehow outdone them all.

Lucius frowned. 'I don't see anything.'

'Shakri allows her servants perfect vision, and I also see nothing,' Altibus agreed.

'Nonetheless, they're there. You'll just have to trust me,' Jack said.

The Scourge grunted. Trust a demon? Did he think all mortals were as puggled as the idiot-god Jack purported to follow?

Jack arched one of his eyebrows questioningly. 'You have something to say holy Consort? Don't be shy.'

The Sergeant, Altibus and Lucius all tensed, fearing how the Commander would react to such overt antagonising. Scraggins stopped cleaning her whiskers with her paw and crouched low in Altibus's lap with eyes half closed.

The Scourge lifted his chin and rolled his head round on his neck. One of his vertebrae cracked into place and he sighed. That always managed to make him feel better, even if it made others wince. Calmer now, he regarded Jack without blinking. 'I was wondering, demon, what would happen if you were unable to sow the seeds of division and chaos? Would you somehow be lessened by it?'

'I am a man of manners, unlike some, Scourge!'

'Come now, Jack, you are no man at all. Need I remind you, you are a demon? You thrive on the anger and rage of others, do you not? You can tell us. Do not be afraid. We are your friends!'

Jack was no longer smiling. 'Is this how you tried to sweet-talk Shakri, Scourge? No wonder your relationship was an abject failure.'

Altibus looked to the Sergeant, but the Sergeant shook his head.

'Please, good minstrel, there is no need to search for another subject. We are not singing of my life with Shakri. We are telling the tale of Jack O'Nine Blades, are we not? We are warning the audience against a demon who would drive them to the sorts of wanton and self-destructive acts that would separate them from their very selves. There is even a moral lesson there that would please the temples, for it teaches us all to guard against a wayward temper and to seek self-mastery through piety. Is that not how the ditty goes? Do I have it aright?'

Jack's summery disposition passed into winter and his blueberry eyes withered on the bush. The black void now gazed back at the chips of black diamond that were the Scourge's own eyes. 'I do not seek to undo this creation, Scourge, but it seems you constantly do. Do you set yourself in opposition to me once more? Come then, set to! Let us fight again, and this time you will not find me so playful.'

'Scourge, do not do this!' Sergeant Marr warned, a terrible premonition clear upon his face.

Scraggins leapt clear from Altibus's horse and straight onto the Scourge's. She butted the Commander under the chin with her head and demanded affection.

The Scourge threw back his head and laughed, and the sound echoed off the mountains. ' Be sure Jack – though that cannot be your real name – that I will fight you one day. But I will not do so now, as you have yet to scale that rock and pull us all up by rope. If it is chaos, death and destruction you want, then you will have more than you could ever hope for once we face these magicians. When all is settled with them, then, demon, we will have a reckoning, you and I.'

Jack began to speak in a language none of them understood. Scraggins's hackles rose and she hissed. She popped her claws and slashed the air. Her green eyes shone in the same way as the priest Nostracles's jade amulet once had.

Deep scratches appeared across Jack's throat and he clutched at it in panic. The void left his eyes and the pleasing blueberry colour returned. A fawning smile quivered on his lips. 'Of course, of course!' he warbled. 'That's as we agreed. All very reasonable! I'm not sure I'll be able to haul those horses up though, heh, heh! I think Altibus has been a little generous with the feed, eh?'

No one laughed or said anything. They simply watched as Jack got down from his horse and skipped across the lightly packed snow without even leaving a footprint. He assessed the wall for a second and nimbly began to pick his way up the cliff. Elfin as he was, his strength easily outstripped his body weight, and he climbed with an effortless grace that meant he scaled the wall as quickly as he would be able to walk the same distance on the flat.

'Don't fall, Jack!' the Scourge heckled the demon, and the acoustics of the place made it seem as if an entire host shouted the same. 'I'd hate to be cheated of my reckoning.'

'Scourge, what do we do with the horses? Set them loose, tether them?' the Sergeant asked.

'Best not to tether them in case there are wolves or mountain cats around. Prey will be in short supply in such weather. If we leave what feed we have for them here, they will have enough for some days, and a ready supply of water from the stream. And if my horse is anywhere in the area when we return, then it will come at my call. Your mares will likely stay close to my destrier as well.'

'I will cast Shakri's blessing upon them so that they will be free from exposure for a hand of days,' Altibus offered.

The Scourge liked the idea. 'That would be a worthwhile precaution, good Altibus. Just do not tire yourself too much with your use of priestly powers. You have been using them much of late. We do not know what challenges still lie ahead of us, but I suspect you will be required to exhaust all your reserves.'

Altibus gave a small, serious smile. 'Yes, Divine Consort.'

'Altibus, *Scourge*, *Guardian* or *Old Hound* will suffice. No more of this *Divine Consort*, for it is no longer my place or privilege,' the Scourge murmured while scratching a purring Scraggins behind the ear.

'Yes, Div-… Scourge!'

'Lucius, you're the lightest of us. You're up first. Then the two of you can pull up the Sergeant.'

'I'd better go last then, as it might need all of you,' Altibus said, patting his ample girth jovially.

They saw to the horses and were then up the cliff in relatively short order. Jack lowered them one by one down the other side, the Scourge going first so that the others could remain with Jack, keep a watchful eye on him and ensure he didn't get up to any shenanigans with the commander's safety.

Once they were all down, they began to follow the ravine through the mountains. The going was fairly slow, since they had to travel along one of the slopes to remain above the deep snow filling the bottom of the pass. But at least they had no trouble with knowing which direction to take whenever the ravine met a bisecting pass, since the tracks of their enemy were clear.

'You would think they'd make some effort to disguise the route they'd taken, wouldn't you?' Sergeant Marr observed. 'Without these tracks to follow, we'd be lost in this labyrinth in no time and I'm not sure how long we'd then be able to last.'

The Scourge had been thinking something quite similar to the soldier. 'They're either in a great hurry or they are arrogant enough not to care if we follow them or not. The way they killed Orastes's guards back in the palace and the things they did to the people of Swallowdale show a casual contempt or complete disregard for life.'

'It beggars belief,' Altibus said faintly. 'Surely they must value their own Shakri-blessed lives. If they value that life and offer the goddess the thanks and worship She is due, then surely they will hold the life she has created elsewhere as sacred. How can they not see that their acts are a sacrilege against the goddess? I cannot comprehend it. It is completely without logic. They cannot be rational or sane. They must have run mad. They have killed without reason. Even a wolf only kills because it needs to eat. These magicians we pursue can have no place in this realm if they kill for the simple enjoyment of it.'

'Hmm,' Jack mused. 'Why is it most of the temples describe actions they do not understand or condone as lacking in logic, irrational, insane or mad? If the actions were truly as described, then they would be sacred to Wim, one of the pantheon. Would you challenge the pantheon, Altibus? I think not.

So, please, do not call our enemy insane or mad. It is an insult to those who are truly insane or mad, or those who pursue the divinity of chance and the random. I do not quibble with you here, either. I think it would be a mistake to underestimate our enemy. They have been deliberate and calculating in everything they have done thus far. They have a purpose, although it may not yet be clear to us.'

'I have to admit that Jack is right on that score,' the Scourge said thoughtfully. 'If we continue to underestimate the enemy, then I fear it will be our ultimate undoing. They have been at least one step ahead of us at every turn. They have outwitted, outfought and outpaced us so far, but that's because we have allowed them to anticipate us and lead us into dead-ends and traps. Perhaps we need to be more cautious, not go blundering ahead or rushing in as Saltar did.'

'Caution is one approach,' Jack agreed, 'if we have the time to spare. Otherwise we can prevent them anticipating us by being more random and unpredictable in our actions.'

Sergeant Marr tilted his head at Jack. 'I'm not sure how to go about being more random and unpredictable.'

'I'm not surprised. You're far too reliable and steadfast ever to be of much use to Wim,' Jack tittered. 'You're quite impious in that respect, Sergeant, but I can't blame you. You have been bullied terribly by the army and the demands of the other temples, who insist on constant obedience or compliance from their followers. I bet they even have you believing that if you work and train hard enough, you can make your own luck, don't they? Have you ever said a man makes his own luck, Sergeant? You do know it's blasphemy, don't you?'

The Sergeant looked guilty.

'It's alright, Sergeant. As I said, no one can blame you. And I am not your judge.'

'Can we try both approaches at once?' Lucius asked brightly, just saving himself from slipping on some scree. 'Oh dear, I really have not brought the most practical footwear for this expedition. Anyway, can a few of us try a more cautious and planned approach, while a couple of others try a more unpredictable approach?'

'We might be best splitting up?' Altibus suggested.

'I can live with that,' the Scourge said without apology. 'When we get the chance to separate, Lucius and Altibus will need to decide for themselves if they go with the Sergeant and me or whether they go with Jack. Good, now let's see if we can't move any quicker, shall we? A bit of running might warm us all up, and there aren't too many more hours of daylight.'

Altibus groaned and surreptitiously used his powers to put renewed strength into his legs. He told himself it was only fair, since he was having to carry Scraggins within one of the folds of his voluminous robes.

Some time later, as dusk was beginning to fall, they found the way blocked by a difficult escarpment. On the top of it was the outline of a huge, ornate oblong of a building.

'It looks like a mausoleum,' Altibus puffed.

As they watched, silhouetted figures shuffled forwards. They lined the top, moving backwards and forwards slightly.

'What are they doing? Looking for something?' Lucius whispered.

'No!' spat the Scourge. 'They're swaying about in order to keep their balance.'

'Drunk?' Jack asked in confusion. 'Dizzy with altitude?'

'Idiots!' muttered the Guardian. With exaggerated slowness, he explained: 'A person's muscles atrophy and begin to waste away within hours of their dying. Once they are raised, therefore, their body struggles to keep its natural balance.'

'Animees!' Altibus gasped. 'Shakri preserve us! It's the worst of blasphemies!'

'You don't say!' the Guardian replied.

Jack and Lucius couldn't help snickering. The poor light hid the priest's blushes.

The Sergeant checked his weapon. 'How do we deal with them?'

'Not with traditional weapons, that's for sure,' the Scourge replied. 'Waste of time. I've got some water blessed by the temple of Shakri, so we can use that if we have to defend ourselves. Altibus, can you bless the water in everyone's bottles as well?'

'I think mine's frozen. I could try and warm it by putting it inside my robe next to my body.'

'It's quicker if you use your piss or spit into a bottle. But, look, I don't care how you do it, just sort yourself out. Now, I'm hoping we won't have to use any of our water on these stinking corpses, as the accursed necromancers animating them will know as soon as we do it. I'm also hoping none of the animees were raised while still fresh, as then we're sure to move faster than them and be able to dodge around them.' The Scourge looked at the portly Altibus dubiously. 'Will you be able to keep up?'

'Yes, Divine Consort!'

'Good. I don't know what we'll find if we get past these animees, so I guess we'll have to play things slightly by ear. Let's try and stay together as much as possible though, as it's our best chance of survival if we're faced by larger numbers. If you think prayers will do you any good, now's the time to say them. Ready?'

They ran to the escarpment and began to make their way up as quickly as they could, hoping that none of the animees above would notice them. Jack pulled away from the others, but the Scourge and Sergeant made steady progress not far behind. With his nimble fingers and long levers, Lucius did not struggle too much, and even Altibus seemed to be coping, although the impossible strength of his arms suggested he was using more than a little priestly advantage.

Jack sprang over the top. His voice crowed and drifted down to the others: 'I will lead them a merry jog, my friends, fear not!'

'J-!' the Sergeant began but suddenly had to secure one of his handholds so as not to slip.

'I should have tied us all together by ropes,' the Scourge decided vehemently. 'And the rope I would have fashioned for the demon would have been a noose for his neck. By the rotting, fly-infested arse of Lacrimos, he's a constant liability!'

'He's a demon,' the Sergeant agreed.

Unleashing a stream of choice epithets under his breath, the Scourge pulled himself up and over the crumbling edge of the escarpment. There were only a couple of dilapidated animees dragging themselves along the ground to be seen. 'Come on, let's get the others up,' he said, giving the Sergeant a hand and then uncoiling a rope to throw down to the others.

When they were all up, they hurried across the top of the arête. Laid out below them was the wide mountain valley of the Brethren. Visible against surrounding snow, there were thousands of small homes organised in clusters. Candle light twinkled here and there. Through the descending dark, and despite an overcast sky blocking out stars and moon, they still could not miss the mighty black peak that rose at the centre of the valley and loomed over the habitations spread all around.

'Oh my!' breathed a startled Altibus. 'So much life, even here amongst these inhospitable slopes. Shakri's creation is a truly wondrous thing! It just takes your breath away.'

'I wish it would take your breath away, priest!' the Scourge said sourly. 'We don't have time for this. Everybody start climbing down. If anyone below us bothers to look up, they're bound to see us against the sky, and we're not behaving like your typical animees. The dead do not tend to stand around taking in the view and passing comment on nature's beauty. So get down that slope before I throw you down it, priest!'

Jack came skipping out of the night. 'Here I am!'

'Great, that's all we need,' the Scourge muttered.

They descended in fairly short order and took a moment to rest and take stock at the bottom. Altibus's chest began to squirm and then Scraggins leapt out of his robes. With a sniff, she raised her tail in the air and trotted off into the dark.

'Scraggins!' the Sergeant hissed, not daring to call out too loudly.

'Perforce, I must follow her!' Jack bowed. 'My friends, here is where we part. I hope to see you in better times. Adieu, sweet Scourge! Do not be too lonely or cold without me!'

'Good luck, Jack!' Lucius said earnestly.

'Ah, good Lucius, it is my dearest wish that one day we make beautiful music together, you and I.'

'Good riddance!' the Scourge said to Jack's retreating back. The minstrel waved without looking back. Then he stuck out his posterior, blew a raspberry and disappeared from sight.

'Scourge,' the Sergeant prompted, now all business. 'Caution dictates that we try and learn something of this place before attempting anything else. What say you we choose one of the more isolated houses and force our way inside?'

'Excellent, Sergeant. Lead on.'

'What if there are occupants?' Altibus asked Lucius, who shrugged.

'Why? You wish to lead on the torturing to be done, priest?' the Scourge said over his shoulder.

'Surely not!' came the priest's high-pitched response.

'Surely so,' the Scourge said grimly. 'These people are our enemies. They have stolen the Battle-leader's son, destroyed Cognis, if I do not miss my guess, slaughtered villages of innocent people and killed the Battle-leader himself, if Lucius is right. They will receive no mercy from me, and as much as they have shown the Memnosians. Torture is the least they deserve. If you do not have the stomach for it, priest – as that girth of yours comes from nothing more than self-indulgence – then you may as well start climbing back up that slope right now. The Battle-leader is dead, so you are released of your duty and vow. I'm sure none would call it cowardice. After all, we all know the servants of Shakri are not permitted to kill, that their hands and consciences are always bound, bound as if they were slaves, mindless slaves without wills of their own. And what of you, Lucius?'

'I have endured much torture,' the one-eyed musician said without hesitation. 'I learnt a number of techniques from Voltar himself that may be of use to us,'

'Really?' the Scourge said rhetorically, the musician rising in his estimation. 'Then let's be about our business.'

Shivering, but not because of the cold, Altibus followed along after them. 'You have shamed me, Divine Consort. Forgive me. I will follow you and help in whatever way I might.'

The Scourge nodded. 'I could not ask any more of you than that, good priest. You have come further than I could ever have imagined. This way.'

They were forced to move relatively slowly, to reduce the sound of their feet crunching on the snow, although the wind was loud enough to cover the worst of it, and to avoid turning any ankles on the rocky paths. When they were forced to enter the shadow cast by one of the houses, the darkness was all but complete and they stretched hands out to avoid bumping each other.

'It seems they all go to bed at pretty much the same time,' Lucius whispered. 'It's a bit eerie with no one about and no sound coming from any of the homes, isn't it?'

'Unnatural if you ask me,' the Sergeant whispered back.

The Scourge indicated a house set slightly apart from the others. They picked their way towards it and moved under its eaves. Like all the other houses, the shutters on its windows were fastened closed against the elements, but light gleamed gently through the cracks between shutter and wall.

The Guardian beckoned the others close. 'We all go in through the door quickly. We three will subdue those within as quickly as we can. Altibus, you'll come through last – make sure you shut the door behind you.'

They nodded and followed his lead. He crept to the door and put his hand to the latch. Taking a deep breath, he depressed the lever and hit the wood of the door with his shoulder. It flew open and he tumbled inside. One of his hands went to the stone floor of the room inside, but he kept his feet under him and his sword was up and ready in an instant. The Sergeant was right on his heels, then Lucius. In rushed Altibus, pulling the door to as he came.

A couple and their teenage daughter sat frozen at the wooden table in the centre of the one-room cottage. They were a bizarre tableau, for they showed no awareness of the four men who had just burst into their home and were now standing, weapons bared, looking at them in mystification. There were a few lit candles on the table, but the hearth was empty and cold.

The Scourge waved a hand in front of the eyes of the man at the table. 'Hello? Can you hear me?'

The man blinked but otherwise gave no response.

'Are they-are they animees, do you think?' Lucius queried.

'They're as alive as you and me,' Altibus whispered, though why he whispered he wasn't sure.

'It looks like some sort of trance,' the Sergeant said. 'What shall we do, Scourge? Hole up here or try another house?'

The Scourge rubbed his chin. 'I suspect all the houses are the same. I've never seen the like.'

'Maybe I can reach them,' Lucius offered, tugging the cover off his greater lute.

'Worth a go, I suppose,' the Guardian shrugged.

The royal musician tightened the strings on his instrument and plucked them experimentally a few times. Then he settled himself against a wall, took the weight of his lute on the inner thigh of one leg and trickled some notes into the air. The strings were cold and sounded slightly brittle, so he was forced to slow the sound until it all but froze in the air. It hung for a second, and then cracked like ice on a puddle as weight is brought to bear by a young boy on his way fishing. He has a long, sharp knife at his belt so he can cut through the thick ice on the lake and drop his line down through the hole to the dark and silvery depths below. His grandfather has warned him to wait a few more days until the surface of the lake will take his weight, but the boy is full of the confidence and optimism of youth and life.

The three mountain people at the table smiled vaguely and turned their heads slightly towards Lucius.

The sun shines down on the boy and he takes a large, glittering icicle from a tree that he passes so that he can wave it as a shining sword. He fights through the snow and it covers his clothes. He wears it as his armour. Fearlessly, now, he approaches the lake and all its promised dangers. He strikes at it and cuts a round shield for himself from the lake's covering. He stands tall and proud.

The small family were now rapt. The Scourge, the Sergeant and Altibus held their breath as they listened.

To the boy's own mind, he has conquered the lake, and he demands it offer up its bounty to him. Rather than the few fish he would normally have, he shouts he will have them all. The boy rails so loud that the lake finally notices him. It hears his impossible desire and begins to laugh. It laughs so hard that it cracks the ice covering its belly. The hole, you see, that the boy has cut for his shield and line has weakened the surface covering.

Nothing in the room moved. The candle flames and the shadows on the wall held still.

With an icicle as glittering sword, with snow as shining armour, and with thick, rounded ice as shield, the boy-warrior plunges into the dark and silvery depths of the lake. The boy's grandfather comes to see if the boy will return. But they say the boy still fights and the grandfather yet waits until this very day.

Gently, Lucius placed the flat of his hand on the lute's strings, and all was done.

'Why do you stop?' asked the man.

'Did the boy ever defeat the lake,' asked his daughter.

'No, child,' Lucius said softly.

The Scourge cleared his throat. 'What is it that you do hear, goodman, sat with your life-mate and child?'

'Why, we wait for the word of our god. We wait to fight those who come. A great army, so they say. It will be glorious, and all for the glory of our god.'

'Who is your god? And where can we find your black-robed magicians?' the Scourge hurried, but the man's head had returned to its earlier position. He stared blankly ahead once more. 'By the divine, unending orgasm of...'

'No, Scourge!' Altibus forbade him severely.

For once, the Scourge bit his tongue. He sighed. 'Well maybe we should just wait until...'

He suddenly went blind. It wasn't that the candles had gone out so that he could only see shades of darkness. There was only the total black of the void. It filled his head so that even the colours of his thoughts and imagination were reduced to little more than the spark of Shakri's gift. Even before the others cried out, he knew they were under a magical attack, for he had experienced something similar when he and Saltar had faced the magician Visier. He faintly heard a boot scuff against a rock outside.

'Nobody move!' the Scourge ordered his companions. 'If you value your lives...'

... and then he could no longer hear his own voice either. He screamed for all he was worth, but in vain. He hung in space, completely lost, worried he was about to lose his entire grip on himself. He gritted his teeth and gripped his sword so hard it hurt. At least he still had his sense of touch. He drew one of his long daggers and crouched.

He knew there were senses beyond the physical. Some called it instinct, some telepathy, some prescience, some magic. He thought of it as some sort of sympathetic resonance or attraction shared by the divine spark and electricity of all living things. He fancied he could sense where his fellows were in relation to himself. He had a physical awareness of their presence and proximity. And now he sensed a new presence.

He cast his knife into the dark and swiftly drew the other one. He did not know if his first dagger had found the enemy, but he was fairly certain he had not hit either Lucius, Altibus or the Sergeant in error.

The sort of cough that suggested fluid in the lungs came to him. His hearing had returned! He knew he must have thrown true. He tried to sense another target.

'Put up your weapons or the fat one dies!' came a hate-charged command. 'Do it! Now!'

The Scourge wrestled with himself for a few seconds and then threw down his blades with a snarl. Immediately, he felt heat and cold shooting through his gut. He recognised the feeling. They'd stabbed him! He played his role and fell into a seated position on the floor, which took his hands back closer to his discarded steel.

His sight returned and he whipped his knife across the room through the neck of one of the black robes entering the room. 'Gkk!' the magician gasped, and then blood spewed from his mouth.

'Incompetents!' raged the commanding voice of before. The owner, a young, anaemic-looking magician, uttered a foreign syllable and touched the Scourge on the arm. The Guardian lost co-ordination of his body and flopped onto the flagstones like a fish landed on a riverbank. Out of the corner of his eye, he saw the Sergeant was also on the ground.

The lead magician turned to Altibus. 'You are a priest, are you not?' he asked shrewdly.

'I am,' Altibus replied bravely. 'I serve Shakri, Mother of All…'

'Silence. Every priest that dies is another blow against the pantheon. Kill him!'

'No!' Lucius shouted, but apparently could not lift his arms.

A magician standing behind Altibus drew his knife across the priest's neck, held him for a second as he struggled and then threw him to the floor in sneering disgust.

'Noo!' Lucius cried again and twisted his torso this way and that, but his limbs would not obey him. He was grabbed and pushed roughly to the floor.

'I'll kill you, you bastard!' the Scourge ground out between his jaws.

The anaemic magician crouched down by the Scourge, stuck a knife in the Guardian's chest and twisted it. The Scourge didn't flinch. 'Huh! Amazing. Not an animee and not a magician. Plenty of blood but apparently undying. So what are you?'

The family of mountain people continued to sit at their table, unaffected by the death and horror surrounding them.

'I'm your mama with face-paint on and I wish I'd had a miscarriage!' spat the Scourge.

There were laughs of disbelief from the other four magicians in the room.

'Shut up!' the anaemic one screamed as he rose, spittle spraying each of them. 'The Lords will be interested in this one. Take him to one of the cells beneath the pyramid. Bleed him every minute or so and he shouldn't give you too much trouble. If he speaks, cut out his tongue.'

'Yes, Refus!' they murmured. 'And these two?'

'I will anoint the soldier with my blood so that he may serve the Three. And the tall one, I don't know. What are you?' the leader asked, looking down at Lucius.

'A musician.'

'A musician?' the leader repeated incredulously. 'You are of no value. Kill him.'

'No!' said the man at the table sternly.

'What?... I mean, what is your will, divine one?' Refus yelped.

'He amuses us. Bring him to us!"

They half-dragged and half carried the unresisting Scourge and Lucius from the house. The Scourge's eyes took in the sorry sight of Altibus on the floor, a shocked looked on the priest's round face but peace in his final gaze. This man who had never harmed another creature in his life or asked for anything himself had been murdered without hesitation or regret. This priest who had spent his life in the service of all living things had ultimately been rewarded with nothing but mockery, contempt and a meaningless death. Feeling a responsibility more painful than any knife he'd had to the gut or chest, the Scourge made a silent vow to himself.

❧ ☙

They'd arrived back in the valley to a rapturous, and enraptured, welcome from the Brethren. Larc and Vasha had quickly become a nuisance to the magicians who carried them on their mounts and were more interested in waving to the crowds than being concerned with whether the youths sat behind them were managing to keep their seats or not. Larc leapt down from his rider, who gave him a glance, shrugged and then rode on. Then he ran along the path, edging between crowd and procession.

'Vasha! Come on!' Larc called.

She saw him and looked down nervously at the long drop from the top of the massive beast on which she sat.

'Come on! I'll catch you!'

She bit her lip and then swung her other leg over the saddle so that she was ready to jump. She leapt with a small cry, and was suddenly in his arms falling back into the crowd. None of the Brethren shouted at them, for they were too busy calling out to their infant god.

'Are you alright?' she asked anxiously.

'Cuts and grazes, that's all,' he winced. 'Had worse.'

A middle-aged man near them started tearing at his clothes with a long knife.

'What's he doing?' Vasha asked, scared.

'I-I don't know!'

Purple blood began to streak the man's grey shirt and his eyes rolled back in his head, but he didn't stop slashing at himself. A young girl raked at her face with her fingernails, as if trying to tear the skin and flesh from her skull. A seductive voice entered Larc's mind, promising him immediate entrance to heaven if he would but end his limited, unhappy life. He would know the divine will, join the Unity, take his place with the Creator. Knowing he committed blasphemy, but unable to prevent what was an involuntary reflex, he shrugged mentally as his grandfather had taught him a lifetime ago and threw off the invading mind.

He grabbed Vasha's hand. 'Run!'

Twenty metres on and Larc risked a glance backwards. No one was pursuing them. No one even appeared to be watching them. They hid behind a house to catch their breath. He didn't delude himself – they'd be able to catch him with relative ease on their massive beasts. He was Owned and should accept that. He'd willingly bound himself to the Lords when he'd reached adult age. He must stay true to that vow, or what sort of man would he be? He'd be without honour and his word would mean nothing. His *life* would mean nothing. He'd be reviled by his own people and he'd feel only shame. What would his grandfather think if he saw all that Larc had done? He might excuse Larc's initial flight from the valley, putting it down to grief and youth, but he would be intolerant of his current wilful behaviour. Larc leaned against the wall and kicked at the floor disconsolately.

'Are you alright, Larc?' Vasha asked gently.

Larc smiled bleakly at her. 'Come on, I'll show you my home.'

He led her on a weaving path that soon had her turned around. How did he know which way to go? All the houses looked the same to her. Then she noticed a regular, black peak rising over everything, and that they were largely keeping it to their left.

'What's that, Larc?' she asked.

He looked up and scowled at the dark landmark. 'You don't want to know.' Then he brightened a bit. 'Here we are!'

He took her inside a small house that was not too dissimilar to the others. She stood near the door and looked round curiously. He hovered near her, clearly wondering what she thought.

'Oh, Larc, it's lovely. Those curtains are such a pretty shade of green.'

He smiled proudly. 'Thank you. It's a bit dusty, I'm afraid. Sarla made the curtains! She… she liked… the colour green.'

She felt terrible for him. And out of place, as if she were intruding.

'I… I haven't been here since… since that night,' he said, his voice breaking.

She looked around the house again, desperately looking for something else she could comment on to distract him or change the subject. Her eyes alighted on a small crib made of newly carved wood. Oh no! He followed her gaze and shook.

He walked quickly across the room, picked up a bucket and said gruffly without looking at her: 'I'll get some water from the river. I won't be long. You stay here!'

She stayed where she was near the door the whole time he was away. She didn't want to disturb anything because it would be like sorting through his private memories, stirring up his grief or spoiling things that were sacred to him. When he returned, he looked a bit better.

'I'm sorry,' he said. 'I hadn't anticipated what it would be like coming back here. Please, sit! I'll light a fire and make us a herb tea.'

A while later and they were both sipping too-hot tea. Amongst most people, an awkward silence would then have developed, but she had always been able to talk to him. 'Oh, Larc, what are we going to do?'

He looked at her, wanting to tell her that everything would be alright, just as on that night when he'd promised he'd never betray her again and that he would do all he could. He wanted to reassure her that they could live in his little house and be happy picking flowers, collecting herbs, hunting rock-rats, herding goats, curing hides and making clothes every day. It was the secret wish of his heart, but it could never be, not whilst the lost god, the Lords and the magickers were the ones to decide everything about his life. Oh, they promised happiness, safety and rebirth, but they had allowed his wife and child to die and he had seen in the attendant magicker's eyes the confession that it was all a lie. He had heard the god peddling the same lie, promising him paradise in return for his own death. He had seen the Lords torture the Builder and his child beyond bearing. He knew he could have no life of his own while the god, the Lords and the magickers sought to increase their power at the expense of the lives of those they Owned. What could they do, though?

'Vasha, we will have to go to the pyramid,' he decided. 'We have no choice.'

'The pyramid? Is that the strange mountain-?'

'Yes. We must not let anyone see us, so we will wait until it is dark. It will be dangerous, Vasha. You can stay here if you like.'

'Can't you stay here too? Just the two of us. It will be nice.'

He looked at her sadly. 'Bad things are going to happen, Vasha, I just know it. Like what happened to your god, Cognis. Maybe if we're still alive when it's all over, then perhaps we… could…' but he tailed off.

'I understand,' Vasha replied resolutely. 'We will go to the pyramid then. Are we looking for the Builder? But isn't he dead?'

'Then why do they keep him in a cage?'

With his one eye and through the bars of the cage, Saltar watched the rock-rat come sniffing through the straw littering the dungeon floor. It smelt his blood and entrails. It came across the thick glistening worm of one of his intestines and began to gnaw on the soft tissue. Ah! How it hurt!

He did not understand how he still lived, in many ways did not want to live, given how it had become an unending torture. *Irreducible*, Cognis had called him, and it was clearly both a blessing and a curse.

There was something in him that could not be undone by anything in this realm. What was it? He looked inside himself and found the raging centre that had made him berserker at certain times, brutally defiant at others, and relentless and unyielding throughout. It crackled with an unquenchable heat and energy. Where the life of most in this realm was but a spark, this was a sun.

He reached for it, but it burnt him. His mind could find no connection with it. There must once have been a connection or organising magic, but it was now broken, just as was his body. And why would he want to reconnect to that body when it was a pained and miserable thing? Why would he seek any magic that might resurrect him so that he could then die horribly again in this cage? Why?

He'd been aware, throughout, of the events going on around him. He'd understood how they'd violated his sweet and innocent Orastes, giving the Unity a gateway into this realm. He'd been appalled as he'd learnt the full extent of the three necromancers' dark desires. He'd been sickened as he'd watched the mountain people sacrifice their life force to the Unity. And he'd been saddened as the possessed adult body of his son had urinated on him.

He felt the urine on him still. It was hard to ignore, for he could both smell and taste it, but more than that it was still charged with the overflow of life. Intoxicated and surfeited with the energy he'd drunk, Nylchros had carelessly excreted the excess and bathed Saltar's wrecked body in it. His body absorbed it and he felt his extremities tingle. The rage within him flared in answer to the magic's call and connected with Saltar once again.

Waves of pain crashed over him and he thought he must die in the next instant. Every bone in his body was broken or crushed, and he felt each one of them. Every organ was punctured or ruptured, and each of them tortured him. His heart fluttered and then stilled. The rock-rat screamed and died, its spark of life leaving it and drifting to Saltar in the cage. His heart lurched and began to beat irregularly. The moss on the walls of the dungeon shrivelled away and a haze shimmered towards him. Then, the Battle-leader's heart began to beat like a war drum.

Chapter Fourteen: For The End Of Days

The Chamberlain shuffled slowly through the resting troops towards Kate's group of commanders. The ichor in his veins had thickened because of the cold. It pained him to move too quickly and his mind was dopey, lacking its usual hard edge. Experiencing such torpor, he would have little chance of survival once the fighting began, so resolved to avoid the melee as far as possible. Besides, there were plenty of inconsequential mortals around who seemed willing to put themselves in harm's way instead of him. Their lives were of little value compared to his own, so let them have their moment of glorious and gross stupidity.

'Well, have you discovered who it is trying to kill me?' Kate asked him blandly, interrupting the conversation she'd been having with others.

General Vidius was too wily to show any reaction to her question, the Chamberlain noted. The eyes of a number of the officers and high priests widened slightly, though whether in amazement or panic, he wasn't sure. Surely there wasn't a wider group conspiring against Kate, was there? No, he discarded that idea, since a large group wouldn't be able to organise themselves effectively without the spies he had in the army finding out.

'No, milady. It appears many would have had the opportunity to slip the poison into the cordial, albeit my staff did not notice anyone out of the ordinary in the proximity of the tents that day, hmm? I therefore suppose that the handmaid poisoned the cordial herself, as Sister Spike has already intimated, yes?'

Kate's green eyes tightened slightly. The Chamberlain realised he wasn't telling her anything she didn't already know. She thought he was prevaricating. Curse his sluggishness! He'd better get to the point soon, or give her something new, if he wanted to avoid testing her temper. When had he become so nervous of her, he wondered to himself, but decided to leave it for another time, if there ever was another time, if they all survived the coming battle.

'Chamberlain!' she prompted him, bringing him out of his fugue.

'Sorry, milady. Forgive me… hmm? Milady, I have something new.'

'Well, out with it.'

Interesting. A few of the officers had shifted their weight on their feet at that point. Were they nervous of what he was about to reveal? None of them seemed to have tensed enough to be about to attack anyone, however.

'In questioning my staff, I learnt that the handmaid had a brother in the Guild of Holter's Cross, hmm? The night before the attack, no one can remember having seen Islaine.'

'That's right!' Kate recalled. 'So she may have been meeting her brother? I see.'

The officers and high priests murmured amongst themselves at this revelation.

Carris arrived with four horses in tow. 'Thank you, Chamberlain,' Kate said thoughtfully and by way of dismissal. She wondered if Grandmaster Thaeon had anticipated the plans she and Vidius had discussed concerning the Guild. Perhaps the old crow had read significance into their declining his invitation. Or had she and Vidius been overheard that night? Could Vidius be in league with the Guild?

'What is it, man?' the General asked Carris, exerting some authority in front of his fellow officers.

'Milord, these horses were found nearby. Feed had been left for them.'

'The stallion is the Scourge's!' Kate exclaimed. 'They're alive and they got this far then! But I don't see the Battle-leader's horse. What has happened to him?' she asked in confusion.

'Milady, his horse may have gone lame, we cannot know,' the General said matter-of-factly. 'They may have ridden two to one horse. Clearly, though, the wall forced them to go on foot from here – perhaps we will be able to see how many of them there were from the tracks on the other side.'

'So will we be forced to leave several thousand horses here also?' Kate said with concern. 'Will we not be able to take our cavalry with us?'

'Milady,' spoke up the lumbering high priest of Gart. 'We will be able to exhort the holy Firmament to clear a way for us… or at least I think so.' He knuckled his brow in some sort of salute or sign of respect.

She nodded and smiled in gratitude. 'Please, attempt what you can. It may be the saving of this army.' Then, to the wider group of high priests, she called out: 'Know this! The power of all the priesthoods are beginning to fail!'

The high priests didn't look shocked. Instead, they surreptitiously began to size each other up, especially the high priest of Aa, who always looked for new opportunity.

'Know also that I will not tolerate any infighting. If I suspect one of you of conspiring against your peers, the General will start seeing to battlefield court marshals. Yes, instant executions! Your example should be the divine pantheon. Save for Shakri and Lacrimos, the pantheon do not fight amongst themselves. It would be the end of this realm were they to do so. Similarly then, if you become divided, I believe that will also see an end to us.'

Brother Hammer could not hide his displeasure.

'That goes double for you, Brother Hammer. I know it is contrary to your calling, but you must hold any grudges you have against the other temples in abeyance. Your energies and focus must be bent towards our common enemy. Do I have your vow?'

'I make vows only to my god!' Brother Hammer replied pugnaciously. But the fact he fought within himself was also clear to them all. His mortal reason warred against his unquestioning dedication to his god. His personal battle was an exaggerated version of what all the high priests must be going through, she realised. Kate could not help feeling the most sympathy for Brother Hammer amongst all those assembled. 'Yet, like the good servant of holy Gart, I will do my best. I would only ask then that we advance upon the enemy as quickly as we may, since that will reduce the chances of my committing any acts of treason. The feuds of my temple are sacred to us, you must understand.'

'Indeed,' Kate agreed. 'We will march through the night, I hope, so that we come upon the enemy while we still have some of the powers of this realm intact. General?'

Vidius pulled a face. 'I have sent scouts over the wall. They report it will be a long march indeed. Our troops have already marched the day through. They will be exhausted by the time we reach the mountain valley tomorrow. But there is nowhere to rest between here and the valley, anyway, so they will be fatigued when we arrive in any event. It could be that our speedy arrival will ensure we still have the priestly powers required to secure our victory. We face formidable blood-mages, so I would not want to be without our priests.'

'It is decided then,' Kate concluded. 'We march.'

The mountain shook and cracks began to appear in the wall. The huge hands of Gart's high priest trembled as he strained to remove the tonnes of earth blocking their path. The priests of his temple knelt in prayer and supplication around him, lending him all the support they could. Furrows appeared in his mighty brow as he pitted himself against rock that had been formed and placed by the most titanic forces the realm had ever seen.

Kate and her commanders had retreated half way down the mountain but even so felt the tremors of what was happening above them. Small stones and pebbles jumped up from the floor as if alive. Then a seismic shockwave hit them and they all staggered as the cliff yawned wide and roared like an angry stone beast.

'I can't hold it!' the high priest cried and a river of earth and shale slid towards him and his followers. They ran, but a young priest was caught up in the deluge and swept off the path. He plunged screaming to his death far below.

Gart's rage and thunder that mere mortals would think to change what he had set in place gradually subsided and the dust cleared. Kate's army crept nervously back up to where the wall had once stood.

'I am sorry for the loss of your brother,' Kate said to the bent back of the high priest.

'There is always a price to be paid, milady,' said the high priest in a tired and gravely voice. 'He had a worthy grave, taken to the earth's bosom by Gart's own hand. The holy Farmer planted this young priest in the soil Himself, milady.'

General Vidius, who was listening carefully, nodded. 'I will have my officers spread such a sentiment amongst the troops so that they will not take the death as an ill omen. We do not want morale to suffer if it can be at all avoided.'

Kate knew that the General was only doing his job, but she didn't like the cynical way in which he saw and interpreted everything. Yet it meant he and those who followed him were rarely caught out. She disliked him intensely but respected his ability. Perhaps, then, she was as cynical as he was in having him lead her army. Shrugging to herself, she told him to give the order.

'Forward!' he shouted, though his voice seemed but a whisper after they'd all heard Gart speak.

They pushed into a snow-filled ravine and rode two abreast or single file. Large beasts had clearly come this way, although what they were she could not fathom. She scanned for footprints and spied some indentations on the slopes above the deep snow. It was impossible to tell how many travellers had come this way on foot, whether Saltar accompanied the Scourge or not. She half hoped that they'd reach the valley to find her husband and the Commander of the Guardians had already annihilated this Nylchros, killed the three necromancers and their pet magicians, and retrieved Orastes. But it could only be a fantasy, for neither Saltar nor the Scourge had any magic to speak of at their command. Remarkable though the pair of them were, they would not be able to stand against the near-divine and magical. She'd heard from Carris that some priest of Shakri had joined Saltar's group, but such a pacifist would be next to hopeless in any test of arms.

It all begged the question why Saltar and the Scourge would press on, when confronted with such an enemy. Did they really not know what they faced? Or was it male ego driving them on? Saltar could certainly be the most stubborn man in the realm once he'd decided on something. And the Scourge took so many risks, with so little concern for his own safety, that he could only be considered reckless. Well, if either of them turned out to have been in any way responsible for harm befalling her child, then there would be no forgiveness. Ever. She would spend the rest of eternity punishing them for it as well.

She checked over her shoulder that Sister Spike, Strap and Mordius were nearby and asked General Vidius, who rode next to her at the head of the line, in a loud voice: 'So, General, were you involved in any way in Islaine's attempt to poison me?'

Unperturbed, Vidius answered her: 'Milady, I was not. If I wished to see you dead, milady, then dead you would be.'

'And what method would you think to employ?' she asked him as if doing no more than commenting on the weather.

The General laughed. 'A strange game to be playing, but perhaps nothing else really suits in the hours before a life-and-death battle. At such a time, all things seem strange and surreal. The trivial suddenly comes into immediate focus and is of the utmost importance and value. And the previously important becomes all but meaningless. Enemies become friends, friends become enemies. The living act like the dead, our plans seem chaos, and madness seems the most reasonable course of action. It is when the glory of divine Lacrimos is most clearly seen by us mortals. What method would I seek to employ, milady? Surely you jest! We are at *war*! In the heat of battle a wise man swings his sword at everything around him, and only then wonders what was friend and what was foe. I could cut you down in the midst of a fray and all would swear blind I sought to defend you. I could proclaim you our talisman and thrust you into the thick of the fighting where there is more steel than air. If I wished to be more indirect, I would cunningly move our troops so that you were stranded apparently by chance amid our enemy. What method would I think to employ, milady? It would be a greater challenge to attempt to ensure your survival. And what method would *you* think to employ, milady, to ensure just such a survival?'

'Why, General, from what you say then the best way to ensure my survival would be to see to the deaths of everyone else. If friend would strike friend, then all are my enemy.'

Mordius coughed.

'You have something to say, good necromancer?' Kate asked.

'Go on, Mordius!' Strap urged him.

'Well, the General makes a point that causes me some concern. His description of battle is no doubt accurate, but it has echoes of everything becoming one. Such a turn of events can only be in the Unity's favour. A similar thing happened when we confronted Voltar's army in front of Corinus, did it not, General?'

'Aye, it did,' he conceded uncomfortably. 'But what else can we do?'

'Perhaps we should not allow ourselves to be drawn in too far,' Mordius suggested. 'If we become completely embroiled, we may be playing into the hands of the Unity. Perhaps we should attempt to keep a part of ourselves separate, keep a part of ourselves back.'

'What say you, General?' Kate asked.

Vidius closed his eyes in contemplation, as if visualising how it would play out for a second. Just how many wars had the man seen in his lifetime? Kate wondered if he'd actually lived as long as Saltar. Finally, he said, 'There are of course many tactical advantages to be gained in keeping troops in reserve, so that they can be used to bolster troops that would otherwise fail, or to give us increased speed and flexibility in redeployments. However, that would only be delaying the inevitable, as the reserves would still ultimately engage the enemy. If you are proposing that we keep back some of our force no matter the situation, then I cannot see any value in our being below full strength. Having said that, the priests of Shakri will be of little value once the real fighting begins. I see them as playing the role of physick and little more. Would that suit?'

Kate thought about it and decided that really it was appropriate the priesthood of Shakri be kept back from the Enemy. After all, they represented the wider creation that the Unity ultimately sought to possess. 'Yes, they must be kept back, and also protected. Mordius, you and Strap can lead the defenders, yes?'

'We can spare you a hundred men,' the General added.

'I can do that,' Mordius agreed.

'If it's all the same to you,' Strap piped up, 'I'd prefer to stay away from these priests of Shakri. They take a very dim view of my being an animee. Whenever I try explaining to them that I'm not too happy about it either, they offer to anoint me with blessed water. Why don't I be your bannerman, Kate, as I once was for Saltar?'

Kate looked to Sister Spike, who nodded silently. 'Very well, the job's yours. A word of warning though. My personal guard are only permitted watered-down wine.'

'What! That's barbaric!'

⁂

They reached the escarpment with the dawn. General Vidius didn't delay in calling Kate, the Chamberlain, Strap, Mordius, Sister Spike, Carris, the mercenary captains, Sotto for the Outdwellers, the high priests and all his commanders to a council of war. From this point onwards, Kate would allow him to take the lead, as his knowledge of warcraft far exceeded everyone else's combined. They all had bags under their eyes and a few of the younger officers could not stifle their yawns.

'Wake up, all of you!' the General shouted. 'At attention, you men!'

The officers present started, raised their unshaven chins and saluted smartly.

'The troops take their lead from you! You're a disgrace!' he snarled. 'Half of you are so backward that you'll be dead and judged by Lacrimos before you even realise the fighting's started. And death is probably too good for the other half of you, you misbegotten, mage-loving wretches! You wouldn't even get jobs in the Accritanian army… though you, Persaline, are pretty enough to serve as one of their camp whores!'

No one laughed. Ikthaeon and the high priest of Gart looked shocked. Brother Hammer and the high priestess of Lacrimos smiled. The rakish high priest of Aa studied his fingernails.

'What, do you need to see blood before you understand there's a war afoot, that fathers, sons, mothers, daughters, friends and comrades will soon be crying into the face of chaos for someone, anyone, any*thing* to help them put their guts back in, to stop the blood squirting out of their wounds, to tell those they care about they love them, to reassure them that it will all be okay and that the gods will look after them? Is it blood you need to see? The very same blood that the mages will turn against us? Then bare your arms, you men, and let's have it out! I will bleed you dry and then you need never fear they will have your own bodies revolt against you! Bare your arms, I say!'

The officers began to roll up a sleeve each. Vidius pulled out his stabbing sword.

'Hold out your arms! That's an order! Any man who does not hold out their arm will have it hacked from his body. Hold it up, I say!'

Then the General walked without stopping down the line, drawing his blade across the back of each arm as it was held up by his officers. None of them flinched.

'Now you can see your own blood! You have felt the pain of it being released from you. You have seen it *betray* your body as it runs free and weakens you. And you know it will *not* return. But are you really lessened? Or are you better off without this thing that will betray you time and again? So do not be afraid to bleed, you men of flesh and bone! Blood is the betrayer! And the mages of blood that you fight against are its masters! They are the ultimate betrayal! They are betrayers of this realm! They are betrayers of the pantheon! They are betrayers of their own mortality! They are betrayers of all living things! They are betrayers of their own bodies, and the bodies of every man, woman and child in this realm! *And by their magic, they would make betrayers of us all, do you hear?*'

'Answer me this!' he roared, no trace of the refined and cultured noble left in him. There was the sort of harmonic about his voice that Kate had never heard from a human body. He seemed a terrifying demon at that moment.

'Would you be betrayers!'

'No, General!' the officers shouted, their eyes alive now.

'And are you afraid to bleed!'

'No, General!' they cried with passion, and Kate, her heart pounding, could not help joining in.

'And will you show mercy to these mages of blood, who would betray you!'

'No, General!' they all yelled, high priests included.

'Then ready yourselves, you men of flesh and bone, for we strike within the hour! We are not afraid to bleed, you men of flesh and bone, for we will give these mages so much of our blood that they will drown in it! Men of flesh and bone, are you ready!'

'Yes, General!' they roared in reply.

'Dismissed!'

Vidius signalled for Kate's cadre and the high priests to remain with him, however. 'We have seen no enemy scouts, but we have seen movement at the top there. It is likely they know we are coming. Ikthaeon, can you tell how many are up there?'

Ikthaeon frowned. 'There cannot be many. I do not sense much life there.'

'Really?' the General asked distractedly. 'High priest of Gart, I presume the valley is beyond. Can you tell how wide this barrier is? Could you bring it down like you did the other?'

The hulking high priest concentrated for a second or two and then reported: 'I would estimate it to be a hundred yards at the top, more like a hundred and fifty at its base. I'm afraid we do not have the strength to level it. And I suspect this is also some sort of magical barrier. We could certainly undermine it, but then we would be climbing unstable slopes.'

'A tunnel?' the General asked quickly.

'Given time,' the high priest pondered. 'But the wider you want the tunnel, the longer it would take, perhaps up to a day.'

The General did not look happy at that. His face returned to normal and he turned to his adjutant, a decision clearly made. 'Bring up the light infantry. Have one legion ready to storm the climb, the others ready to follow in after them.'

'Yes, General!'

'General?' Kate asked quietly.

'We will have to try and take the barrier. It is the higher ground and of prime tactical advantage. It seems the only way to do it is to try and overrun the enemy.'

'We lose our cavalry then?' Kate asked.

'It appears so. If we can hold the top though, we may be able to buy the high priest of Gart enough time to complete his tunnel.'

'I'm not sure how much of our priestly powers will remain a day from now,' she cautioned.

'Indeed. Then we storm that climb and get our priests over the other side as quickly as we can,' he shrugged. 'It's a blow not to have our cavalry. We will turn our riders into foot soldiers, but they have neither the equipment nor the training of our true infantry. Even the Outdwellers will probably be more effective. So I will hold back the foot-cavalry as long as possible. Oh, and you will have to pay the mercenary cavalry extra to fight on foot.'

Kate shrugged. Money was meaningless now. 'Why advance initially with only one legion, General?'

He sighed with irritation, though it did not seem entirely directed at her. 'If we have seen movement above, then we must assume they have seen us. Yet Ikthaeon says there aren't many of them up there. Well, why aren't there? They could hold that barrier against our entire army with just a thousand of them repelling our climbers.'

'Unless the enemy are not large in number?' Kate suggested. 'They might be relying on magic more than anything else.'

'Maybe the General said. 'It just doesn't feel right, that's all.' His adjutant returned at that moment. 'Trumpet the advance! Have the other legions roaring them on. The battle-cry is Dur Memnos as usual.'

❦ ❦

'Come on, you dogs!' Persaline shouted as he led his legion into a run in the grey dawn light. 'What are you waiting for, your nurse to come change your swaddling clothes?'

War horns brayed around them and their comrades cheered. They raced for the escarpment, every man wanting the claim to fame of being the first up. Thirty of forty feet above them, they saw the line where sky met cliff top. They crawled and leapt towards it for all they were worth, muscles straining, lungs burning. Those with shining metal breastplates saw them scraped and scratched. Persaline's beautiful black boots quickly became marked and scuffed, but for once he didn't care. Battle had been joined! Their cause was just! Their blades were sharp! The legendary Green Witch and General Vidius were with them! The priests of every temple were with them. The gods themselves saw to their protection. This was what it was to be alive!

Dust drifted down into his eyes, and he instinctively wiped his face on his tunic. He blinked furiously, but it didn't clear his vision. He felt his eyes beginning to stream. If anything, his sight got worse. He heard his men mutter and complain around him.

He paused in his climb, freed one hand and rubbed vigorously at his eyes. The pain became so intense that he could no longer keep them open. The hand he'd just used felt sticky. Cracking open an eyelid, he saw there was blood on it, a lot of blood. A red tear dropped from his cheek and onto a rock. He was crying tears of blood!

'Help!' he cried out, but there were others calling too. What was happening? This was not how their glorious charge was meant to be.

Persaline reached for his handhold again. He couldn't find it. One of his boots slipped. He compensated by shifting his weight to the other foot, but that then went out from under him. Unable to hang on by just one handhold, the legion commander fell. His head broke open on a rock, and his beautiful face looked skywards with that final question, why?

❦ ❦

General Vidius snapped his eyeglass closed and cursed.

'General, what is it? Why did those men fall? Why have others stopped climbing?' Kate asked urgently.

'There are a handful of the enemy in black robes up there apparently tipping something down on the men. I don't know what,' he blinked.

'What do we do, sound a retreat?' Kate asked, wiping away tears.

The high priest of Gart raised his head curiously. 'There is earth in the air,' he rumbled. 'Powdered gemstone. The wind carries it!'

'What are you talking about?' the General asked brusquely, rubbing at an irritation in the corner of his eye.

'General, there's blood on your cheek!' the adjutant said in alarm.

'Everyone close your eyes!' Kate yelled. 'Now! And don't rub them. Do it! Pass the word, quickly!'

The shout went up, and soon the whole army was wailing and groaning, their panic and pain echoing off the ravines around them. Hundreds of horses bucked and reared, threatening to stampede.

'Cover the horses' eyes!' the officers shouted.

Men were bumped to the ground and trampled under hooves. Many handlers and riders were forced to open their eyes to try and calm their thrashing horses, and is so doing sacrificed their sight. There was pandemonium. Some of the troops furthest from the climb turned to flee.

'Hear me, servants of Gart,' their high priest bellowed. 'Create magical lodestones to draw the powdered stone out of the air. Use whatever magicks you can. Increase the powder's density so that it falls out of the wind. Exhaust your powers if you must. We must not fail!'

Brown-robed priests of Gart hurried to obey. There were only twenty or so of them but they spread themselves as far as they could amongst the five thousand men.

'Adjutant, are you there?' the General called.

'I can hear you, General!'

'Pass the word that all is well. The priests of Gart will save us. Start the chant, *All is well!* Quickly, man!'

'I will do my best, General!'

Then priests of Shakri were moving amongst them. They'd been able to heal their own eyes and were now seeing to those worst affected, as were priests of Malastra.

'Messengers!' the General soon shouted, finally able to look round. Several youths ran to his side. 'You, relay to the cavalry officers that we will fight this war afoot. They are to put down whatever horses necessary and release those that cannot be calmed. Go! You, tell the commander of the second legion that he is to charge the climb on the first trumpet, and the commander of the third legion is to charge on the second trumpet. Go! You, inform the high priests of Shakri and Malastra that they are to retrieve any survivors from the first legion on the third trumpet. Go!'

Having sluiced water in her eyes and deciding she was okay, Kate came close to the General again. 'Should we not retrieve the survivors first? Regroup? Count our losses?'

The General looked at her blankly. 'What care we for the number of our losses? If we do not take this climb, the realm is lost. Only morale and momentum will see us succeed now. Regroup, and the men will see it as retreat. They will begin to look around them and realise how many comrades they have lost. Their heads will drop. And then, milady, we will have lost this war before even a single enemy has been struck!'

The second legion of light infantry had now marched forward. A trumpet sounded and the five hundred men broke into a screaming run. The third legion marched forward to wait their turn to shout in the face of death.

Kate had seen war before, fought in the middle of it, but never seen it carried out like this. She'd never had to command an entire army, never had to make decisions that she knew would consign large numbers of people to their deaths. She'd never had to treat life with the same casual disregard as the General now did. Rationally, she understood that he maintained such a manner so that the horror of what he did would not destroy him and leave the army leaderless. Emotionally, however, it was completely inexplicable to her. Yet wasn't this what she'd wanted from the beginning? Hadn't she resolved to see to the death of every man in these mountains? She began to realise she was not the same sort of monster as Vidius. He gave her a look as alien as a lizard's. She began to wonder just what she'd unleashed in putting the army in his hands.

Razor-sharp stone discs came angling out of the sky and into the onrushing second legion. A dozen men fell, one disc slicing halfway through a man's neck and then careening off to hit another in the face. Another wave flew in and cut down the same number again. Fifty or so had died before the legion reached the climb. As the soldiers began to scale upwards, rocks the size of melons were thrown down on their backs and heads.

A trumpet sounded and the third legion poured forwards. Stone discs came spinning towards them, but not as many as before, for clearly the enemy was now split between the two legions.

'They are nearing the summit!' Kate said, shielding her eyes against the rising sun. There was a roar from the waiting Memnosians as the first man made it over the top.

The General didn't answer, just kept watching the action through his spyglass. The white and grey robes of a hundred or so priests of Shakri and Malastra had now shuffled forwards. Anxiously, they watched the swarthy man with the largest of the war horns wrapped around his waist and shoulder. And still the General held them. Now that the two legions were on the climb and the cheers of the army had abated somewhat, the pleas for help from the first legion could distinctly be heard. Obeying their natural instinct, some of the priests had begun to wander forwards.

'Adjutant, have Sotto of the Outdwellers bring his people up as quickly as they can! They are to have their water bottles blessed by the priests of Shakri. Move, man!'

Minutes later, Sotto and Dijin had joined the General and Kate.

'There are large numbers of the enemy up there, but Ikthaeon sensed very few who were actually alive,' the General explained.

'Animees!' Kate said grimly.

'Sotto, your people are the quickest we have. I need them up there with blessed water at the double. Clear the undead if they're impeding you, but the magicians in black robes must be the main target. Understood?'

'Yes, General, we can manage that. You don't want any prisoners, I imagine.'

'Absolutely not. Do not let any magician live a second longer that necessary, for they will create havoc in that second. They will not easily be taken either, so you will need to take them off-guard or swarm them under. Go now, and may Shakri protect you!'

Sotto nodded and turned away. Dijin hesitated and performed a creditable bow. 'Come on, Dijin! There's killing to be done.' The ogreish Dijin laughed heavily and skipped off after his friend.

The Outdwellers were soon on the move and scampering up the climb as if it was something they did nearly every day, like taking a morning walk or having breakfast.

'Right! Now we move the entire army up,' the General told his adjutant. 'Inform the commanders and high priests accordingly. Spend time corralling the horses if they must, but I don't want too many men left here and I don't want it to take more than ten minutes. Get to it! Milady, shall we advance together?'

⁂

The fighting once they reached the top was ugly. There were crowds of animees hemming them in against the drop. The more Memnosians that pushed their way up, the more of their comrades who were pushed into the waiting, tearing hands of the undead. They were packed in so tight that the Outdwellers couldn't get past the second and third legions to use their water blessed by the temple of Shakri. In the end, the bottles had to be passed forwards to those at the front, and that began to relieve the pressure. The line of animees, deep though it was, broke.

The Outdwellers began to dodge past the infantry engaged in one-to-one battle and seek out the black robes. Sotto spied one at the corner of the giant building on top of the plateau. He dragged Dijin away from the animee he was happily dismembering with his bare hands and tried to direct his attention towards the magician.

'Sotto, do you think these animees are good eating?'

Sotto sighed, knowing he had to give his friend a sensible answer if he was ever going to get him to change tack. 'Can't you smell them, Dijin? They're old. Won't be good for your stomach. But that woman in the black robes over there is fresh. It's okay to eat her. She's the enemy.'

'Really?' Dijin asked dubiously. 'But she's alive, Sotto. I'm not allowed to eat people who are still alive.'

'Dijin, my friend, this red rag I'm wearing means I'm in charge. I make the rules, see? Today, it's alright to kill people in black robes. I promise. You won't get in trouble. The Green Witch says so.'

A wide grin opened up Dijin's face, revealing the rows of tombstones he had for teeth. 'Oh, in that case, let's go! My stomach's rumbling.'

Suddenly, Sotto was having to run to keep up with his friend. The magician saw them making for her and directed animees into their path, but Dijin battered them aside and hardly slowed. One jumped onto his back and sank its teeth into his shoulder. He swatted it away as if it were no more than a fly. The magician's eyes widened in fear and she screamed for more of the undead to protect her from the behemoth. Dijin ploughed on regardless, Sotto darting along in his shadow.

The blood-mage then changed tactic. She began to chant a spell at the huge Outdweller and he seemed to lose direction.

'Feeling sleepy, Sotto,' he mumbled.

'I thought you were strong, Dijin! The other Outdwellers will think you're weak, won't they?'

Anger blazed in the giant's eyes and he shouted: 'Dijin is the strongest, Sotto! I will show you!' He smashed his way forwards with renewed vigour, coming within a few strides of the mountain mage.

The woman suddenly had a small knife in her hand. She cut her palm open, planted it on Dijin's outstretched arm and uttered a single guttural syllable. Dijin froze and began to topple over, immobilised by the magic. Quick as a flash, Sotto darted round his friend and slashed his thin blade across the blood-mage's throat. She grabbed at her neck, but could not stop the blood spilling between her fingers. She fell to her knees and then pitched over on top of Dijin. A number of animees near them collapsed with her.

The large Outdweller surged up from the ground and looked round in confusion. 'What happened, Sotto? Oh, we killed her. Can we eat her now?'

'Tell you what, Dijin, here's another idea. Let's kill another one and then we can eat two at once.'

'Oo, yum! Yes, let's! You *are* clever, Sotto. Quick, though, before the others get them and want them for themselves. Should we take this one with us in case someone tries to steal her?'

'No, Dijin, she'll only slow us down. Besides, no one will dare steal her. I'm the leader, remember! Look, there's one! Quick, get him!'

And so, the few blood-mages on the plateau were systematically hunted down. A few retreated into the bowels of the House of the Dead and blocked the path to them with hundreds of the dead.

'Take the first room and hold the door to the next chamber!' the General ordered. 'Get some firebrands lit! Start setting the decomposing bodies alight and throwing them into the second chamber!'

His men wasted no time obeying him.

'Withdraw the men from the room and barricade the main doors! If the inferno doesn't take these mages, then the smoke or lack of air will.'

'Smells good!' Dijin drooled to Sotto as an aroma of roast pork began to fill the air. The House of the Dead boomed as the flame exploded into one chamber after another. Its walls cracked with the intensity of the heat, part of its roof fell in and columns of thick, black smoke rose into the air to cast a pall across the sun.

With the giant pyre behind him turning the blue sky to shadow and replacing the sun with its hellish blaze, the General moved his army to the edge of the plateau and looked out across the valley of the Brethren. It was white with clean snow. To the onlooker, its quiet houses, trickling rills and herds of goats on distant slopes would have given it an almost idyllic, innocent feel; until the eyes of that onlooker took in the giant, black pyramid overshadowing it all with a brooding menace. Its apex stood higher than where they were on the plateau.

'This is the point of no return,' the General said quietly to Kate and her cadre.

'What do you mean?' Kate asked.

'Once we descend into this cauldron, they will have us with our backs to the wall. We will not be able to run and there are certain wheeling troop manoeuvres that will be denied me. We will have to stand toe-to-toe with the enemy and give better than we get. If the tide turns against us, then we will be slaughtered to the man. There will be no escape. It is an all or nothing battle, and not the sort any commander who hopes to fight another day wants to enter into. Only the most desperate of commanders would commit to such a battle.'

'These are the most desperate of times, General. Not to descend will see the pantheon decline beyond a critical point. Everything we know will collapse in an instant. I cannot imagine the reign of terror that would then follow. We must enter in, General, if we are to have even a fighting chance. And if there is *no* chance of survival, then I would prefer to die with a sword in my hand and looking the enemy in the eye!'

She looked round her cadre. 'Are we all in accord?'

Mordius nodded with more steel in his gaze that she would once have expected.

'Nothing to lose, have we?' Strap smiled.

'If we must, we must, hmm?' the Chamberlain said twitchily.

Sister Spike showed her small, pointed teeth. 'It is my holy duty to exact whatever retribution I may in the name of Incarnus!'

Carris saluted. 'As you command, milady!'

'Well then, call our commanders to us,' the General instructed his blood-smeared adjutant, 'and we will see to the disposition of our troops, as I doubt the enemy will give us long to organise ourselves once we are upon the plain. They will not harry us while we hold the higher ground and are still descending, for they will fear we have a large number of archers at our disposal. As it is, we have only a hundred, but they will serve as deterrent enough against too many testing sallies by the enemy. I will leave the archers permanently stationed on the plateau during the fighting, as they will be our one advantage, at least while the supply of arrows holds out.

'I will take Memnosian infantry and foot cavalry totalling two thousand and hold the centre,' General Vidius informed the assembled officers and luminaries of their host. 'The priests of Shakri will be behind us and help recover the injured, hopefully so that they can fight again. Milady and her cadre will lead the Outdwellers, five hundred foot cavalry and the other priesthoods on the left flank. The mercenary captains will take the right flank with their thousand-strong force.'

No one needed it pointed out to them that they'd therefore lost a thousand men in taking the plateau.

'Once we're onto the plain, I fully expect the enemy to rush us, as they will not want to risk our getting in amongst the houses half a mile hence. They will hope to keep us pinned against this wall and without room for manoeuvre. If we reach the houses, they will not be able to present a united front. Our aim is to force our way through to their seat of power, the black edifice that eclipses the sky.'

'People of Dur Memnos!' Kate then spoke up, and all stilled to hear her. Even the wind quieted so her words would reach the furthest man. 'We are the chosen of our gods! They are our shields, armour and weapons! They are the air in our lungs, the thoughts in our minds, the light in our eyes, the faith in our hearts! We are their children, the thoughts of their minds, the light shining from their eyes and the love in their hearts! If I speak blasphemy, then it is because mortal words cannot encompass their divine truth. We know it is their will that we do what we do, for they have spoken to us through their high priests. We descend now for the pantheon. For the pantheon!' she yelled and punched her fist into the sky.

'For the pantheon!' General Vidius echoed and raised his fist.

'For the pantheon!' hollered the men until their voices were hoarse and had shaken the heavens themselves.

⁂

The Scourge was in a foul mood, again. The twisted mages had hung him up and stuck more than a dozen blades in him. They'd torn deep rents in his flesh to be sure his blood would continue to flow. They'd cut, carved and sliced his body as if it were the carcass of an animal. His bile, urine and blood was half an inch deep on the floor of his cell.

'My love, what have they done to you?' came a familiar, mocking voice.

'By the self-impregnating bastards of the holy hermaphrodite Malastra!' the Scourge swore. 'That's all I need! What do you want, Jack? Let me guess, you've come to gloat, sing me a ballad or recite me love poetry?'

Jack simpered. 'Not quite. No minstrel likes to perform for a bad audience, my love.'

'Then what do you want? And how did you get in here?'

'As you are so fond of reminding me, my love, I am a demon. The lock has not been devised that can keep out Jack O'Nine Blades. No, I have come to ask your advice. And if you will not speak it, then I will read it in your entrails.'

The Scourge yawned.

'Ahem! So, my love, here it is. The Green Witch has entered the valley with her army, but I fear she will not fare well. My question to you, therefore, is would it help her cause if I released you? It would not suit me to see her fail, you see.'

'Kate is here? You troublesome dolt! Of course I will do what I can to help her. It's why I came to this benighted valley in the first place, as you well know. I have to attend to the killing of a particular magician first, however. I have sworn it.'

Jack tilted his head in question.

The Scourge sighed. 'Jack, a magician called Refus killed the good priest Altibus without a qualm or moment's thought. It may mean nothing to the amoral creature within you, but I must do this to honour his memory. And I have vowed to do it. Again, it is something that would mean nothing to a quixotic creature born of chaos.'

'Have you ever visited the demon realm, my love?' Jack asked softly. 'Its beauty might surprise you. It shifts constantly, but its chaos is not unfettered. My kind has been known to honour vows. Is Jack O'Nine Blades not sworn to serve Wim? I have remained true to that vow.'

'Ha! A vow to serve the fickle god is no vow at all.'

'See it as you will, my love. Simply know that I was pleased Altibus did what he could to help the followers of Wim in the forest. Simply know that I understand the desire for revenge, for that is what you seek. I would also happily kill this Refus, but it strikes me as being far from the best use of the time remaining to us.'

The Scourge laughed dismissively. 'You talk of selfish motivations, demon, all you are really capable of. I speak of doing something because it is right, because of purposes and principles that are larger than the desires of an individual. Such purposes and principles are the foundations of this realm. It is because they are meaningless to your kind that you have no place in this realm. It is because of them that I must ultimately hunt you down and snuff you out.'

Jack's nostrils flared in anger, his eyebrows dropped and he opened his mouth as if to show fangs. His face was transformed, as if it was but a translucent mask for another beneath. 'Alternatively,' he growled, 'we could spend the time seeing if you might actually be killed, my love! If you ask me, those magicians lack a bit of imagination when it comes to what can be done with a blade.'

There was a hiss down near Jack's feet and he jumped back in fright. Scraggins wove her way back and forth through the bars that stretched from floor to ceiling and made up one wall of the Scourge's cell. She sat down, curled her tail around her front paws and glared up at Jack.

Jack looked like his fey minstrel self once more. 'Oh, alright, alright! I'll let him out, Scraggins! It was a jest, nothing more. Honestly, you're getting quite tetchy in your old age, almost as crotchety as the Scourge actually. Maybe he's rubbing off on you. Look, no hands!'

The door to the cell clicked and swung open unaided. The demon tiptoed through the muck on the floor of the cell and touched the manacles around the Scourge's wrists, by which he was suspended. The Guardian splashed down onto the floor, his limbs without the strength to support him. His head flopped into the viscous gore that had originally come from his body. Despite the stench, all he could do was lay there.

'Sorry, Jack, it looks like I've fouled your hose,' he managed.

The minstrel rolled his eyes but did not retreat. 'I was going to offer you one of my knives, Scourge, but it seems the magicians have thoughtfully left you with more than enough. Here, let me help you!'

Jack grabbed the handle of one of the knives stuck in the Scourge, twisted savagely and pulled it free.

'Ahh!' the Guardian screamed.

'Shh, my love, we do not want to wake the house. And 'tis but a prick! You did not make such noise when it first went in, surely? My, you are quite unmanned.'

Jack pulled out the other blades and dropped them in a pile next to the harrowed Scourge. He then produced a needle and thread and roughly sewed up what flesh he could. He looked critically at the Scourge. 'Well, there's little more I can do. I must leave you now, my love, now that I have played my part. There is much that is amoral and quixotic that I must be about. Think well of me!'

With that, the willow-the-wisp minstrel disappeared into the darkness of the corridor outside the cell. Scraggins sniffed at the Scourge a few times and gave him a lick with her rough tongue, which made his hand tingle.

'Thanks!' the Scourge murmured as the feline turned and went to keep an eye on the demon once more. The Guardian couldn't help wondering just who was pet and who was owner when it came to Jack and Scraggins.

⁂

The Memnosian army arrayed itself in good order at the foot of the plateau. The sun reached its zenith and began to overheat the men in their armour, despite the snow still on the ground. The slight breeze made their flags snap and crack, a red fist on a white field in the centre of the host, a black hawk on a green field on the left flack, and three gold coins on a sky blue background on the right flank.

His mind's eye at the apex of the quartz pyramid, Nylchros considered these strange puppets while scratching his crotch far below. Why were they just standing there? Where was the cowardly pantheon? Was the army just waiting for the pantheon to arrive?

He decided he was probably best off using the Brethren to attack before the pantheon arrived. After all, the sooner the life of this realm was sacrificed, the sooner it would be a part of the Unity. For the briefest moment, he considered consulting the petty Lords of this place about the decision, but it rankled having to bow to the knowledge and will of another. He ordered the Brethren to attack at once.

Down on the plain, Kate herself wondered why they were waiting. Surely they could have reached the houses in the time they'd stood here. She looked round her cadre in frustration.

It was the Chamberlain who answered her: 'Milady, we daren't risk a charge without knowing the full strength of the enemy, yes? We may reach the houses to find the enemy fully prepared. A trap, hmm? What if they have archers hidden on every roof? Or we might begin a charge only to find they respond with their own charge, except they will have cavalry while we only have infantry. If their cavalry catch us out in the open, we will easily be undone, hmm? Best, then, to remain here, where we will have the advantage of our archers and will have some opportunity to adapt once we know what faces us, yes?'

'If we sit here twiddling our thumbs for much longer, our priests will be too weak for it to make any difference, Chamberlain!' she groused.

'I'm sure the General will seek to provoke the enemy somehow soon, Kate,' Strap said soothingly.

But she did not want to be soothed. She needed to be ready, at fighting pitch. She'd keyed up the troops, and they were as eager as her to have it start. The hairs on the back of her neck stood on end as they did when the air was charged with an approaching storm.

She heard thunder in the distance and looked around for signs of lightning, but the sky remained clear. A band of darkness clouded her view of the houses. Could storms be so low-lying in the mountains? But the sound echoing off the walls of the valley changed and she wondered if it was actually the roll of war drums she heard. No, hoof beats!

'Archers, fire at will!'

'Spears and pikes to the front! Plant those butts to the ground and hold them steady!'

'Javelins to the second and third rows!'

'Be ready!'

Kate and her cadre were jostled backwards, all except for Strap, who had Kate's giant flag strapped to his back and was ready with his bow for whatever came towards them. Was it his imagination or did the ground tremble slightly? Nerves and excitement, he told himself. His mouth was dry, even though he knew that wasn't possible in an animee. Or were life and death already collapsing one into the other?

'They've got cavalry!' shouted one man.

'They're-they're enormous!' another shrieked.

'They still won't have dicks as big as mine!' one boasted, to laughter from his comrades.

'Hold your ground!' officers shouted harshly.

Now all could see what rode towards them. Their mounts were four times the size of a normal horse, and they seemed much more savage. Thick foam streamed from the sides of their mouths and into their manes of black fire. Their teeth threatened to crunch through the thick metal bits with which their riders controlled them, their eyes flashed with the lightning Kate had searched for before, and they had the sort of musculature more suited to a hunting predator. The giants on their backs were no less fearsome. They wrestled their mounts with hands so large and powerful that just one could completely encircle a normal man's chest and crush it without effort. Their arms and chests could surely collapse the houses in the valley just as easily. Most terrifying of all, however, was the blank look on each of their faces. To them, the defenders were nothing, without strength of any significance, without lives of any meaning. The enemy rode towards the Memnosians as if out of a nightmare.

'Hold!' Kate found herself screaming, though whether in fear, to bolster the courage of her men, as a desperate plea or in prayer, she could not tell.

Arrows flew from the plateau, many of them finding marks, but they were little more than pins or splinters to the silent riders and their mounts. Not one of them was brought down. The charge did not slow even a fraction.

'Brace yourselves!'

The cavalry smashed into the centre of the Memnosian army, killing several hundred of General Vidius's troops in an instant. Of the two hundred or so Brethren cavalry that had attacked the army of four thousand, only five fell during this first attack. Their mounts had been impaled on spears that had by chance found their way past the slabs of rock hard muscle just beneath their skin and into their mighty hearts. But the unhorsed riders did not hesitate to take their own terrible toll. They wielded swords as along as the Memnosian spears. They swept them left and right, scything down several men at a time, separating countless legs from torsos and heads from shoulders. One of these Brethren was finally brought down by a soldier rolling bravely under the flat arc of the enemy's weapon and then rising quickly to gut him. Another was brought down by a javelin spearing through his eye, into his brain and out the back of his head. And the other three were finally surrounded and brought down from behind.

By then, however, the cavalry had already wheeled and started another charge. One hundred hit the centre of the army again, while fifty punched into each of the flanks. The Memnosian lines were wrecked in seconds. The giant beasts stamped Memnosians under their enormous hooves, stove in their chests and crushed limbs with their kicks, and crunched down on heads with their terrible jaws. Their riders hacked left and right till their swords were dripping with gore and almost too slippery to hold.

Strap released an arrow and took a rider in the eye, but the rider was unfazed and carried on slashing with the same mechanical action. Strap drew again immediately and hit the same rider through the heart, which finally put an end to the eerie automaton. He tried to get another arrow from his quiver but he was suddenly crushed by the press of men seeking to move back out of the range of the Brethren monstrosities. Several soldiers were trampled and killed by their own comrades.

As one, the cavalry turned and rode back to start another charge. The Memnosian dead lay everywhere.

'They act in concert, hmm?' the Chamberlain observed as he worked with Carris and Sister Spark to keep their troops from crushing Kate, their own commander, to death. 'They are directed by one intelligence, yes?'

'Tell us something useful!' Kate cursed him. 'We're being slaughtered! They're going to beat us with a mere handful of riders!'

War horns rang out from Vidius's point of command and ordered the flanks to advance.

'Finally!' Kate said, echoing the thoughts of everyone. 'Advance! Troops to the far left at the run, troops near right at walking pace!'

'This is fun, eh?' whispered a divine voice in her ear.

'Aa!' she said in delight as she beheld the small figure perched on her shoulder, a figure no one else could see. 'I'd almost given up on receiving any direct help from the pantheon.'

'Wouldn't miss it for the world, and I mean that quite literally!' the Holy Adventurer replied, pursing his lips. 'Given that you've put my entire priesthood in harm's way and that that could see an end to me, I thought I'd better come and check how things are going. Making a bit of a hash of it, aren't you?'

It dawned on Kate that, in bringing the entirety of the priesthoods to this wretched valley, she might indirectly end up being responsible for the demise of the entire pantheon. She almost collapsed with the horror of it.

'Oh, I shouldn't worry about it, if I were you! The others were livid of course, and I wouldn't have put it past one of them to try and assassinate you, but you didn't have that much choice, after all, and it could well be that you're right that this is the only real chance we'll get. Besides, you know me, I love the foolhardy bravery of it all, the devil-may-care risk, the absurdly high stakes, the glorious drama! You've really outdone yourself this time, my dear! Ooh, look lively, here they come!'

Apparently oblivious to how the flanks were working to corral them in the centre and then take them from all sides, the Brethren thundered back into the Memnosian ranks once again. The riders didn't try to turn away this time, instead cutting their way into the troops wherever they were thickest, in order to cause the most damage and mayhem. The fighting now began in earnest.

At least a dozen riders in Kate's vicinity suddenly turned their heads at the same time and looked at the flag on Strap's back, and then directly at her. They spurred their beasts towards her.

Realising what was happening, Strap shouted, 'Guard the commander!' but it was clear the horsemen would reach her before enough bodies could be placed in the way to prevent them from doing so. He released an arrow into the eye of the nearest beast and, as it raised its head in pain, shot one deep into its chest. Its front legs collapsed and its rider was catapulted to within ten yards of Kate. Metal rain suddenly filled the air and the Brethren died with a dozen spikes through his neck.

Another rider closed in. A brutish Outdweller stepped into its path and delivered a colossal blow to the horse between its eyes, which pole-axed it on the spot. It fell on its side, trapping the leg of its rider beneath it. A small Outdweller darted in and slit the rider's throat. Kate realised she was looking at Sotto and Dijin, but she suddenly lost sight of them in the melee.

The next rider that came for her was tackled by the Chamberlain, who scuttled under the belly of the charging horse to avoid the rider's swinging weapon, came up the other side and was suddenly all over the enormous Brethren. The Chamberlain's hands moved too quickly for Kate to follow, but the effect was immediate and the rider sat paralysed in his saddle. The horse bucked, aware of the alien thing upon it, but the Chamberlain stuck to it like glue and would not be dislodged. Then the horse lost its own ability to move and fell to the ground.

She dared not watch a moment longer, however, as two riders converged on her at once. Strap was ridden down by one of them and a massive sword split Carris's head completely in two.

'No!' cried Sister Spike and threw herself at the Brethren responsible. The mountain man pulled his massive blade free of Carris's body and caught the priestess round the head with the flat of it. She reeled and stumbled, which was all that saved her life from the next swing of the outsized weapon. Sister Spike was now on the rider's offside, so the rider swung his fist the size of a boulder and bashed her into the ground.

'Oops!' Aa breathed on Kate's shoulder.

Kate ducked and the sword of the other rider missed her head by a whisker. She released the bolt of her crossbow blindly and heard it thud home. She rolled and came to her feet, only to have an avalanche of weight floor her. The bolt she'd fired had buried itself in the face of the Brethren she'd been fighting, but he'd then toppled down on top of her. She tried to heave him off her, but there was just too much of him. She looked around in panic, knowing she would now make for an easy kill and that there were riders still coming for her.

'Aa, where the hell are you?' she coughed. 'I could really do with some help round about now!'

A shadow fell across her and she hiccupped in fear. The priestess of Lacrimos stood over her, in an umbra of darkness. She was alone, for there were no others in her temple of course, death ultimately being a lonely and solitary experience. The priestess pointed her finger at the rider menacing them and black tendrils shot out to wind round rider and mount. Dark magic covered them for a second and then dissipated, leaving only skeletons and the odd scrap of flesh left on the bone.

The seven remaining riders arrived and attacked the priestess all at once. She did not resist them, instead allowing their blades to pass through her flesh time and again.

'Holy Lacrimos!' she called. 'I sacrifice my life and its magic to this final spell of living death! Embrace me, beloved Lord!'

The priestess of Lacrimos rose into the air and kissed one of the riders. His life passed out of him through her kiss of death and he slumped in his saddle. She drifted to another, then another. They tried to cut her down, but their blades went through her as if she were naught but a shade. She was the ghost of a life and the shadow of death itself. As the last rider died, she faded away on the wind.

'Needing a hand, are ye, lass?' boomed a deep voice, and a huge, gauntleted paw lifted the dead Brethren off her and helped her to her feet.

'Incarnus!' she wheezed at the juggernaut. 'You took your time!'

'Hmmm. The balance is close to collapse. I fear that my entering in now will it tip completely. You know me, I'm always up for a fight, but I may find my end here on this battlefield. Nonetheless, I have been forced to enter the fray, in part because of my nature but also because we cannot afford to have you die now, Kate. So enough of these empty words, lass, and give my war hammer a target!'

Numbly, Kate pointed at the rider nearest to them and Incarnus lumbered towards him. He hefted his enormous war hammer and bludgeoned horse and rider into the mud and snow, smearing red for all to see. His eyes smiled out at Kate through the visor of his helmet and demanded another victim. She pointed quickly and the invisible engine of destruction annihilated another rider. She pointed at another.

To the eyes of the Memnosians, Kate would point at one of the Brethren and then rider and mount would inexplicably receive a sledgehammer blow out of thin air. A ragged cheer started to go up each time an enemy was bashed in, along with chants of 'The Green Witch!' It became their battle-cry and the Memnosians set about the Brethren with renewed purpose and determination. A battered Strap rejoined her and her flag was hoisted over the field again.

The priesthood of Malastra cast withering plagues and enchantments at the Brethren, priests of Aa danced back and forth with their rapiers to unstring mounts and riders, the priests of Gart made the earth underfoot treacherous for the horses, and the red-robed priests of Incarnus worked in attack groups with their vast array of devastating weapons and techniques to bring down one enemy after another. Brother Hammer and his temple fought as if possessed, for they felt their god moving amongst and within them.

There were less than a hundred of the Brethren left but they came together and had no trouble clearing the Memnosians around and amongst them. Deliberately, the riders ordered themselves and spurred as a single unit, without any signal being given, at Brother Hammer and his priests.

The behemoth Incarnus loomed over the red robes and swung His impossible hammer back over His head. He demolished the lead rider, pushing him several feet down into the muck. He hauled his weapon up and to the right, scattering a knot of the Brethren. The other riders made it into the war priests, however, so that the god dared not swing too freely again lest He kills His own followers.

The air became the sharp edge of a killing blade and everything was painted red. The towering Brethren, with their untiring strength and wide reach, and the quick, skilled priests of vengeance were evenly matched. They set about killing each other with efficiency and an almost suicidal lack of fear.

As priests and riders fell, Incarnus began to materialise on the field, first as a shadow, and then a full, physical manifestation. He roared with divine rage at the Brethren, bursting their eardrums, but the bespelled warriors ignored the blood trickling down the sides of their faces and pressed on.

Then the unthinkable happened. A blow was landed on Incarnus by one of the largest of the Brethren, denting the deity's armour. The god backhanded the warrior, mashing his face in with His iron hand. Another rider landed a blow, hacking into the god's lower back from behind. Incarnus leapt into the air, span and kicked the enemy fully twenty feet. Riders clattered him from both sides at once.

All the red robes were dead now, Brother Hammer lying with four giant bodies around him, but thirty of the mountain men still remained. Without hesitation, they set upon Incarnus. The god grabbed a head in each hand and smashed them together so hard that bits of skull and grey matter rained down on the Memnosian troops fifty yards away and the concussion forced the other riders to rear back for a second. Yet they did not blink and came in with hooves flying and blades chopping.

The Memnosian host stilled as they witnessed the impossible and irrational destruction of their spirit. The blows clanged across the field as holy Incarnus was undone upon the anvil of the mountain. There, beneath the unblinking eye of the midday sun, they pounded the deity until there was nothing left of Him save for a few metal plates.

Tears filled Kate's eyes and she cried like a young girl who has just lost her father. The sobs racked her body and she fell to her knees in despair.

The remaining thirty riders turned together and looked towards the priesthood of Aa. They put cruel spurs to the bleeding sides of their ravenous beasts. The Memnosian host wailed in agony.

Then, the detritus and slurry around them began to stir. A giant cadaver hauled itself out from under the bodies littering the plain. The dead Brethren began to climb to their feet and search for new victims.

And the disembodied laughter of Nylchros filled the valley.

❧ ❧

With his one eye, all he saw were the stone walls and the stone floor. But the white rage within him saw the organising magic and force within the metal bars of his cage, and began to draw that force towards him. The metal turned brittle as he absorbed its strength, and then disintegrated into a powder. He was free, at last.

He was still bent and crushed though, lacking the energy to repair himself fully. His rage tried to draw from the rock around him, but the substance was too obdurate. He could not shape and mould it to his will in the same was as he could the metal. Was there also some sort of magical ward on the stone? It seemed to block his sense of what lay beyond the cell as well.

Saltar cursed silently – for his palette was broken – and did all he could, which was wait and endure the inhuman suffering.

At some point, although he did not know how much time had passed, a sound came to him from somewhere. He sensed movement. The rage within him flared hungrily, insisting he snatch at the approaching life force while he could. After all, it was probably one of the blood-mages who held him prisoner, and all they deserved was death. Yet instinct warned him not to strike too quickly.

The person was close to him now, almost on top of him.

'Saltar, it's me, Larc!' whispered a small voice. 'Are you alive? Can you hear me? My friend Vasha is watching the end of the corridor to warn us if anyone comes. We were stopped by one of the magickers before, because the Owned aren't allowed near the pyramid unless they wear the clothes of an attendant. But we told him Refus had ordered us to take a message to one of the Lords. All the magickers are scared of Refus, so he let us go.

'... Saltar, I'm sorry that I tricked you, truly I am. I'm one of the Owned, you see, and the Lords caught me. It's forbidden to leave the valley and they could have killed me for it, only they threatened to kill Vasha instead and said I had to... and... anyway, I'm sorry!' he said sadly.

'I don't know what to do now, Saltar. Can you talk? I don't think you can stand, can you? Should I try and carry you out?' the boy asked, gently touching the Battle-leader. How it hurt! 'You're heavy, but if Vasha helps me then I think I can manage. Are you in pain, though? I don't want to hurt you even more by moving you, but you can't stay here like this.'

Much as it grieved him, Saltar knew he would have to absorb the life force of this young innocent. The rage was greedy for it, but Saltar fought it and drained only as much as he could without killing the boy.

Larc groaned and faltered. His eyes were heavy and he slid down the wall until he was sitting next to Saltar. He suddenly looked years older, unutterably weary.

'And I am sorry, Larc, that I have had to take from you in this manner, without your permission,' moaned Saltar. It was a few seconds before he had the breath and strength to speak again. 'I will return it to you as soon as I may. I need you to do something for me first, though. Find me one of these so-called magickers and bring them here. Tell them I wish to reveal a secret to one with magical understanding in return for mercy. Can you do that?'

The youth nodded slowly and slurred: 'Vasha will do it. She is brave, and I do not think I can make it further than the corridor.' He wiped some dribble from the side of his mouth and then crawled on hands and knees out of the cell.

More time passed and then an adult voice echoed along the corridor. 'What's this Owned doing here on the floor in the way, girl?'

'Please, milord, he's tired. The outsider is here, in this cell, milord,' came a young, female voice that was presumably Vasha's.

This time, Saltar made no effort to control the ravenous rage within him. It leapt onto the magicker as soon as he set foot in the room. It laid him bare and then sank merciless teeth into his heart. It ate out his vitals while he was still alive and then gnawed on the marrow of his soul until it fled screaming from Shakri's realm. The magicker's empty husk then thudded to the floor.

Scintillations of light bathed Saltar and he mended and unfolded himself. The pain left him and his mind finally cleared. Recreated now, he stood and gifted back to Larc the life force he'd borrowed. The youth grinned with endorphin-driven ecstasy as his body coursed with energy and potential once more.

'Thank you, both of you, Vasha and Larc. I will not forget your bravery. Now, there are terrible things which I must attempt before it is too late. The two of you should find somewhere safe while you still can. Do you have a place you can go?'

Vasha nodded for them. 'Yes, milord. I hope you find your son, milord!'

A sad look passed over the Battle-leader's face. 'Thank you, Vasha. So do I. This is a very bad place, I think. Come along!'

They went along the small, stone corridor and climbed some steps to higher levels where daylight flooded everything. Saltar squinted, happy in the moment. It was amazing to be himself once more, to be able to walk, to breathe the sweet air, to turn his head. He felt so light, so powerful! He was charged with a magic of sorts, whether it was Shakri's magic or not, he wasn't sure. And it felt *right* to have it at his command somehow, as if it had been something he'd possessed in a previous life but then lost. It completed him. A part of him had been locked away in the dark for the longest time, and had now been released to take its first hesitant, tottering steps into the light. It was a type of revelation or enlightenment.

If he concentrated, he could see everything shimmering with its own energy or magic. He could almost touch it, almost taste it in the air. He waved his two young friends goodbye and sent his mind questing outwards in order to orient himself.

He was in a pyramidal building as far as he could tell. It was made of a strange substance. Sometimes, his thoughts would disappear when they met the rock, and sometimes they would be reflected straight back at him. The place was a labyrinth of angles, planes, dead-ends, echoing chambers and bottomless wells. He felt the resonance of individual life forces all around him, some of the signatures far stronger than others, not that he recognised any of them. The closest major signature was in a small chamber above him, so he chose a corridor that sloped upwards and started his ascent.

The life force apparently sensed his approach and came quickly to meet him in the confined space of the corridor. There were now windows, only lit torches in brackets spaced periodically along the wall. Out of the darkness and into one of the pools of light came the Plague Victim. He grinned like a ghoul, and the air around him became cold as he drew in what energy it had. The flames on the nearest torches dimmed and almost went out. His gnarled hands shook with what was either a palsy, desire or rage. His red-rimmed and rheumy eyes stood out from his face and saliva strung across a mouth of brown teeth as his white tongue moved like a worm in mucus.

'How delicious!' he gargled.

'How disappointing,' Saltar replied without any display of emotion. 'What a tawdry and ragged thing you are, after all.

The Lord of the Brethren lashed out at Saltar, seeking to paralyse him. Saltar felt his blood and heart slowing. He remade his body and slipped free of the necromancer's magic. The Plague Victim sought to blind Saltar, but Saltar could sense the energies eddying all around him so well that it was as effective as vision. Then the magician tried to swell Saltar's gorge to try and choke him, but Saltar no longer depended on air for his life. The Lord tried to block Saltar's sense of feeling, but the white rage within Saltar would not be gainsaid. The enemy struck at all of Saltar's senses with pain, to overwhelm him, but the Battle-leader had suffered pain in the cage far beyond the human and mortal, so remained unfazed by anything the magician tried now.

In desperation, the Lord then tried to draw Saltar's life force from him, pulling harder and harder. He clawed and strained, capillaries in his eyes and on his forehead bursting and washing his face in blood. Saltar resisted him with little effort and then, when the necromancer was at his most exerted and open, released a bolt of energy wrapped in the licking flames of his white rage. Saltar was momentarily weakened by it, but his enemy was flung to the floor to writhe in magical flames. His screams were hideous.

'It's what you wanted,' Saltar observed.

The creature who had fed off others for thousands of years twisted in the coruscating flames and finally died. Saltar turned away.

'That's one!' he said grimly.

Nylchros laughed madly as he watched. 'Another member of the pantheon gone! The mighty Incarnus laid low by these little armies of puppets. How weak and pitiful my children are. Did they think they could dethrone their own father, the Creator? Did they think to subvert the supreme will of he who gave them life, a life of his own body and design? I should have been more watchful. In loving them too much, I gave them a sense of being special, of being different. I allowed them a sense of self and the selfish. I have been too indulgent a father. The fault was not mine, however, because their wills were their own, so their crimes are their own. Their punishments must be their own, and this time I cannot play the indulgent father. Their acts were treasonous, and the punishment for treason is always death and unmaking.

'The Brethren I will now direct at the puppets of Aa. Aa is a vain and strutting fool. He is the epitome of my children's selfishness and self-importance. Brethren, there they are. At my command, you will…'

Lucius lay in one of the corners of the main chamber, listening to the crazed, naked youth talking to no one and everyone. The musician had been brought here in the night and forced to play hour after hour. Nylchros had demanded one song after another, until Lucius had exhausted his entire repertoire and been forced to improvise. His fingers had bled on the strings and cramped. When he'd started to make mistakes, Nylchros had flown into a foul rage and would have killed him were it not for the apparent arrival of Kate's army with the rising sun. The Unity had become distracted and distant as he'd filled the minds of the Brethren and directed them in the fight.

Lucius could tell it was not going well for Kate. He knew her defeat must be close at hand. Even the gods were falling! His mind swam with a lack of sleep and it took him a few attempts to pick up his lute with his stiff fingers. He struck a discord on the strings and the perfect harmonics of the chamber helped it to swell and grow. He'd made Nylchros laugh, cry and experience a hundred emotions during the night, so he prayed he would be able to affect the Unity as much now.

The youth shook his head, bothered by the sound, but returned to guiding the Brethren. Lucius struck more discords and disrupted all order in the chamber. Even the musician's own thoughts no longer made sense to him, and he used that state to continue the anti-harmony. The youth fell off the altar where he'd been standing. He rose and staggered towards Lucius, hands stretching out to throttle him. The musician hit him with a screech of insanity that threatened to fragment the Unity.

The youth howled in agony and wove randomly about the chamber. He covered his ears with his hands and recovered something of his equilibrium. He ran at where Lucius was sitting and threw himself into the air. He crashed down on Lucius, using his body and momentum as a weapon. The frame of the lute snapped and Lucius cracked Nylchros over the head with the remains of it.

The musician used the opportunity to slip free of Nylchros and ran for the far side of the chamber, knowing he could not prevail in any physical contest. Unexpectedly, however, Nylchros simply glared at Lucius and returned to his position on the altar beneath the apex.

Lucius knew that each second he could keep Nylchros off-balance would be another second of life for Kate's army. With no other instrument left to him, Lucius attempted to use his voice to create disharmony and dissonance. Although he had perfect pitch, he'd never been the best of singers, lacking vibrato and the ability to hold notes long enough so that their echoes would layer or create counterpoint. It took him a few attempts, but he finally found a discord to trouble Nylchros.

The Unity's brow cracked and he turned eyes picturing the cataclysm on Lucius. The musician shrank in terror and considered fleeing the chamber, but knew he owed Kate and Saltar his life. He was prepared to give it. Deliberately, Nylchros climbed down from his altar and stalked towards the quickly cornered Lucius.

This is where I die, Lucius told himself.

Inexplicably, Nylchros tripped and Lucius, seeing his chance, ran around him to the far side of the altar. It had bought him only a few seconds more life, but how he valued those seconds! The Unity's eyes narrowed and his hand shot out. He pulled someone bodily out of the air and held them dangling by the throat. Nylchros smiled evilly.

'What do we have here? Why, it's Wim the witless! You offend my eyes, you unkempt buffoon!'

Nylchros tightened his grip suddenly and snapped the struggling god's neck. Then he dashed him into the hard floor.

'Come, musician, will you not sing a paean to your dead god? Will you not try an anthem, a eulogy or hymn to the dead? How about something epic about the fall of the pantheon? Come, fit your doggerel verse to my eternal judgement and be found lacking. No? Then the last sound you make will be as you perish. What key will you die in, do you think? What will your final note be? Let us find out!'

Lucius hardly listened. He stood transfixed by the sight of the dead god. How could it be? Gods couldn't die! Chance could not end. If he were to toss a coin, would it forever come down on the same side? Would it even come down? It made no sense, there was no reason. He did not notice Nylchros approaching him.

'Not so fast, little Nylchros! There is much fun to be had yet!' sang out a merry voice and Jack skipped into the chamber with Scraggins close on his heels. 'If the voice of my good friend Lucius does not please your ear, then perhaps mine will.'

The minstrel brayed forth the sounds of the chaos realm, tapping his foot and clapping his hands in false time.

'Demon!' Nylchros hissed. 'There's nothing for you here. Desist or I will see to your realm once I have done with this one!'

Scraggins slashed with her claws and lacerated one of Nylchros's calf muscles.

'Arrrgh! And what is this? Your familiar?'

'Oh, no, no, no! That is a cat, and probably the deadliest creature in this realm. I'd say you're in real trouble now!' Jack taunted him.

❧ ❧

'Get those priests of Shakri up here, Mordius!' the General bellowed as the Brethren dead started to rise. 'Adjutant, get that order relayed! I don't care what we promised about keeping them back. If they don't get here now, we're finished.'

'Yes, milord!'

'There's only a handful left! Stand firm and the day is ours!' the General shouted at his troops, trying to instil some fight, hope and belief back into them. He suspected it would prove impossible, though, now that their god of anger, hatred and revenge was dead. In truth, although he was not of their kind, he too was shaken to the core by what he had witnessed. Life in this realm was even more fragile than he'd thought. It was like one of those desert seeds that lay inert for years waiting for a single hour of rain in order to grow rapidly and burst into bloom, only then to wither and die just as quickly under the unforgiving sun. A brief moment of beauty and then dust, unless the flower had managed to produce further seeds in its short span. 'You men, form up there! Priests of Aa, it is this sort of danger that you were born to face! Be ready!' Men and priests raised their weapons, but they did so uncertainly and without much obvious intent.

The General looked around the field. There were as many dead or injured as there were standing. His calculating mind figured that each of the Brethren had accounted for ten of his men. If the dead could not be put to rest quickly, then he'd have far fewer than half of his original men left. It was hopeless. He wondered how he could best effect his escape before it was too late.

'Milord, they're stopping!' one of his few remaining officers shouted.

The strains of a cacophony came to General Vidius on the wind, replacing the sinister laughter he'd heard not moments before. The Brethren had lost their impetus it seemed. Intelligence had returned to the eyes of the giants, but with it had come confusion. They did not know where they were or what they were about. They sat on their mounts stupidly, weapons slack in their hands. Their huge mounts, suddenly without a firm hand to their reins, began to rear and buck. A good number of riders were thrown out of their saddles.

'Kill them all!'

The Memnosians needed no second bidding and set upon the disorientated Brethren with relish.

'Form up, ready to advance! Sound the war horns!'

Kate looked up and watched as the enemy was finally cut down. Mordius led Shakri's priesthood into the thick of it and saw to the laying to rest of the Brethren dead.

Strap was standing over her. 'The left flank will be awaiting your orders. No doubt the Outdwellers won't agree to take another step unless it's at the direct command of the Green Witch. It's probably best if you're standing up when you give your orders too. More dignified than sitting there in the mud, don't you think?' He offered her his hand and pulled her up.

'Cr-Crossbow?'

He put her weapon back in her hands.

'Th-Thank you, Strap. Chamberlain, find Sister Spike and get her to a physick. She should be laying around here somewhere.'

'Yes, milady, with pleasure, hmm?' the courtier bowed elegantly, hardly a splash of dirt on him.

'Form up! Foot cavalry to the fore! Outdwellers and priests following behind! Be ready to advance!' she shouted, her voice becoming less shaky with each word.

The war horns trumpeted and they moved at a run for the line of small mountain homes. They were met by an assortment of bewildered women, children and the elderly. They clutched simple weapons, but clearly did not know how to use them to any real effect. A few were run through by panicking or overeager troops before the officers realised they were not facing any real threat and ordered the Brethren to be simply disarmed.

The Memnosians advanced amongst the homes of the Brethren in good order until they came to the edge of the precinct of the mountainous black pyramid.

'Priests to the front!' General Vidius commanded.

Arrayed on the steps up to the central building were over a hundred black-robed blood-mages. Standing above them was a vast individual with all-seeing eyes. As each Memnosian met the gaze of this Lord of the Brethren, they lost their own volition and allowed their weapons to clatter to the stone floor. The dark chorus of magickers chanted with one voice.

Kate was yanked down and to one side before she could fully take in what confronted them.

'Wha-?'

'Shh!' said a serious-faced boy.

'What's happening?' Strap asked, unaffected by the Lord's magic.

'I know you!' Kate gasped. 'You're the high priest of Istrakon, aren't you? What are you doing here?'

'Saving you from looking into the fat man's eyes. I have been exploring, milady. There is no way past these magicians. If you wish to find your son, then come with me. There's a back-door.'

'There's a back-door?'

'There's always a back-door.'

'Kate, do you want me to come with you?'

'No, it looks like they're going to need you here. You're in charge!'

'Thanks, I don't think!'

⁂

Saltar had quickly got turned around in the pyramid, despite the advantage of his magical senses. Now he thought about it, perhaps it was those senses that were getting in the way. He realised that the building had probably been designed to confuse just such a magical intruder as himself. He kept thinking he was heading for some chamber, only to find he'd entered another blind alley and that there were no signs of secret entrances or rooms to be found.

He finally chanced across an attendant replacing one of the wall torches and ordered her to lead him into the main corridors of the pyramid. She obeyed without question. She led him back and forth, down and then back up, and brought him to an intersection of two major corridors. To the left and in the distance was the main entrance, the right led to the central chamber from what he could tell. His senses jangled and he could tell that one of the more powerful energy signatures was hurrying towards him from straight ahead.

'You're not going to want to be around for this,' Saltar said, shooing the mousy attendant away and taking the corridor in front of him.

Eventually, a shining skull came out of the gloom. His face was little more than a tissue-thin tracery of blood vessels, such that even in the poor light Saltar could see substances moving sluggishly within the man's skin. Much of his eyeballs were visible, making them seem too large for his head.

The Skull stopped. 'Can it be possible?' he asked through clicking jaws. 'I would be intrigued to know what magic could raise you up like this.'

Saltar stared at the maniac who sought to make small-talk of torture and ruination as if they were fellow academics. Mastering his rage, he answered: 'I will tell you that if you tell me where my son is.'

The Skull steepled his fingers together before him and touched them to non-existent lips. 'Ah, well, as to that, it would depend on how you would see your son. His body is whole and hale, and to be found in the main chamber, but I think you'll find his spirit or essence, I don't know which term you prefer, is lost to you. It was necessary, you understand. And you?'

'Did I tell you about the magic I used? Forgive me, I misspoke. I will rather show you. I am also wondering if it's best to kill you quickly or slowly. I would enjoy doing so more slowly, of course, but I find myself quite busy and pressed for time at the moment.'

'Then let us dispense with this idle chatter, by all means, for I too have other things to attend to. I must join my brothers on the steps outside. They are in the process of destroying the last of the Memnosian army. Most of them are dead already, you know. They were fun while they lasted, but there's not much fight left in them now. I suspect the Green Witch has already fallen as well. She was your wife, was she not? I must say, you haven't really done a very good job of protecting your family, have you? Still, you are just one man. What difference can a mere mortal make? As the death of countless, anonymous mortals has shown throughout history, a mortal life means nothing. But to be more than mortal? Ah, that is where meaning begins! That is where true life begins! Were you but to see that and join us, Saltar, then your wife and son could be yours once more. Did you not wish to see them again?'

There was truth in what the Skull said, Saltar knew that. Indeed, he'd thought such things himself upon occasion. Yet it always came down to the issue of what the aggrandisement and elevation of an individual cost. Look at what Voltar had been content to sacrifice in order to see his life come so close to being immortal. Look at what these necromancers had already cost the realm so that they might rise above their own mortality. Join them? No, it would be a capitulation, and look at what they'd done to him last time he'd capitulated. They'd caged him. Cognis had been right to criticise him for allowing that.

'You said, magician, you needed to join your brothers on the steps outside, to destroy the last of the army. I'm afraid that won't be possible as I've already killed one of your brothers. He looked ill anyway, as do you incidentally.'

'What? Oh, I really would have preferred it if you hadn't done that! Still, what's done is done. Years beyond counting I'd known him, but familiarity breeds contempt as they say.'

The magician waved his hand negligently and dozens of illusions of himself appeared up and down the corridor. 'Now, now! I know you're thinking about murdering me. You can't hide such a thing from the Master of the Mind.'

'I seek to hide nothing, magician. Come, let me show you that magic I promised!' Saltar smiled. He did not attempt anything as elegant as he had with the Plague Victim. He simply opened himself and allowed the white rage to vent out of him in incandescent sheets and waves. It swept away all in its path, not even allowing the necromancer the dignity of a dying scream. A scattering of burning cinders drifted towards the ground, all that remained of the Skull.

'That's two!' Saltar said, stalking away.

❧ ☙

The two thousand Memnosians standing around Strap had frozen. Their weapons had fallen to the ground from slack hands.

The blood-mages continued to weave their magic and now drew blades for the letting of blood. They intended to slaughter everyone!

Strap did not hesitate. He nocked an arrow to his bow and drew a bead on the gargantuan mage at the top of the stairs. In his youth, Strap had hunted cannibal mountain tribes and troglodytes with his bow in much worse winds than this. He was not about to miss such a large target in this sheltered valley.

He waited for the swell in the air to subside and then released his arrow. It hit the mage high up in his distended gut. Strap whipped another arrow out of his quiver and into place before any sort of shout had gone up.

He released again, but this time one of the smaller magicians wandered across the arrow's path and took its point to the temple.

'There must be an animee amongst them!' a blood-mage on the step directly below the Lord shrieked. 'Find him, quickly! Or find the necromancer! Use your blades! Milord, perhaps we should retreat into the pyramid?'

Strap ducked his head down and ran in a half-crouch between two ranks of troops until he was twenty metres from his previous position. He did not want them converging on him before he'd had a chance to release a few more missiles at the exaggerated stomach of the Brethren Lord. He stood and released.

This time, the Lord raised his hand and deflected the arrow while it was still yards from him and into one of his black-robed underlings.

'There he is!' they bayed.

Strap prepared to run again, but then became aware that the mages were under attack from elsewhere. A black, gangly frame arched and levered amongst the robes, pricking and stabbing at several of them at a time. Whenever the stick-insect touched one of the magicians, the black-robe would fall to the floor a second later and start having some sort of fit. In next to no time, a dozen of them had been brought down.

'It's the Chamberlain!' Strap said to himself. 'That means there can't be any blood in his veins. Not surprised really. He always was a creepy and bloodless sonovabitch! Just glad he's on our side.'

Strap released more quarrels, this time at the blood-mages seeking to get past the Chamberlain. He hoped that it was only his imagination that the Chamberlain was beginning to slow.

In the bedlam, the spell binding the Memnosians had begun to unravel. The troops were looking round woozily.

'Reassert the spell!' the Lord boomed. 'Find the animee and pin him to the ground with your longest blades. I will protect you from any arrows he has left. Surround that one there and harass him until he falls.'

Strap wondered what gods of the pantheon were left to whom he might pray. Yet all their priests had been rendered powerless. There was no one left in the entire cosmos to help him.

✱ ✱

The Scourge leaned against one of the pillars supporting the massive lintel above the entrance to the pyramid. He fought for breath but didn't even have the strength to win that battle. This is worse than being an animee, he decided, at least they can keep going when they have to.

The host of blood-mages had their backs to him. There seemed to be all sorts of bother going on, but the largest of the mages, who was also nearest to him, blocked most of his view.

An arrow came winging in. Did his eyes deceive him or was that Strap. About time he showed up and started earning his keep. What was wrong with the Memnosian troops?

'There must be an animee amongst them!' a blood-mage shrieked and then turned to address the big one. It was him, the one the Scourge sought! Refus.

All other thought went out of the Scourge's head. He ignored the import of Refus's words, he paid no attention to the kafuffle going on amongst the magicians, he was deaf to the Lord's shouted instructions. His only thought was to kill the Shakri-cursed magician who had so casually ordered the death of the bookish cleric Altibus. It had nothing to do with the torture that the magicians had put the Scourge through in the cell – after all, it seemed he couldn't die, and he was old enough and ugly enough to put up with most sorts of physical pain. No, Refus had to die because of the purpose and principles the Scourge had tried to explain to the demonic Jack O'Nine Blades. There was no place in this realm for any creature who acted based solely upon the motivation of their own selfish desire and whim. Absolute selfishness could not be allowed to replace morality, law and respect for the life of others. Otherwise, anarchy, death, despotism and the apocalypse were all that could follow. Beyond all that, Altibus had been the Scourge's friend, and no one killed one of the Scourge's friends and got away with it. It was something the Scourge did not compromise on, not that he compromised on much.

He pushed himself away from the pillar and lurched towards Refus, concentrating with all his might on keeping the dirks in his shaking hands. He wove like a drunk who'd been locked into a distillery overnight. He smiled at the idea, and then shook himself. He could not afford for his mind to wander as well as his body right now, for it would all be won and lost in this next moment. The bespelled Memnosian army, Strap, the Chamberlain, Kate – was she in there somewhere? – all would be lost if he could not hold himself together for just a few more seconds.

He did not understand how it had all come down to this, how Shakri had contrived to have him here at this precise moment. If that cow had been manipulating him all along then… then… oh, what was the use? Of course she'd been manipulating him! She'd always manipulated him. It was what the gods did. They just couldn't help themselves. They interfered, meddled, dabbled, manipulated, conspired, contrived and frustrated. No wonder the balance had been so easily upset. The gods only had themselves to blame, damn them.

Realising what rode on his next strike, he dimly wondered if he should go for the Lord rather than Refus. He didn't know. Oh well, if he was about to make a mistake of apocalyptic proportions, he doubted he'd be around for long to regret it.

'Now don't go anywhere, fat boy! I'll be with you in a minute. I just have to see to this demon-whore first.'

He stuck one of the dirks into the middle of Refus's back and cut across the blood-mage's throat with the other. The Scourge sawed deep in case Refus had some ability to heal himself. His blade reached the magician's spine, which was always the difficult bit. The Scourge worked to flex the bicep and tricep of his arm that little bit more, and finally crunched his way through the magician's brain stem. He held up Refus's decapitated head and lobbed it into the middle of the appalled group of magickers.

'Who's next? Since you've waited your turn so nicely, how about you, big boy?'

The Lord's eyes bored into him and sought to wrest control of the Scourge's body from him.

'What's the matter, magic not working properly? That's because your idiot mages drained me of pretty much every drop of blood I've got. Come on, don't be shy!'

The Lord tried to draw the Scourge's life force from him.

'I don't know what you're trying now, but you'll get nothing from me save a swift death… well, swift*ish*, once I get my feet to obey me.'

'Rush him!' ordered the Lord. 'He is weak. He can hardly stand.'

'Ha!' grinned the Scourge. 'I have killed gods while in a worse state than this. In fact, I think I was even drunk when I last killed Lacrimos.'

Two hefty mages intercepted the Scourge before he could reach the Lord. They stuck knives into him and bore him to the ground. He struggled with them but they pinned one of his arms each. His head reared up and bit one of the mage's arms. The man screamed and punched at the Scourge's head with his free hand. The Scourge would not relinquish his bite and the mage finally had to release the Scourge's arm. The Guardian plunged his freed knife into the mage's exposed armpit and then rolled aside as the dying man pitched forwards.

The Scourge was now laid up against the knee of the other mage, who still had one of the Guardian's arms pinned. The Scourge bit the offending knee and, as the mage shunted back, twisted free. He rolled onto one of his own knees and then drove his head up under the mage's chin. He blocked the mage's arms with his elbows and then slammed his knife into the man's chest.

Another mage came in and kicked the Scourge in the stomach. He clung onto the leg and began to claw himself up him.

'Get off! Noo!' he squealed as the Scourge pulled yet another blade from where it was tucked through his belt. 'Please! Have mercy!'

The Scourge stuck the knife into the flesh of the man's thigh.

'Aiee! Lord, save me!'

The Scourge now had a grip on the mage's front and hauled himself up as the mage was dragged down. The Guardian dug his blade into the v of the mage's neck and shoulder and then slowly pushed down on it with his body weight while the mage tried in vain to push the Scourge's arms and the knife back up.

'I don't want to die!' the blood-mage wheedled and then coughed blood down his front.

The Scourge gained his feet and swayed like a centuries' old animee. He stretched his chest and arms and then roared at the line of blood-mages, who now hung back from him.

He turned back to the mage who'd just died and spat on him. 'Don't want to die? You should have thought of that before you decided to kick Shakri's Divine Consort in the stomach, now shouldn't you? It's not exactly respectful, now is it? I'm all but a demi-god, you know, and I'm extremely pissed off with the lot of you!'

The Lord had backed away and was now nearly at the pyramid's entrance.

'Where do you think you're going, laughing boy? Move quickly for such an overblown gut-bag, don't you? Come back here and face me like a man!'

All the blood-mages were now streaming back into the pyramid. Straps arrows took a few in the back.

'Seal the portal!' boomed the Lord.

The blood-mages still outside cried for their fellows to wait, but the door clanged shut with half a dozen trapped without. The Scourge, unable to stay upright any longer, fell flat on his face. The Brethren mages edged towards the prostrate Guardian.

Suddenly, a black spider was scuttling amongst them and unstringing their limbs.

The Scourge looked up into an ugly, sallow face. 'I never thought I'd hear myself say this, but it's good to see you, Chamberlain!'

❧ ❧

Kate crept through the small tunnel in absolute darkness. She'd cracked her head on the roughly carved roof once and since then kept it low and her elbows tucked in. Every now and then, she felt a change in the air to left or right and knew they'd reached a turning or intersection. At such times, the boy priest would hang back to guide her. She had no idea how he could find his way in this murk. Could he actually see or was he using some priestly power gifted to him by Istrakon, the elusive god of thieves? She resolved to stay on the good of this god should they ever see Corinus again, as the followers of the boy god could find their way into any place of their choosing.

They finally entered larger tunnels, with a smooth finish to walls, floor and ceiling. She straightened up and circled her head on her neck to try and work the kink out of it. It wasn't long before they entered corridors where torches were maintained. And occasionally they traversed chambers where daylight shone through the semi-translucent black quartz and gave everything a mystical, smoky quality.

'I will leave you here, milady,' the boy priest bowed.

'You mentioned my son.'

'Straight on and next right.'

'Where are you going now?'

'To realise a return on my labour and the risks taken thus far. It is a requirement of my calling, you understand. Besides, my part has been played, and there is no help I can offer you against what you now face.'

Kate was fearful. 'Is it so terrible?'

The boy priest chewed the inside of his cheek and looked at her with sympathy. 'I pray not, for the good of us all. Farewell, milady!'

He ghosted away and she lost sight of him in the half-light within a dozen yards. Kate checked the bolt was still in its groove in her crossbow and moved forwards.

She knew there would be plenty of killing to be done before Orastes was returned to her. In many ways, she looked forward to the slaughter to come. She relished the prospect of bathing in the blood of her enemies. She would be happy to see it dye her green leather red. Yet it would hardly be punishment enough for what they had done to her. She didn't care that they'd slaughtered innocent priests and citizens of Dur Memnos. It hardly mattered that they'd desecrated temples and been responsible for deicides. Nor was it that they'd torn apart her loving family and used her innocent child for their own ends. No, the offence that they'd committed that was beyond all compass was to bring her to this place and time, with this crossbow in her hand, to face the task of killing her own son. For if Orastes had indeed become the vessel for Nylchros, as Mordius suspected, then she could not and would not show her son a moment's mercy. She would treat him in the same way as she would deal with those magicians who had brought her here.

What sort of realm was it that would demand a mother kill her own son? Not a realm worth saving. A mother that killed her own child was no mother at all, and might as well never have had the child. If she had to kill him, then she would, but would then see to the destruction of the realm and its gods herself if she could. A realm in which a mother was no mother and a child was better off not being born was not a realm deserving of life.

Resolved, but fearing every step forwards she took was a step closer to the end of all things, she jerked and stuttered into the corridor to the right. What else could she do? Thousands upon thousands of Memnosians had died so that she – just one woman – could be crouched in this ill-lit corridor on her own at this time with her crossbow in hand. Gods had died to see her across this valley and into this pyramid! She'd helped instigate and had overseen many of the terrible sacrifices made by this realm. She could not betray everyone and everything by letting fear and indecision get the better of her now. She could not remain cowering here in this corridor, even if it seemed preferable to facing the dreadful task ahead.

She looked into a large chamber, where a madcap scene was being enacted over and over. A naked youth was taunted alternately by a willowy man and a black cat. The man would sing in a flat, screeching voice until the youth made to stop him, at which point the cat would run at the youth from behind, scratch him and set up an awful yowling. The youth would then make for the cat, at which point the willowy man would run at the youth from behind, slash him with a knife and start his deafening yammer once more. They played it out again and again, a head-splitting clamour always kept up. If ever the youth came close to catching man or cat, a tall man – Lucius! – in the corner would manage a few tortured choruses to set the youth's teeth on edge and drag him away from the others. The four characters seemed trapped in some ever-repeating loop, stalemate or tension.

She suddenly realised what she was seeing: some microcosm of the balance itself. Lucius must represent mortal kind, but what forces did the other three characters represent? She could not fathom it. Dare she enter in? Surely she would tip the balance in doing so, she just needed to make sure it tipped the right way!

Where was her son, she asked herself desperately? It couldn't be this tormented, bleeding youth could it? Why would three forces be fighting against the one unless that one was the Unity who used Orastes as his vessel?

Kate raised her crossbow, levelled it at the youth and stepped across the chamber's threshold. 'Lucius!' she shouted. 'By the fecundity of Shakri, what's going on?'

'Kate!' he squawked. 'Shakri be praised!'

The others stopped and stared at her. She gazed at the willowy man and the cat. It took all her courage to meet the eyes of the youth... those baby-blue eyes that looked at her with love and need, that did not judge her, that mixed something of both Saltar and herself and embodied the beauty of their love for each other. There could be no doubt that it was her beloved Orastes, her dear son. He looked at her in the way only a son could look at his mother, and she saw the telltale beauty spot below the left eye that confirmed him to be Orastes. She could not hold her crossbow steady.

'Are you Kate, beloved of Saltar?' asked the willowy man, and bowed slightly. 'Milady, I am Jack, a follower of Wim! Nylchros,' and here he sneered at Orastes, 'has just murdered the Divine Jester. The body is behind the altar there. Milady, you must shoot him while you may!'

'He's right, Kate!' Lucius called. 'Shoot him, now!'

Her crossbow shook so badly that even standing just twelve feet from the youth, she wasn't sure she would be able to hit him. She did not want to do this. It was wrong, surely!'

The youth's eyes pleaded with her. 'You are the mother?' he said softly. Her son spoke to her! How he had grown! How handsome he was. She was so proud of him that she thought her heart would burst. Tears filled her eyes. 'Have you come to see me, mother?'

'Kill him!' Lucius shouted. 'You know me. Trust me now. It is not Orastes. Shoot, Kate! Do not hesitate! Do not hesitate!'

But she did hesitate. How could she not? If she shot him and the realm was saved, how would she then be able to live with herself? She knew she could not. How could she betray one of this realm's most fundamental principles? For was Shakri not only the goddess of creation but also the goddess of love? She would not want her to break the bond that connected mother to child, a man to a woman, and the mortals to the gods, would she? Surely such a betrayal would only help to end the balance anyway! She was increasingly certain that shooting her son was the last thing she should think of doing.

And yet they said it was *not* Orastes! They said he'd killed holy Wim. Lucius had never lied to her, and the youth had not refuted the claims of the willowy man. She knew that the owners of this pyramid, the Brethren and Nylchros, were determined to put an end to the pantheon. Cognis was gone and she'd seen Incarnus dismantled. She *must* stop them. She must kill Nylchros.

She was caught in a paradox, just as the four characters she'd first seen in this chamber had been trapped in a repeating loop. Many a time she'd heard Mordius say that the fundamental nature of magic was paradoxical, and that when the paradox unravelled, the magic unravelled. Dare she do anything that would end the paradox and perhaps the magic of the balance? How could she take the precipitous action of killing her son? Or was it precipitous not to do so? They couldn't remain like this, cancelling each other out forever, as it was not a life of any sort. She wished Mordius was there to tell her what to do. She wished *anyone* was there to tell her what to do or to do it for her. She didn't want to be here. She wanted to be somewhere safe with her babe in her arms snuggled against her bosom.

'Shakri, help me!' she screamed upwards, and it echoed around the eternity of the chamber.

The black cat yowled in agony.

'Quickly, Kate, before it is too late!' Lucius cried.

'Give me the crossbow!' Jack begged.

Kate fired. Nylchros screamed like a young child and fell to the floor. It physically hurt her to hear his screams. She nearly dropped her weapon to cover her ears.

The youth rolled over to face her. 'You bitch! How dare you shoot me!' he demanded, clutching his thigh where the bolt had buried itself. 'You will die for this! I will have you tear out your own womb before this is done!'

Kate didn't recognise him anymore. His voice was wrong. His eyes held nothing but storm-clouds. This was not Orastes, this was not her son! How could she not have seen it before? Though it grieved her, she began to crank back the draw on her crossbow. Her son was dead; he could at least be laid to rest with dignity and reverence. She would not have his body abused by this abomination. She felt relieved now she had made her decision. She pulled another bolt from the leather holster at her waist and prepared to fit it to the groove of her weapon.

'Pathetic mortal! You will have no place in the Unity. You will be consigned to an eternal isolation, if your simple mind is equipped to last that long.'

It slotted into place and she raised the crossbow so that it was aimed at his head. She walked towards him and crouched. The tip of the bolt was a few feet from his forehead.

'Any last words, dear one?' she whispered.

The Unity glared into her eyes and started to absorb her mind. With a sigh, she pulled the trigger.

❧ ☙

Heritus stormed into the main chamber, having already sensed what awaited him. Had he underestimated the Green Witch? No, he'd always known it would not be easy to overturn the entire realm and reality that had created him. He'd plotted and planned for millennia, but that was as nothing compared to how long the likes of Nylchros had waited and schemed. There'd always been an element of doubt… until he'd felt Nylchros break Wim. It would all be so much easier from hereon in, as if there were only a finite number of pieces to this child's puzzle and only one way in which they could fit together to make up the only picture that had any sense of sense, coherence or cohesion. At last, certainty and inevitability had been introduced. His victory was assured. A specific number of chemicals had been combined, and there could only be one result.

He almost slowed as he entered the chamber, so sure was he that there would be no need to hurry. But it was a good job he didn't, for the Witch was crouched before Nylchros, her crossbow cocked. How had she found such an advantage? The musician and the minstrel were of no consequence, so how had she… the cat? He did not know how it had come about, but he knew he must act in the instant.

His will was immediate. His will was all. The trigger was pulled. The draw kicked and sped and the bolt forwards. Heritus forbade it, turning the pyramid against it, turning the air to diamond. The bolt punched forwards and froze just as it had begun to create an indentation in Nylchros's forehead and break the skin.

Nylchros fell backwards and rolled free. The remaining fifty or so magickers filed in and stood round the walls, although they no longer filled the walls like they once had.

Feeling faint from the considerable exertion of stopping the bolt in midair, Heritus ordered a nearby magicker to immobilise the witch. The magician looked terrified and opened and closed his mouth without a sound coming out. Heritus realised the magicker probably hadn't yet mastered the blood-magic concerning movement.

'What are you then? Sight, hearing, smell, taste, what?'

'Sp-speech, Lord!'

'Speech?' Heritus sneered. 'That's not even one of the senses. You're no use to me. You will give your life force to Nylchros, should he request it.'

'Yes, Lord!'

Heritus raised his own power again and cast an immobilising web over the musician, the minstrel, the cat and the troublesome Green Witch, who had already begun to reach for one of her crossbow bolts. He immediately felt giddy and depleted. He was over-exerting himself, he knew, but also knew that without doubt now was the time to use whatever reserves he had. Things had been so close to spiralling out of control! It should not have been possible for it to happen; it should all have played out with absolute predictability. There must be another element here that he had not anticipated. But what was it? Surely not the cat? The cat's tail was still twitching – the web he'd cast clearly hadn't been strong enough, but the animal could not otherwise move. All was under control, he reassured himself. He was jumping at echoes and shadows of the past, at bad, old memories, that was all. There was nothing to fear in a cat's twitching tail. This was the moment. Now!

'It is fitting…' Heritus, one time acolyte of Harpedon, and Lord of the Brethren, boomed in godly tones.

'Kill her!' demanded Nylchros and ran at Kate with his hands curled into claws.

Curse the tempestuous wretch! 'Nylchros, you will be still!' Heritus shouted in anger.

The Unity pulled up short and glared furiously at Heritus. 'It is my will that she dies. At once! I demand it. You will make it so.'

It had been millennia since anyone had spoken to Heritus is such a manner, and he didn't like it. He was tempted to teach the impudent pup a lesson, but he was not sure he'd be able to maintain the immobilising web at the same time. In addition to that, he still needed Nylchros to bring the rest of the realm under his control. He therefore curbed his temper. 'She is of no threat to us. *No one* is a threat to us anymore. See here, all the forces of this realm are gathered in this one chamber and we have won. We stand at the nexus, the centre of the Pattern, at the tipping point of the balance, and we are the ones still moving, we are the ones who decide all things from this place forward.'

'I do not see how,' Nylchros frowned.

Heritus smiled. 'All life is here, Nylchros. Do you not yet understand the nature of the feline who has been tormenting you all this time? Have you not wondered where Shakri has been hiding Herself?'

The Unity's eyes widened in comprehension and wonder. His face went through an acrobatic series of expressions and then he was laughing uproariously. He laughed so hard, he began to cry and hold the stitches in his sides. Blood trickled from his nose, eyes and ears. He ejaculated mightily across the altar of the pyramid.

Behind them, someone cleared their throat. 'Ahem!'

Heritus frowned.

'Sorry to interrupt the party!' Saltar said from the doorway, his voice as flat and lifeless as it had ever been when he was an animee.

Nylchros recoiled as if burnt. Heritus's tongue became thick in his mouth. The magickers ran to each other in panic, trying to organise themselves into attack groups of complementary skills.

'The father!' Nylchros gasped. 'Tee hee! Now we are one happy family.'

Saltar stepped into the main chamber of the pyramid of black quartz. En masse, the dozen or so magickers closest to him fell to the floor dead. There were no lights, no shouts of warning, no death rattles. Their animation simply ceased between one blink of an eye and the next. Saltar took another step round the chamber, the dead zone surrounding him travelling with him. Another half dozen magickers fell.

Instinctively, Heritus and Nylchros backed away. The death hanging in the air was palpable. It was an emptiness like an ache in the heart. When they extended their senses towards it, those senses disappeared as if they'd never existed. It was a nullity that threatened the Unity itself.

'Father, what is it you do?' Nylchros challenged Saltar.

'You are no son of mine,' Saltar replied dispassionately. 'You may have the body of my son and bear features in common with me and Kate, but they do not belong to you. You have stolen these things. You are nothing but a common thief in the night. And sneak thief that you are, you then think to replace the husband in his bed or the child in its cot with a changeling or simulacrum, hoping to inherit by these means the family's entire estate, title and legacy. You seek to dispossess us of ourselves, our realm, our birthright. But we have seen through your masquerade and know you not to be true. What role will you now take on? The robber baron? The lost god?'

'Blasphemer!' yelled one of the magickers furthest from Saltar. 'I will not hear you speak such words in the inner sanctum of our temple. I will sacrifice my own life force before I will allow it!' With that, she let her life spill into the air around her and sent lightning arcing into Saltar. The crackling energy blinded everyone in the room and left patterns burnt into their vision. The air smelt of ozone.

Saltar was unmoved. There was no mark on him. He pointed at the now haggard looking woman and she fell dead. The blood-mages jumped back from her body, fearing death's touch.

'Bind him!' Heritus ordered the remaining magickers, no trace of alarm in his voice, although there were beads of sweat on his brow.

As one, the magickers extended their weaves of magic towards the Battle-leader. He smiled and, one by one, gathered up the thread of magic from each magician as it reached him. When he had them all bunched in his grip, he began to pull. He hauled all the magic they had out of them. Some realised what was happening and tried to pull back, but it was too late to do anything but slow the inexorable force extracting their souls. Depending on the nature of the magic they were using, their centres of mortal power were drawn out through head, heart or loins, and then the divine magic Shakri had gifted them so that they might first know life followed. The deaths of the magickers when Saltar had first entered had been sudden, painless and silent. Those who died now suffered terribly. Their souls were harrowed up and pulled thin as if on a rack. Their tortured screams were an agony to hear. Nylchros cringed and clapped his hands over his ears, Heritus struggled to keep his own magic in place. Finally, all the souls had been snapped, broken, torn away or scattered. Every magicker was dead. All was silent again.

The Unity sprang up onto the altar and stared hatred down on Saltar. 'You are wrong, pathetic mortal! This body and realm *do* belong to me. They were made from *my* original being, from *my* substance. It was my own children, the pantheon, who stole it from me. They took what was not theirs to take. They had no right to anything except what I chose to give them. I now reclaim what is mine. I *will* have this realm. It is my will.'

The arms of Nylchros shot straight up into the air and he began to draw down life force from the apex of the pyramid. A cascade of energy wreathed him in gold and he grew beyond all human proportion and compass. There were wails from outside the pyramid, and Saltar knew that Nylchros was taking all the life force from those he Owned. He must be killing them in their thousands. It was a genocide!

Nylchros stretched his giant golden limbs, glorying in their power and effervescence. None could look upon him and not be blinded. He was the centre of the sun, the essence of purity, living omnipotence in the realm of his pantheon. He towered thirty feet above them, the physical barrier of the walls of the pyramid nothing to him. He passed through them as if they were no more than air.

Heritus threw his arms up to shield his eyes. Kate and the others forgotten, he now used whatever magic he had to protect himself. He could withstand any onslaught, but not if his powers were divided. Kate, Jack, Lucius and even Scraggins were forced onto their stomachs and faces, unable to stand before the self-proclaiming and manifest majesty of the Unity.

Heart pounding at seeing his beloved forced to grovel on her belly before such an abomination, Saltar directed his dead zone so that it disrupted the flow of life force to Nylchros. Twin orbs of liquid gold turned to regard him. 'You dare! Kneel before me and all might yet be forgiven. Refuse and I will grind you under my heel, ridiculous and presumptuous creature!'

'I will not capitulate again. No submission, no quarter, no compromise and no pity. I am not of this realm. I will *not* be reduced by you. Know me! I am the *Builder*! This realm was recreated by *my* will, and that will cannot be bowed by you. Leave this place! I forbid it to you! It turns against you!'

'So be it!'

A golden hand came down and flattened Saltar into the ground. Giant cracks appeared in the black crystal all around the fingers of the celestial being. Sharp edges lacerated the hand and black blood ran into one of the floor channels, but Nylchros did not seem troubled. He lifted his hand away.

Saltar stood. 'I am stone.'

The Unity grabbed the Battle-leader, ran with him far to the north and plunged him into the heart of a volcano. The god's skin burnt to a crisp, but he continued to hold Saltar in the lava. The god's flesh melted away and he withdrew his skeletal fingers before the whole hand was lost.

A glowing figure clambered out of the inferno. 'I am fire.'

Roaring with rage, Nylchros picked up his nemesis and dove into the deepest ocean with him. Surely nothing could survive the impossible pressures here. Their membranes would be burst and crushed in a second. The god held him there for an age, until one of his own divine lungs had collapsed. Then Nylchros drove for the surface. He dragged himself up onto the strand of a beach. He'd risen too quickly and his ears and eyes fizzed as unequalised internal and external forces threatened to tear him apart.

Saltar walked out of the sea. 'I am water.'

Whimpering, the god took up his tormentor and leapt skywards. So high they went, there was no more air to breathe. The mortal must die in such a place. Nylchros floated there for an eternity, until his brain began to suffer damage. Then he hurtled back to earth, his body flaming as he re-entered the atmosphere and then smashing deep into the earth.

Saltar was before him still. 'I am air.'

Crying with pain, Nylchros dragged Saltar down into the ground. He crammed earth into the mortal's nose, ears, mouth and anus. He buried him under the weight of the world and then its core his tomb. The god had used his own body as a tool to work the earth and most of his bones had broken. Where his body had repaired itself, the bones had not healed straight. The twisted, deformed god crawled slowly back up to the surface. He headed for his pyramid again, praying it could return him to his former glory.

Saltar was waiting for him. 'I am earth.'

'Mercy!' pleaded the ruined creature.

Nylchros realised something was crawling up him. He turned his head to see what was on his upper arm. A chaos of claws landed in his face and scrabbled at one of his eyes until it had been shredded. He whipped his head back the other way, flinging the cat off him. An arrow sailed in from the side and unerringly took out his other eye. He howled blindly.

Nylchros now crouched so that he was entirely within the main chamber again and protected from any more arrows. He summoned the last of his magic to him, but the musician played his infernal lute so that the god stayed vulnerable. Then the minstrel danced in and kicked the god in the testicles. Kate's crossbow took Nylchros in the throat and he collapsed into a foetal position, no other way to save himself from further harm.

'Nylchros, you will leave this place!' Saltar commanded him. 'You are dissipated. Remain, and you will be ended! Release what life force still remains to you and be gone!'

Keening for his loss, the smouldering chunk of flesh that had been on the verge of ruling the entire realm forever more gave up its life. As the last of its energy drifted into the ether and the charred remains of Nylchros twitched for the last time, Saltar held the body at the point between life and death. He looked at Heritus and unmade him in the blink of an eye.

'That's three!'

Saltar drew on the life force released by the Lord's passing and used it to refashion the body of his son Orastes. A two-year-old boy lay before him.

'He's not moving!' Kate cried.

'We need Mordius!' Saltar replied urgently.

Chapter Fifteen: When We Will Be Made Anew

Mordius brought Orastes to them, cradling the happy, burbling boy in his arms. The necromancer beamed at Kate and Saltar, his joy and relief plain to see.

'It was just like raising an animee, easier actually! Here you are!'

He held the child out to Saltar, who moved to take him, but Orastes screamed in terror.

'What's wrong?' Saltar asked in panic. 'Kate, you take him!'

Kate did not move. She seemed unwilling to touch her son.

Mordius pulled Orastes back into his chest, turned the child's face away from the Battle-leader and the Green Witch, and jigged the infant up and down in a comforting manner. Screams became wails, became sobs, became a brief cry or two.

'Kate, why didn't you take him?' Saltar asked in confusion.

She shook her head. 'I-I…'

Mordius looked from one parent to the other and then back again.

'You take him!' Kate said.

At a loss, and clearly becoming upset, Saltar looked to Mordius for help.

'Saltar,' the necromancer said gently, 'I think Orastes's body may be giving him stray memories about what you did to Nylchros. He will be alright given time. Just be patient.'

'You must hold your son! He needs you!' Saltar demanded of Kate.

'Saltar,' Mordius said again. 'I think Kate also needs some time. I think we're all shocked by what's happened to us. You too, Saltar. You're reacting as you always do – with anger and agitation. Others will react in other ways – with a feeling of numbness and listlessness. Be patient or you will make things more difficult than necessary.'

Saltar sighed sharply. Then he took a more deliberate breath and released it slowly.

Orastes made a bit more fuss and Mordius said, 'I think he's hungry. Kate… would…?'

Kate shook her head without looking at her son, folded her arms across her armoured breasts and turned away slightly.

'Well, then,' the necromancer smiled. 'Maybe there is one amongst the few surviving Brethren who can help. I will take Orastes with me for a while, now that you know he is healthy and bonny. I think you two need some time alone. Good night!'

The necromancer withdrew from the antechamber, leaving Saltar looking at his wife with a tragic concern. The Battle-leader couldn't speak, couldn't move. The misery on her face hurt him far more than the Lords or Nylchros had. It felt like he was trapped in an even smaller cage than before. He did not know what to do. Always before in his life, he'd known what to do – he'd fought harder, come up with new stratagem or found some sort of saving magic. He wanted everything to be alright more than he'd ever wanted anything, but this was the first total defeat he'd known.

'If you won't hold our son, will you not at least hold me?' he managed in a strangled voice.

She did not respond for a long time. When she finally looked at him, it was without love. He recoiled from her, afraid.

'How could you allow this to happen?' she accused him venomously.

'I did everything I could!' he pleaded. 'He is returned to us!'

'How could you let him be taken from us and turned into that… that *thing*!' Kate screamed. 'How could you? How could you make me *kill my own child*?' she wept. 'That pink worm is no longer my child! He is dead!' she snarled.

'No, no! Don't say such things!' he begged, shaking his head in denial. 'You saw him! He is beautiful! He needs you, Kate. *I* need you!'

'Oh, why did I ever listen to you! What possessed me to put aside my armour and lay with you! I was a fool to think we could ever have a family or be happy!

She lashed out and caught him a stinging blow across the face. He reeled back and she came in with a kick to the stomach. She pulled a knife from the top of her boot.

'How could you do this to me!' she screeched and launched herself at him.

Timing his grab precisely, he caught her wrist, forced it up above her head, doing the same with her other arm, and then pushed them back behind her so that she was pinned. He held her in a tight embrace.

'I love you, Kate!'

She bit at his face and he forced his forehead against her cheek so that she could no longer attack him. They stayed like this for hours, until all was dark outside the pyramid, and even blacker within.

In the first few hours, she struggled, but gave up eventually for it was futile. He would not release her. As dawn began to approach, she was shaking. Was she cold? He realised she was crying.

Some time later, she asked: 'What, will you hold me forever?'

'Yes.'

A pause.

'Forever and ever?'

'Longer if necessary,' his voice smiled in the dark.

'Why would you want to put up with me for that long?'

'You are everything to me, you know that. Our life together, our family; it completes me. Without you and Orastes, there is nothing. I have no reason to build, to fight, without the two of you. You understand?'

Another timeless pause.

'Then I will hold the child and we will be a family,' she said without joy, 'but do not expect me to lay aside my armour again.'

He nuzzled her ear. 'Not even if I ask nicely.'

'Never!'

He blew gently. 'All our enemies are dead. I have killed them all. You are safe with me here. You do not need your armour.'

'N-Never!' she groaned although her body seemed intent upon betraying her.

He nipped at her ear lobe playfully. 'We cannot be touched by any unless we wish it. Not even the gods can gainsay us for some while yet. Incarnus has fallen, Kate. There is no hatred left, nothing needing revenge. There is only our love for each other and our child now. In reclaiming our son, we saved the realm. In remaining true to our love, we survived where our enemies could not. Shakri, the goddess of love and creation survived, yet Incarnus did not. So who does your armour protect you against, Kate?'

'You!' she said huskily. 'It protects me against you! I hate you!'

She melted into him, into the darkness and into oblivion. Their passion for each other was such that it could have birthed whole worlds that night.

❧ ❧

There is an hour of the night at which men find it almost impossible to stay awake. In some cultures, it is called the hour of the wolf, in others the hour-when-dreams-come, and in one or two the hour of the demon. It is the time when the night is at its most dark and still. It is when the different realms of existence are at their closest, and some believe that very small or powerful creatures can temporarily co-exist in realms, or even cross from one into another. It is when seers and prophets have their clearest visions. Practitioners of the black arts are at their most powerful. Mighty warlords are at their most vulnerable and artists are at their most tortured and inspired.

It is a time when wise men are safe asleep in their beds in tightly secured rooms. It is a time when only the lost, the hunted and the hunter are abroad.

As the night reached this hour, Jack O'Nine Blades padded softly up the stairs to the pyramid, through the portal and into the main chamber, from which issued the magical summons. He knew it was not Shakri who called him, for She usually appeared directly before him to make Her petty wishes and demands known. She liked to confront him as if in some sort of reprimand for his very being and nature. No, this summons was quite mysterious, while at the same time naggingly familiar. He'd been tempted to ignore it – anyone with magic enough to call him was likely to be dangerous and therefore best avoided – but the summons was insistent. In addition to that, of course, there was then his damnable sense of curiosity. Although it made life much more interesting, it also always got him into trouble and would probably see an end to him one day.

The main chamber was lit by a torch on each wall, but the flaming brands had burnt low and no longer reached the shadowy pool at the centre of things. Jack set the peripheral shades in the place to shifting gently and then slipped in amongst them almost invisibly.

'Ah, there you are, demon!' a smooth voice noted. 'Thank you for coming!'

'Who are you?' Jack O'Nine Blades asked the darkness surrounding the altar.

There was a soft chuckle. 'If you knew, you would not presume to ask anything of me. But I am feeling indulgent… and time is short.' A figure stepped forward into the half-light.

Jack peered ahead nervously, but continued to move within his own concealing shades lest he suddenly be attacked by the stranger. He made out a non-descript, middle-aged man. Too non-descript? The hairs on the back of his neck rose. What did he face here? Was it too late to flee?

'You may call me Vidius, demon,' the man said velvetly. 'I am a Prince of the Nihil.'

Jack whimpered in fear, shielded his eyes and bowed low.

'Enough of that, demon. You have permission to look upon my person.'

'Your will, master!'

'Let us behave as friends, demon, for not all Princes choose to make their will, power and rule manifest in the manner of the old laws. Are we not in a different realm entirely? Are things not different here? Are *we* not different here, demon?'

'Yes, master. I will behave as your friend then, master!' Jack said straightening up slowly. Then, as per his nature, the cunning aspect of his mind began to stir. What advantage could he gain through the favour of this Prince? He waited silently upon the Prince's pleasure.

'You will open a gate to our realm so that I may pass through,' Vidius informed him.

Jack knew that the one to hold a gate open could not be the one to pass through it. It was a magical impossibility. He knew of demons who'd tried and had managed to get halfway across the threshold before the portal had snapped shut and cut them neatly in two. The Prince needed him, and had told him as much. Jack decided he could risk a question – otherwise he was unlikely to gain anything from this encounter.

'Master, why would you want to return our realm?'

Vidius did not answer at once and Jack feared he'd overstepped the mark. He held his breath. Finally, the Prince condescended to answer him. 'How long have you been here, demon?'

'Some centuries, master.'

'And though you are free of the demon realm, is this realm giving you what you'd hoped? Or do you constantly have to hide your true being in the shadows? Are you not constantly afraid that one of the gods here will find you out?'

Jack bit his lip and stood on one foot.

'Ahh! I see one of them already has. Which one?'

'Shakri!' Jack whispered.

'Idiot!'

'Yes, master. I was careless. I was d-drunk!'

Vidius chuckled. 'I understand. I actually killed my first body with a taste I developed for Stangeld brandy. Remarkable, the effects such substances have on the mortal body and mind.'

'Yes, master. I am free of Her now, though. I have preformed my service and can roam the realm once more.'

'As a homeless vagabond, demon. You will be circumspect for a while, but then become complacent and be caught again. And then you'll be even more circumspect, until you're afraid of your own shadow and will want to fade entirely from existence. That is why I return to the demon realm.'

The Prince was not telling him everything, and Jack knew better than to challenge the Prince's decision on that. The Prince had told him enough. He had successfully identified Jack's own need and implied that the Prince might be of a mind to help him. He would get nothing more.

'I am yours to command, master.'

'Then open the gate. Enough energy lingers here and the nature of this structure will also help. Hear me well, demon! You will open a gate on this spot, on this night, every year hence. Do you understand?'

'Yes, master. Even if they destroy this place, I will find a way.'

'And I will seek to reward you upon my return. Let us begin.'

❦ ❦

The Memnosian troops had been so exhausted that they'd been able to do little more than send up a ragged cheer at news of their triumph and then find themselves somewhere out of the cold to sleep. Many of the Brethren had mysteriously died during the titanic struggle that had apparently gone on inside the black pyramid. The few that had survived had hardly warranted a guard. So it was that the remaining Memnosian troops had occupied the empty houses of their foes and laid aside their armour, very few of them bothering with either fire of food.

They emerged now into the morning light, stiff-limbed and blinking, to face the aftermath of the previous day's terrible fighting. Brethren bodies lay all around, though most looked peaceful in death. Beyond the houses lay over three thousand Memnosian dead, not one of whom by contrast had had a peaceful death. It seemed wrong somehow that the enemy had suffered so little even in defeat. It seemed wrong that the victors, those still living, should face scenes even now as horrific as any to be found in Lacrimos's realm.

No one could face the task of starting to pile up the dead in pyres. Besides, there seemed to be very few officers left to be giving orders. A rumour started that the General had disappeared in the night, but few of the troops had known him, so most shrugged at the information. Besides, the Green Witch had survived, and she was their talisman. And hadn't the Builder materialised at the last moment or something? There were tales that the Battle-leader and Vidius had once been enemies on the battlefield when Voltar was King. Perhaps the Battle-leader had settled an old score.

There seemed to be priests of Shakri and Malastra everywhere, tending to the sick, bringing food to those who were too numb with shock to help themselves, calming the belligerent and gradually raising the spirits of even the most downhearted. It was clear that the powers of the priesthoods had returned stronger than ever.

Word came that the commander of the Guardians ordered everyone to assemble in the temple precinct by noon. In the absence of any other command, soldiers, Outdwellers, priests and mercenaries began to drift towards the muster. As comrade met comrade along the way, they rediscovered their sense of shared direction and remembered who they were. By the time they came to the precinct, soldiers were straightening their hair and cleaning their faces, weapons and buttons in case there was to be an inspection. The injured were helped along by everyone. When the rays of the sun made it over the roofs of the surrounding houses and welcomed them into the precinct, the volume of their voices rose, jokes were exchanged and laughter was heard. The Scourge waited for them on the steps of the pyramid, saluting them all. They lined up before him proudly and came to attention.

Saltar and Kate waited inside the entrance to the pyramid. She wore her green leather, for fear the army would not recognise her otherwise. He wore baggy, grey vestments that he'd found in a pile in what looked to be a servant's quarters.

'Are we ready?' Saltar asked his son, who sat straight in Kate's arms and smiled at his parents. 'Did you feed him?' he asked Kate.

'I know how to be a good mother to our child, thank you very much!' Kate growled.

Orastes mimicked Kate's growl and frowned at Saltar.

They couldn't help laughing. 'His mother's son alright!' Come on then.

They joined the Scourge on the steps and looked out at the upraised faces.

'So few!' Saltar murmured.

Kate nodded. 'It was barely enough. We sacrificed a great many and a great deal.'

Saltar sighed and lifted his voice. 'People of Dur Memnos, I come to thank you. I come to praise you. I come to mourn our losses!

'Thank you for returning my son to me! Yet he was not why you fought.

'Thank you for honouring your oaths to the flag and marching forth from Corinus. Yet it was not for the kingdom that you fought.

'Thank you for hazarding your lives to defeat our enemies. Yet you did not fight merely to defeat them.

'I praise your bravery. Yet that is as nothing.

'I praise your loyalty. Yet I insult you by doing so.

'I praise your fellowship. Yet you will hate me for it.

'So what is it that unites us? Why have we fought? What is it that I thank and praise you for? Why is it that we mourn for those we have lost?

'It is because of the things that define our innermost selves. It is our hearts, it is the things we love. It is because of such love that we will sacrifice everything to protect certain things, build others and destroy others. In that, we are like the gods, and that is no blasphemy. For are we not creations of the gods? Are we not invested with aspects of them… *all* of them?

'We are one with the gods' design and one with this realm. Our will is one with the gods' and the intention that drives the realm. Our cause was holy, it was just. It was to preserve the right of any man or woman to exercise their free will, to love another and to build a family. It was to preserve our right to *be*, to exist without permission to breathe, to live without bending knee to another before we form thoughts in our own minds.

'This is what we have fought for! *This* is why we were prepared to die! *This* is why we mourn those who died to save us! *This* is the kingdom we have built and defended! Dur Memnos! Dur Memnos!'

The two thousand roared their answer and their voices filled the valley and Needle Mountains. Surely they were heard even beyond the mountain range.

'I too would like to thank you,' Shakri whispered seductively in the ear or everyone assembled there. She glided out of the pyramid, intoxicating every mind. Her exquisite form conjured physical desire in men and women alike, Her perfume was a drug to enhance and befuddle the senses, and the air that caressed Her body then teased the erogenous zones of the audience. The people began to come towards Her, desperate to touch and consume Her. They shoved, jostled and rubbed up against each other, experiencing paroxysms of pleasure at the bodily contact.

The only one who seemed unaffected by Her presence was the Scourge. 'She just can't resist upstaging everyone, can she? Has to steal the moment and be the centre of attention,' he muttered.

'Stand back, all of you,' She purred. 'Be at peace!'

They could deny Her nothing and eagerly showed their devotion through obedience.

'Goddess, I am here!' Ikthaeon, Her high priest, called desperately.

Kate rolled her eyes.

Shakri smiled. 'He has a way about him that is not to everyone's taste, daughter, but he is ultimately a good man. Ikthaeon, dear, be silent, would you.'

'Then it was not him who tried to have me assassinated?' Kate asked.

'No, daughter, but in truth I am not sure who it was. What I can tell you is that it was not one of my children, although many were tempted.'

'Who then?' Saltar asked curiously.

Shakri arched one of Her eyebrows at him. 'I thought you might have a better idea than me. The disappearance of Vidius concerns me, but without Cognis I am blind.'

'I may be able to help there,' Saltar replied. 'Larc, Vasha, are you here?'

There was a ripple in the crowd and the boy and girl stepped forwards.

Saltar nodded at them. 'I would especially like to thank you two for freeing me. Were it not for your actions, I do not think we would all be standing here today. Vasha, were you not an acolyte of Cognis previously?'

'I was... milord!' the girl said nervously, her cheeks colouring prettily.

'Then you are the best equipped to found a new temple in His name. Will you take on this new task for Dur Memnos? Would you prefer it to be in Corinus or here in the mountains?'

Vasha looked at Larc in silent question. He looked abashed, but said in a clear voice: 'I can help you rebuild the temple where you used to live. And my people can help. If you stay here, then we can be... be close to each other.'

Shakri smiled down upon them. 'And you will be happy together. The two of you have my blessing. You will have many healthy children.'

Vasha's face went crimson at that, but Larc puffed his chest out like an eagle's. A few soldiers near him clapped him on the back.

'And see,' Shakri said, 'here is Sister Spike. She will re-establish Incarnus for us.'

Kate beamed when she heard the woman who had once been her bodyguard was still alive and well. There were not many Kate could trust well enough to call friend, but Sister Spike was one of them. Furthermore, the priestess was the first *female* friend Kate had ever had.

'I'm sorry for the loss of Brother Hammer and all the other members of your temple,' Kate said.

Sister Spike accepted the words with a nod. 'Of course, but their lives helped exact revenge upon our enemies. And their deaths were blessed, for they fought side by side with His holy vengeance. Kate understood the priestess's refusal to yield to emotion. Even in victory, she would not allow her guard to drop, would not allow joy to distract her or the grief of lost comrades to undermine her. She remained the weapon and shield of Incarnus. It was reassuring to Kate, for it meant the god she loved so well was not entirely lost. 'Sister, I would ask something of you on behalf of the kingdom, just as we prevailed upon dear Larc and Vasha. Once you have re-established your temple, will you undertake to train an elite Memnosian guard? Will you train my son in the martial disciplines once he is of an age?'

'I would almost consider it my holy duty,' Sister Spike bowed and stepped back.

'Jack!' Shakri sang. 'Come out, come out, wherever you are! I know you're here. It's your turn.'

Looking wary, the minstrel Jack O'Nine Blades slid between the various priests clustered near the front of the assembly and presented himself to the ruling party. The Scourge's nostrils flared in anger, his brows became a storm cloud and his hands instinctively went to the handles of his long blades. Shakri ignored Her consort.

'People of Dur Memnos,' She zephyred, 'you are not deceived. This is the songster who has preserved many of your ancient tales. Tales about him have grown up in turn. As your soul, he has lauded, bedevilled and saved you. He has been my mercurial emissary in recent times. Single-handedly, his quixotic nature has safeguarded the will of Wim in this realm, without which the Lords of the Brethren could not have been defeated. Call his name now!'

'Jack O'Nine Blades!' the valley shouted in joy.

Jack threw his whole body into grandiose bows. He back-flipped and somersaulted into them, playing to his adoring public. Then he outrageously poked his tongue out at the Scourge.

'Calm yourself, Janvil!' Shakri sighed.

'Don't call me that!' the Scourge snarled.

'I know your nature demands you finally hunt Jack down, but now is not the time. I cannot allow it. I promised him his freedom. He shall have it.'

'I will give him an hour's head start,' the commander of the Guardians ground out.

'You priests,' Shakri said to those present. 'Many of you have disapproved of Jack and his kind in times gone past. You will no longer do so, for he is in many ways like you. As you are priests to the gods, Jack is a priest to mortalkind. You will render him help or sanctuary should he ever request it.'

The high priests present nodded solemnly. Jack stepped up into the air and skimmed above the heads of the Memnosians. Barely a hair on anyone's head was put out of place as he flew towards freedom.

Long legs pounded after him. 'Jack, wait for me!' Lucius cried, his greater lute banging against his back as he went.

'Quickly then, musician, for the Scourge will be hot on our heels and looking to spoil our fun.'

'We'll need another musician to sing Orastes to sleep at night,' Kate frowned.

'Well don't look at me!' Saltar spluttered. 'I am capable of many things, beloved, but music is not one of them. I would prevent our child ever sleeping again, that or give him terrible nightmares.'

'Janvil!' Shakri pouted playfully. 'Will you not give up testing your manhood in this aggressive and obsessive manner? Forget Jack. Your energies could be put to much better use as my consort. Do you not miss the fun and games we used to have together? If you prefer me more girlish than womanly, you just have to say so!'

There were a few catcalls from amongst the soldiery. The Scourge turned on the men, refusing to be embarrassed. 'She threw me out. She sought to manipulate me even when I was back in Dur Memnos. None of that may surprise you. What it may surprise you to learn, however, is that Jack O'Nine Blades is a demon!'

There were murmurs amongst the crowd.

'How else do you think he has survived for so long? Shakri used him just as She used me! If you think that's funny, then so be it. But I am sworn to hunt down this demon, to safeguard the good people of this realm. Yes, to guard them, for I am a sworn and true Guardian. I guard our people when the gods are otherwise engaged, distracted or uncaring. Who here would prefer me to give up my vows, principles and calling?'

Only the wind answered him.

'Then I will hunt down this demon and I'll have no one mocking me for it, do you hear!'

'Oh, Janvil, you can be so serious and such a grump sometimes,' Shakri tinkled. Bewitched by Her once more, the assembly couldn't help laughing at the Scourge despite the words he'd just spoken. 'I cannot allow you to be invulnerable to harm anymore, now that the balance has been restored, you know that? You will be careful, dear one, won't you, for me?'

'Ha!' the Scourge scoffed. 'I will be my own man again!'

'Of course, once you die, you'll be returned to me anyway.'

'Then I will do all I can to stay alive for as long as possible!' the Scourge sniffed.

'Excuse me!' Saltar interrupted. 'Before we all die of old age, could I just ask you, Shakri, how you knew we would need the Scourge's help to defeat Nylchros? How did you know to return him to us exactly when you did?'

She smiled coquettishly. 'Now that would be telling! A girl has to have her secrets, you know. Eh, daughter?'

'Don't drag me into this!' Kate warned the goddess.

Orastes became restless and began to grizzle. Shakri approached him and touched him tenderly on the brow, instantly calming him. 'It grieves me how much you have suffered, little one. Come, accept my blessing and you will never know illness in your life.'

Orastes's face became beatific and his eyes drooped. He snuggled into Kate's chest and fell asleep contentedly.

Kate watched him for a second and then looked up at the goddess. 'Thank you!' she said.

'But of course, daughter. You will always have a special place in my heart, you know that. You sometimes seem to forget it, though, and worry me greatly.'

Kate took the reproof. 'This realm can be an unforgiving and cruel place. Sometimes, it is only the unforgiving and cruel who survive.'

The Mother of All Creation looked genuinely sad for a second or two. Hardened soldiers started to cry at the sight of it. Then she brightened: 'Yet there are two more I would like to thank. Mordius and Strap, step forward, please!'

The necromancer and the Guardian made their way to the front. Strap winked at all his friends and nodded to the Scourge. The Old Hound returned the gesture.

'The two of you,' Shakri announced, 'undertook the most difficult trial of all those gathered here. In fact, I was not sure you would survive.'

'I didn't, as it happens!' Strap commented.

'Shh!' Mordius reprimanded him.

'It's alright, Mordius!' Shakri reassured him. 'It's in his nature. Strap is what I made him still. And it is good that he is, for it makes it all the easier to return him to life without upsetting the balance too much. Mordius, I relieve you of the burden of keeping Strap animated. Strap, you are free to live again.'

'Jolly good!' Strap observed. 'That means I can join Janvil... sorry, the Scourge!... on the road again, just like old times.'

The Scourge looked at Mordius. 'Does he still talk too much?'

'Oh, yes,' Mordius sighed. 'You can be sure of that. Not even death could shut him up!'

'By the fetid, arse-eating breath of Lacrimos!' the Scourge cursed.

'Come now, Old Hound, don't be such a grump!' Strap chided him. 'You know you've missed me.'

'People of Dur Memnos!' Saltar shouted over them all. 'We will see to our dead and then we will go *home*!'

They all cheered.

'Can we get someone to eat, Sotto?' Dijin hollered over the din. 'I'm famished. Listening to so many words makes me hungry.'

Shakri commanded their attention one last time. 'My people,' She said gently. 'I love all of you.' Her eyes rested on Mordius. 'If ever your need is great, call on me and I will do what I can.' She looked last at the Scourge. 'I even love you, my sweet Janvil!' Then She faded from view.

❧ ❧

Saltar stood contemplating one of the throne room tapestries that had survived the attack by the man of magma a lifetime ago. It showed the scene of a battle from ages past, the name of which had long since been forgotten. Most of the colours of the weave had faded to grey and he did not recognise the rugged landscape of the setting.

As he looked closer, he saw smaller stitches had been used to create the faces of all the warriors. It made for a level of detail that allowed him to make out individual expressions. Curiously, all the troops in one army looked lunatic or frightened, while the troops of the other force seemed to be frowning. The first army was led by a blindfolded man on a giant, pale horse, while the opposing leader had horns – or was that his helmet? – and sat astride a black beast *en rampant*. There was something alien about the armour and features of the second army. The artist who had made the tapestry must have had an imperfect understanding of anatomy, as many of the members of the alien army had their limbs articulated in impossible ways. Perhaps there'd been more than one artist, for the members of the first army all appeared to be functioning properly.

The eyes of the horned leader glittered – presumably, silver thread had been used. In the unsteady torchlight of the throne room, Saltar fancied the leader's eyes were moving and hungrily taking in the enemy arrayed before him. The leader's army was bunched up behind him. They fought to be at the front. Several of them were biting one another. One seemed to be devouring the hand and forearm of another. Had they been starving? Certainly, many of them were lean, and their numbers were far greater than the enemy's. It would have been difficult to feed so many in the barren landscape.

The alien force spread all the way back into the distant hills. Many were clustered around one place in particular. Was it a cave they were all emerging from? A tear? A portal of some sort? He leaned closer, trying to make it out. The scene was so crowded, his view was obscured. He wished he could move some of them aside, but more and more of them came through. There was no end to them. What chance did the blindfolded leader have? Surely none. Was that why the artist had covered his eyes? Was it some sort of retrospective metaphor or comment rather than a literal depiction?

The portal called him back and he gazed into it. His mind's eye imagined movement beyond. Vast, unseen forces were readying themselves to come through as soon as the gate could be widened enough. What prevented them, Saltar wondered. Ah, there were magicians in the blindfolded man's army. They bore rods of power rather than blades and held them up as part of some great incantation. They inscribed runes in the air and chanted words of power. His eyes flicked from one to the other, faster and faster, trying to read and understand their spell.

There was a sudden knock at the door and the moment was lost. Saltar blinked, moved back from the tapestry and turned his back to it.

'Come in!' he called.

The large doors swung open and Mordius came inside. The guards outside closed the doors behind him.

'Ah, Mordius, my friend! Come join me in a goblet of wine. I've got some rather fine Jaffran red. I know it's your favourite.'

They seated themselves, clinked goblets, swallowed a mouthful each and enjoyed a moment of companionable silence.

'There were moments when I thought I'd never have my family safely home again. I thought you and I would never get to share a toast or drink together again,' the Battle-leader said quietly.

'You and me both,' the necromancer replied softly. ' I don't know how you did it…'

'How *we* did it!'

'Very well. I don't know how *we* did it. Even the gods were powerless. It's a terrible thing to see a god die. I had no idea they were so… so fallible. You know, when I was in the Old Place, the witch suggested the gods were little more than magicians, magicians on a par with the Three.'

Saltar rubbed at his eyes. When was it he'd last slept? He sipped some of his wine before answering. 'You have just spoken one of the most terrible of blasphemies. Every temple would see you hung for speaking such words. Yet I heard the creation story from Lacrimos's own lips. He suggested that this realm was little more than a spell woven by the pantheon.'

Mordius gulped audibly. 'B-But you know what that means, d-don't you!'

Saltar rubbed at his brow. 'I haven't thought it through. Go on!'

'Well, all magic is paradoxical in nature…'

'You've said as much several times.'

'… and it eventually unravels itself. If this realm is indeed a spell, even one of the most complicated ever wrought, it will ultimately unravel. Worse than that, its tendency will always be to unravel.'

Saltar took a slow, deep breath. 'Then tell me, good Mordius, are we forever fated to fight against that tendency? Twice in three or so years we have saved this place from fragmentation and annihilation. Will we have to go through the same thing a few years from now? Will we have to repeat and repeat? Now I recall, the nature of the spell is self-replicating and propagating. Perhaps by definition we go through the same cycle over and over.'

Mordius nodded gloomily. 'It makes sense. After all, it is called the cycle of life. Shakri's creation, the life that dies and is then born again, is precisely that repetition. What can we do? We dare not break the cycle, surely, for that would break the spell that holds the realm together. It would be suicide.'

'Give me another drink! Thanks. Do you know what, Mordius, I'm not sure I've got the energy to go through something like this every few years. And we can't take the losses. What remains of our army? Virtually nothing. If the Guild of Holter's Cross were of a mind to attack us now, we'd be entirely wiped out. No, we must find a way to protect ourselves and pre-empt the next unravelling.'

Mordius sat forward in his chair. 'How? You have thought of something, I can tell. What is it?'

Saltar smiled conspiratorially. 'Mordius, I have a task for you.'

'Name it!'

'You must build a cadre of magicians. Seek out those with potential and begin to train them in the ways of magic. You may want to start with the boy Larc. There is something special about him. How else could he have resisted Nylchros's call, when every other Brethren bowed to his will? And investigate

Lucius, if you can track him down. I don't understand how he's always there at the most crucial moment.'

Mordius was taken aback by what Saltar proposed. 'You want me to become a full blood-mage?' he whispered. 'It is outlawed. If the temples…'

'Leave the temples to me. Come to that, leave the gods to me… and Kate. Anyway, we will have a period of grace, I'm sure. And you will start your work discretely, of course.'

This was the moment that Mordius changed. No longer was he the small, eager to please, timid, sometimes cowardly individual he'd always been. At last he knew his own mind. At last he was the person he was always meant to be. 'When do I begin?'

'Well, let's at least finish this fine jug of wine first, eh?'

With some effort, Mordius relaxed into his chair. He held his goblet in both hands like a scrier and drank every few seconds or so, his eyes distant. His mind raced with ideas, implications and possibilities. After a while, he asked, 'So just what did happen to Nylchros?'

Saltar shrugged. 'I'm not sure really. Maybe Samuel's gnawing on him as we speak.'

'Samuel?'

'Hmm. One of the lesser gods, apparently. He chewed on my intestines.'

'Your intestines?'

'Have you ever heard of the Prison of All Eternity, Mordius?'

'The Prison of All Eternity?'

'Hmm. You know what? I think we're going to need another jug of wine.'

❦ ❦

The next day, despite the amount he'd consumed with Mordius, Saltar felt better than he had in a long time. He'd managed to get a good number of hour's sleep. Then he'd spent the morning with Kate and Orastes. His son had grinned at him and said, 'Dada!' for the first time… at least, that was what it had sounded like. It had done Saltar's heart good. He felt light, almost human again. They'd put Orastes down for a nap and Kate had then gone for her weapons practice with Sister Spike, as she did everyday, with an almost religious zeal.

With time now available to him, Saltar knew he would have to have the one conversation he'd been putting off. He went to the throne room and sat in one of the comfortable side chairs to wait.

Some minutes later, the door opened and the Chamberlain slid stealthily inside. He eyed Saltar and approached cautiously. The man-spider knew that his usual fawning act was not what was required now. He lowered himself into the chair opposite the Battle-leader.

'How stands the army?' Saltar asked peremptorily.

The Chamberlain twisted his head. 'It licks its wounds, as any wounded creature would, hmm? With the mercenaries and Outdwellers departed, we barely have a thousand men. It could hardly be termed an army, in fact, hmm? It is a fighting force of little consequence.'

'Then it needs to become a force of consequence, Chamberlain.'

'As you command, milord.'

Saltar sighed. 'Which officers still survive? What of Sergeant Marr?'

'He survived. He is confused, but will become himself again in time. I am not sure what the mages did to him, hmm?'

'I'm glad he is still with us. We can ill afford to lose good men like him. I will see him promoted several ranks when he is ready to return to duty. And Kate tells me you were of particular help to our cause, Chamberlain.'

'Perhaps,' the Chamberlain conceded. Events took on a certain momentum and direction of their own, which inevitably swept me along with everyone else. I am wise enough to know that it is futile to resist the tide on such occasions, hmm?'

Saltar knew that it was time to cut to the chase. This stilted back and forth really wasn't getting them anywhere. 'Are you irreducible in this realm?'

The man-spider's tongue darted out between his pointed teeth and he licked his thin lips. 'I have not heard it described thus, but were I to die here, it would not be my end. I could return... as could you. You and I have known each other here in this realm for millennia, although I seem to retain a better memory of it than you do, hmm?'

Saltar hesitated and then asked: 'Can I trust you? I have been told that we have deliberately been given personalities, you and I, that will antagonise one another. It is to prevent us sharing knowledge and becoming too powerful. There are some things that I know and remember that you do not.'

'Ahh! I had not realised that. It makes sense, hmm?' the Chamberlain said, his body twitching with what was presumably excitement. 'Can you trust me? Let me put it this way: in my saying no, you can at least trust my honesty.'

'I suppose that'll have to do. Are you aware of any other irreducibles in this realm? If we all know different things but learn to trust each other enough to share them, then I believe we will finally be restored to the beings of power that we once were.'

The Chamberlain blinked. 'The only other irreducible I knew of was Vidius, hmm?'

'What happened to him?'

For the first time in Saltar's memory, the man-spider looked confused. 'I-I am not sure. I do not think he resides in this realm any longer.' Then the Chamberlain gasped. 'If he has gone to a realm where he might be fully restored, we will ultimately be in great danger. He is different to you and me, you see. He believes in nothing, hmm? He is a destroyer!'

'What do you mean?' Saltar asked, the hairs on the back of his neck standing on end.

'I-I cannot remember!' the Chamberlain wailed in distress. 'And if he has taken a vital piece of knowledge with him that we would need to restore ourselves, then we are surely lost!'

Saltar gripped the arms of the chair in which he sat. He was not one usually given to fear or panic, but it threatened him now. It was inside him and fighting against his control like a demon seeking possession of his body. His voice was choked and he didn't recognise it as he said: 'I will search out what irreducibles I may, while you must rebuild the army, Chamberlain. Do not focus on recruiting large numbers – our population is already sparse enough – rather, increase the prowess of those we have. See what skills and secrets we can learn from the Outdwellers, the temples, Accritania, Holter's Cross and Jaffra.

'I am visited by a vision! I see only war in our future! We will not be able to hold our cities. We will be hunted. We will become a scattered population of spies, assassins and rogue warriors. Is this what I have brought us to, Chamberlain? Have I put this realm on the path to becoming an eternal hell? How could I do this to our people? How could I do this to my family?'

The Chamberlain had drawn his legs up into his chair in an effort to make himself as small as possible. 'How long do we have?' he yelped.

Eyes staring like a prophet's, Saltar replied: 'I fear it has already begun!'

Here ends Book Two of the Flesh & Bone Trilogy,
which continues with Book Three,
Necromancer's Fall.

About the Author

A J Dalton is one of the UK's leading authors of metaphysical fantasy. He has worked as a teacher of the English language in Thailand, Egypt, Poland, the Czech Republic and Slovakia. The influence of these diverse cultures lends a rich and vivid quality to his prose.

Necromancer's Betrayal is his second novel. He has also written a number of articles and short stories. He currently lives and works in both Manchester and London.

To find out more about metaphysical fantasy, the writing of A J Dalton and getting published, go to http://metaphysicalfantasy.wordpress.com.

Lightning Source UK Ltd.
Milton Keynes UK
UKOW040646040413

208655UK00001B/42/P